The Cuckoos of Batch Magna

The Cuckoos of Batch Magna

The Batch Magna Chronicles, Volume One

Peter Maughan

W F HOWES LTD

This large print edition published in 2019 by
W F Howes Ltd
Unit 5, St George's House, Rearsby Business Park,
Gaddesby Lane, Rearsby, Leicester LE7 4YH

1 3 5 7 9 10 8 6 4 2

First published in the United Kingdom in 2019
by Farrago

A CIP catalogue record for this book is available
from the British Library

ISBN 978 1 52887 861 6

Typeset by Palimpsest Book Production Limited,
Falkirk, Stirlingshire

Printed and bound by
T J International in the UK

MIX
Paper from
responsible sources
FSC
www.fsc.org   FSC® C013056

For Honor and Hugo
Both my worlds

A BEGINNING

In his bedroom in Batch Hall, the old squire, General Sir Humphrey Myles Pinkerton Strange, lay propped up on his pillows, his breath struggling with the illness in his chest. On the bedside cabinet sat his copies of Surtees and Beckford, and the stud books he'd asked his housekeeper to bring up, pedigrees of hunters and hounds going back to his great-grandfather's day.

As master of the Batch Valley Chase, in his old yellow hunting waistcoat, and with a threadbare shine on his ancient silk topper, the General had taken his last field through a covert four years before, sitting his hunter cavalry style as always, straight as a young dragoon. But had to be helped onto his mount to do it, bundled onto it, an old knight, stuffed with straw, and had seen the charity then, and the impatience, in people's eyes. He never hunted again after that, and had felt age like a wound ever since.

A wound he suspected that, this time, he would not be getting up from. And serve you damn well right, he told himself.

His housekeeper said it would be the death of

1

him. Standing about in a November drizzle after the Cenotaph service last year with all the other silly old fools, gossiping over the hipflasks as if in the mess, umbrella furled still because he was in town, the breast of his Gieves overcoat heavy with medals. Medals which went back to the pounded mud of Passchendaele, and a young moustachioed captain of the Cavalry of the Line eager to get there before Christmas, before it was all over.

When his father, Sir Cosmo Strange, the man who brought the paddle steamers to the village, died, the villagers and tenant farmers, and the heads of each estate department, including the senior master of the Cluny Steamboat Company, a half-pay Royal Navy captain from Cardiff, had followed his coffin, and the three shops the village had then had closed for the day. And soon it would be his turn. And who was there now, to follow him?

The General absently stroked his old gundog, Snipe, quietening him, the dog moving restlessly next to him on the bed, retrieving again perhaps in his sleep. Annie and Owain would look after Snipe, he had no worries there. It was the estate, or what was left of it, that concerned him now.

It was not how he had wanted it to be, how it should be. But he had outlived his three sons, losing one in the Second World War, another to a hunting accident in the Fifties, and the youngest at sixty, after a stroke. And his siblings and his wife had also died, had also gone before him.

He had two daughters alive still, and grandchildren

and great-grandchildren, boys among them, but the estate was entailed, and his will had to follow the rule of descent. That line, in this case, stopping at a great-nephew, someone he had never met. A stranger soon to be among them, soon to take what was left.

The General lay back on the pillows, feeling suddenly weary of it. An old man, left behind in a house full of the past. Outside the room the lost lands, and the cries of peacocks walking the ruined walls of the gardens. And a world that was all in his head now, the memories of it all that was left.

Christmases when it always seemed to be snowing, home from school in the holidays with his brothers, piled in the back of the covered game cart from Church Myddle station. The carols around the big outside tree, and liveried carriages and motorcars lining the drive, when the house was lit like a cake and waltzes were played, and the faces, all seen again, all danced with again, of the girls he fell in love with each year at the party in the servants' hall.

Out on a winter river with his first gun, a Wesley Richards 28-bore he almost slept with, for wigeon and teal and snipe, and the Boxing Day coot shoot. And cock pheasants on January mornings iron with frost, gloving his hands with the warm wings of the birds between drives, when the fires of the Stops burnt like polished copper through the trees.

And helping with the hay in summer, the carts of Home Farm piled high with it. Memories of dust and the heated scent of sweet vernal grass, and the bite of cider cooled in a jar.

He saw his wife again as if for the first time, across a dance floor in the London season, in a white presentation dress and Prince of Wales feathers. And on her favourite bay, clattering out of the stable yard in wide skirts and a bowler hat and veil, and rode again with her on a good scenting morning, with the hounds in full cry and a horn calling. And remembered walking the root fields on September afternoons with his head keeper, and his sons when they were young, out after a few early partridges or pheasant along the hedgerows, and teaching the boys to spin for pike.

And memories of his own father, happy as a boy himself among the hissing steam and coal dust, firing up a boiler on one of the paddle steamers, or pacing the landing stage, fob watch in hand, checking and rechecking the time with mysterious urgency. And opening up the steam whistle full throttle, as if to alert shipping, as they puffed importantly upriver, piling up smoke and stampeding sheep and cattle along the grazing meadows.

The Cluny Steamboat Company. Mad, all quite mad. And all such fun.

The day trips to Water Lacy and back, the Two Shilling Dips, as they were called, the paddlers crowded with villagers and farm workers in their Sunday best, with bottles of beer and pop, and sandwiches made for the trip, churning the water white around Snails Eye Island. And the Moonlight

4

Excursions, when courting couples found the shadows on deck and coloured lanterns lit the murmuring, soft summer darknesses. And in the last war, after the company had bankrupted itself, local men rode their decks in the uniform of the Home Guard, patrolling the river approaches, ready to stand between Batch Magna and the Nazi jackboot.

And now another enemy perhaps waited. And this time one the village could do nothing about.

A brittle winter sun lit the large, leaded bow window in the room, the curtains open on a view of the hills which sheltered his valley. Its light the colour of gemstones in the frieze of armorial glass along the top panes, warming the centuries, the patina on floorboards of estate oak.

It had faded from the room by the time Annie Owen, the General's housekeeper, carrying a tray of afternoon tea, entered it again. And by then the hand that had been stroking the last of his dogs, the veins standing blue on it, had been still for some time.

CHAPTER 1

Phineas Cook woke in the bedroom of the *Cluny Belle* to the sound of a cow browsing on the other side of the river.

He got out of bed and pushed the bedroom window fully open. The cow, a large moon-faced Hereford, had made her way down the bank from the field there, and was in the shallows, among the reeds and budding water-lilies, champing on a few young stalks of meadowsweet, and up to her udder in a river mist.

The mist lagged the trunk of a goat willow uprooted during a recent storm, and hung in drifts above the meadow where the shapes of more cattle loomed. A moorhen croaked above the murmur of the river dawdling on its way to the fish weir, and something small made a splash. And in Mawr Wood next to the meadow, birdsong simmered, calling from the tender new green of sycamore, hazel and alder.

He could smell and feel it waiting in the mist, the promise of heat, of summer, at last.

He rummaged through the clothes piled on a chair, and pulled out a sweater and jeans. On the

7

bed, Bill Sikes, six muscular stone of white boxer with the face of the spike-collared dog in a cartoon backyard, lifted open a suspicious eye.

'Up!' Phineas told him. 'And next time stay on your own bed,' he muttered as he went through into the sitting room.

He found the socks he wanted on a hanger, above the stove he'd had alight only yesterday against a river chill. The stove, large and pot bellied, sat in the centre of the room, its chimney fed into the paddle steamer's original stovepipe funnel, sending up smoke again from it, and the heat banging and knocking through the pipes.

He marched back into the bedroom in wellington boots to pull Sikes off the bed, ignoring the panto-mime curses, the fearsome-sounding growling and snarling, upper lip rigid over teeth polished with spittle.

Phineas paused out on deck, out into a world wrapped in mist and silence. A dog somewhere on the other side of the valley barked steadily on into it, and in Mawr Wood on the opposite bank, rooks in the tops of the big sycamores stirred and bickered, damp-throated in the mist. And upstream of the wood, from one of the fields on the river that side, a horse whinnied, the sound rearing in the still air, and he heard the drumming of hooves as it broke into a gallop, kicking up its heels and bucking because perhaps it was young and simply had to. Or, for all he knew, it was something that went on at first light every morning in summer.

Placidly grazing or under a saddle for the rest of the day, for that brief time, perhaps, that brief summer dawn on the river, it ran and danced to a different tune.

The mist had rolled up to Batch Magna's High Street, and as far as the castle above the river, the last grey wisps of it drifting among its ruined stone like cannon smoke, like the ghost of old battles. The trees on the lower slopes of the hills were ragged with it, and it was as if snow had fallen elsewhere, the hawthorn of the valley piled with blossom. A green and white scented world that seemed to have bloomed overnight.

The ground in front of the *Cluny Belle* had once been a small cider orchard. Some of its ancient trees stood still, mossy and lichen stained, and bent as if by winds. A few of them, brought down by the years and the weather, slowly growing back into the earth among nettles.

Home Farm had used it during lambing and it still had a few sheep out on it, fleece-fat ewes with their spring lambs, like stones in the mist.

Sikes ignored them. Head and scut of a tail down, he waited resignedly for Phineas to open the makeshift gate of a pallet top secured with orange baler twine, and went through it as if to his doom.

In the lane he headed for the next best thing that time of a morning to a bed or sofa, Phineas's car, parked half up on the verge. An old Frogeye, a canary-yellow Austin Healey Sprite, made for summer and the top down. Sikes liked to see the world go by when he travelled in her, sitting upright in the passenger seat, sticking out his head when they hit the open road, trying to bite the wind.

Phineas called him away, and waited then, when he saw the bulky figure of Owain Owen ambling along Upper Ham from the direction of his own boat further downriver, beyond the pub. Owain was carrying a rod and an old wicker fishing creel on his back, Bryn, his Welsh collie, quivering with anxious excitement at his heels.

'Like a bloody heron, you are, Phineas, standing there,' Owain said when he came upon him, Phineas's tall spare figure in the mist.

Phineas nodded at the gear. 'Off after a drop of breakfast, Owain?'

'Chub, boy. You got to be up early to catch a chub. I spotted – Bryn! Doolally bloody animal you, heel!' Owain growled, his dog all over Bill Sikes in a demented burst of energy, while the boxer stood there, glumly.

Rod or 12-bore, both in his master's hands had the same effect on Bryn. The collie went into the water for the fish Owain caught, bringing them in alive and flapping, and dropping them like pheasant at his feet. It was Owain's boast that when it came to fish or bird, his dog had a mouth as soft as a woman's.

'I spotted a likely-looking chub hole the other day. Up past Padford Bank.' Owain lowered his voice as if the fishes could hear. 'And the water's settled again now. Be clear as gin under that lot. And that'll be lifting soon. Then it'll be a hot 'un. And what about you then, boy? What got you out of bed this time of the morning? Somebody set fire to it, did they? Or haven't you been in it yet, is that it?'

He peered over at Phineas's bedroom, bolted like the rest of the living quarters on to what was left of the PS *Cluny Belle*'s upperworks. 'On your way back, is it, from somebody else's?' he said, and raised his bushy eyebrows a couple of times suggestively.

Phineas smiled as if indulging him. 'No, Owain, I'm on my way *out*,' he said patiently. He nodded at Bill Sikes. 'You'd think I was taking him to be shot, but we're actually off for a walk. A spot of shore leave after all that weather. Now summer's decided to turn up. And as you say, it will be hot later. No, all that other sort of business is in the *past* now, Owain,' he said, shaking his head with a chuckle, as if gently chiding him for not keeping up.

He regarded his friend earnestly. 'Quite frankly, Owain, I don't think it's overstating it to say that you see before you a changed man.'

'Oh, ah,' Owain said.

'A more adult, responsible model, even if I do say so myself.'

'Oh, ah,' Owain said again.

'Sally, Sally has made – you've met Sally?' Phineas broke off with a small quizzical frown, his tone suggesting that if Owain *had* met her then no further explanation should be necessary.

'Ah, at the pub,' Owain said.

'Yes, well,' Phineas said simply, 'she has made me see things differently.'

'Oh, ah,' Owain said.

'Made me more . . . well, more adult and responsible.'

'Where is she, then? Still in bed? Knackered, is she?' Owain said, peering past him again at his bedroom, his eyebrows going up as if at the thought of one woman heroically supplying all that Phineas had regularly been getting from what at times seemed like a steady stream of them.

'No, she's not in *bed*! Here or anywhere else. If you must know, she's on a week of nights, helping out at Kingham General. Ministering to the sick. What I meant was, was that she's made me see things in a different light, simply through being the sort of person she is – a mature, responsible woman. Mature and responsible. There's comfort in those words, Owain. Words to come home to, a rest for one's weary head after slogging away on the primrose path, as Shakespeare had it. A puffed and reckless libertine who reaks not his rede. Well, whatever a rede is, I've decided it's about time I reaked it.'

Owain was staring at him. 'You're not thinking of getting married again, are you?'

Phineas looked startled. 'What! No – no, I'm not *thinking* of getting married again. No, it's simply as

I say, these days I'm taking a more adult approach to life. There are people, Owain,' he went on confidingly, his tone suggesting that Owain might find this hard to believe, 'who have expressed the view that I lack a sense of what they describe as responsibility. That, in their assessment, it's about time I started taking life a bit more seriously. The weightier approach is called for, that seems to be the general consensus. In short, they consider that it's about ruddy time I grew up. And what's more, Owain, quite frankly, they're right! They are *right*. I see that now,' he added into the middle distance, the light of the new maturity in his eyes.

'Well, I don't know. And what's Pugh the Pew going to do? He'll have to start buying the *News of the World.*'

'That gossip shop. It's only because nothing ever happens here. Elsewhere I'd be regarded as being near celibate.'

'Oh yes,' Owain said with interest. 'Where would that be, then? London, is it?'

'Anywhere with a bit more to it than one shop and a pub. Where people are too busy living their own lives to concern themselves with those of others.'

'Oh, you're right there, boy. Nothing to bloody talk about, they haven't, some people round here. Or think about. Sex on the brain, they've got. *Sex* on the bloody brain. But what do you think of the old suit, then?'

Owain pulled in his stomach to get a better look

himself, peering down at the lovat-green tweeds he was wearing. 'It was the General's. Sarah, his granddaughter, she gave it me. Gave me all his shooting clothes. Savile Row, they are. *Savile Row*. In London. And they fit. Well, apart from the sleeves, that is. And the trousers, like. As you know, he were a big man, the General. Still, Annie'll sort it all out one of these days.'

The sleeves came nearly to his knuckles, the waist, even on Owain's ample front, tied like a sack with a large buckled belt.

Owain pointed at his wellingtons, the tops of them turned down. 'And these socks I have on are hand knitted. Like walking on moss, they are. He liked to look after his feet, the General did. Pity he didn't pay the same heed to the rest of him. God bless him.'

Owain's Welsh-dark liquid eyes turned mournful. 'The old love. It's not the same round here without him. Not the same.' He shook his head. 'I never thought I'd be that sorry to have a glass in my hand.' Owain, who had been a head keeper on the estate, and the General's loader until the old man had to give up shooting, had been invited up the Hall with Annie, his wife, after the funeral.

Phineas had drunk to the old man himself, along with most of the village and valley in the pub that day, remembering him with affection. And like those who had known him all their lives, he realised that he had somehow come to believe that he would always be there.

'Has the estate been settled yet?' he asked.

'Well, the valuers have all finished, like. But no, no one seems to know yet what's happening. Myself, I reckon Sarah'll get it. Everyone else is either dead or too old. There's no money as such, so I don't see the boys being interested, except maybe to sell what there is left. Something the General would have thought of, you can be sure of that. And Sarah's not only the eldest grandchild, she knows her way about, like. She practically ran the place when she was working in the office. She'd sort things out. She nagged him enough about it when he was alive. So did I, about the sporting interests, and that. But as long as the old man could get out with a gun and had a drop of some-thing left in the cellar he just didn't care, not after Lady Phylldia died. God bless 'em. And he would know he could trust Sarah. Oh, she might have to sell off a bit more land or whatever to pay death duties, and all that. But everything else would stay as the General wanted, I'm sure of that.'

Phineas looked doubtful. 'I've yet to meet a woman, Owain, who was content to leave the furniture where she found it.'

'Well, we'll see. Tell the truth, I don't see it mattering to us much who's in charge of things. I mean, all this'll still be here, no matter what.' Owain's hand carelessly took it all in, the greening hills of the valley growing out of the mist, the sleeping village, and the castle on a hill. And their home, the river.

'Anyway, if I do get something in the bag, come and have a bite later. Wasting away you are, according to Annie.'

Phineas thanked him. 'As long as I can bring the wine,' he added.

Owain laughed. 'Annie's bloody medicine! Have a drop of this, she says, do you good. Must have got half the village legless on it in her time. The old vicar as well on a couple of occasions,' he said, not without pride.

During a recent gathering on the Owens' boat, the *Felicity H*, Annie had brought out some of her homemade stuff, bottles of blackcurrant whisky, rhubarb brandy, cherry and apple port, and red mead, all innocently labelled, like jam.

Phineas had been there before with Annie's brews, and not for the first time in his life told himself afterwards that he should have known better.

This time he'd managed to get back to the *Belle* without falling into the river, either off their deck or tacking into it off the bank, but he had no memory of doing so. He'd come to on his sofa, looking up with a sort of wonder at Bill Sikes looking down at him, the dog's breath friendly with the smell of one of the bones he had buried, the folds of his face like a fall of warm gentle snow.

After leaving Owain, Phineas went past Batch Hall and up Roman Bank, a lane running between fields, the verges, in front of hedgebanks cut with slate and dry stone, tall now with summer, with cow parsley and hemlock and goutweed, and with a smell to them like wet iron in the damp and mist.

And from somewhere behind him a cuckoo called abruptly, an urchin sound, like a bit of street corner mischief, following him mockingly. And he heard in it as he always did the taunting, near demented glee of a bird that knew something nobody else yet knew, but any day now would.

At the top of the hill, Phineas left the road and crossed the two humped fields called Peny Brin, Bill Sikes, with a sudden show of interest in the morning, scattering rabbits feeding among the moon daisies and buttercups, Phineas's boots shining like wet tar in the dew. And up into Cutterbach, a stretch of ancient woodland flushed each September by the Batch Valley Chase, home to badgers and owls as well as foxes, and fallow deer, relics of an ornamental deer park and a time when the Strange family and the village were young still.

They were on the very edge of the wood over-looking the valley, on a ride rutted with the recent weather and punched with the hooves of horses, when with no hint of its coming, the sun rose, and hung there, burning the trees on the skyline black, before ballooning above them as if released, a cock somewhere below crowing as if caught napping as its light swept across the valley.

Phineas felt it touch his face, warming it like a

cow's summer breath, fragrant with flowering grasses and meadow herbs and clover. With all the scents of summer ripening in the valley, under a creamy, blue and white marbled sky.

He stood looking down at the scene, as if coming on it for the first time. A field of buttercups seemed to slide, glistening, off the side of a hill, as if melting under the sweep of the sun, and among the trees above them the pale fire of rhododendrons. The meadow grasses falling away below him glinting here and there under frail webs of dew and mist, catching the light like things hidden. And the river, smoking in the sudden warmth, with the houseboats, the four paddle steamers that had once plied the home waters and a Victorian Thames, now tied permanently to the land, held there on their ropes, and the island called Snails Eye sitting at the heart of the river, where it bulged on a meander like a lake.

The small black and white farms of the valley among orchards, and the houses and half-timbered cottages of Batch Magna, a Marcher village, the cross of St George, flown from the Steamer Inn, a riposte to the red dragon of Wales above the door of the Pughs' post office and shop. The cricket field and pavilion behind the churchyard, and the great, immemorial yew, the centuries in its vast girth corseted with rusting iron bands, shading a church which bore in its nave the marks of Norman chisels, and among its gravestones a sundial which told the time in Jerusalem.

And the tall, star-shaped chimneys and gabled black and white timbers of Batch Hall, home to the Strange family for over four hundred years, set with Elizabethan ornateness in what was left of its park, its lawns, under horse chestnuts heavy with bloom, running down to the Cluny. And the castle, a fortress once against border incursions and the forces of Cromwell, open now to Welsh rain and rabbits, the loopholes in the ruined towers blinded with creeper, its red sandstone turning to coral in the sun.

The forgotten country, this part of the Marches had been called. A country largely ignored by the rest of the world, apart from a trickle of tourists on their way to somewhere else, and the odd company rep who had taken the wrong turning, in a place with need for few road signs. A valley lost among its ancient wooded hillsides and winding high-banked lanes, on a road to nowhere in particular.

Phineas had arrived there by accident, after taking a wrong turning himself, when on a road to nowhere in particular. And five years later was still there.

He thought occasionally, in a vague sort of way, about moving on, getting back to what he vaguely thought of as the real world. But there never seemed to be any particular hurry to do so.

And that of course was the *trouble* with the river, as he'd had occasion to point out before, to himself and to others, sparing no one. Whether boating up and down it, or simply sitting on it, there never seemed to be any particular hurry to do *anything*.

Well, now he had the feeling that all that was about to change. That now, with the General no longer at the wheel, they stood exposed to more unsettled weather. That the real world, which had always been over there somewhere, beyond the blue hills, was perhaps about to come to them.

He whistled for Sikes, busy putting up a few panicking pheasants and the smell of wild garlic as he blundered through the undergrowth after the scent of fox or badger.

They had walked this wood together in all the seasons. In autumn, when it ran like a damp fire through the trees, and in weather that had shrivelled Sikes's testicles as he padded warily through undergrowth crackling with ice or got himself buried in snowdrifts along the rides. The winter bareness like a ruin now in early summer, overgrown with new growth, letting in the sun and with the sound of birdsong up under its roof.

The sunlight lay among the drifts of bluebells and red campion, and reached with long slender fingers deep into the wood, where the new grass and ferns were tender in the shade between trees. And above him, high in the green and golden heart of an oak, a blackcap opened in sudden song. The sweet, poignantly brief notes flung, carelessly, on the morning air like a handful of bright coin.

CHAPTER 2

'An American? As squire!' Mrs Medlicott looked flustered, her English rose complexion reddened in patches by the sun as if she had been roughly kissed. Warm air, sprayed round the room in waves from an electric fan on the shop counter, teased the loose pink ribbon on the straw hat she hoped wasn't too young for her.

'Oh, yes. An American. He gets the lot, he does. Title and all. We heard it from Mavis Thomas, the cleaner from the pub,' Mr Pugh said, with a touch of astringency on the word pub. 'She got it from one of the women who did at the Hall, who got it from Annie Owen. And *she* got it from the horse's mouth – from the family. He's the General's great nephew. The grandson of the General's younger brother. The one who went to live in America sometime in the Twenties. The *Roaring* Twenties,' he added, as if inviting them to make what they would of that.

Across the other side of the small shop, perched with guinea-pig plumpness behind her post office counter, his wife was busy with more of the gossip that had been flying about the valley and village all day, adding to it, and passing it on with the stamps and postal orders.

'Sounds interesting. Might wake things up a bit round here.' Clem, the Honourable Clementine Wroxley, had stopped off for an ice-cream, leaving the engine running on the hunt's big Land Rover, an old post office workhorse with heavy lifting gear on the back, the throb of the diesel engine seeming to pump more heat in through the open door of the shop.

Clem used her rolled-up shirt sleeve as a purse, flexing a tanned muscular arm to tuck her change away. She was joint master of the Batch Valley Chase, and dressed for work in stained tight breeches, her boots bringing in on them the smell of that morning's mucking out at the hunt's stables and kennels at the other end of the village. A tall, straw-haired girl, with a nose delicately broken while point-to-pointing and determinedly female in make-up not always carefully applied.

'Can't stop,' she said between vigorous licks of a vanilla-and-strawberry Monster Double-Decker. 'Got a dead ewe and heifer waiting at Upper Rea. Leave them lying about too long in this weather and they'd have to be jolly well shovelled up.'

It was part of Clem's job to clear the local farms of dead stock, to be fed to the hounds. And if the part-time kennelman the small hunt employed wasn't there when she returned, she'd skin and butcher the carcasses as well, in full make-up as usual, wielding a hacksaw and siding knife among the blood and gore.

'That girl!' Mrs Medlicott said faintly as the door of the Land Rover was slammed shut.

'But what about the eldest grandchild, Sarah?' Tom Parr wanted to know, frowning at what he'd been listening to. 'What about her? Why didn't her get it? I don't understand.'

Mrs Medlicott was nodding vigorous agreement. 'Yes. Yes, I must say I thought she would have inherited. Everyone did. She farms herself and she's worked in the estate office. She could certainly run it as well as any man. Better in fact. And, well, surely that would have been far more appropriate.'

Mr Pugh, back from his storeroom behind the counter with replacement tins of Tom Parr's shag tobacco, was humming a hymn in short fierce bursts between sucking on an extra-strong mint, and Mrs Medlicott caught the smell of the drink she knew he kept in there. Mr Pugh regularly punished a Nonconformist conscience by drinking in what he still thought of as secret, and had further torment waiting for him in the storeroom in a collection of top-shelf magazines hidden behind the canned goods. Both of which activities had long been known to his wife and, through her, to the entire valley.

Mr Pugh, crunching on the last of his mint, took his time, arranging the rest of the tins on the shelf, and taking Tom's money and giving him change first.

And then he regarded them judiciously.

'That has nothing to do with it,' he announced. '*Nothing* to do with it. The inheritance has to follow a certain line of descent. A *certain* line of descent.' Mr Pugh was adamant, his raised finger rigid. 'That is the rule.' He sniffed. 'He's dead now, the General's younger brother. So is his son. So *his* son inherits, see. The grandson. The General's grandnephew. That is how these things work. Enshrined in praxis and usage immemorial,' he added, a man who only took the bigger books out of the lending library, no matter what their content. 'It's called,' Mr Pugh ended solemnly, 'entailment.'

'I still say it should stay in the family, the proper family,' Tom Parr muttered obstinately, beaten by all the words. Tom, an old man in a white cotton sun hat and a flannel vest, was aged like wood from the sun and his vegetable garden in one of the Masters' Cottages, his scrawny arms a deep, dull polished brown, and gnarled like willow roots. He was a retired mechanic and one of the few villagers living who had worked on the paddlers when they were the Cluny Steamboat Company, as fireman and engineer. A hero then to small boys, and the village girls who sighed weekly in the threepenny seats at the Kingham Odeon, with his Ronald Colman moustache and nautical sweater, and a fireman's cap worn at an angle, swaggering up the High Street as if he had a parrot on his shoulder.

After Tom had gone Mr Pugh started emptying Mrs Medlicott's basket, while keeping an eye on a grubby little girl loitering casually by the open display of sweets at the front of the counter. He'd been watching her.

Peering out earlier, beyond the glare of a white-washed wall topped with gillyflowers, and a Walls ice-cream sign, he had seen her lift her baby sister up over the gutter to pee. Then he'd heard the door of the telephone box open just out of view, as she checked it for any change that might have been left. She was off the boats, a water gypsy, one of Jasmine Roberts's lot. Her mother had come in with the rest of her brood for the post office, to cash another giro, no doubt. He'd like to see them all moved on, all the houseboats got rid of, the things that went on there.

Mr Pugh paused with a pound of Glamorgan sausages in his hand, suddenly stung by his thoughts.

'A big noise, the American is, by all accounts. A tycoon, a magnate – a mogul, he is!' he said, as if addressing Mrs Medlicott, but slyly aiming it at Jasmine Roberts on her way to the door, and missed the lightning raid on the jelly babies, a grubby little hand scooping a fistful up and shoving them down the front of a pair of pink cotton knickers.

'He'll make a few changes round here, you'll see. Oh, yes, you'll see – *you'll see*,' he called after the Roberts's clan as they straggled out, his voice rising with chapel fervour and the extra large Bells whisky he'd helped himself to.

And a few days later Jasmine *did* see, as did the others. The same letter, which, as a psychic, she said she had known was coming, arriving at all the houseboats.

CHAPTER 3

The heatwave that Batch Valley had been drowsing under for the past week continued. Turtle doves in the hawthorns on Snails Eye Island called, endlessly, into it, and the weeping willows were drenched with summer, trailing their branches in the water-lilies and sweetgrass, and their own reflection.

Onboard the *Felicity H*, Owain and Annie Owens' second youngest daughter, Ffion, was taking advantage of the weather and a day off work, and shallow diving off the starboard paddlebox, slipping as clean as a seal into water that was like a second element to her.

She had been born on the paddle steamer and had been swimming in the River Cluny since the age of five, when the children used to put to sail in a tin bath, brandishing wooden swords under a cardboard Jolly Roger, putting flotillas of ducks to rout, and sending moorhens diving, tails up, for cover.

Sleek with water, she climbed back up the steel ladder fixed to one side of the vented, fan-shaped paddlebox, the heat of the day waiting for her like a warmed bath towel, drying the river chill on her.

The PS *Felicity H*, her name painted with fairground flourishes along the arches of her two paddleboxes, had been the flagship of the old CSC, named after Sir Cosmo Strange's wife. Before being converted to a houseboat with the other paddle steamers in the late Forties, in the largely vain hope of catering for duck-shooting parties, and then for holidaymakers who came in even fewer numbers, she had served variously as a storage shed, hay barn and as living quarters for estate workers.

The original houseboat's steel and wood upperworks were built fore and aft of a funnel that was painted still in the company's livery of dark gold and Trafalgar blue, and offered then a double bedroom, sitting room, kitchen and a bathroom, with a shower and hip-bath. Over the years, as the children had come along, Owain had added a further two large bedrooms on top, the uptops, as they became known, reached by companionways, their roofs smelling now of sun-baked tar.

When high winds hit those rooms on the shallow-draught vessel, the children, tucked up in their bunks in the rocking and swaying darkness, squealed and screamed as if getting their money's worth on the big dipper.

Standing on the deck matting, Ffion brushed the river from her dark hair and adjusted the top of a scarlet lycra bikini, her firm young breasts tanned to shades of honey brown and cream, and pearled with moisture. From the shade under a table, where her mother and her eldest sister, Bryony, sat drinking tea, Snipe, the General's old gundog, who had decided that Ffion was his replacement, thumped the deck with his tail.

Ffion was leaning on the rail, eyes half-closed against the glitter of water and sun, its light falling like rain on the river, when she heard the post van pull up.

She glanced over at the two women. Bryony had her baby son on her lap, spooning him pureed pear from the village shop, while her second youngest splashed noisily and happily about in a patched rubber dinghy that had once kept Bryony herself quiet, aided by Cadi, Ffion's youngest sister.

'It's the post. I'll get it,' she called, slipping into a pair of flip-flops against the heat of the metal deck.

It was the second post of the morning, a second offer of hope.

The two women had exhausted the latest gossip on the American, and Bryony had returned to the new mail order catalogue she'd brought over. The green acacia chairs and the matching table they were sitting at were from another one of her catalogues. Suburbia, as seen in the Patio Living pages, had come to the river and was well represented on all the boats, finding a second home on their decks for anything from a complete dining-table set ("with stylist parasol"), to garden lanterns ("for that exclusive Mediterranean ambience").

And while Bryony went on about the shoes, her mother watched as Ffion strolled casually towards the gangway with Snipe in tow, and wondered again who the boy was.

She's sitting about like a fire waiting to be lit, Phineas Cook had said a few weeks back, when Ffion, slumped in an armchair, was deep in an adolescent sulk over something or other. And although, as far as she knew, her daughter had never had a serious boyfriend, and wouldn't be drawn on the subject, Annie now suspected that someone had provided the match.

Out of sight of the two women, Ffion hurried down through the sprawling plot, scattering chickens, ducks, and honking geese, an Anglo-Nubian milking goat, knuckled down in the long grass, looking snootily amused by the sudden disturbance.

An old gamekeeper's field hut, with rusty iron wheels and a stovepipe, rotted in an amiable sort of way under a crab apple tree, and what was left of a Fordson tractor, half buried in the grass. There were wooden Tate and Lyle sugar boxes for hutches, and several old, iron-framed wooden railway containers, bought by the estate when the local branch line closed, and used as sheds for such things as the deep freeze. Stacked odd lengths of timber and stove logs weathering under wraps, sheets of rusting corrugated iron, coils of old mooring cable, a ruined punt, and the bones of a beached sculling boat with grass growing through it, and a fridge.

The postbox was nailed on one side of a five-barred gate. There were two letters in it, both for her parents.

Nothing for her.

But she had known there wouldn't be. She had been telling herself all sorts of stories about their future together since he'd left, but she had known that all along. Known as soon as he'd left, the moment he'd left, that she was never going to see him again.

She tried not to cry, walking slowly back up to the boat. The hurt and humiliation, and the anger she felt with herself, making her look somehow much younger than her sixteen years.

Lieutenant-Commander James Cunningham, DSO, DSC and Bar, RN (ret), was scribbling away in what he called the wardroom, a room that in part had once been the wheelhouse of the PS *Batch Castle,* when the post van arrived unnoticed. The Commander was busy replying to another letter from his bank.

He wondered sometimes what was going on out there. Once he had someone called a bank manager who fussed over his financial health like a family doctor, and if he needed to chide him then at least did so in a literate and recognisably human manner. Now he had somebody calling herself a customer service executive lecturing him in letters that read as if they'd been dictated by a Dalek.

The Commander paused to relight his briar, and then looked at his watch again. He frowned and checked it with the old gimbal-mounted brass captain's clock on a bookcase. There were some mornings when the sun took longer to move over the yard-arm than others.

Phineas Cook, as Warren Chase, the crime writer, in a Gent's Superior Panama, and with a Gauloise at a hard-bitten angle in his mouth, was working on the deck of the *Cluny Belle* under a Martini parasol, courtesy, along with the table, of the weekly installment plan and Bryony Owen, the woman who had introduced Batch Magna to life on the never-never.

He was hammering out his thoughts on an old heavy Underwood typewriter, instead of something more advanced, because that's how Detective Inspector MacNail of Scotland Yard would have done it, the words going in like punches.

He stopped typing to fend off another caddisfly, then swatted at something on his neck.

Under the table Bill Sikes simmered noisily in the heat, tongue lolling, the smell of drying river silt on him attracting more flies. The dog, who liked a swim, had been in earlier and had then come out through a stand of reed and silt some yards astern of the boat.

At that moment DI MacNail, with only his fists

for protection, was on the top storey of a deserted East End warehouse, waiting for a Dragon, a Triad gang boss, and two of his henchmen to come up and get him.

Three against one, and the gangsters armed with Chinese chopping knives, weapons they were experts with. Things were looking up for MacNail.

MacNail, according to Warren Chase, had eyes the colour of rust on barbed wire, and a face that had been kissed by Glasgow steel, the marks of a razor slashing striping one cheek. And now, as MacNail heard their soft tread on the stairs, the detective grinned carelessly, in the darkness. Life was a game to MacNail, and one he always won. Life, when Warren Chase was writing it, did as it was told.

Phineas's eyes were narrowed over the page as the murderous thugs crept nearer. Then the flies and the smell finally got to him. He shoved the deckchair back.

'I'm trying to work here! Trying to get the rent paid. And look at the mess you've made!' he snapped at the dog. Sikes had waited until he was back on board to rid himself of most of the water and silt, spraying it round the deck.

Phineas was on his way to the kitchen for a bucket of water to wash the dog and deck down with, when life, of the sort that even Warren Chase could no nothing about, arrived in the shape of the post van.

33

CHAPTER 4

Phineas walked along Upper Ham, and through the door of what was once the ticket office and waiting room of the Cluny Steamboat Company, to reach the *Batch Castle*, and out onto the landing stage, all now part of the paddler's plot and moorings.

Both the building and landing stage looked much as they did in the photographs on a wall in the lounge bar of the Steamer Inn. There was a wooden triangular pediment still under the eaves, like that of an old branch line station, hanging baskets of geraniums, hollyhocks and foxgloves in the beds, and begonias blooming in the fire buckets. And a Victorian lamp-post that had once flared in the river mists, a yellow rambler climbing still up one side of the office door, and crimson roses under the windows, the heated air velvet with their scent.

Phineas found the Commander standing at the starboard rail of the boat, bracing himself on his good leg, a pair of marine binoculars trained steadily on the wooded hills on the other side of the valley, as if watching for the smoke of the enemy.

He lowered the glasses when Phineas came up the gangway, and wiped at the sweat on his brow with the back of his hand.

'A buzzard,' he said. 'Hear it whistling? There's a nest up there somewhere. I love to see them soar, riding the sky, so effortlessly. And so free. I shall reserve a second life, after first returning as an otter, and come back as a buzzard.'

He glanced at the letter Phineas was holding, the white envelope red-franked with the name of a firm of Kingham solicitors. 'Ah, I see you received the same signal, my boy.'

'So it's not just me?' Phineas said, stuffing the letter into his shirt pocket.

The Commander smiled. 'No, old chap, it's not just you. Ours came in the same post. As did one for the Owens. And presumably Jasmine's been paid off as well.'

'A hell of a blow!' Phineas said, and looked at the Commander as if waiting to be told otherwise.

The Commander nodded solemnly. 'As you say.'

'And completely out of the blue.'

'Oh, completely,' the Commander agreed.

'Jasmine's not there, by the way. Or at any rate her car isn't. I was going to give her a shout.'

The Commander motioned towards the living quarters. 'The first lieutenant,' he said, meaning his wife, 'is in there now, ringing both you and Jasmine. Annie's with her.' When storm threatened, those on the river tended to turn for the lee of the *Castle*.

'And you've been given the same notice on your moorings?' Phineas asked.

The Commander nodded. 'Three months.' He and his wife, Priny, were the only ones to own their boat, buying it out of what was left of a venture farming edible snails in Cornwall, something else which had ended in a lively exchange of letters with the bank. 'They don't say what they'll do if we haven't moved by then. Sink us, I suppose.'

'Well, at least he's given us good notice. Two months more than he was legally obliged to. Which is decent of him.' Phineas thought again. 'Or is it?' he asked himself suspiciously, seeing that it involved business and lawyers.

He decided it wasn't. 'He's probably got his own timetable. Besides,' he added indignantly, 'the estate owes the Owens a bit more than that. A damn sight more than that!'

'Oh, I quite agree. I quite agree,' the Commander said, peering at his wrist watch.

'And what about you, James, you and Priny? What will you do?'

'Emm? Oh, well, we'll have to sell her back to the estate – always providing of course that they want her back. Or we could arrange a tow – *if*, that is, we can find somewhere to tow her to. And *if*, that is, we had something to steer her with. The old duck certainly couldn't go anywhere without a push of some kind.' He looked at Phineas, as if Phineas had suggested she might. 'There's not enough of her plumbing left for anything else.' The *Castle* was also the only one of the paddlers to still have the remains of an engine.

'Although I'd dearly love to be able to do that for her. To take her out as she arrived . . . To put a fire in her again . . . smoke and steam in the air . . . her wheels churning the water white round Snails Eye . . .'

The Commander's good eye was distant and full of it.

Then he remembered Phineas. 'And what about *you*, Phineas? What will *you* do, my boy? What are *your* plans? Will you stay here? Move on? Have you given it *any* thought at all yet?' he demanded anxiously, making up for it with a flurry of concern for his friend.

'No – I don't know, James. I don't think I'll stay. Not now. I mean, it won't be the same, will it?'

'No, old man, it won't be the same. Not the same thing at all.'

'And what about Annie and Owain? And after all this time.'

'It's an outrage. No other word for it.'

'And Jasmine and her family,' Phineas went on. 'Where will Jasmine go, with . . . with all those children of hers?' he said vaguely, never sure, like most people, like Jasmine herself seemed not to be sometimes, quite how many that meant.

'As you say. As you so rightly say, my dear chap. Where will they go? Where *will* they go? It's appalling, appalling.'

'And what's he going to do with the paddlers, that's what I'd like to know? The notice doesn't tell us much, does it? Just that he wants vacant possession. So what is he going to *do* with them?'

'What indeed. What indeed, my boy. That's the question,' the Commander said, frowning about him. '*That* is the question . . .'

He found his stick on the deck table, a heavy blackthorn, cut and shaped for him by Owain Owen, the handle, with a shine stroked into it from use, carved into a badger's head. He then fished about in his trouser pockets, searching for his fob, before remembering that he was using his wrist watch this morning. Life had suddenly become rather hectic.

'What indeed. What indeed, my dear fellow,' the Commander muttered, studying the watch face.

'That's it!' he said then. 'Wardroom's open.'

He was wearing a pair of creased white ducks, with a Royal Yacht Squadron necktie for a belt, and what was left of his hair sticking out in the heat in damp, greying, tufts. He had his head to one side slightly, favouring his good eye. Phineas peered at the glass one.

The Commander's leg had been shattered when, as a wartime naval pilot on the deck of his carrier, a Swordfish aircraft, coming in after him, and with the pilot wounded, had landed nose down, shredding the air with splinters from the wooden propellers. When the same accident later caused him to have an eye removed, the Commander commissioned a miniaturist to paint a collection of plain glass ones, depicting naval battles and landscapes that spoke of England, and one flying the Union Jack when a bit of swank, a bit of defiance, in the face of whatever was called for.

'The Stubbs,' the Commander told him. *'Huntsman and Horse.'*

'Ah,' Phineas said.

Phineas followed his friend up the steps to the wardroom, a room stuffed with books and bottles, and copies of ancient charts, like storybook charts, marked with brimming treasure chests and spouting whales, and warnings of monsters, and cherubs with winds on their breath. Here, the Commander pursued his theories of such things as the nature of time, and of moons that had shone down on this planet before, and monsters that still lived here, and the location of lost Atlantis.

Carrying their drinks, they came out into the dazzle of sunlight and white-painted upperworks as Priny and Annie Owen left the sitting room opposite.

'Ah, there you are, darling,' Priny said when she saw Phineas. 'Jasmine's not here,' she added to her husband. 'She's gone to Shrewsbury for the day, the babysitter tells me.' She smiled at Phineas. 'What is it about your legs, Phineas, that reminds me I was once a mother?'

Phineas frowned down at his legs, in a pair of white shorts. Annie laughed. 'It's because they need fattening, like the rest of him.'

'I was hoping,' Phineas said, 'they'd look less sort of obvious, once they got a bit brown again.'

'Leave the man's legs alone. He's got a perfectly good pair,' the Commander told her. 'The sort of knees that helped carve out an empire. His shorts could do with a press, and his hair's too long, I grant you. And he needs to straighten up a bit, stop slopping about the place. But his legs will do.'

'At least he's got the sense to wear a hat in this heat,' Priny told him. 'Put yours on, James, please. You'll boil your head.'

The Commander had caught the sun on a trip yesterday in their mahogany dinghy, pulling strongly upriver, with a lunch hamper in the stern. His leg, which rarely failed to let him know it was there when on land, forgotten.

'I can't, Number One, you've hidden it. She's always hiding things,' he told Phineas. 'Something to do with her age, I expect.'

'Where's Owain?' Phineas asked, while Priny located the ancient red-and-white striped rowing cap her husband had left on a deckchair.

'Helping out on a pigeon shoot over at Boden,' Annie said. She smiled sympathetically at him. 'You've got notice as well, then, Phineas?'

Phineas nodded. 'Yes. He hasn't wasted much time, has he? And to not say anything to you when he was here!' He shook his head. '*Incredible.*'

'Oh, I'm sure he didn't know it at the time, Phineas. He couldn't have.' Annie looked appalled at the thought.

'He's a businessman, Annie. A money man. To them, people go in one drawer, profit in another. And they *never* confuse the two.'

Annie had met the American at the Hall when he was over briefly to inspect his inheritance, and had liked him, as he had seemed to like her. She hoped he hadn't known that one of the house-boats was hers, that with a few impersonal words that weren't even his own, he was pulling over twenty years of family memories up by the roots.

'And Owain doesn't know about it yet?' Phineas said.

She shook her head. 'No. No, none of them do. Not yet.'

He saw she had been crying, the kohl she wore on her eyes smudged, and never very good at that sort of thing, made an awkward job of hugging her.

'Drinks!' Priny said brightly, looking at their glasses. '*What* a good idea.'

'Where's Pink Gin?' Phineas asked when they were seated. Pink Gin was the Cunninghams' aged mongrel, a dog who, when the drinks came out, usually liked a drop of something in her bowl.

'Too hot for her, darling,' Priny told him. 'She's getting rather ancient now, I'm afraid.'

'She's inside,' the Commander said. 'Dreaming of past glories. Ratting and rabbiting in her sleep.'

They were sitting at the round white plastic deck table, under a large, Patio Living pink-and-white striped parasol, an oasis of shade and the chime of iced drinks.

Priny lifted her glass. 'To survival.'

Like her husband she was good at that. Priny couldn't be kept down for long, no matter what the weather. Even Hitler, with his promise to bomb Malta to dust, couldn't do that when she nursed there during the worst of it. Not *even* the matron of her hospital could do that.

She was wearing a wide-brimmed sugar-pink straw hat, and what she called her mad old bag spectacles, emerald green, with two electric-blue butterflies perched on the frames, crimson lipstick to match her nail extensions, a poppy print shirt and floral Capri pants. A party of one in full swing, a Plymouth gin in one hand, a cigarette in an amber holder in the other.

'I'm just surprised the General didn't do anything about all this in his will, you know?' Annie, who'd been thinking about it, said. 'I mean, it's not just us, is it. It's the paddlers, and all that. Part of the history of the place, the old CSC. Our old tub was named after his mother.' She shook her head. 'Just didn't think, I suppose. That would be it. Poor old love.'

'It's this place. We are children here!' Phineas cried suddenly. 'Strolling heedlessly along, smelling the flowers and admiring the view. With no thought of what might be on its way round the next bend.'

He shook his head incredulously at the sheer *folly* of their ways. 'Well now it's here,' he said, looking at them accusingly. 'Now it has found us.'

Phineas's newfound maturity, worn over the past

few days with a solemn, aloof sort of air, like that of a visitor from an enclosed order to the frivolous world he'd left behind, was now less in evidence. His expression, as he gazed hotly out across the water, more that of an aggrieved teenager who had done what he'd been told to do, had taken a more mature, a more serious, responsible view of things, and had ended up getting evicted.

'Bound to happen sooner or later, I suppose,' the Commander said equably, tamping his pipe down. 'It's the times, my boy, the times. *O tempora o mores*. The new order. It goes under different names but always calls itself progress, and we are in its way. And the last sad squires ride slowly towards the sea, and the new lords take the land. Lords who look at our labour and laughter as a tired man looks at flies. With bright dead alien eyes. Something like that.'

He put his pipe in his mouth, and then took it out again. 'Come to think of it, I had a letter from one of them only the other day.'

Priny laughed, the sound pure bottled nightclub. 'James thinks the bank manager's been taken over by an alien.'

'It's the only possible explanation,' her husband said.

'That's what happens, darling, when you leave your hat off in the sun.'

The Commander ignored her, and lifted his glass. 'Here's to the General,' he said, and winked mysteriously at Phineas.

Annie laughed then, suddenly, at her own thoughts, and wiped at her nose with a hand. 'He'll go mad, Owain, when he hears. Go *mad*, he will. Probably take an axe to the old boat, the work he's put in on her. He only got round to finishing the paint job a couple of months back, her letters and scrollwork and all. Hopping, he'll be. Bloody well *hopping*.'

'Perhaps that's what we should do to all of them,' the Commander said. 'Rather than simply hand them over. Hazard them ourselves. Sink them. Blow them up. Send them to join their sister ship, the *Sabrina*. Better that than into the hands of the enemy, and god knows what indignities. It could be said we owe them that. Both the little ships and the General.'

The PS *Sabrina,* the old Roman name for the River Severn, and the vessel that had made the full complement of the CSC, had blown a boiler two years into service, when her crew, in an attempt to beat a previous time from Water Lacy, tried to shovel more speed out of her than her maximum eight knots safely allowed. She lay upstream of the *Cluny Belle* now, a diving board for generations of village children, and with moorhens nesting in her broken wheels.

'What, a few limpet mines on their hulls, you mean, James?' Phineas asked with interest, remembering a film he'd seen recently on television.

The Commander shook his head. 'No. No need for that, old man. A few sticks of something in the bilges should do it. Linked to a central detonator.'

'A plunger. Yes, yes, I know,' Phineas said, nodding at it.

'Then *bang*!'

The Commander leaned towards him. 'And we're far enough away from the village not to cause civilian casualties or to take the Masters' Cottages or the pub up with them. The General wouldn't want that. No, it would just be our party. Us and a plunger. Bang!' he said again, the huntsman's pink in the Stubbs like blood in his eye, the good one with enough blue life in it for two eyes, twinkling away, signalling devilment like a ship's lamp.

'At night, of course?' Phineas said. These things were always done at night.

'Well, of course at night, old chap. Not a lot of point in fireworks during the day now, is there.'

The Commander's head reared at a sudden thought. 'Of course! The very thing. The very time. On the day of the regatta. A grand finale to the fireworks. It could scarcely be more appropriate. The little ships started the whole thing, let them finish it. Let them have the last, loud word. Eh? *Bang . . .!*'

'I think,' Priny put in, 'that perhaps we should try something a little less explosive first, darling.' She could never be entirely sure with either of them. There was a part of her husband, she always felt, that had yet to return from the war. And Phineas, despite being in his middle thirties, had

45

still to grow up. 'And do bear in mind, James,' she told him, just in case, 'if you are inclined to get any silly ideas, that the *Castle* is all we have in the bank at present.'

The Commander sighed heavily. 'Yes, I know, Number One, I know. I'm sorry, Phineas, old man. It's age. It makes misers of us,' he said dolefully. 'Counting out our lives in small change from a thinning purse.'

Priny ignored it. 'We'll meet tonight. In the pub for the happy hour, and see what we can come up with. Jasmine should be back by then. I'll pop round and leave a note for her, in case we miss her, and she throws a drama.'

Annie finished her wine. 'And I'll get over to the Hall now, see what else I can find out.'

'What shall I do?' Phineas wanted to know.

'I've got you down for keeping an old party company over another glass in the wardroom,' the Commander told him, getting up stiffly with the aid of his stick.

'It's not over yet, Phineas my boy. Not over yet, my dear fellow,' he said then, quietly, confidingly. 'Did I tell you that a few days back I saw an otter? No, not a mink,' he insisted, as if Phineas was about to suggest it might be. 'A mink is much smaller and a darker brown. No, it was an otter. On Snails Eye. Disporting itself on a bank there. Sliding down a mud run and splashing away without a care in the world. A lord of time, with a fine set of whiskers.'

The Commander stopped and looked at him.

'Time for animals like the otter, you see, Phineas, is different from, for example, time for a farm animal. On the whole, time for farm animals stands still, scarcely moves from where they're grazing. If we were able to represent it on a clock face, you would see that in the evening, when it's time to sleep, the minute hand had barely moved from where it was in the morning, when it was time to start eating. Which of course is how it should be.'

The Commander started and stopped again.

'Time for wild animals, on the other hand, you see, my boy, is almost *constantly* on the go. Here and there, this way and that. It leads them by the nose, as well as the belly. And when they're not questing or eating, or engaged in sundry other matters, then they're squabbling. And when they're doing none of those things, they are playing. And then they are lordly, lordly. Time for us, Phineas, we humans, is a poor shackled thing in comparison. We are tied to it from birth, and burdened with its future as well as its past. The baggage of our lives, and our fears of what might be. And the usual spree of youth aside, we spend it with one eye on the clock. Unlike animals such as the otter, who chuck it about as if there were no tomorrow. Which of course, for them, there isn't. They live only in the present. They cannot *know* time and so are free of it. And lords of it. With fields of time, seas and rivers of time, and all the skies to play in.'

47

The Commander shook his head with sudden impatience. 'Anyway, anyway,' he said, moving again, and as if Phineas had diverted him. 'The point is – the point is, my dear Phineas, that I have never, in all my ten years on this river, seen an otter here before. Never.'

He stopped again, and sighted Phineas with his good eye. 'You do realise what this means, don't you?' he said. 'It means, it means, old chap,' he explained patiently, when Phineas appeared to have no idea, 'that the General is once more among us. And *why*? That's the question, Phineas. That is the question, my dear old fellow. Why? Why *now* of all times?' the Commander asked, and winked.

CHAPTER 5

The village pub, the Steamer Inn, a paddler puffing away on its sign, was built in 1662, and called the Black Boy, in honour of their restored monarch, Charles II, until Sir Cosmo brought the boats home.

When in London, and if not at his club or discussing vintages over a glass of Oloroso in Berry Bros & Rudd, Sir Cosmo had spent his days riding up and down the Thames on the new fleet of paddle steamers, owned by London County Council and run like a bus service between Hammersmith and Greenwich. He had found heaven there, in a drizzle of steam, soot and spray, lost to the music of the wheels and the sound of a twin cylinder compound diagonal engine hammering away.

And then, after a couple of years of steadily falling receipts, the LCC decided to cut their losses and sell.

And on the day of that sale Sir Cosmo, nagged to London by his wife for a much-needed meeting with his accountants, came across it in the ironed pages of *The Times* when breakfasting at his club on the morning – the very *morning* – he was to deliver himself and his finances into the hands of bean-counting abacists and scriveners, intent on getting a tighter grip on the estate's purse strings.

He was not, he told himself, a fanciful man, but if this was not fate, then he'd very much like to know what was. And if, in the arithmetic of that notion, it didn't add up to a paddle steamer service on the River Cluny, then he'd very much like to know what would.

He was among the first at the sale on Westminster Pier, coming on the entire fleet of thirty paddlers tied up along the river on that mid-December morning with all the wonder in his eyes of a small boy in his first toy shop.

Christmas, for Sir Cosmo, had come early.

He bought five of them, the smallest vessels of the fleet, at a combined cost of nearly six thousand pounds. And could only wonder that money, mere money, could buy such things.

Not that Sir Cosmo had any money, or at any rate none to spare, but scribbling down a few figures on the back of an envelope, he had beamed with satisfaction on the result. Arithmetic wasn't Sir Cosmo's strong suit, but even he could see that ferrying people, goods and livestock between Batch Magna and, say, Shrewsbury, came to a good deal of profit, whichever way you looked at it.

He worked out how he was going to pay for them on the other side of the envelope, selling off another slice of his estate there.

He telegraphed for a team of estate workers to

50

entrain for London, to be instructed with him in the mysteries, the wondrous mysteries, of a paddle steamer, and with one of his keepers acting as fireman, took the wheel of the largest vessel, earmarked as his flagship and already renamed the PS *Felicity H* after his wife, in an attempt to placate the tiresome questions she had no doubt waiting for him.

Trailing smoke and white water, they paddled their way downstream to Gravesend, to the River Medway and dry dock in Chatham, where they were partially dismantled and hauled over to the railhead on steel rollers for the journey to Shrewsbury, borne there on a train pulled by an engine called *Progress*.

In Shrewsbury, they were put together again and their fires relit for the twenty-odd-mile journey down the Severn, to the home waters of the River Cluny. There, they closed stations and shovelled on more speed for a finishing flourish, panicking cattle and horses along the water meadows, and flooding the banks with their wash.

Half the county, and a good bit of Wales, had turned out to greet them. The village school declared a day's holiday and the children lined the banks in their Sunday best, each, in an excess of excitement, given a little flag of empire to wave. Bunting was hung throughout the village and the flags of two countries flown, and the Silver Band from Church Myddle, waiting with the mayor and the local press, tuned up on a hay wharf that was soon to be the landing stage of the CSC. The bouncy, sea-brisk notes of "Hearts of Oak" struck up on the approach, when the steam whistles of the tiny flotilla opened full throttle, screaming above the cheering and the music.

Photographs and other memorabilia of that time looked down silently now from a wall of the bar where the present-day occupants of those boats had gathered. Copies of sailing bills and freight charges, advertisements and tickets, and photographs of the paddlers and their crews, and Sir Cosmo in a top hat among the Sunday bowlers and best bonnets, and the first herd of sheep being loaded, dogs low at their heels.

They were sitting in the bay window, which looked out over the small terrace with its summer chairs and tables, the upended mahogany sculling boats for hire on the slipway below, and the river. And now, after discussing the eviction notices and the news Annie Owen had brought back from the Hall, a small silence had fallen over the table.

'Are they all right, Jasmine?' Phineas asked then, nodding at two of Jasmine Roberts's young sons, grimly trying to strangle each other on the floor.

'Stop it, you two! Get off him, Thorin!' she hissed.

'They're at that difficult age,' she explained. 'Halfway between their aether body and their astral.'

'Ah,' Phineas said.

Jasmine had been doing readings in Shrewsbury, the result of a recent ad in the *Shrewsbury Gazette*, introducing her "world famous psychic powers", with a special rate for pets.

She had read for six adults there, and a canine client called Coco, a great dane stretched in elegant decline the length of a chaise longue, her brown eyes regarding Jasmine with ineffable yearning – ineffable, that is, to anyone else.

There were times when Jasmine didn't have to bother making up things, and she knew almost immediately what ailed the animal, even if she did spin the "consultation" out for an hour. Coco was broody, and if the owner wasn't going to let nature take its course, a course Jasmine herself had always been enthusiastically inclined to take, then she suggested surrogates, a few large soft toys for her to mother.

All in all it had been a successful day, even allowing for Coco's special rate, with enough now in her handbag to pay off some of the final demand she'd stuffed in the back of a kitchen drawer, something to throw the electricity company to stop them cutting her off again.

And shoes, there's be enough now as well for new shoes for Arian and Morwen, she thought with satisfaction, singing softly to herself as she walked up the gangway of the *Cluny Queen*, and found the solicitor's letter and Priny's note waiting for her.

She rounded everybody up and mustered them on deck, as if checking for casualties, or survivors, as if disaster had already struck, as in a way it had. She did so out of nothing more than an instinct for drama that had to go somewhere, had to *do* something. With no babysitter available for the evening, and without stopping even for a cup of something, she had then headed back down the gangway for the pub, carrying the baby and with her brood in tow as if leading them to a place of safety.

Careful not to wake her daughter asleep on one arm, Jasmine reached with a plump hand dressed with fish and abraxas rings for her pint of Black Boy bitter, her breasts, under her working dress of voluminous purple silk printed with stars and moons, rainbows and comets, filling the blouse like pillows.

'Well, I don't know about the rest of you, but my letter came as no surprise, I can tell you. I've known for days, I have, that it was coming. I just didn't see yours as well, I'm afraid,' she apologised. 'Otherwise I would have warned you all, of course. Terrible news, it is. *Terrible*,' she said, with a relish for even her own disaster. 'Homeless now, we are.'

She smiled with sudden brightness at another two of her brood eating crisps at her feet. 'Still, never mind, we can always drown ourselves, can't we, little ones.'

'I was hoping for a royalty cheque,' Phineas said to no one in particular.

Her daughter stirred and woke with a cry, and Jasmine tossed her Egyptian charm necklace over a shoulder.

'There, there, little heart, pert bach, there, there,' she cooed, popping the top buttons of her dress like peas, and fumbling for one of her generous bosoms. Her daughter fastened lustily on it, and Jasmine gazed down at her feeding head, her long hair, the colour of coal, falling like a curtain over the scene.

'I saw it all one night in a dream, I did,' she crooned, rocking gently over the infant. 'I dreamt that the letter blew in like the seven ears of corn, like locusts sent from Moses, on a bitter East wind, the wind of destruction, and pressed itself against my forehead. And I read it then, through my skin,' she said, and gave a little shudder.

Rumour had it that the baby was the work of a slaughterer and butcher from the valleys who passed this way regularly, killing and jointing cattle for the home freezers of local farms, and whose van had been spotted twice parked up for the *Cluny Queen*.

'He was just dropping in a bit of meat he'd promised me,' she'd said afterwards.

'Quite, darling,' Priny had replied.

The Commander shook his head. 'The poor General. To have his name associated with such an act of vulgar greed. Little wonder that he's restless,' he added, and winked conspiratorially at Phineas.

Annie had learned at the Hall that the American heir was submitting plans for a riverside holiday village with a paddle steamer theme to be built on the combined plots and moorings, news that by now, of course, was all round the village, the valley.

'Nice weather for ducks,' George Bishop had smirked when he came in. George was busy with his own plans, to put up a bed and breakfast sign, ready for when the future turned up in Batch Magna by the coach load.

'The Yank's got to get planning permission for it first,' Owain Owen growled. 'Can't just walk in here and build what he bloody well likes, doesn't matter who he bloody is.' Owain's chest had caught the sun again, rearing out of his shirt and a pair of the General's braces like an inflamed bull's.

'Of course he can't,' Phineas said. 'The reason, no doubt, he's given us three months' notice instead of one. He can afford to. It will take at least that for it to go through planning. And meanwhile it makes him look good.'

'Crumbs from a rich man's table,' Owain growled.

'A sop to Cerberus,' the Commander added.

'We could get up a petition,' Annie suggested. 'For the planning people, like. It probably won't help us, I know, but it will at least show how people feel. There's bound to be more people against it than for it, surely? I mean, be like bedlam it would here in the summer. Like Piccadilly Circus.' To Annie, who had only seen Piccadilly Circus, only seen London, on television, it came to the same thing.

'Good idea, darling,' Priny said. 'And we could

56

lobby our MP, that tall girl, the one who wears all those ghastly-coloured suits. Be rather like attacking them with a bunch of delphiniums but it might help get the local press interested.'

Priny herself was wearing a dress that looked more suited to a Kensington cocktail party, and a rope of pearls that had been across the odd pawn-shop counter a few times in the past, in exchange for what she and the Commander called marching money.

Phineas had remarked how grand she was looking. I *am* grand, darling, she'd told him.

'That's the stuff,' the Commander said. 'Lob as much as we can at the fellow. Any more suggestions?'

They looked at each other.

Phineas, feeding the last of a packet of pork scratchings to the two dogs under the table, had nothing to add either. As far as he was concerned it was already all over. The real world was already on the doorstep, with words like area regeneration and maximising potential in its briefcase.

'Myself, I'd like to drown the bloody man,' Owain said.

'Oh, Owain!' his wife protested.

'What do you mean – oh, O-*wain*?'

'Well!'

'I would! I'd like to drown him, and that's the bloody truth of the matter.'

'He means well.'

'Something I find far too many people mean today,' the Commander muttered.

'Duw,' Owain growled at her. 'You soft woman!'

Annie was also an obstinate one once she'd decided she liked someone. 'He does,' she insisted. 'He has the good of the estate and village at heart, really. He talked about that, about bringing money into the area, and that. I just didn't know that evicting us and all the rest was going to be part of it, that's all.'

'Damn busybodies are everywhere these days,' the Commander puffed crankily on. 'Earnestly knowing what's best for the rest of us. One can't even get a weather report without some impertinent comment or other as to how one should or should not dress if one is out and about, as they put it. Out *and* about, indeed!'

The Commander snorted, his good eye glaring. Tonight, his glass one, like rallying colours in battle, was flying the flag. 'And if they're not busy knowing best, then they're banning something. And if they're not banning it, they're modernising it, whether it wants it or not. We are once again in the hands of busybodying puritans. Puritans, bounders and blighters, and now this damn vulgarian from the colonies! I second Owain's idea. Let the fellow face the consequences of his own actions.' He shifted abruptly in his chair, his leg troubling him.

They were in the bigger of the inn's two bars, a room of worn Welsh slate flagstones and high-backed settles, under beams of estate oak, a summer urn of foxgloves and bracken standing in the hearth of a fireplace big enough to stable a pony. It had been the thought of pubs like this that had helped keep the Commander going through the worst of his war. While waiting with stretched nerves in the Ready Room, or utterly alone in the cockpit of a Swordfish or Dulmar, with all that sky and an enemy waiting. He had kept an image of such places, an image of home, close to him, like a photograph kept in a wallet. As far as he'd been concerned it was what they were fighting for.

'We could do it on one of the paddlers,' Phineas said, his eyes narrowed with plot. 'Invite him aboard on some pretext or other, and finish him then. Knock him out, and tip him over the side. He wasn't pushed of course. He fell. And must have hit his head on the paddlebox on the way down, poor chap. We could easily make it fit forensically.'

Owain came closer, a Welsh conspirator. 'He was inspecting the boats, wasn't he. And must have leaned over too far, like. Saw him then, we did. When it was too late, like. Drifting down to Prill Weir, he was. Like a dead sheep.'

With a practised movement Jasmine hiked her baby on to the other breast. 'An accident. A tragic accident,' she intoned.

'Regrettable, but there you are. These things happen,' the Commander said briskly.

Jasmine brightened. 'Then perhaps Sarah will inherit.'

'Be the end of our problem,' Owain murmured seductively at them.

Priny changed the subject, like an adult with childish talk getting out of hand. What, she wondered brightly, as if inviting them to wonder with her, did the American intend *doing* with the boats. 'That's the bit no one seems to know anything about.'

'They'll be given to the tourists to play with, that's what will happen to them,' Owain scowled. 'Holidaymakers, wearing plastic caps with Captain written on them. That's what it'll come to, you'll see. I'm only glad the General won't be here to see it. Break his old heart, it would. *Break* his heart.'

'The General didn't mind holidaymakers back then, did he. You remember,' Annie said.

'That was different,' Owain said.

'Not that he got any, mind. Well, not many. I remember that,' Annie went on. 'Years ago, that was. It was a big thing then, when we were young, to have holidaymakers – *strangers*, turning up. We used to come down and have a good gawk at them. There was nothing else to do. And, well, I mean, if it didn't work then why's it going to work now? You remember that, Owain. Course you do. I used to watch him about the place,' she told the others. 'Had my eye on him even then. He used to smell of skinned stoat, stink of it, he did sometimes,' she recalled fondly. 'He was keepering then, see.'

'Well, you could earn your beer money, couldn't you, with stoat skins in those days,' Owain said,

60

mellowing with memory. 'We used to send them to Birmingham, to a fur and feather merchant there, batches of them. We had rabbits all over the estate then, see, used to drive 'em with dogs, we had so many. And stoats like rabbit.'

'He used to come courting with half-a-dozen of them, for mam,' Annie said. 'And a brace of pheasant on Sundays. But that was when I was older, like, and he was completely free again. I made sure of that. Oh, no, I wouldn't trespass.' Annie, who was nearly twenty years younger than her husband, was Owain's second wife.

'But was he worth waiting for, Annie?' Priny asked. 'That's the thing. Or would you like to tell me later, darling?'

'Yes, what we want to know, Annie,' Phineas said, 'is if you knew then what you know now, would you have thrown the old chap back?'

Annie studied her husband, head on one side, while Owain bridled under the scrutiny.

'*No-oo*,' she said then, on a long breath, eyes narrowed sexily at him, and reaching across, tickled him under his chin. 'Not my old pike.'

Jasmine's laugh started somewhere in her stomach, the sound like a heavy engine turning over, and then catching, until her whole body rocked with it, almost shaking the baby loose.

'Don't say anything interesting till I get back,' Phineas said a while later, when the conversation had moved on to what sort of day they'd all had, and the rest of the village gossip. They were like a family, it seemed to him, leading separate lives in separate rooms, but always with the warmth of a kitchen there, and a glass or cup of something to share when needed.

Up at the bar he was served by Lucy, an ash blonde who'd arrived a couple of weeks earlier from the Welsh side of the border, and who lately had been looking in his direction.

She looked again now, when she gave him his change, her eyes signalling promise like a lure from the rocks. She counted it out slowly, in a low, light voice, like fingers walking, tantalisingly, on his skin.

Phineas concentrated on his change.

For one thing, there was the homicidal Carl, her boyfriend, and the pub's chef, a man who had once chased a critical diner from the pub with a boning knife. And then there was Sally.

When Jasmine had last read the tarot cards for him, just before he'd met his new girlfriend, she'd talked of calmer weather on the way in affairs of the heart. And he'd thought, wouldn't it be nice, just for once, to have a relationship that didn't end in tears and the sound of breaking crockery?

And now there was Sally. Sally and the new Phineas, who thanked Lucy politely for his change, paying her as much attention as he would have Patrick or John the barman. It was all the same to him now, he thought, sitting back among his friends, wondering if it showed.

Later, with yet another pint of the local Sheepsnout

cider in front of him, its name stencilled on the wooden barrel like a warning, he looked with a sudden fierce rush of love at the others. What fun it had all been, what fun. Lord! The times we've had together. What a jolly life it must be, Mole said, living by the river. By it and with it and on it and in it, Ratty had replied. It's brother and sister to me, and aunts and company, and food and drink. It's my world, and I don't want any other. Lord! The times we've had together.

'No!' he cried suddenly, as if in his sleep, and then glared at them. 'No! Damn it, we will fight! We will fight and we will win! We'll drive them from the river. From *our* river!'

They watched with surprise as Phineas stood, and draining his glass like a salute, lurched off in the direction of the lavatories.

Lucy, picking up glasses from the tables, was leaning across one of them to wipe it, her breasts buoyant in a silk vest, a miniskirt riding up over gleaming tanned thighs.

Phineas looked tormentedly towards the rocks for a moment. Then with a sound like a groan, plunged through the door into the corridor.

Zipping himself up before leaving, he almost walked into the condom vending machine.

They were the last out of the pub, which largely kept its own hours, out into a sleeping world, the village and valley deep in darkness.

Patrick, the landlord, saw them out through a

side door into the car park. 'See you tomorrow,' he whispered, and closed the door after them.

'Cut adrift,' the Commander said as the bolts went home in the silence, and lifted his voice in one of the songs Patrick had been banging out earlier on the piano.

'*Shhh!*' Priny said.

'*Shhh!*' Lucy the barmaid said, and giggled.

Phineas smiled fondly down at her, and drew her closer. He really could not *think* why he hadn't got round to this before.

'Where to now?' the Commander enquired brightly.

'Home,' Priny said.

'Nonsense, Number One,' her husband said, looking about him as if to see what else the night might have to offer.

'Home, Cunningham,' she said firmly, taking him by an arm. 'I don't want you getting your feet wet on me quite yet.'

The lights went out downstairs and the others straggled after them round to the front of the pub, their feet scrunching on the gravel.

'*Lead kindly light*,' the Commander sang out, '*the mariner home across the . . .*'

Priny gave him a dig with her elbow. '*Shhh!*'

'*Across the storm-tossed sea!*' the Commander finished. 'When you're an admiral,' he told her, '*then* you may tell me what to do.'

He sailed on for a few more yards, listing slightly, and then stopped.

'I know. The very thing! Let's wake Mr Pugh. Invite him back for a nightcap.'

'Home, James,' Priny said.

'Let's show him Lucy's legs,' Phineas suggested, and Lucy giggled again. 'Eh?' he said, laughing with her. 'Eh? You naughty girl!'

'*Shhh!* You'll wake Carl,' Priny warned them.

Phineas halted abruptly. 'Right. Thank you, Priny. I will. Which is his room? Show me the blighter's room!'

'It's that one.' Lucy, who lodged in the village, pointed out one of the bedroom windows. 'He always sleeps with his window open. Winter and all. He's a fitness fanatic, he is.'

'And mad as your bloody hat with it,' Owain said.

'Yes,' Annie said, 'perhaps we ought to go home now, Phineas, bach. Come on now, there's a love.'

'Yes, come along, Phineas. There's a good chap,' Priny said briskly.

'What! And show my back to that pot burner. That scullion! That – that Frenchman!' Phineas said to a cheer from the Commander.

'Shhh,' Priny said, digging him again.

'He's English,' Lucy said.

'That swill bucket! Beetle head!' Phineas went on, getting into his stride, and swaying as he tried to focus on the darkened window, his voice rising. 'Cockroach! Piddle-faced dish of cat's meat! What! Have him come down here! I'll cudgel him like a dog. I'll break my sword on the rogue!'

He looked at Lucy, holding her to him like a prize. 'And my sweat will be the tears of his once love, weeping in her tenderness for his death.'

'*Ahhh,*' she said.

'Come on, Phineas,' Owain said, pulling him by the arm. 'Before he gets his trousers on.'

It was Owain's turn to stop a few moments later. He held up a hand. 'Listen!'

'*Shhh,*' Lucy said, and giggled again.

The night was sultry and utterly still, the air holding the heat of the day like a cooling stone. A tawny owl called between silences, the cries drifting raggedly across to them from Mawr Wood. The light of a battered-looking full moon shone like blue frost on the slate of the village, and on the bright fields, the drifts of shadows under trees and the fat summer hedgerows piled as soft and as black as soot.

'Lovely, isn't it,' Owain said, more to himself, and breathed deep of the river-scented night. 'Lovely, it is. Lovely. Lovely, lovely, lovely,' he chanted mournfully, waving a hand at it as he made his way down towards Lower Ham and the *Felicity H*, adrift and a little unsteady, Bryn his collie at his heels.

'Don't forget lunch tomorrow,' Annie called back to them, going after him.

After saying goodnight to Priny and the Commander, the other two walked on slowly past the *Cluny Queen*. Jasmine had left the pub much earlier, a sated, sleeping baby slumped on one arm, the rest of her family following like a brood of chicks, and the paddler looked becalmed now in the night, deep in stillness and shadow, the upper-works bleached by moonlight.

Phineas waved a hand in the manner of Owain. 'He was saying goodbye, Lucy. Owain was saying goodbye to it. The way it is.' He stopped and regarded her solemnly. 'Because no matter what happens, Lucy, no matter what happens now, it will never be the same again. No. Not the same, Lucy. Not what we meant at all,' he said, shaking his head and swaying off course. 'Not what we meant at all.'

'I know, darling,' Lucy said, steering him back, and then losing him again as he dived for a bush and pushed his head into it. Something he often did when drunk, and for reasons which always escaped him the next day. It was a sallow bush, threaded with honeysuckle, and he came out with a sprig of it caught in his collar.

He lowered his head like a cow and looked at her, his eyes foolish.

'Pribbles and prabbles,' he said, and Lucy giggled. 'Cobwebs and doorknobs. Moths and mustard seed,' he said. 'Benabbled, dibbled and faddled. Undone I am. Drunk on moonshine and Lucy, and sweet summer buds, de-da, de-da,' he said, and waggled his head at her. And then he lifted his arms and spread them, sharing it with the village, the valley. 'I know a bank,' he roared, 'whereon the wild thyme blows, where oxlips and the nodding violet grows. Quite over canopied with lush

67

woodbine, with sweet musk roses and with eglantine. There—'

'*Shhh!*' Lucy hissed, looking at the small, darkened terrace of Masters' Cottages opposite. 'Come here,' she said, and pulled him to her. 'Kiss me,' she said, and pushed him back into the hedge, melting into it with him until they were still, one shadow in a pool of shadows, the air oiled again with the sudden scent of honeysuckle.

The lights of the two other paddlers were out as well by the time they reached the *Cluny Belle*, lingering in more shadow on the way.

Sikes had gone ahead, wandering off after they'd left the pub, and was now sprawled on deck, looking as if he'd collapsed there out of boredom.

Phineas put him in the kitchen, and gave him what was left of his favourite dried pigs' ears as a sop. When it came to a show of human affection, Sikes was a dog who liked to join in.

Lucy was standing at the rail of the *Belle*, holding her face up to the moon as if to the sun, its light falling like dust in the air. The river was sluggish with light, stirred with it midstream to a thick inky silver, and black with shadows under the trees.

Lucy turned and eased the scooped neck of her vest away from her skin. 'Phew!' she said. 'Hot, isn't it?'

She peeped over at the canopied hammock from Patio Living.

'I sleep on the deck in this weather,' Phineas said, and smiled at her without knowing it. He rather liked the way the moon warmed the hollows of her neck and made inviting shadows of her breasts and waist.

She pouted up at him. 'Not very big, is it,' she said and, lifting her throat, touched delicately at it, at the sweat on it, with her fingertips, as if with scent.

'And what's in there, then?' she wanted to know, looking over at the sitting room. Phineas showed her.

'I've often wondered what they look like inside,' she said, after he'd turned on the light, and not looking at the room, looking at him.

He showed her the bedroom next.

She slipped away from him once they were inside, teasingly, giggling, and was undressed by the time she reached the bed.

Phineas followed, getting his jeans tangled up in a frustrated struggle with his deck shoes, and stumbling into the bedside chair, and then the bed. Before finding Lucy in the dark, the sudden, satiny warmth of her skin against his.

'Hmmm,' she breathed a few moments later. 'There's nice!'

CHAPTER 6

An hour after that, the fishes dropped to the bottom of the river as the glass fell, and the heatwave broke suddenly in a summer storm. The thunder crashing and stumbling across the valley, setting the cock pheasants in Mawr Wood off crowing, before following the river out on its way to the sea.

Ffion Owen, who had cried herself to sleep and wondered if her heart was broken, woke to find that summer had turned to a grey dawn rain falling, drumming lightly on the felt roofs of the uptops and peppering the river. From somewhere nearby a starling sang, damp spluttering bursts of half-notes, like water being blown from a whistle.

Leaving Snipe sleeping on at the bottom of it, Ffion got reluctantly out of bed.

She had her toast and tea standing up in the kitchen, dressed in a bright yellow waterproof and her riding hat, and minutes later was pedalling down the deserted High Street, head down against the rain, to her job in the hunt's yards.

The kennels smelt of soiled bedding straw, piled, dripping wheelbarrow loads of it, and the swill of disinfectant. The air busy with the rattle of pails and the slap of water on stone, as the hound lodges were scrubbed and scoured, the released hounds piling into the yard, clamouring to get at the morning.

Clem Wroxley, in a flat cord cap, the collar of an old riding mac up, was standing no messing about in this weather. She knew the name of each hound, all fifty of them, and let them know it when she was in charge of the morning walk, using only her voice to control them as they swarmed into the lane that led to the yards, spoiling up it as if for the chase.

By the time it was the turn of the hunters to be exercised, the rain had stopped, leaving rivulets sparkling like broken glass down the sides of the hill lanes, the sun climbing in a glowing, water-colour sky.

Clem and Ffion were walking the last of them back down to the stables, followed by Clem's two dogs, dawdling on behind. The air smelt of the warmed damp summer earth, of tangled creepers of honeysuckle in the hedgerows and meadowsweet on the banks, and the heated smell of nettles drying.

Clem stopped and stood in the stirrups, easing the bladder of her hunter as he peed in a cloud of steam. Ffion reined in with her and batted a few flies away from her face, the tail of her mount swishing. She was on a grey, the smell of the yellow mud drying on its legs and belly attracting more flies.

'He couldn't seem to get going at all,' Clem said, talking about her date the night before with a horsefeed rep. 'Talk about slow. Terribly wet, you know?' She turned and frowned the question at Ffion.

Ffion wondered if Clem had then offered to arm-wrestle him, and laughed suddenly, and without meaning to.

She sniffed and wiped at her nose with the sleeve of her sweater, the end of it coming unravelled. 'Sorry, Clem,' she said. 'It's just that, well, he does sound a bit feeble.'

'Yes,' Clem said, mollified. 'Yes, that's precisely what I thought. Come on, George,' she added to the horse. 'Give it a shake, and let's get going.'

'Perhaps he's married, and had an attack of the guilts.' Ffion refused to be completely cynical about men.

Clem frowned again. 'Well, he might be, of course. Still, whatever. Doesn't make one feel exactly . . . I mean, it's not as if I threw myself at him or anything like that. I only really agreed to go out with him because of his tie.'

'His tie?'

'The way it swung when he walked across the yard. It's a weakness of mine, men striding about with their ties swinging. I know it's daft – what are you laughing at?' she asked curiously. Humour was something Clem was not always sure about.

'I'm sorry, Clem . . .' Ffion started, before spluttering with laugher again.

Clem stared at her, and then giggled. The both of them laughing then, and neither entirely sure why.

'We shouldn't laugh, really, poor man,' Ffion said, dumping it on the horsefeed rep. 'He can't help it if he's a drip.'

'You can say that again!'

'Coming to lunch today?' Ffion asked her then. Clem lived on her own, in a caravan behind the stables, and regarded the *Felicity H* as a second home.

'Yes, please. I'll bring my things, shall I?'

'Good idea,' Ffion said. 'The water should have warmed up a bit by then.'

They turned into the lane leading to the yards, the big horses shouldering their way down it, sending a startled dove crashing out of an over-hanging oak.

Out of sight above the open fields, larks sang, their darting notes endlessly threading the air. Since she was child Ffion had thought of that sound as a sort of conjuring trick, a trick of delight, their song somehow becoming one in her young imagination with a large glitter ball at her first circus, kept magically in the air, its hundreds of spinning, fragmented mirrors catching the light.

She moved her head to avoid the lower branches of a hedge hazel in the narrow lane, the fat leaves sending down a brief shower of rainwater, and brushed it from her face with a hand smelling of disinfectant.

'Clem,' she said suddenly, decided to say. 'Clem, I'm pregnant.'

Clem glanced sharply at her. 'Pregnant?'

Ffion nodded miserably, and wiped at her nose with her sleeve.

Clem's George took advantage of the sudden stop, and pulled abruptly over to the verge to snatch a quick nibble of freshened grass and cuckoo spit. 'Are you sure?' Clem said. 'Who by?'

'Someone I met at a club in Kingham. He was on holiday.'

Clem's saddle creaked as she turned to get a better look at her friend. 'You kept that very quiet. And where is he now?'

'Back home. In London.' Ffion answered the unasked question. 'I haven't heard from him since.'

'The bastard!' Clem said.

Ffion moved forward, sitting dejectedly in the saddle.

Clem kneed her mount on after her. The horse tossed his head, and champed on his bit and a mouthful of green slobber.

'Are you sure?' she asked again, drawing level with Ffion. 'I mean that you're pregnant?'

'Yes. I'm ten days overdue. I've never been that long before.'

'Have you told your parents yet?'

Ffion shook her head. 'You're the only one I've told.'

They walked on in silence. 'First the eviction and now this,' Clem said. 'Oh, Fee!'

And then, a few moments later, she said: 'Well, as regards the eviction, as I've said, you can come and stay with me. Of course you can. I'd love to have you, you know that. And as for the other, well, the first thing to do, is to make sure that you actually *are* pregnant.'

'What, go to the doctor, you mean?' Ffion looked doubtful.

'Oh, there's no need for that,' Clem said airily. 'We'll just buy a preggers test. From Boots. I'll run you into Church Myddle tomorrow.'

'How does that work?'

Clem hesitated. 'Well, to tell you the truth, I'm not awfully sure. I've only really read about it. Perhaps you blow into it. Like a breathalyser,' Clem said, and looked at her friend, as if unsure if she'd made a joke or not.

If she had, it wasn't one Ffion appeared to find amusing. She rode on for a few more yards in a sort of hurt, dignified silence.

Before her sense of humour got in the way, and she giggled. And then Clem joined her, the two friends laughing together again as they clattered through the gate into the yards.

CHAPTER 7

At that moment, in the bedroom aboard the *Batch Castle*, the Commander, black patch pushed up on his forehead, had selected his eye for the day from the box lined with midnight-blue velvet.

After giving it a quick polish on the sleeve of his dressing gown, he held his eyelids open with one hand, and eased it in with the other.

He blinked hard a couple of times, and then peered in at it in the dressing table mirror, a bit of old England gazing back at him. Constable's *Cottage in the Cornfield*, warmed by a sun that would never set.

The tea slopped in the mug when he lifted it, a slight shake to his hand. A bit of a sea running this morning, he told himself. It really was time he started being a little more *sensible* about things, he thought vaguely, looking around for his pipe.

Minutes later he was out on deck, in pressed white ducks, blue deck shoes, and a shore-going Sunday blazer that, like him, had known better days, the black buttons discreetly patterned with the cipher of the Royal Yacht Squadron.

'Splendid, splendid,' he muttered, as if finding all the things that made up his world lined up and awaiting inspection, and unreservedly approving them.

Priny had been up for some time and was busy on the beds above the landing stage with a hand-fork and trug, coughing round her cigarette holder like a sheep, her hair in large orange rollers.

The Commander's good eye shone with love.

He continued his stroll round the deck, breathing in the rain-freshened air as he went, the sun warming his balding head like a benign hand. The Cluny steamed gently in the warmth, the gnats busy in the sunlit air above it, and the fishes rising lazily to feed, and nothing but pleasure waiting around each bend of his day.

Shortly, after selecting a buttonhole, he'd take a stroll with Pink Gin up to the shop for the papers, left in the bin outside by the Church Myddle newsagent, because Mr Pugh would have no truck with commerce on a Sabbath. And then breakfast on deck, reading bits out to Priny – 'Here's a thing!' – over sausages and back bacon, fried toma-toes, black pudding and mushrooms, a slice of fried bread and a couple of eggs, a present from the Owens' chickens. He had never understood how people started the day on less.

And after that a little more work on his Atlantis charts before church.

He had recently come across a new theory that immediately made more sense of the sense he had already made of certain phenomena which, on their own, made no sense at all. He had gone into all this, in some detail, with Priny the other day, using isotherm and isoseismal charts of the area, and his illustrations of the theory of continental drift. But hadn't been entirely convinced that she had altogether understood things.

A heron flapped his way downstream, trailing its legs, and rooks circled in the tops of the big sycamores in Mawr Wood, dry sticks of sound falling in the river air.

The Commander picked up the glasses kept on a rope hook on the side of the boat, and trained them on Snails Eye Island, a regular watch since his first sighting. He swept the bank, and then quartered the water around it, searching for the trail of telltale bubbles left by an otter busy under the surface, or a pair of nostrils travelling along it.

He realised that for some reason he had quite confidently expected to see it this morning. And when he lowered the binoculars felt the disappointment as a child might, and also old because of it, and a little foolish.

He busied himself knocking his pipe out over the side, and filling it again. And then whistled for Pink Gin, before remembering that she, too, was old now. He went in to fetch her.

Phineas Cook came to, opened his eyes, and shut them immediately.

When he opened them again she was still there.

He sunk down in the bed and groaned.

A few minutes later he sat up gingerly, a headache shifting about like loose cargo. He had no idea what time it was. His watch had stopped and the clock he usually kept on a chair beside his bed seemed to have disappeared.

Not that it mattered now. It was too late, whatever time it was. He'd done it now.

He was reminded grimly of *Death Cashes a Cheque*, one of his earlier Inspector MacNail novels, in which a playboy tycoon wakes up after a night on the town, to find a blonde he'd never laid eyes on before dead on his bathroom floor.

Except that he knew who this blonde was. It was Lucy the barmaid. And she was alive and well, and in his bed. On her back, whistling away carelessly in her sleep.

Phineas pulled the sheet up, covering her body almost tenderly. He just hoped that the homicidal Carl would make it quick for both of them.

He sat limply on the edge of the bed, feeling like something Sikes had dug up.

And he had cricket practice this morning, which, with the annual match against Blurford coming up, he must not miss. If he was leaving here, then he'd like to see them put in their place first. And that was *not* posing triumphantly again in the back pages of the local papers.

And then there was Sally – he remembered Sally then, and winced as his headache took a swipe at him.

And serve you right! he told himself, getting to his feet, on his way to get something for it. And then froze.

He had felt the slight movement of the boat that told him someone was coming up the gangway. And doing so slowly and quietly.

Headache forgotten, he ducked across to the window that side and shut it. And then quickly drew the curtains, hands stretched up to them, and on his knees, like a man praying.

He heard the footstep pass the window, and move stealthily along the deck towards the door, an assassin's tread.

The sitting room was unlocked as always. And even were Sikes awake, it was no good expecting alarms from him, not even so much as a single bark.

Sikes considered the world none of his business until he'd had his breakfast.

His jeans were tangled up on the floor, inside out with his underpants showing. Phineas grabbed a pair of corduroys. If this was death on its way in the shape of Carl with something from the knife rack then he wanted to meet it with his trousers on.

He paused then, struggling with the zip, struck by the sudden thought that it might be Sally, showing consideration in case he was still asleep. A district nurse and midwife, she could have nipped over from Kingham, after a night of easing people into this world, or out of it, and hoping for a cuppa and a restful word before home, and finding a blonde in his bed.

Because there would no point in hoping Lucy wouldn't be discovered. He knew that in situations like this women can see through bedroom doors.

He heard the door of the sitting room open then, heard that squeak it gave when it was opened slowly, and thought wildly of the window.

And then pulled himself together. He had never exited through a bedroom window in his life, at least not through his own, and wasn't going to start now.

He pulled on a sweater, and went out to meet whatever was waiting for him, his mouth dry. Where was MacNail when he was really needed?

It took a couple of seconds for the identity of the tall serious-looking youth standing in the sitting room to register.

'Daniel!' he said then, weakly.

'Hi, Dad. I was trying not to wake you.'

He gave a small laugh of relief. 'Daniel, my boy!'

'I rang you several times last night, but couldn't get an answer.'

'No, I was – but, Danny, this is *marvellous*!'

'It was a spur of the moment thing, Dad. I had the chance of an early lift to Shrewsbury from a neighbour. I was lucky then, thumbing from there,' his son said, slipping his rucksack off. 'I got one straight to Church Myddle. Then I remembered the paper van and got a lift in with him.'

'Oh, well done, Dan! And well done, paper man!'

'I didn't expect to be here until much later, on a Sunday.' Daniel stretched and yawned. 'I was going to crash down on the sofa till you got up.'

'What is the time, then?' Phineas asked, combing his hair with a hand.

'I'm not sure. Not all that early.' Daniel smiled in a tolerant sort of way. 'You look like you've had a bit of a late night, Dad.'

'Emm? Well – late-*ish*, yes,' Phineas admitted. 'How's your mother?'

'She's fine, yeah.'

'Good, good. I'll make some tea or something in a moment. But sit down, dear lad, sit down.'

Phineas found another pair of deck pumps under the coffee table and sat down himself to put them on. 'And how was America, Dan? It certainly sounded as if it went well, by your letters. Everybody's had a read of them. Even Sikes. I had to read them to him, of course.'

'Yeah, good. I really enjoyed it. I'll tell you all about it later.' Daniel had recently returned from a semester high school exchange visit.

'Right. Good. Smashing. How long can you stay?'

Daniel shrugged. 'Well, a few days, you know. I'm going to France for a month at the end of next week, with some friends, just bumming around.'

'Quite right, too.'

And, well, I thought I'd come and see you first.'

'And how glad I am that you did.'

Phineas sat smiling at his son, and Daniel sat smiling at Phineas.

And then Phineas found something else to look at, glancing round sharply at the room. 'I don't know, look at the state of this place,' he said, standing up to get a better look, and as if someone else was to blame.

Daniel had never known it look any different, and he supposed that as usual he'd be doing the cleaning up. The way, after each visit, he tidied up the details of his father's life for the benefit of his mother and stepfather, and ended up resenting all three of them.

His mother and stepfather never said anything, but then they never had to. It was all there in the amused, tolerant sort of way they enquired after his father. As if taking time off from their infinitely more together lives to be entertained by a small diversion called Phineas.

Daniel loved his mother and father, and liked and admired his stepfather. And sometimes wondered why he bothered with any of them.

He watched as his father shook his head and tutted, and picked up a couple of books, yesterday's newspaper and a used breakfast plate from the sofa, and put them on the table in front of it, and then found an empty mug to go with them.

'Don't worry, Dad,' he said. 'I'll do it all later.'

'No, don't,' his father said. 'You're on holiday. Relax.' The last time his son had cleaned up for him he'd spent a week after he'd gone searching for things. 'And anyway, surely we've better things to do with our time together than spend it on housework?'

Daniel was his first son, the only child of the first of his three marriages. The one he felt closest to, and had seen the most of over the years.

'It's good to see you, Dan. It really is. Bloody marvellous. It's well over a year now. Must be. And by God,' he added as Daniel stood up, 'you look as if you've grown again!'

Daniel laughed. 'I don't think so, Dad. Not at my age.'

He had Phineas's blue eyes, and his father had a sudden memory of him as a toddler in a London park, lifting him high in the air, his face flushed and laughing above his, and looking as if he had the sky in his eyes.

'Now,' Phineas said, 'what about tea? Better yet, breakfast. Have you had breakfast yet? No, of course you haven't, at your age. Silly question. Let me see, there's coldtonguescoldhamcoldbeefpickl- edgherkinssaladfrenchrollscressand—'

Phineas had to pause for breath. He cocked his head at his son. 'Remember that?'

Daniel nodded solemnly. '*The Wind in the Willows*. Ratty telling Mole what he'd packed in the picnic hamper.'

'Yes.' Phineas smiled. '*The Wind in the Willows*. Well, I'm afraid I've only got eggs, maybe a bit of bacon, I'm not sure,' he said briskly, filling the gap. The years between the child and a loved bedtime story, and the tall young man standing there now, both of them looking embarrassed by the distance and the memories that that distance held.

'That's all right, Dad. I'll just have toast. I'm vegetarian now,' Daniel said.

'Ah,' Phineas said. 'Vegetarian. Right. Good. Well, there's plenty of bread.'

'How's everybody?' his son asked. 'The Owens, and . . .?'

'Oh, just the same. Everybody's just the same. Still afloat. For now, at any rate. But I'll fill you in on all that later.'

'And where's Bill Sikes?' he asked with a grin. 'Still asleep somewhere, I suppose.'

Phineas looked round the room. 'He's in the kitchen,' he remembered. 'We'll wake the blighter up.'

Daniel stretched again. 'And then I wouldn't mind a couple of hours' kip, Dad, if that's all right.'

'Yes, yes, of course, of course. Er . . . right. Well, there's the camp bed, and I've got some sheets somewhere,' his father said vaguely. 'I'd suggest the deck hammock but the church bells will be starting up any minute.'

'That's all right, Dad, I'll just crash on the sofa for now.' Daniel knew that hunting for sheets could take half the morning.

'What am I talking about! Use my bed. I'll turn the sheets round on it. How's that?' Phineas said, beaming at his son. And then remembered who was in it. 'Ah, well, actually, Daniel, come to think of it, my girlfriend's in there at the moment. She's a nurse,' he heard himself say, and as if that somehow explained her being there, and wondered why he had said it at all. 'Her name's Sally,' he burbled on, 'she's a local district nurse and midwife, you know?'

Why did you say that? he asked himself. Why on *earth* did you say that! When Daniel was bound to meet Lucy when Lucy got up, and even more bound to meet Sally, the real Sally later.

His headache had come back. And the church bells had broken out, brisk blows of sound in the morning air as he crossed with Daniel from the sitting room to the kitchen.

Your talent, your real talent, he told himself bitterly, is not for writing potboilers with absurd comic-book characters like MacNail in them. But for getting into things up to your neck, and then shovelling more on top for good measure!

CHAPTER 8

Small riots of children, some of them Jasmine's, and friends of theirs and Cadi's from the village, some Owain's grandchildren from his first marriage, chased round the deck of the *Felicity H*, and jumped from the rail as if abandoning ship, the explosions of spray turning to glittering light in the yelling, sunlit air.

Bryn the collie added to the din, tearing, barking, up to the deck, and then back down again to the riverbank, where more screaming and splashing and shouting of orders was going on in the water at the stern of the paddler. Cadi and a few other children were manning a raft there, made of planks nailed together and floated on oil drums. A blue raft, painted with what was left after the recent job on the paddler, and flying the skull-and-crossbones and red dragon, and with the added importance of an old tractor number plate tacked on the back.

Ffion and Clem Wroxley were both in bikinis. Clem in lime green, the scraps of clinging material busily fielding her curves as she bounded, dripping, back onto the deck from the paddlebox ladder after a swim.

A couple of friends of Iwan, Ffion's second eldest brother, nudged each other as the two girls walked past, while the girls studiously ignored them.

As far as Clem was concerned they were too young, and Ffion felt herself to be beyond that now. She had, overnight, left all that behind. She would, she had told herself, never be young again.

She was thinking something along those lines when her mother found her some time later, and asked her to give a hand with the salads.

Annie's eyebrows went up in surprise when her daughter not only did as she was asked when she was asked, but did it without arguing, without wanting to know why she had to do everything, and wasn't she ever allowed to have any fun, hissing the words at her, intense needles of temper in her dark eyes. But Annie was not to know that tragedy had now set her daughter apart from all that.

Tom Parr had helped fill the big white and gold china salad bowls with produce fresh from the earth of his vegetable garden and the outdoor tap, the bowls waiting, with plates and cutlery, bottles and glasses, on one of the long trestle tables the Women's Institute regularly borrowed for their sales in the village hall.

Tom was sitting in a candy-striped deckchair, with a pipe on and a glass of Sheepsnout cider from the gallon plastic container down by his side. Chickens scratched about in the grass and a river breeze moved gently among the spears of rosebay willow herb growing out of a ruined punt behind him.

Tom had done worrying for now about his future in one of the five Masters' Cottages, all still owned by the estate, and was addressing himself to Phineas's hangover, explaining the quality of it.

'It was a long hot summer last year, see, Phin. That's what done it.'

The Commander, who plotted such things on charts in his wardroom, was able to add that July and August had been the hottest for over twenty years.

Tom looked at Phineas, the glare of age in his eyes. 'Well, there you are, then. Stands to reason don't it. Got the sun baked in it, en't it. Sweetened in heat, it is. The hotter it is, the more sugar in the fruit, the more alcohol in the cider,' he said, as if that should be obvious. 'Here, tek a smell of that.' Tom leaned across and shoved his glass under Phineas's nose.

Phineas was in what Priny called the recovery position, reclining on a sun lounger, with a second glass of Chardonnay and the soothing presence of Sally, looking cool in a blue gingham sundress and espadrilles, sitting on a horse rug at his feet.

'Pure cider, that is,' Tom went on. 'From real cider apples. Sweet Coppin, Sheepsnout, Dabinett, Bulmer's Norman, Rustfair, Michelin,' he said, reeling off the names like battle honours. 'Apples that come over with the Conquest. The Frenchies, like, they brought 'em.'

'And even I have to admit it was damn good of them,' the Commander said from the depths of his deckchair, a glass of it in his hand. 'I've yet to have a dud pint from Dotty's orchards, whatever the weather.'

Tom shook his head. 'There's no secret about making good cider, Commander, if you'm got the right apples, and look after 'em properly. That's the key to it. And her knows all about that. Then you just pulp 'em, and basically leave them to get on with it. They ferment in their own juice, see. Because the yeast is there already, the wild yeast. When I were a kid we used to press 'em in swill bins – after cleaning 'em out first, of course – before casking up. Kill a cat, it would, the smell sometimes. And anything else in the yard what happened to fall in. In fact, dad used to chuck a dead rat in apiece. They all did in them days. Give it a bit of body, like.'

Tom drained his glass. 'Sure you don't want any, Phin? I got plenty here.'

'No thanks, Tom,' Phineas said weakly. 'I think I'll stick with the wine for now, if you don't mind.'

He'd turned up for cricket practice earlier, doing his share out on the field, and at the wicket, each ball on the clean straight bat he prided himself on, ringing in his head like a tenor bell. And afterwards had laid his white-flannelled length out in the long grass and waited to die.

'Poor darling,' Sally said.

'Put hairs on your chest, it will,' Tom told him, topping up the Commander.

'That and the promoting,' the Commander said,

gazing at his glass, 'of that state of reverential wonderment in rapture which an ancient wine, whether of the grape or apple, will lead to. Well you wot, as George Meredith almost said. Your health, Tom.'

'Ah. An' yours,' Tom said.

The Commander looked at Phineas, the sun catching the yellow in his glass eye, shining again on the cottage in the cornfield. 'And in your case, my dear Phineas, having taken my advice and got yourself a nurse for a girlfriend, a little tender loving care as well, eh?'

'He looks more in need of intensive care to me,' Priny said from under the broad brim of a lilac raffia hat, a large Plymouth gin in her hand. 'Now don't let him take advantage,' she added to Sally. 'It's his own fault. He drinks too much.'

'Don't worry, I shan't,' Sally murmured, gazing up at him.

'Emm,' Priny said doubtfully.

Owain, in a vest, belt and braces, a red and white kerchief round his neck, his face streaked with sweat and coal dust from his struggles with the new De Luxe Cook Centre from the Alfresco Dining Experience page of Patio Living, came across with one of his granddaughters, in a damp swimsuit and wearing a moustache of ice-cream, perched on his wide shoulders.

Another of his grandchildren had left the pot he'd been squatting on, and with bare bum warmed by the sun, and his arms held out to catch them, toddled with cries of delight after a line of ducks waddling up the plot.

More shrieking and yelling and barking came from the direction of the boat, while knuckled down in the long grass, Megan, the Anglo-Nubian nanny goat, looked on with ancient, secret amusement.

A gaggle of children, the sun drying the river on them, chased up the plot, and Owain's grand-daughter climbed eagerly down to join them, scrambling down the broad front of her grandfather as if from a tree.

Owain mopped at his brow with a large olive handkerchief, and then swabbed ice-cream from his vest.

He poured himself a glass of Annie's blackcur-rant whisky and lifted it in a salute. 'Here's to Pink Gin.'

The Cunninghams had brought news of Pink Gin's death. The dog had died in her sleep, her death waiting for the Commander when he went in to fetch her for his walk to the shop earlier.

'She's here in spirit,' Priny said, and smiled across at her husband, a conspiracy of loss. She waved a hand at the bottles on the trestle table. 'She wouldn't miss this.'

Annie, arriving for a cider refill, said the food shouldn't be long now, the smell of venison cooking on the river air.

Owain, who could still get within ten feet of a deer without it knowing, had brought back a small roe buck, part of his wages after working on a cull of male deer on a neighbouring estate. It had come out of the freezer kept in one of the old railway containers yesterday, which had then left room for Pink Gin today, her body shrouded in an old bed sheet.

Tomorrow, she would be taken to Kingham to be cremated, and her ashes brought home and scattered along the lanes and on the fields she'd known.

Jasmine Roberts, perched in jeans on a kitchen step-stool near the Cook Centre, began tuning the guitar she'd brought with her, hugging it in her bare, dimpled arms, her long black hair framing it dramatically.

She was being watched by Ernest, a boyfriend from Kingham, a builder, who had built the uptops for her on the *Cluny Queen* to accommodate her children. Who would have built a house for her, a town, a city, with his own hands, brick by brick, had she but asked, or he the nerve to ask her.

A few more people dropped in to sign the petition against the proposed holiday village. Some, they knew, welcomed the news. Dilly, the landlady of the Steamer Inn, it was said, was already measuring up for new curtains.

Miss Harriet Wyndham was appalled by it. 'It's wicked! Simply wicked,' she said, her jowls shaking with indignation.

She sank untidily into a deckchair, a jumble of large straw bag, lisle stockings and thorn-proof skirt, and a blouse of Victorian frilliness, her hair escaping from under a green felt hat with a jay's feather in the band. 'And what does the wretched man intend doing with them?' she demanded.

'That, Hattie,' Owain said, 'we haven't been told. The only words his lordship sees fit to address to us, is to tell us to sling our hook.'

'It's wicked! Wicked!' Miss Wyndham said again.

The only child of a rural dean, Miss Wyndham had met her fiancé while day-tripping on the PS *Cluny Belle* in the heyday of the CSC. He was a young solicitor, free for the day in a boater, and he'd teased her about her hair, the way it kept escaping from under her hat. Miss Wyndham had never been teased by a man before, and had only read about the madness of heart, as she later thought of it, that had made her accept immediately, without even a pretence of demure, his offer of tea when they disembarked at Water Lacy.

Her young man enlisted in a rifle regiment when war was declared in July of that summer, and proposed to her in uniform. Invaded her heart, as she afterwards thought of it. Not quite a month later he was killed at the Battle of Mons.

She still wore her engagement ring, and his signet ring, given to her by his parents after his death, and still lived in the house that had known his voice in the hall for the last time. That had seen him smoking a rather self-conscious pipe in the study with her father. And had watched him dutifully touring the flowerbeds with her mother, before catching his train back.

She had never married. There had been a brief upheaval in the Thirties, when a local vet had admired her, and made her think for a while of what she might be missing, and of the years waiting ahead. But in the end she had turned him down, as she knew she would. Miss Wyndham had already given her heart.

'Perhaps he intends turning them back into pleasure boats. You know, running them up and down the river again,' Sally said, looking on the bright side, something she'd had a good deal of practice at doing since meeting Phineas Cook.

And now, following his eviction notice, she felt there might be more chance of a bright side to look on. She was still uncomfortable about her feelings for him, still under no illusion as to his potential as husband material. But once he was on shore, as it were, it might prove easier to get him into a suit and a proper job.

Tom Parr made a sound like a laugh. 'Tek some money, that would. You'm have to refit 'em all for a start. And who'm you going to get to drive 'em, eh? You answer me that,' he said, and laughed scornfully, indignant for old skills. 'You have to know what you'm doing, you know. A bit more to it than just pressing a starter button and steering, I can tell you.'

'But if that's what he really did have in mind for the old ducks,' the Commander said, his good eye tender with the thought, 'then one would almost be prepared to forgive the man. After all, it was what they were for in the first place. That and a bit of haulage.'

Owain snorted. 'And forgive him for turning the bloody place into a holiday camp as well, I suppose. Duw, man!'

'There you are, Hattie,' Annie said brightly, before her husband could get going, handing Miss Wyndham a glass of home-made cherry port.

'Jasmine has such a pretty voice,' Miss Wyndham said, moving her head in time to it. Jasmine was in full cry, her eyes closed on the words, a song taking her down country roads, her voice strong and true, going straight to the heart of the notes.

'We've got a new jazz band this year, for the regatta,' Miss Wyndham told them. She was an insider, a member of the subcommittee – church fete and flower show – of the Batch Magna regatta committee. 'The Church Myddle Stompers. They are really hot, apparently,' she added, sharing the description with a vaguely anxious air, still unsure quite what that might mean.

'So we are *having* our regatta then, are we?' Priny wanted to know.

'Oh, I hope so!' Sally said. She was new to the area and had been looking forward to it.

Miss Wyndham looked aghast. 'Of course we're having our regatta!'

'That's next year, Priny,' Owain said. 'No regatta. No more river, neither. Not for us.'

'Only we won't talk about that, not today, will we?' Annie said, looking at her husband.

'Quite right, Annie. Fun Order only today,' the Commander agreed.

Priny waved her glass. 'I'll drink to that.'

'And tomorrow a shop doorway. And a mother and children begging on the streets,' Owain muttered obstinately, Welsh gloom darkening his brow.

'Not have our regatta?' Miss Wyndham said wonderingly, the thought still exercising her. She put it to Sally, an outsider among them. 'We've always had a regatta here. It wouldn't be summer without it. We've *always* had a regatta. Well, since the arrival of the paddle steamers, anyway,' she added, strict with the truth. 'The crews started it, racing the barge men from Water Lacy, right up until the company went bankrupt, before the last war. And it went on from there,' she told Sally.

Miss Wyndham glanced across at Tom Parr, who was lifting his glass, sunlight moving in it. 'Only the engineers, who were also the paddle steamers' firemen, were picked to row. They had the arms for it, do you see. And how dashing our men looked!' Miss Wyndham remembered, 'in their Trafalgar blue and gold singlets. And how young.' She paused, lost in thought. And then she said: 'What will we do? What *will* we do?' sounding suddenly bewildered, suddenly lost, and quite near to tears.

While Miss Wyndham blew on a handkerchief edged with lace, Annie poured her another cherry port and invited her to stay for lunch. 'We're having venison steaks in blackberry wine.'

'Ambrosia,' the Commander declared, and advised Miss Wyndham not to deny herself. And the others joined in, insisting that yes, she must stay, while Miss Wyndham, handkerchief balled up in a hand, dithered with pleasure, and felt wanted.

She would, of course, as she always did, accept. Lunch, or any other social occasion at the Owens', the company there, and the latest doings of their children and grandchildren, was a fire which Miss Wyndham, alone with her memories and her cats, warmed herself at for the rest of her week. 'And there's summer pudding for afters,' Annie told her, 'made with raspberries and redcurrants, with raspberry liqueur.'

Miss Wyndham, who insisted in her own kitchen that summer pudding, must *only* be made with raspberries and redcurrants, nodded happily. And Annie's homemade raspberry liqueur. Summer on the tongue, with the extra warmth of one of Annie's alcoholic ingredients. Miss Wyndham felt restored.

With another glass of cherry port in her hand, she looked at Phineas with her bloodhound gaze and asked him if he had seen the Sussex job in the newspapers that morning. Phineas said he hadn't had time for the papers yet, what with one thing and another.

'Horrible business!' Miss Wyndham said with relish. 'A domestic,' she qualified, 'but horrible. Quite horrible.'

She took a sip of her port. 'It is the prosecution's case,' she went on, agitated with pleasure, 'that he, the wretched woman's husband, bludgeoned his wife to death in the kitchen with our old friend, a blunt instrument – they found brain tissue behind the cooker and blood traces on the walls and on the tops of the skirting boards. He had tried, apparently, to clean it off with bleach.' Miss Wyndham chuckled briefly at the murderer's naivety. 'Then, it is further alleged, he cut her up in the bath.' She looked at Phineas, one expert to another. 'More blood and human hair found in the downpipe,' she added crisply.

Miss Wyndham and Phineas shared an interest in murder. The bloodier the better. Happily swapping details of human remains packed away under floorboards, ominously leaking suitcases in left luggage offices, severed heads and torsos wrapped in newspaper like fish, and dealing in all the finer points of trace evidence and forensics.

'Then it is said,' Miss Wyndham went on, 'that he boiled her up over the course of a week in a set of saucepans. Made a sort of soup of her.'

'Good gracious!' Priny said. 'Then what did he do?'

'Poured her down the drain,' Miss Wyndham said with some satisfaction. 'Unfortunately for him the sewage wasn't, apparently, all it might have been, and more of the unhappy woman's passing was found in the pipes.'

Phineas, fascinated, despite the state of his

stomach, had opened his mouth to say something, when he spotted Daniel, who'd been seeing friends in the village, strolling towards them.

He slid down on the lounger. He had been wondering when this would happen, and here it was. His comeuppance. And it found him, as it were, without his trousers on.

Because, beleaguered and hungover, all he'd ended up with when he'd tried to find a story anywhere *near* convincing enough to explain the other Sally to this Sally, was a headache.

CHAPTER 9

Phineas watched his son approach and tried to remember how it went.

Lucy, he could be sure, was safely behind the bar of the pub. But Sally, who had yet to meet Daniel, was here. And Daniel, who had been introduced to Lucy earlier, when Lucy was on her way out, thought Sally was Lucy. Or was it, thought Lucy was Sally? He found he could no longer be sure. And his headache had returned.

'Ah – Daniel, my boy!' he greeted him heartily, a man with nothing to hide, but after Daniel had said hello to the others, he mumbled Sally's name when he introduced her.

But Danny had caught it, and gave a surprised laugh.

'What, another Sally?'

'Yes. Yes, another Sally,' Phineas said, laughing with him, as if finding the coincidence just as amusing, and waited resignedly for him to ask if this Sally, like the other one, was also a nurse.

'I didn't know there was another Sally in your life, Phineas,' Sally said, smiling up at him, one hand shading her eyes.

'Emm? Well, there isn't, darling. Not now. The job's taken,' he said, and tried one of his winning smiles on her. 'There *was*, yes, it's true, there was another Sally, in my life, as you put it, once, at one time, briefly,' he burbled on when she didn't respond, just sat there with her hand up to her eyes, looking at him.

And then Daniel, who didn't know the details but could more or less fill them in himself, came to his rescue and said that he'd been very young then, but the name had sort of stuck with him, you know? He knew he'd be told all about the other Sally, or whatever her name was, later, when his father would sigh in that way of his, leaving Daniel unsure whether it was at his own folly or at a world which burdened him with such problems.

But for now, looking at her, the easy warmth of her smile, he much preferred this Sally.

Phineas put his head back and regarded his son from under the brim of his Panama. 'He's got a remarkable memory, that boy,' he said, his tone managing to convoy both his thanks and, as a father, a reproof for telling downright lies.

'He's also got your eyes, Phineas,' Sally said.

'Apart from the red and yellow bits,' Priny added.

'Have a drink, Daniel,' Annie said. 'What about a bit of homemade? The wine of our welcome, as we say. Drop of red mead, how about that? Do you good, that will. Have you seen Fee, yet?' she asked in the same breath, popping a cork.

'Just to say hello to. I saw her earlier, with Clem Wroxley, when I was on my way in with the paper van.'

'Out with the horses, I suppose,' Annie said. 'She works for the hunt now.' Daniel, who had decided views on hunting, merely nodded. 'They're old pals, Daniel and our Ffion,' she added to Miss Wyndham.

'Yes, I used to see them about together,' Miss Wyndham said.

Annie's expression suggested that Miss Wyndham didn't know the half of it. 'Inseparable, they were. *In*separable.'

She asked Daniel if he wanted to see her latest rescue, a fledging crow she'd found dazed in one of the lanes.

Owain narrowed his eyes at his wife's retreating back. He'd been married to her for far too long not to know when she was up to something.

'And leave my maggots alone!' he called after her, his gamekeeper's soul enraged at doing anything to a crow but shooting it.

'Fed it my maggots from the fridge the other day, she did,' he complained to the others. 'Had to go digging up the bank at five in the morning to get a bit of bloody bait together.'

Annie couldn't see the crow down by the hutches, and started calling it, startling Daniel with the sudden cawing sound she made at the back of her throat.

He was startled again then, when he heard a

younger version of the same call from the lower branches of the hornbeam tree by the gate. The bird had been trying its wings, short erratic hops from the top of the rabbit hutch it now regarded as home.

It came back in, landing awkwardly on top of the hutch, an ungainly bundle of young crow and large wings, and immediately started hopping about, squawking, its beak gaping.

Annie fed it a morsel of cat food from an open tin, pushing it down its flesh-red craw with her little finger. 'Thinks I'm its mam,' she said to Daniel. 'Back to the nest with a nice fat juicy worm.'

The crow swallowed, and then put its head on one side and winked, the milky-blue lid closing and opening slowly again on its eye like a shutter.

'And how was America then, Daniel?' Annie wanted to know. 'We heard all about it, of course, almost as soon as the postman arrived, I should think. Read all your letters, we did. That family you stayed with sounded nice.'

'They were great. Made me feel complete at home. And everybody was very friendly at the school, as well. Yeah, I really enjoyed the visit.'

'Oh, good. And have you got a girlfriend yet then, Daniel? Anybody special, is there?'

Daniel shook his head. 'No, not really, Annie.'

'Well, so I should think!' she said, sounding indignant. 'Plenty of time for that, there is. Don't want to start tying yourself down yet, do you. Not at your age, and with your studies, and all. And how are they going then, Daniel, your studies?'

'Fine, Annie, thank you. Yeah.'

Daniel was stroking the bird's crown with a finger, and the crow had its head down under it, scrawny neck stretched, looking up at him with a coy expression, a threadbare Victorian cleric with an offering of humbleness.

'I know *what* you're studying. *Applied* mathematics,' Annie went on, even more impressed for not knowing what it was. 'Your father told us all about it. And that the university you've been offered a place at, Bristol, is one of the best. Proud of you, he is. What he don't understand,' she added with a laugh, 'is where you get your brains from!'

Daniel covered his pleasure and embarrassment at this by asking if he could feed the bird. 'Has it got a name?' he asked, digging out a bit of Turkey Treat from the tin.

'Howell. After Howell Pugh at the shop. He's like him, isn't he. Like that old hypocrite. Like old Bible face, old Pugh the Pew, aren't you, eh?' Annie said, while pulling the crow's wings out and combing among the shining feathers with a finger, looking for passengers. 'That's it, shove it down its throat, like its mam does with her beak. And what will you do when you finish university, Daniel?' she wanted to know then, as the bird shook its combed wings with an irritated air, and folded them away like an umbrella.

'Well, that depends on my degree. If I get a first.'

Daniel gave a short laugh. '*If.* Well, then I'd try for a masters, and Ph.D. Then a research fellowship.' He laughed again. 'That's the plan, anyway.'

'A *research* fellowship,' Annie said, her eyes wide at the sound of it. 'Oh, that would be something! Well, I wish you all my luck with it, Daniel, I really do. I'll keep my fingers crossed for you. And how long did you say you were staying for then? Because you've grown now, quite the young man, you are,' she went on, without waiting for a reply. 'And well, you don't want to be stuck round here all the time, do you. There's nothing here for young people, there isn't. No. And I'm sure your da would lend you the car, like, if you asked. You've got your licence now, he tells us.'

'Yes, I passed just before I went to America.'

'Well, there you are then! You want to get out while you're here. Go to Church Myddle. Or Kingham. Kingham's better, I suppose, being bigger, like. More what you're used to, I expect. And there's a nice new club opened there, I believe, for young people.'

Annie drew a sharp breath, obviously struck by a sudden thought. 'In fact, come to think of it, that's where Fee goes, I'm sure it is. And well, if it is, I know she wouldn't mind taking you, showing you where it is, like. Course she wouldn't!'

Annie smiled at him. 'Be nice to see you two together again. She often talks about you, Ffion. Oh, look, you've finished your drink. Can't have that, can we. And you on holiday.' Annie pushed the last bit of Turkey Treat down the crow's throat. 'Come along, Daniel, bach, and we'll get you another,' she said, taking his arm.

And the crow, head on one side, closed his eye again in a slow, wide wink.

After lunch, a shirt on over her bikini, Ffion stood alone with her thoughts at the rail of the *Felicity H*, looking out across the river. She had never known anything else but this valley world, these hills which had always encircled and held her safe. Had never known another home but the river. And she was taking a last look at it all, remembering other days, other times, and saying goodbye.

She was going away. She didn't need a visit to the chemist's to tell her what she already knew. And she had decided she was going away. She had no idea where, except that it would be an anonymous city somewhere. And she wouldn't tell anyone. She would just leave one morning, before they were all up. On her own, with a suitcase and her secret.

She had no doubt that her parents, were she to tell them, would offer only understanding and support. But that was not how she saw it. She saw herself pregnant and going away as she had seen herself pregnant and deserted by her man, the father of the child she was carrying, the words like captions in a silent film. In Ffion's dramas, she was the audience as well as the star.

While Daniel, bounding up the gangway some

minutes later, was having quite the opposite time of things.

When he saw her standing at the rail he made a beeline for her.

'Lo, Fee,' he said, parking himself next to her and nudging her with an elbow.

Then he started drumming with his hands on the wooden coping, and making trumpeting noises with his cheeks puffed out.

Ffion looked at him almost pityingly. 'Hello, Daniel,' she said quietly.

'I saw you earlier,' he went on cheerfully. 'When I was coming in with the paper van. You were out horse-riding with Clem Wroxley, on a massive great white thing.'

Ffion, who had returned her gaze to the hills, tried to ignore it, and failed. 'It's riding. Not *horse-riding*. And that massive great white thing, as you call her, is a grey. A grey horse. Only Arab and circus greys are called white.'

'Whatever,' he said easily. 'Anyway, dad said I could borrow the old Frogeye any time I wanted to. I've got a licence now. So how about coming out somewhere one night? Annie mentioned some-thing about a club that's opened in Kingham.'

He glanced at her, down to the tanned bare legs, appreciating again the change in her, the difference a year had made.

Ffion turned large, Welsh-dark eyes on him. 'I can't,' she said softly. 'It's nice of you to ask, Dan, but I can't. I'm not free to.'

'What does that mean? You've got a boyfriend? Well, that's all right, we'll leave it then. I just thought, you know . . .'

Ffion was shaking her head. 'No, it's not that.'

'Well, what is it then?' he asked, looking both impatient and amused. Whatever it was, after a couple of glasses of Annie's red mead he could only wonder what the fuss was about. 'Come on, spit it out,' he told her, thumping the rail coping for emphasis, and Ffion burst into tears.

The tears were real. But this was also Ffion giving herself up to a scene she felt called for them.

Daniel stared at her, astonished, and appalled.

Clem, who'd been flicking through the Sunday papers on a sunbed on deck, rose from it like an Amazon at the sound, and a couple of mates of Sion, Ffion's eldest brother, looked threateningly in Daniel's direction. People had gone in over the side from the *Felicity* before.

Ffion wiped tears from her eyes, and shook her head, letting them know it was all right.

She sniffed an apology to Daniel. And then, eyes brilliant with tears, she smiled at him, the sun coming out after rain.

Daniel, confused even further, then agreed immediately, when by way of making up for it, she suggested that they take one of the boats out.

Here at least was something he could get to grips with. 'And I'll row,' he said decisively.

'Oh, been taking lessons, then, have we?'

'Well, I don't know about lessons but I've been

out a few times since I was last here. At home, on the Serpentine in Hyde Park.'

Ffion looked impressed. 'In a *park*. And what's that then, the Serpentine? A paddling pool, is it?'

Daniel laughed. 'A paddling pool! It's a lake. Massive great lake. Bigger than the river here, I can tell you. And deeper. A paddling . . .!' He saw then that she'd been teasing him.

'Right, come on!' he said, and laughed again, a man with a few surprises up his sleeve.

The boats were up on the bank to the fore of the paddler, under the tilting shade of a couple of alders.

They were followed down there by Bryn and the General's old gundog, Snipe, who decided that that was far enough, and sank down to watch from the shade of the trees.

Ffion suggested taking the small pram dinghy. Daniel scorned the idea with another laugh, and insisted on the rowing skiff.

They pulled the big boat down to the water, and pushed it out before scrambling aboard. Bryn leapt in after them and started running up and down and barking, until Ffion shut him up. She deftly fitted the rowlocks and sculls from the bottom of the skiff, the varnished wood of the oars warm in her hands. Then she sat in the stern, on purple cushions with yellow tassels and piping, feeling like a wife while Daniel did the work.

In the meadow on the other side of the river a chestnut horse, its coat polished amber in the sun, stood, tail switching, watching them, and a couple of moorhens met in a summer fight below the bank there, splashing noisily in and out of the rushes. In the heat of the day the water pushed out by the boat seemed to move sluggishly, reluctantly, the brilliance of the sky vibrating gently in a widening spread of ripples.

Ffion idled a hand over the side, and watched as Daniel frowned over an adjustment he was making to the foot-board, and wiped at the film of sweat on his forehead.

'You want to go upstream, mind. Not down. Or you'll end up on the weir again. And we'll only have to get out and push, won't we, like last time,' she said, mock-nagging him. 'You remember that, now, don't you. Don't you now, Danny, bach,' she went on, as if chucking him under the chin. 'And we don't want you getting your swim-ming shorts wet, now, do we. New, they are, by the look of them. And that nice white polo shirt of yours. Not in this old river, we don't. Not with all the dead sheep floating down it.'

Daniel bent over the oars and ignored her. In other ways, Ffion Owen hadn't changed at all.

He beat the water a little but felt otherwise in charge of things, as he rowed strongly and grimly out to midstream, determined to show her.

He pulled right to turn upriver, and the oar somehow went in much deeper than he'd intended, while the other glided just beneath the surface like a fish, and then leaving the water altogether, waved feebly about above it, the dripping yellow scull gleaming like butter in the sun.

Ffion bit on a giggle and pretended not to have noticed, and he brought it quickly and awkwardly back down, the flat of the blade splashing water into the skiff and setting Bryn off again.

Daniel, his face heated, yelled at the dog to shut up, his tone managing to imply that it had somehow been Bryn's fault, and bent to his work again.

But it had put him off his stroke, as he later had it. The sculls after that seemed to take on a sulky, ungainly life of their own. They tried to jump out of the rowlocks, or went in at different depths again, pulling the boat off course, or skimmed the water, and sometimes missed it completely.

Sweat teased his eyes, and his cheeks were red, as if they had been tweaked hard. He was learning that there are two sorts of rowing. There is rowing on a weekend Serpentine, a novice in the uncritical, splashing company of other novices. And there is rowing under the eye of an attractive girl, and one in whose own hands the blades cut through water as if through air.

Daniel had time to give thanks that the other villagers, all born of course with oars clutched in their fists, kept their boats upriver, above the wreck of the *Sabrina*. Before being made aware that he was not to be short of an audience.

Ffion's eldest brother, Sion, and some of his mates, along with others who had nothing better to do, had been drawn to the rail by the barking and yelling, and were hanging over it, shrieking and shouting things at them.

Daniel put his back into it, desperate to pull clear of them, and this time went in so hard with the left oar that the skiff tilted in that direction. He moved quickly to the right to steady it, letting go of the oar to put out a hand, and the scull slid from its rowlock and started to drift idly away downstream.

In a panic of embarrassment, and to a chorus of jeering encouragement from the rail of the *Felicity*, Daniel stood up abruptly and shakily, and with the other oar tried frantically to punt after its fellow.

It was all too much for Ffion. She started laughing and couldn't stop. She was helpless with laughter, holding her sides and rolling about with it, her feet kicking as if being tickled. While Bryn raced up and down, over the seat and back again, barking frenziedly.

Ffion laughed even harder then, when she saw what was about to happen, when Daniel, wobbling about on the end of the oar, swayed too far over. She was still screaming with laughter when the skiff capsized and the three of them were tipped neatly into the Cluny.

A cheer went up from the paddler, and a body hit the water as the first of the onlookers jumped in to join them, the day loud again with shrieking and splashing.

While on land things were going on much as

things tended to go on at the Owens', to the sound of talk and laughter and the popping of corks.

And Jasmine singing again. Her voice beating above it all, the clear, high notes of "Wild Mountain Thyme" soaring like a released bird into the summer air.

CHAPTER 10

On his first visit to Batch Magna, the newly entitled Sir Humphrey Franklin T. Strange, the 9th baronet of his line and squire of this March, had been driven there from Kingham by the land agent, in company with his mom and the man he called Uncle Frank.

On this occasion he was on his own, and apart from having to remind himself to look right, stay left, stay on the goddam left, was doing just fine.

His large frame never having quite enough room in the driving seat of the hired Ford, he had driven from Birmingham airport to Church Myddle, arriving just as it started raining again, another of the heavy showers he'd been driving through for the past hour.

In the town square, where he'd found a parking space, surrounded by overhanging Tudor gables and Elizabethan half-timbers, a huge copper kettle, polished by the rain, sat fatly above one of the shop doorways.

Sheltering under a plastic raincoat he'd remembered to bring after his last visit, and hoping it wasn't just a shop which sold huge fat copper kettles, Humphrey made a dash for it.

It was a tea shop, or shoppe, as the sign had it. A busy place of tweed and gossip, smelling of damp mackintoshes and coffee, and with a bell on the door which tinkled when he entered, and waitresses in black and frilly white.

Humphrey ordered a pot of tea and sat listening to the accents around him, the Welsh lilt among them breathy with scandal. On one of the walls was scrolled something about Pailin, the Prince of Cake Compounders, and how, *The mouth liquefies at the very sound of thy name.*

And boy! He didn't know who Pailin was, but they weren't kidding. There were thick pastries with rum syrups, and cream topped with chunks of icing, mounds of sweet chestnut puree, whipped cream and grated chocolate, and gateaux stuffed with jam and cherries, and more cream.

And no Sylvia here, adding up the calories and ready with the latest on blood sugar. Or Doctor Frieberg pointing out what he was really putting into his mouth. According to Doctor Frieberg, the Park Avenue analyst Sylvia had recommended he see, what he was really eating was failure – or was it success? Was he eating because he wanted success but feared failure? Or wanted failure and feared success? He'd never been sure about that, and he was frowning over it again now, in a vague, inattentive sort of way, while keeping an eye on the cake trolley.

He was served by a young Welsh girl, as plump as a cake herself, with creamy skin and cheeks buttoned with dimples.

Humphrey said he'd have that and that, please, a slice of this, some of that, and one – no, better make it two, of them. Oh, and one of those, as well, if she didn't mind. And sitting back, tucked his napkin into the collar of a shirt with palm trees and a sunset on it.

Back at the hire car, parked in front of a red sandstone building called the Council House, he noticed the town's arms and motto above the door in dark blue and gold. *Fidelitas Salus Regis*. In the town's loyalty lies the King's safety.

He'd seen the translation on the tea shop menu. This area had stayed loyal to the crown during the Civil War, he had the ruins of Batch Castle to show for that. And he remembered the family story, from a time when he considered the whole thing, Hall and all, just that, a story, that after the Restoration the English King, Charles II, had once stayed at Batch Hall, the ancient seat over there in England and the bit that was in Wales, of the Strange family.

Humphrey sat in the car for a few moments, chewing on a cigar and thinking about it.

Yeah, he might do that. Have a Charles II Room or something, when the Hall was turned into an hotel or country club, or whatever it was decided was most likely to show the biggest returns. He left stuff like that to his Uncle Frank, who was back home now, busy putting an investment package together.

The same Uncle Frank, he liked to remind himself gleefully, who had once hired, then fired him, and who now worked for him. It couldn't be neater if he had arranged it himself.

Uncle Frank, who was not Humphrey's uncle, but a cousin of Humphrey's late father, had been a last resort for Humphrey's mother, in despair at her son coming home with yet another career in bits. Frank was the boss of a small Wall Street brokerage, and reluctantly, under pressure from Humphrey's mom, had found her son a place in it. And Humphrey had bounded into the job as he usually bounded into things, like a large, wet puppy, showering people with yet another new enthusiasm, and how this time this was it, this is what he'd been looking for all along. The world of daring young men flying by the seat of their pants, the world of wheeling and dealing, of money markets and fortunes made on the turn of a financial index. This, Humphrey had decided, was where he lived. This was coming home.

He had christened Frank "uncle" then, when he was offered the job, slapping his back and telling him to leave it to him.

Frank had no intention of doing anything of the sort. He kept Humphrey firmly where he could see him. And that, as far as Humphrey soon came to realise, was just what was wrong with the old firm. That same stick-in-the-mud, wishy-washy sort of attitude that had kept it sitting on the runway while others took off all around it.

And then Uncle Frank went to Europe on a business trip. And Humphrey got the company airborne.

Sitting at Frank's desk in his Atlantic Sports Club tie and Wall Street suspenders, one of Frank's reserve Havanas in one hand and the phone in the other, and using a complicated combination of the Super Bowl, World Series, and New York Yankees stock market theories, based on game wins and losses over the past five years, and sold to him for a snip by a guy in a Wall Street bar, Humphrey blazed briefly but spectacularly across the financial skies before falling, equally spectacularly, to earth again, taking Frank's reputation for cautious dealing, and a large chunk of investors' money, with him.

That had even quietened Humphrey down for a while. He got a job in a diner after that, reaping what he'd sowed, as Shelly, his mom, told him when he complained, glumly learning his lesson working as a short-order cook.

And then came the letter from the lawyers, and his life turned into a movie.

He even got the girl. Sylvia, a Wall Street super highflier, a woman Humphrey, as an underling in Frank's office, had regarded with an equal measure of lust and awe. Won from the top floors of Snell and Bloomfield, carried away from under the noses of hotshots and Upper East Side Ivy Leaguers, and soon to be his. Sir Humphrey and Lady Sylvia Strange.

He laughed suddenly and loudly at it all. And clamping the cigar between his teeth, gave a couple of blasts at absolutely nothing on the road ahead of him.

CHAPTER 11

Six or so miles out of Church Myddle, Humphrey picked up a signpost for Batch Magna, just as, on cue, the sun came out and the rain stopped, the last of it turning to brittle silver in its light.

He sailed off, whistling cheerfully, and starting vigorously on songs he then almost immediately forgot the words to, with the windows down, and the sun shining, and the birds singing.

He felt he was on vacation, and at the same time truanting, taking time out from Frank and the serious business of making money, and even from Sylvia.

He might, he decided, do a bit of the tourist thing this time, see a bit of the old country before saying goodbye to it. It needn't get in the way of business. He could still keep his eye on the ball and the bottom line, Frank's parting shot of advice to him. And when he got to the Hall the first thing he'd do would be to ring Sylvia.

The road twisted and turned its way down into Batch Valley under high-banked hedges, the Ford bouncing like a New York taxi cab over ruts and potholes, and Humphrey hoping nothing was coming the other way on the bends of the narrow lanes.

He scattered a few pheasants wandering about on the road, flustering them like elderly maiden aunts, as he hugged it round the edge of a wood. And up and over a hill, a small, perfectly shaped hill, like a hill in a storybook, down to a crooked junction of three lanes.

And not a signpost between them. And he couldn't remember which direction the land agent had taken last time.

He moved the cigar about in his mouth, and then guessed the middle lane, which at least seemed, more or less, to go in the sort of direction he thought he ought to be going in.

The road dipped suddenly, jolting the car's suspension and lifting his stomach, and then swept in a wide confident arc to the right.

He followed it, straight into a farmyard, scattering geese and chickens, and collecting half a dozen sheep dogs, barking and leaping up at the car. A cab-less tractor with a smoke stack, its seat padded with sacking, sat in front of the farmhouse as if waiting for someone. But the house, its half-timbers of English oak blacked with pitch under a roof of Welsh slate, stayed silent.

He reversed out, followed by the dogs, and back at the junction tried the lane that went more or less left.

And some time later, after travelling along lanes

that kept dividing up into more lanes, and then dividing up again, found he'd guessed himself back to another part of the Church Myddle road.

He sat for some moments, looking at it. The world was still going on out there, a truck and a couple of cars passing. Here, he hadn't seen another soul since turning off.

He went back down the hill he'd just come up, and tried the lane he'd noticed on the right, on the other side of a dog-leg halfway up it.

It was little more than a track, overhung with dripping trees and patched here and there with hardcore and tarmac, and puddled with rain-water. It cut through more woodland running along the side of the hill, and was forded in places where streams ran across it, the dense woods either side when he slowed ringing with birdsong. Before the road dropped down to the fields again, and left him there.

He stopped at the first field gate facing down the valley, in the direction he was sure he wanted to go, and got out. He had an idea.

A herd of sooty brown-black sheep had their heads down to the rain-freshened grass, and a feeding crow rose when he appeared, and flapped lazily above them.

He balanced his weight shakily on the middle cross-pieces of the gate, and found the landmark he was looking for piercing the summer green, the tower of St Swithin's parish church, the highest point in Batch Magna.

Gotcha! he said, clambering down, and determinedly heeling the butt of his cigar out, set off for it.

He would have been happier finding a right turn a little way along, going down into the valley, but the road went straight on. Until it went left. In the direction again of the Church Myddle road.

Humphrey came slowly to a halt and sat, fingers drumming on the steering wheel.

He leaned suddenly forward then, and peered through the windscreen. Fifty or so yards up from him there appeared to be a turn-off, going right.

Keeping an eye on it, he pushed the gear home.

It was another overhung potholed track, and it took him through another stretch of woodland, and then down again under the sheltering hedges of more fields.

And along more lanes, hillocky with sudden dips and rises, the road constantly seeming to be turning back on itself, before shooting off in another direction, twisting and turning as if the very lanes themselves were lost.

He knew by now that either he had long overshot the village or he'd been going round in circles.

He was looking for another gate to peer over, coming round yet another bend in yet another lane, when he saw ahead of him what he at first took to be a farmworker, doing whatever it was farmworkers did on their knees on verges.

Drawing nearer he saw that it was a woman.

Miss Wyndham, a keen amateur botanist, was kneeling among the summer grasses, with a magnifying glass and a handbook of wild flowers, examining a patch of dry-stone walling.

When the Ford pulled up and Humphrey got out, she glanced round vaguely, and as if resuming a conversation, said decisively: 'Moss campion. *Silene acaulis*. Unmistakably so.' She rapped the open pages of her field book with the glass. 'No doubt on it.'

Miss Wyndham gave a short laugh and shook her head. 'I know it's not *supposed* to be there. North Wales is the nearest it's *supposed* to be. Rather like, one has to say, Colonel Ash, who's *supposed* to be an expert on local flora. But it's not up a mountain, is it. Where, as a species of alpine plant, we all know it should be. So of course it *couldn't* be moss campion, could it.'

She gave another little laugh. 'Well, it is!' she declared, snapping the book shut, and in a sudden flurry of activity struggled untidily to her feet, her reading glasses dropping to the end of a length of black cord worn round her neck.

'Moss campion,' she added faintly, and swayed alarmingly.

'Are you all right, ma'am!' Humphrey said, starting towards her.

'Emm? Oh, perfectly, thank you. Perfectly. It's age, you know. Everything takes that much longer to catch up.'

Humphrey nodded at her bicycle lying nearby

125

on the verge. 'Tough going, too, I should think, ma'am, on these hills with that.'

'What? Oh, I push it up. Always do. Then free-wheel down.' Sometimes Miss Wyndham pushed it up *only* to free-wheel down. 'Although I really must remember to get the brake-blocks fixed one of these days,' she muttered to herself, before remembering her manners.

'Well, at least it's stopped raining. Although, there's more to come, apparently. Heavy intermittent showers into the evening, according to the weather forecast on the wireless this morning. Although I have to say that that isn't what my barometer indicated. Set fair for the day, *it* said. But then it always says that.'

Miss Wyndham's mackintosh was stuffed into the wicker basket of her bicycle but she still had her black sou-wester on, or had forgotten to take it off. Her blouse was buttoned up to its pie-crust collar, and the front of her green twill skirt patched with damp. She tucked an escaped hank of hair behind one ear and took an abrupt deep breath.

'Oh, how *good* it all smells. And how glorious everything looks now.'

The trees dipped light, the sun striking more liquid sparks from fields and verges, and the tops of hedgerows. From up in a field maple a mistle thrush broke into song, and Miss Wyndham lifted her face to the sudden shower of notes as if to the sun.

And then she looked abruptly at Humphrey. 'I sheltered from the worst of it,' she added gravely.

'It stopped just as I got here. Then I got lost.' He shook his head. 'The lanes around here . . .'

'Yes, they can be quite confusing. People have been known to get lost. *I* have been known to get lost. And I've lived here all my life. It's all to do with what Mr Rhys-Thomas calls original purpose. Many of them were green lanes, you see – old track or cart ways, prehistoric, some of them. And drovers' roads, of course, and bits of Roman road, and coffin routes. All adopted into the local road system. And you should bear in mind,' Miss Wyndham advised him, 'that the standard width of a cart in those days was only four feet. That should explain a few things. But I really can't help you further there, I'm afraid. As I say, you need Mr Rhys-Thomas, our local historian, for that. He'll tell you all about it. Now he really *is* an expert.'

Humphrey smiled at her. 'It sounds fascinating, ma'am, but right now I'd settle for finding the way to Batch Magna.'

Miss Wyndham looked startled. 'Batch Magna?' she said with surprise, and Humphrey wondered just how far he'd strayed.

'It's over there,' she said, pointing, and as if now there might be some doubt about it. 'Down there. On the right.'

'Well, I guessed it might be in that sort of direction,' Humphrey said. 'But it's getting to it.'

'Oh, that's *quite* simple,' she said, sounding relieved. 'Just continue on along here. Turn right, first right. Then first left. First right – No. No, wait a moment. *Second* right. I do beg your pardon. First left, then second right. That's it. Then a few yards on you take another right, and then a sharp left. Then simply follow the road all the way round, all the way round.' Miss Wyndham's hands were on the handlebars of an imaginary bicycle, steering her way home. 'Ignore the turning on the left, it's a farm track. You'll then come to a fork in the road. Take the right hand lane, and then a left, and then right again. Follow that down, and then . . .' She thought again. 'No, no, my mistake. Forgive me. No, right again first, after the fork, and *then* left. That's it. And then another left, followed by a right, and then left again. That will take you down Hollow Oak Hill. Follow the hill down' – Miss Wyndham's hands twisted and turned down Hollow Oak Hill – 'all the way down, all the way down, to Monk's Bridge, the humpbacked bridge. You turn *left* then, on the other side of it, and follow the road round, all the way round, and into the village.'

She stopped, as if catching her breath, and blew a strand of hair from her face.

'You can't miss it,' she added with mild reproof.

Humphrey got paper and pen from the car, and asked Miss Wyndham would she mind saying all that again. Miss Wyndham did so, while Humphrey, repeating it carefully after her, wrote it all down, and then drew a map for good measure.

'You're an American, aren't you?' she asked then, shyly. America to Miss Wyndham was still Liverpool during the war, when she did her bit there in a factory after the death of her fiancé. It was the place still where dreams came from, on Saturday nights in the local Regal, when the smell of machine oil and the banging of the presses could be forgotten. And the tears she sniffed back in the darkness were not for her own loss, but for other people's happy endings.

'Yes, ma'am.' Humphrey saw her glance again at his shirt, and smiled. 'It's Hawaiian.'

'*Hawaii*!' Miss Wyndham closed her eyes and swayed to the word as if to music.

After she'd declined his offer to put her bicycle in the back of the car and give her a lift down, he thanked her again and they said goodbye.

'Do have a good holiday!' she cried on a note of sudden gaiety. 'Or vacation. I'm sorry, I should have said vacation.'

Humphrey regarded her over the roof of the car. 'Thank you, ma'am, but I'm not on holiday, or vacation. Well, not really. Not officially, anyway. I'm on my way to Batch Hall there. On business.'

Miss Wyndham opened her mouth to speak, and then closed it.

'You are not,' she said then, slowly, regarding him with her bloodhound gaze, 'you are not by any chance Humphrey Strange? *Sir* Humphrey Strange?'

Humphrey admitted that he was, his small

self-deprecating laugh at least partly meant. Even he was given at times to consider it lousy casting.

Shy by nature, and with an intense dislike of confrontation of any sort, and most particularly with a stranger, Miss Wyndham found it within herself to do her duty.

Her considerable bosom lifted in outrage, she told him just what she thought of the eviction notices and his plans for the river front. Of his despoiling of history, and of a way of life entrusted to him.

'You have sold, sir,' Miss Wyndham, a clergyman's daughter, pronounced in a tremulous parting shot, 'your birthright for a mess of pottage.'

She watched Humphrey's car until it had turned off, following the directions she had so obligingly provided, a map handed to the enemy. And then made a dash for her bicycle.

She had no idea what she was going to do. No idea what she *could* do. But she did it anyway. Quivering with excitement, she hiked up her skirt, and peddled furiously after him.

Humphrey's ears burned, as they always did when he was angry, all the way down to the narrow humpbacked bridge.

He couldn't see much of the river, just the glint of sunlight on it as he started over. But he heard it, some bird on it, honking, he was in the mood to think, in a deliberately derisory sort of way.

Humphrey roared over the bridge, not caring if anything was coming the other way, crossing it like an invasion.

In the High Street, he pulled up with a squeal of brakes outside the shop and post office, his first visit to it. On the flag of Wales above the entrance the red dragon hung damply after the rain, as if doused.

Mrs Pugh had already cashed up and was upstairs, and her husband was about to lock up for the day, when the door opened and Humphrey's bulky frame filled the doorway.

The shopkeeper blinked at his shirt.

'You still open?' Humphrey asked without preamble.

'Always time to serve a customer, sir. That is what we are here for,' Mr Pugh said with dignity.

He was right out of picture postcards, but he thought he still had a few of those tea towels left, with a map of the Marches on them, and Shrewsbury tea caddies, and a whole box somewhere in the storeroom of souvenirs from Wales. It wasn't every day he was sent a tourist.

'We pride ourselves on that, sir. On our service to the community, and of course the wider world. Service before profit. That is our watchword and our motto,' Mr Pugh said sternly, making his way to the counter. 'Service before profit. Now, sir, what can I do for you?'

Humphrey moved his head to avoid a rope of wellington boots, hanging with various other goods from the ceiling, the soles on them like tractor tyres. 'Got any candy?'

'Candy?' Mr Pugh said blankly. He'd been wondering whether to push the tea caddies or the Welsh music boxes first. Although judging by the man's shirt, he thought that perhaps the novelty leeks might be more up his street.

'Candy, candy,' Humphrey said, looking at the shelves behind the counter, and then pointing.

'Ah,' Mr Pugh said. 'Chocolates. Yes, I see. Black Magic, is it?' Mr Pugh only sold Black Magic. He had three boxes on the shelf, left over from Christmas and Mother's Day. 'Very popular, they are, sir. *Very* popular.'

Humphrey said he'd take two. Mr Pugh got them down and surreptitiously wiped the dust off on his khaki shop coat while fiddling with the white paper bags kept on a piece of string below the countertop. The shopkeeper had a few yellowing strands of hair plastered across his scalp like flattened winter grass, his cheek hollows and bony nose threaded with broken veins.

'Staying in the area long, are we, sir, may one ask? Or just passing through, is it?' he asked, and bared his teeth like a horse.

Humphrey said no, he was staying here – for now. He'd decided that. As soon as he'd got the bottom line squared up he'd get back. Back to where people knew which side their goddam bread was buttered on.

'At the pub, is it, sir?' the shopkeeper wanted to

know then. Under cover of a few adjustments to the bagged chocolates, Mr Pugh was busy putting two and two together.

'No,' Humphrey said baldly. 'Batch Hall.'

He knew it!

'Then does that mean, sir, does that mean, may one enquire, that one has the honour of addressing Sir Humphrey Strange, ninth baronet, master of Batch Hall, and squire of this March?' Mr Pugh smiled coyly at the American, and then sniffed, sharply, as if at his own hypocrisy.

Mr Pugh's head was English but his heart was Welsh. And after a lifetime's servitude a source of rebellion when alone in his storeroom, the fierce whispered words of revolt like an outbreak of mice then among the stacks of cornflakes and washing powder. And to Mr Pugh, whose heart lived still in the shadow of Batch Castle, the squire was always English, even when he was an American.

Humphrey said yeah, yeah, he was Sir Humphrey Strange, 9th baronet, and all that stuff. On his way to foreclose on a few more mortgages, to turf a few more pensioners and widows and orphans out onto the street. It was just a pity it wouldn't be snowing while he was doing it.

Mr Pugh looked aghast. He assured Sir Humphrey that if he was referring to the eviction notices then he would have Sir Humphrey know that he was doing the community a service. Yes, sir, a service! The things that went on there. Gypsies, that's what they were, water gypsies.

'And the drinking! I have seen the empties myself. Cirrhosis-on-Cluny, one of their number, a certain Commander Cunningham, has called it. In this very shop. And he should know. And sex!' the shopkeeper cried suddenly, and Humphrey blinked, and caught the smell of strong mints.

'Oh, yes, sir! Sex. You only have to take a walk along the Hams in clement weather to see what goes on in that department. Naked men and women I have seen, laughing and chasing each other round the deck like Sodom and Gomorra. Now you, Sir Humphrey, have come among them. Now they are to be confounded. Now they shall be oppressed and spoiled evermore!' Mr Pugh declaimed with the heat of familiarity, the torment to be found in Deuteronomy and the Curses for Disobedience.

The shopkeeper inclined his head. 'Welcome, Sir Humphrey, to Batch Magna,' he ended solemnly, and sniffed

Humphrey wasn't at all sure what the guy was on about, but he was quite taken by it. He said it was a pity other people round here didn't think like that, and was moved to tell the shopkeeper that he hadn't expected a band playing and the flags out when he arrived, but he had at least hoped for some understanding of what he was trying to do, some grasp of economic reality.

Mr Pugh was shaking his head slowly and implacably at it. 'You will never get through to them, sir. *Never*. Living in the past, they are, some of them. Living in the past. And of course for some of them it doesn't pay to do anything else, does it. Take, if you will, the late General's housing scheme and the estate cottages. His kith, the old General used to call them. Which is all very well, sir – in its time. In its proper squirarchical context,' Mr Pugh qualified, his ill-fitting teeth taking the words like fences. 'And I can tell you, sir,' he confided, 'I can tell you that some people think *scroungers* would be the more appropriate appellation. Oh, yes!'

He held up a sudden hand, as if in protest. 'And I yield to no man, mind, in my respect for the old squire. No man! My father, the late Mr Pugh, had the honour of serving Batch Hall for over forty years, and when I took over I made sure things were kept up – and saw it as a privilege, sir. Oh, yes. A *privilege*,' Mr Pugh insisted, and sniffed again.

He asked Humphrey if he'd heard anything from the council yet, about the planning permission, like. Humphrey said he hadn't, but the decision was due soon, and that's what he was here for, to make sure it didn't get stuck in some in-tray. He was used to that, getting things done, putting a bit of zip into things.

'Well, sir,' Mr Pugh was able to tell him, 'you might like to know that I have personally written a letter to them, strongly recommending your proposal. *Strongly* recommending it. As I said to Mrs Pugh, the future has arrived, carrying a banner.

Progress, that is the word we must march behind now. In step with you, sir, and the rest of the world.' Mr Pugh's finger pointed the way. 'Progress and modernisation, they must be our watchwords now, sir, isn't it. Progress and modernisation.'

And profit. And Mr Pugh was provoked again by thoughts that had provoked him even in chapel, perhaps particularly in chapel. The new shop extension, with queues of holidaymakers at the three tills. And the girls on them. Girls like those in the supermarket in Kingham, in their short tight nylon overalls. Wicked girls, he'd no doubt, painted like sin, and in their hands the lure of money.

When Humphrey had gone, Mr Pugh locked the shop door, and moving aside the cardboard display sheets behind the glazed top, turned the sign to Closed.

And then he pushed his nose up against the glass, his face framed with sheets of hairnets, balloons, plastic farm animals and soldiers, and throat drops for sailors. Watching with a small, hidden smile as old Batch Magna, in the shape of Miss Wyndham, at the end of her brave, pointless dash, wobbled exhaustedly up the High Street on her bicycle.

CHAPTER 12

Humphrey was whistling away again, after his talk with Mr Pugh, turning into the lane for Batch Hall, the tall, star-shaped chimneys appearing and disappearing between the trees.

The General's housing scheme the shopkeeper had mentioned hardly mattered. It was the estate cottages, the pensioners that Humphrey, out of guilt, had made light of evicting, that was the bit he didn't want to think about.

The housing scheme allowed local people to buy estate homes at well below market value, with a legal tie that, if they sold, they sold back to the estate. For generations it had kept house prices down and a community together, and eventually of course it would have to go. The houses, whenever they become available again, sold on the open market. Which, as nothing had moved for years, was comfortably in the future. Batch Magna, as Frank had said, was obviously one of those hick spots where people hardly ever got off the tit.

But the estate pensioners would have to be given notice to quit. The cottages would be rented out, either as holiday units or on the open market, or sold. As Home Farm would have to be sold, to offset the mugging he'd had from the British Government, the size of the death duty they'd hit him with. In this goddam country they did their best to make *sure* you couldn't take it with you.

Humphrey took out another cigar out of the glove compartment, approaching the entrance to the Hall, and then changed his mind and put it back.

The lion and otter rampant surmounting the gate pillars of the Hall were yellow with lichen, the walls either side, cut from the same quarry that had built the castle, and put flags on the Hall's roofs, crumbling under a blanket of ivy. He'd rather have liked to have given a toot on the horn here, and have someone nip out from the lodge to open up for him.

But the tall wrought-iron gates that once had been run back to welcome carriages and the first motorcar of the valley, had long stayed open, rusted on their hinges. The lodge itself half buried now in bramble and nettles, and with its roof timbers exposed, the bones of another age.

The house waited, hidden behind a bend in the drive and screens of rhododendron and the great ancient beech trees he remembered, their bark like elephant hide. And he smiled when he saw it again, as he had done the first time he'd set eyes on the Hall. There was, he thought again, something a bit loopy about the place.

It formed three sides of a south-facing square, an Elizabethan confection, striped this way and that with black half-timbers on white, reminding him of the liquorice squares when he was a kid.

The chimneys and red sandstone roofs needed work on them and the walls a fresh wash of lime, and the timbers re-pitching. And age had settled the grand end gables out of true, giving the whole a tipsy look, a foolishly happy, disreputable sort of air, suggestive of a down-at-heel aristocrat, ruined but jaunty in a battered silk topper and with a bottle in his pocket.

His cousin's green Land Rover, still badly in need of a wash, was parked in front of the main doors. He'd been hoping she would have gone by now.

Sarah made him feel like a brash American, a clumsy colonial among Old World furniture, stuff that had always been there. But above all, she made him feel like an interloper, a usurper. It was, everybody seemed to agree, Sarah, the General's favourite granddaughter, who should have inherited.

He found her in the kitchen, a large room with flagged floors and soapstone sinks, which immediately echoed when he entered with the barking of her dogs, until Sarah shut them up, startling Humphrey by doing so with a single, sudden loud yelp.

She'd left her muddied wellington boots on the steps outside the main doors, and was sitting in socks and a brown bib overall at a long pine table in the centre of the room, an empty tea mug and a couple of farming catalogues, and a tin of roll-up tobacco and cigarette papers in front of her.

She had one of the dogs, a young Jack Russell, on her lap and was combing through its coat with her fingers. She also had a horse-print scarf on, ready, pointedly, to leave, the scarf framing tow-coloured greying hair and a pale face, the well-bred cheekbones reddened with weather.

Humphrey made a show of looking at his watch.

'Gee, Sarah, I'm sorry. The flight was late in, crosswinds or something. It was good of you to wait.'

Sarah's gaze met his shirt without flinching, and took in his plaid golfing pants. 'There should be some family member here when you arrive,' she said, as if instructing him on a point of etiquette.

She cracked the flea she'd found between two fingers and put the terrier down.

'Normally, Humphrey, one wouldn't mind. But John's away, which means I'm practically on my own, with two cows about to calve down and the usual hundred and one things to do about the place.' Sarah and her husband farmed in Cuckington, near Kingham.

'Yeah, well, as I say, the flight . . . And then, when I *did* get here, I went and got lost.' He laughed, inviting her to find it as amusing as he seemed to.

Sarah ignored it. She stood, and the terrier and the two other dogs, a black Labrador and something shaggy with a look of greyhound about it, took it as a signal for more barking, until Sarah did her yelping thing again.

Humphrey paused with them, and then started talking about taking wrong turnings and going round in circles again.

Sarah waved it aside as something that couldn't be helped, and got on with things that could.

Hers was the sort of voice that had ruled in the far-flung households of empire. It had been there when bandages were rolled in Kensington drawing rooms, and had spoken again when the right thing needed to be done in yet another war. Her world in this life was the farm, and dogs and horses, and the Bench and various charity committees, a world ordered with the same brisk lack of fuss.

'I've left a list on the table of where things are and how they work, including instructions for the central heating – such as it is – should the rain continue. It's an ancient and rather erratic contraption, but it does help with the damp. There's food in the refrigerator and clean sheets in the bedroom you stayed in last time, the master bedroom. Mrs Thomas will feed the cats – there's several about somewhere – and the peafowl. You might tell her, when she comes in in the morning, that I've put a new bag of maize for the fowl in the dairy. All the house keys are in the key-cupboard by the door there. They're all labelled.'

'Mrs Thomas?'

'She cleans at the pub.' Sarah said, padding over

to a sink with her mug. 'She'll be in every day while you're here, to do a bit of cleaning and basic cookery. Her wages will paid out of the estate account, along with various sundries connected to your visit. I don't think there's anything else. But you have my number if there is.'

'What happened to Annie, the other house-keeper. She leave?' Humphrey asked.

Sarah, gathering her things together, paused and considered him.

And then smiled slightly, and with some relish. 'Annie Owen? Yes. Yes, she left. Quite suddenly, too. Odd, that, isn't it. Leaving like that, after all these years. Simply because you're evicting her and her family from their home. A home promised by the General, by the estate, for life. I wouldn't have thought Annie could be so petty. But there you are.'

'Oh,' Humphrey said, still holding the boxes of Black Magic he'd brought in with him, one of which had been for Annie Owen.

Sarah considered him further. 'You didn't know, did you. Do you know any of their names, the people you're evicting?'

'Well, I . . .' Humphrey started, and then shook his head. 'No. No, I don't,' he said, looking, in his shirt with palm trees on it, like a holiday that had suddenly been rained on.

Sarah told him. 'And Jasmine Roberts is a woman with . . . with a large family,' she said vaguely. 'And still no idea where they're all going to live. And the estate has nothing else available for them. For any of them.'

She looked at him, questions in her mind about people such as Mrs Parks, in her nineties, an estate cottager who had started work at fourteen in the Hall, and Tom Parr, and Mr and Mrs Tranter, seeing their last days out together in another of the Masters' Cottages. Questions she would not allow herself to ask.

'Well, it won't change anything – it *can't*,' Humphrey said, 'but I'll go and see Annie Owen tomorrow, and the others on the houseboats. Explain why I'm doing it. Why I *have* to do it.'

'I hope you can swim,' was all Sarah said on her way out.

The Jack Russell claimed the passenger seat in the Land Rover, while the two other dogs went in the back, among the empty feed sacks, oil cans, tractor batteries and coils of fencing wire.

Sarah paused, her hand on the ignition key, and allowed herself for a few moments to dwell on things that couldn't be helped.

Batch Hall was a delight to look at, of course, a beautiful house. But it was just that now, a house, had been just that for a long time. A beautiful old house, creaking with age and silence, like a museum. And she was seeing it as a home again, with a family to shelter, the sound of their lives rising through the empty floors, like smoke in its chimneys, warming it.

And she was glad again that she didn't have to

make the decision she would have made, would *have* to have made, had she inherited.

Estates these days were given with one hand held behind the back. And as far as this estate was concerned she knew just what that hand held, not the least of which was seventy-five percent death duties. People had assumed she'd wanted to inherit. And people had been wrong.

The General had never discussed it with her, that hadn't been his way, and when she was told that it had passed to a distant cousin, an American, her feelings had been complex and mixed. Feelings that went back to the roots of her family in this place. But chief among them, after a first, quite illogical, reaction of disappointment and loss, had been relief. Relief that she wouldn't have to carry the burden of it all. And that she wouldn't have to sell Batch Hall to help meet that burden.

Perhaps one day, she thought, she might even tell him that.

Humphrey remembered too late that he'd forgotten to give Sarah the second box of Black Magic, listening to the sound of her Land Rover fading, leaving him alone in the kitchen, alone in the house.

After a lifetime spent living with New York outside the window, all he could hear was silence.

He jumped at a sudden banging and gurgling in the water pipes, and listened intently for a few moments to what he was sure were footsteps

144

upstairs somewhere, and once a car horn, sounding quite near, he thought.

And then silence again.

Humphrey reached for one of the boxes of chocolates and, quietly, opened it.

CHAPTER 13

In the early hours of the morning, when rain clouds hid a new moon, and Sir Humphrey complained in his sleep of the two boxes of Black Magic he'd left empty downstairs, darkness was kind to Batch Hall.

It hid the broken flags of its roofs, and smartened up the facade, and trimmed the lawns that ran smoothly down to the river again. It softened the ruin of its terraces and walls, and tidied up the gardens, and re-roofed the lodge with shadows.

The village of Batch Magna lay shuttered in it, the lamp-less High Street lit only with the light from the telephone box burning outside the post office and shop.

And on its river only the Commander was awake, one eye staring at the ceiling. Next to him the comforting form of Priny breathed steadily in her sleep.

Thoughts which knew their place during the day tended to get a bit above themselves in the dark watches. Thoughts of what sort of future they were making for this time, now that they were both holed a little, both a little rusty with years.

And what the loss of this place would mean to them.

The Commander peered at the alarm clock on his bedside cabinet, a birthday present from one of his grandsons. Bought with saved-up pocket money, and an eight-year-old's unshakeable conviction that granddad would like it.

And he was right. Granddad did like it. It was a proper alarm clock, looking as an alarm clock should look. A large brassy affair with two bells and a hammer on top. The sort of clock that when it goes off in a cartoon bedroom is propelled into the air by its own loudness.

It had a round, plain fat face, and the Commander had no doubt that if it could speak it would natter away in a cheap and cheerful sort of way all day, were he to let it.

But all it had to say for itself now, in a rather glum sort of way, was that it had just gone three o'clock. The Commander decided to get up.

He walked up and down the deck a couple of times to get the circulation going. And then stood stiffly at the riverside rail, leaning on his badger-head stick.

Darkness sharpened the sounds of the river, its murmurings and the gurgling of snagged currents. And made small night mysteries of a sudden rustling among the reeds, and the chatter and squeak of some animal on a bank, and what might or might not have been a wind lifting in the willows, and things that go plop in the water.

But he was listening for something else, hoping to hear what he was sure he'd heard a few nights back at around this hour. The shrill whistling of otters. Two otters. He was sure of that. And sure he hadn't imagined it.

One had been on or near the island and one further upstream, and they were calling to each other. A bitch, perhaps, coming downriver with her favours, and a dog, his otter, the one he'd seen playing on Snails Eye, swimming to meet her.

He'd taken the dinghy over to the island the next day, on his own, and without telling anyone what he was doing, his second time to do so. But still could find no signs of a holt, or otter spraints or food leavings along the banks.

The Commander stood for some time at the rail, shivering now and then in the river chill. A gaga old party, he told himself, wandering abroad in his pyjamas, his head stuffed with otters and thoughts of the future.

Which was where Priny found him a while later, and suggested that, now they were both up, she make tea.

Afterwards, she told him that she'd wash up the tea things first, before following him to bed. And after drying them, she cleaned the sink, and then the worktops, before starting on the cupboard doors, and then getting the mop out. She was thinking about the future, the same future that she'd pooh-poohed when the Commander had sat fretting about it. The same future that had troubled his good eye and was now getting the kitchen cleaned.

Something will turn up, she told herself again, as she had told him then. And James had testily agreed, she was right, something *would* turn up. The question at their age, he'd insisted on pointing out, was what?

And whatever it was, it would mean leaving this place. That was what they really meant by the future. Because even if they *could* stay, they wouldn't, not now. What they had here would be gone. But they would never stop wanting it back, no matter where they were. Whatever else that future held for them, it would always mean that, always mean loss.

It would also mean selling the *Castle*. They hadn't been able to find moorings elsewhere on the river, and without power to move on, and keep on moving until they did find somewhere, they didn't see there was anything else for it.

Tom Parr had been aboard several times to poke about at what remained of the engine, he and James with their sleeves rolled up, banging the odd bit of rusty pipe with a spanner and shaking their heads over it.

As long as they washed their hands before they came to the table, Priny was quite happy with them playing with it. She knew as well as the Commander that it would probably take more than the boat was worth to bring her to full power and river worthiness.

Which hadn't of course stopped either of them talking about leaving on her. Talking about moving again, remembering other times, the fun of it then, and as if leaving now wouldn't matter. Ignoring the tedious, practical details, the "hows?" and "what withs?" All that sort of thing belonged in the real world and, for now at any rate, they were still on the river.

And as for the "where to?" well, they'd know that when they got there. As they had known it when first arriving in Batch Magna, on their way like Phineas to nowhere else in particular, falling into it one winter's day off a valley road, with the scent of woodsmoke over the village and the Steamer Inn just opening. And waiting for them, tied up on the river in showy, amiable decline, the surprise delights of four Victorian paddle steamers.

But tonight the real world loomed. And in the real world the most they could hope for was that the estate would want the *Castle* back, and feel obliged to pay what they had paid for her. Which wasn't much, but would at least give them marching money.

Only this time they knew they wouldn't be marching far. This time, wherever they ended up, it would be somewhere quite predictable. At their age, and with their means, there could be few surprises left.

Some sort of old folks' accommodation, she supposed, in Church Myddle or Kingham, and she'd play whist, she also supposed, while knowing perfectly well that she'd do nothing of the sort, even if she knew how to play it. And it would be handy for the shops and library, and the doctor's and the chemist's. And the undertakers.

The sort of move in fact they ought to have considered making anyway. It was only sensible, really, at their age, as their eldest daughter, Charlotte, had been pointing out for some time now.

Charlotte only had sensible views. Her father usually immediately found something else to think about when she aired them, while her mother listened with a half-smile transfixed somewhere between alarm and boredom. Charlotte had been born sensible and had stayed so, down to the sensible knickers she no doubt still wore. Priny could only wonder where she got it from.

Back in the bedroom she tucked her sleeping husband in, a nurse's hands at work briskly on the covers. And then stood for a few moments watching him as he slept, that familiar determined set to his face as he did so making him look curiously young and pugnacious, as if sleep were a duty he took jolly seriously.

She smiled at herself then, getting in next him, at her own thoughts. Even on only one headlight, it was quite astonishing what that twinkle of his could still do to her.

And at your age, too, she told herself, cuddling up to him.

In her bedroom in the house in Petts Lane off the High Street, Miss Wyndham was also awake.

Suddenly and violently awake. Chased from sleep by a washing line of Hawaiian shirts intent on strangling her, while the Brides in the Bath murderer, Joseph Smith, grinning with maniacal relish, played "Nearer my God to Thee," on the harmonium.

It was dining too late on too much Welsh rarebit that had done it, she told herself, her heart thumping. Or reading too late in bed, finishing just this last page. Dipping into one of her bedside favourites, books on old friends such as Jack the Ripper, stalking again the night-time cobbles of Whitechapel, and Christie, busy with his rubber tubes and Friar's Balsam and Cream, and Dr Palmer, and Crippen in his cellar.

Or thoughts perhaps of a murder much nearer home?

Miss Wyndham drew a sharp breath and clutched the bedclothes to her.

She had stumbled – as she thought of it afterwards – on a plot to murder the new squire, Sir Humphrey Strange. The conspirators were all known to her. Indeed, were all friends of hers. Friends of summer days down by the river, and snug winter evenings when all was battened down, as the Commander put it, and when many a good table and cheerful conversation around a sitting room stove had lit her way home. And now the talk was of murder.

And Miss Wyndham had done more than merely stumble on the plot. She had contributed to it.

They were all there, on the *Cluny Belle*, having

afternoon tea on deck, when she'd returned a new work on forensic toxicology Phineas had lent her.

And when Jasmine Roberts had mentioned a boyfriend in the stripped pine business, and suggested a tank of paint remover, or whatever he used, if they needed to get rid of the body, Miss Wyndham had been all too eager to add her bit.

She had cautioned them to bear in mind Haigh, the acid bath murderer, who had put too much confidence in a drum of sulphuric acid to dissolve his last victim, and learned too late that a couple of gall stones and a full set of dentures had remained to accuse him.

None of it had been meant, of course. It had all been a sort of joke. British humour when up against it.

Or had it?

Miss Wyndham shivered with sudden fear.

Or was it excitement?

She had had just enough energy left after her encounter with the American earlier, and her subsequent dash for the village, to stagger home to her cats and an extra schooner of sherry. But she thought now that, exhausted or not, she should have found the strength somehow to carry on to the river. That she should have warned them.

Or him.

Out in the night, an owl called across the sleeping village, and was answered by another, and Miss Wyndham slid further down in the bed.

CHAPTER 14

Murder was the sort of thing that occurred to Humphrey, as well, much later on that morning. Standing on a pair of library steps in that room at Batch Hall, with a book in one hand and his mouth open.

Murder done, horribly, to somebody else, outside, in the Hall grounds somewhere.

Age creaked in a floorboard or a ceiling joist, and he jumped as the grandfather clock on the landing gathered with a rattle of eighteenth-century machinery, and struck the hour, a light sprinkling of notes falling in a silence smelling of old books and Mrs Thomas's beeswax polish.

And then he heard it again, and much nearer the house this time. A scream, rising in great pain or anguish, the sound surely of someone being killed, or a mind lost.

The skin of his scalp rose with it and he dropped the book.

Earlier, in his Yankees dressing gown, Humphrey had sat in the chill of a cavernous bathroom tiled in cabbage green, waiting for the water to heat up as it gushed and spat in spurts from a brass tap the size of a standpipe. Before remembering that he'd forgotten to switch on the immersion heater not less than one hour before, as detailed in the list Sarah had left him. He also remembered that he hadn't made his phone calls last night. He'd sat in front of the television instead, eating chocolates and not feeling well.

He'd phoned Sylvia first, on her personal office number, confident of getting her there.

She was always there. She even had lunch at her desk. When there was no reply he tried her apartment, and let it ring, vaguely anxious now. And when she finally did answer, he'd barely got a couple of words out before she wanted to know who had been a silly Humphrey. And while he was thinking about that, went on to tell him. He had, she'd said, without raising her voice, forgotten about the time difference. That while it may be nine o'clock where Humphrey was, it was only four in the morning where Sylvia was.

He'd heard her use that voice before on others who had erred, the sweetness in it hitting his teeth like ice-cream straight from the freezer.

He was still digesting the experience when Mrs Thomas, the temporary housekeeper, arrived.

Mrs Thomas hadn't known what to expect. Her experience of Americans was limited to the films and television but she found Humphrey, who had decided it would be more proper for his visit to the paddle steamers to wear his Brooks Brothers executive suit, vaguely disappointing.

She also thought he seemed a bit subdued. Although a breakfast of back bacon and double egg, pork sausages, mushrooms, tomatoes and fried bread, seemed to do the trick. She'd polished and laid out the silver in the first-floor breakfast-room but Sir Humphrey said that if it was all right with her he would eat in the kitchen.

He'd picked at his plate at first, but was soon tucking in and chatting away. He told her all about his adventures in the financial skies of New York, and how he'd escaped from life as a short-order cook to emerge triumphantly as Sir Humphrey of Batch Hall, while Mrs Thomas said, go on! and strike me! and well I never! and poured more tea for them both.

The pork sausages, she told him, when he'd singled them out for particular praise, were home-made, from Stretch's, a butcher in Church Myddle, and she strongly advised Sir Humphrey to have nothing to do with Mr Pugh's bacon or his pork sausages. Mr Pugh got them from Morgan's, in Penycwn, on the other side of the border. Mrs Thomas, who before marriage had been a Miss Hooper, a farmer's daughter from this side of the border, said she had nothing against the Welsh as such, she'd married one. But even Mr Thomas had to admit they knew nothing about pigs. They must have plenty of fat on them for a start, and Mr Stretch wouldn't let one across his doorstep unless it had been castrated first. That's why, of course, Morgan's pork always smells of you know what.

She'd picked up one of Stretch's pork pies for his lunch, she told him, filled on the premises, they were, and big as dinner plates, and she had steak and kidney pudding with dumplings in mind for tonight, if that suited.

And Humphrey, a long way from home and his mom's kitchen, nodded happily, and said that it suited just fine.

He'd followed her about after that, while she did her cleaning, hearing all about the people on the houseboats, and the petitions they'd got up over his plans, plans which she said she agreed with, by the way. And the public meeting in the village hall, who was for it and who was against it. Among the for its was a man from the Church Myddle Chamber of Trade, very impressive, he was, with a wall graph and calculator. And Commander Cunningham, who of course was against it, and who, if you asked her, had had one too many, which wasn't anything new, said that what they would lose couldn't be calculated, nor demonstrated on a wall graph, or something like that, and then went on about otters.

Which was all very well, but progress is progress, that's what she always said, and had Sir Humphrey anyone in mind for doing the cleaning in the holiday village yet? Humphrey said he hadn't, and absently agreed that if the plans were passed Mrs Thomas and her extended family of daughters and daughters-in-law could do it.

Mrs Thomas, having suddenly been handed a

career as a cleaning contractor, said she'd pick up some nice cream cakes as well, while she was at it, and a couple of packets of Shropshire Dunks, double milk chocolate biscuits, for a special treat for his tea, if that suited.

But Humphrey scarcely heard even that. He was thinking about the paddle steamers again, the thought of the visit he had to make a dark cloud on the horizon of his morning.

After Mrs Thomas had left, and because it was still too early to ring his mom, he decided to call the agent managing the planning application. The plans for the holiday village had had their mandatory public airing, and having been passed by Batch Magna Parish Council, were now in the hands of the final authority in the matter, the District Council.

Oddly enough, the agent, a man with a hopeful smile and a taste in spotted bow-ties, had been, he said, about to ring him. Not that he had any news for him, Humphrey was to understand, but just to bring him up to date on what wasn't happening. Which in his opinion was sometimes just as important to a client as what was. And the first thing he had to say was that they hadn't had the formal hearing yet. But having said that, they were in the right corridor, as they say in the Town Hall. Now it was simply a question of the right desk, if Humphrey followed him. The second provisional submission stage before the formal submission for approval by the Planning Committee proper.

He assured Humphrey that things were moving,

if not actually on the move, if Humphrey took the distinction. It was just that, with a submission of this size, there was bound to be a bit of shunting about, a bit more toing and froing than usual between departments, if Humphrey saw what he meant.

Humphrey said he did, and then, after putting down the phone, stood frowning at it.

After that, he couldn't then think of anything else that needed doing. Which left him free for his visit to the houseboats.

He decided on another wander round the house first.

Portraits of his ancestors lined the carved Jacobean staircase, oils in the manner of Gainsborough, a small gallery of squires and their families in silk waistcoats and dresses, with lapdogs and fowling pieces, and a young Sir Humphrey, the late squire, standing behind his wife, Lady Phylldia, and their children on a chaise longue in the drawing room.

The rooms, mute with dust sheets, were filled with a past he felt an intruder among. The anonymous faces in family photographs, a group on the river, a school cricket eleven of long ago, and the General in uniform, the Highlands of Scotland and the Italian Riviera between the wars, and memories of Edwardian tea parties in the summer shades of the horse chestnuts on the lawns.

And on a secretaire in the General's bedroom,

with a sudden shock of recognition, a photograph of his own father, a father he knew only from photographs. He was in company with the General, standing on the top of the small fan of steps in front of the great oak doors of the Hall. It was dated 1940, and his father was in Royal Air Force uniform.

Humphrey knew the story. In company with other Americans of his generation, his dad had defied the Neutrality Act and arrived that year in England, via Canada, to train as a pilot with one of the newly formed American Eagle Squadrons.

He took the photograph into his bedroom, ready to take back with him, to take home with him.

He wandered about the rest of the house after that, wandered through its past, a visitor there without a guide. Through anonymous rooms smelling of damp, with blown and peeling wallpaper and sagging ceilings. The day and night nurseries, and what had been the schoolroom, and the servants' bedrooms under the eaves, rooms murmuring with pigeons and with buckets placed to catch the rainwater. The billiard room, the still room, and gun room, the servants' hall, and the butler's pantry, where a cobwebbed crate of pale ale empties had still to be returned, and mice had shredded the newspapers lining the cutlery drawers.

In the library across from the kitchen, with its impression on the faded wallpaper above the mantelpiece where the last of the Stubbs had been, Humphrey found other things to delay him.

Leather-bound volumes of *Punch* and the *Illustrated London News* to leaf through, and *Country Life* and *Horse and Hound*, and Burn's *Justice of the Peace and Parish Officer*. And he had just climbed the library steps to try a top-shelf row of parish histories, when the morning was rent with the sound of screaming.

Humphrey wasn't the bravest man he knew. But he felt that something ought to be done about it. And as, for now, he was the householder, he supposed he ought to be doing it.

Reluctantly he climbed down and went off to do it.

The screams seemed to have come from the back of the house. He walked down the hall into the drawing room, and picking up a poker on his way through, opened the French windows out onto the balustraded terrace.

He blinked in the sudden sunlight, the air dusty with the scent of geraniums, an overgrown bed of them below the terrace, among other overgrown beds of pansies, saxifrage, antirrhinums and alyssum, gillyflowers and love-in-a-mist. Tudor flowers, first grown there with magic and the health of the household in mind.

And his mouth dropped open a second time that morning, as around the corner of one of the box hedges, grown to shelter the beds, and half buried now in a pale pink rambler rose, strutted a peacock.

Dipping its crested head as if to the crowd, he walked with theatrical pomp up the terrace steps, a bedraggled-looking opera king, his gorgeous train of tail feathers, eye-studded and tipped with gold, muddied round the skirt after the rain.

When he saw Humphrey he paused on the landing, and cocked a brown eye at him, demented looking and sly with enquiry.

Humphrey felt like a messenger, and one with nothing to say. If it had been the sort of fowl he'd thought Sarah had meant, he would have made clucking noises at it. Now all he did was gape.

The cock, still keeping an eye on him, began to paw with his large claws at the ground, as if about to charge or fly at the intruder. And with a swishing sound like a curtain going up, slowly lifted his huge train of feathers, and fanned them, their startling, iridescent beauty like a trick done by mirrors, over and over, in the shining brilliances of blue and gold and green.

And then the peacock screamed again. His head held back and abandoning himself to it as if to grief, shrieking on higher and higher notes at the flightless sky, a mad king singing of exile.

And then seemed suddenly to lose interest in the whole thing, the show over. His tail came down like a curtain on it, and he began pecking prosaically at the grass growing between the stone paving of the landing, the sun oiling the quivering blue and green of his crown feathers.

Humphrey, feeling he had been dismissed, backed from his presence.

CHAPTER 15

Humphrey stopped off at St Swithin's on his way to the river, telling himself that this was something that *had* to be done. That *should* have been done on his first visit.

There was nothing else for it. The houseboats would have to wait.

He looked hopefully at a few graves when he got there, before aimlessly following the path round to the rear of the church. And he found someone then, in a corner of the churchyard, an old man standing in front of what appeared to be a brick outbuilding.

From high in the yew a wren opened in sudden, loud song, scolding him as he made his way between headstones etched with lichen, and mossed and ivy-clad stone coffin lids, the air sweet with a recent cut of grass that looked scythed.

And he saw when he reached there that that was where he wanted to be. That what he'd taken to be an outbuilding was a burial vault, built of the local red sandstone, and carved into the ornate top of the front wall, under an urn and grapes decoration, was the shield of the Strange family crest, his crest.

The old man was wearing a dark blue serge suit for his visit to the churchyard, and collar and tie, a mop of yellow-white hair sitting on his head like smoke.

Humphrey exchanged greetings with him, and remarked on the weather, as he had learned to. The old man was rolling a cigarette, stiffly, his fingers bent and with a shine on them like claws.

'That last entry was the old squire here,' he said, watching Humphrey peering at one of the vault's two name plaques, the General's inscription added to the stone with new pink precision.

'The General, as he was known. They had a job getting him in there. Big man, he was. It's subsided a bit at that end, see. Time, I suppose, and water seepage, and that. And the entrance slab was jammed. They had to dig him in round the back at the end.'

The old man laughed as if clearing his throat. 'Went in through the tradesmen's entrance, you might say. That'd have tickled him, that would.'

He lit the thin pipe of tobacco with a match, his weathered cheeks caving in as he sucked on it.

'And you keep it tidy, huh?' Humphrey said.

'Only when I'm here, like, after I've looked in on the wife. The odd weed coming through and that,' he said, nodding at the strip of raked gravel surrounding the vault behind low-slung loops of rusty iron chain.

'His granddaughter, over at Cuckington, her drops by regular. He's with his wife now, the General. Lady Phylldia. Pneumonia, her died of. Pneumonia with complications,' he intoned. 'There's more of the family in there, going back centuries. Strange Corner, this is – that's the family name, like,' he assured Humphrey. 'There's some of their servants here as well, outdoor and indoor. There's Cradoc over there, Cradoc Benbow, an old head gardener of theirs. Natural causes, he died of. I used to play dominoes with him regular in the pub. And Mrs Bowen the cook. And old Mr Peel, their last butler. Cancer, that was. Cancer of the bowels. He was in church a week before he went, doing the plate as usual after the General had read the lesson. Three months later the squire followed him.'

He'd been glancing at Humphrey, a stranger, out of the corner of an eye, and now said, 'Anyone you know here, is there, sir?'

Humphrey hesitated, and then said, no, there was no one he knew. He was just passing, and had stopped out of interest.

'Cause I know 'em all here, I do. Know 'em all. Family, friends, neighbours. Got the wife over there. Hers was cancer, as well. Cancer of the breast, her died of. And our William's over the other side, a younger brother of mine. Turned his tractor over up on the hills there, with him half under it. Took him hours to die, they reckon, and nobody to hear his cries but the sheep,' the old man said, his voice like a mournful wind. 'Crows had his eyes in the end. And John Hodges down there.' He indicated a row of graves further down that side against the boundary wall. 'Went to school with him, old John. Dropped down dead only a couple of weeks back, he did. In his hen house, on his way in with his breakfast.

'Well, better be getting back, I suppose,' he said, wheezing a little as he bent down to pick up a handfork and the plastic bag he had with him.

'Though the way I feel some days, hardly seems worth it.'

Humphrey stood in front of the vault after the old man had gone, hands clasped in front of him, head bowed, in some vague notion of ceremony, and seeking words for the occasion found he had nothing to say.

He had come to pay his respects to one man, the General, expecting without thinking a single grave, and had found a monument to the name he shared, to its history in this place. And it was as if he were learning about it for the first time, and for the first time was overwhelmed by it.

He had worn his title as if it were something he'd won in a raffle, as if it were something *anyone* might have won in a raffle. He had travelled since that day his life had changed forever on the buoyancy of good fortune and his own natural, large exuberance, and now that had left him, and he had nothing to say.

He was no longer Sir Humphrey Franklin T. Strange, 9th baronet, his name when his time came to be cut with pink precision into the stone of a monument, but Humph, a short-order cook, there to make a fast buck on the back of it.

Yeah, well, all that stuff's the past, and I've got a future to run, he growled then, giving them, and their history, a bit of Wall Street short shrift, and chewed briefly and furiously on nothing, his ears burning.

And was about to leave when he remembered that part of that, more immediate future, was the visit he had still to make to the houseboats, which prompted an interest in checking out the grave of Mr Peel the butler first, and then that of Cradoc Benbow, the Hall's head gardener, and Mrs Bowen the cook, and, while he was at it, John Hodges's new black granite headstone, the man who'd died before breakfast.

Humphrey checked out a few more graves after that, and then found more things of interest to look at in the porch of the church, reading the notices, and the love notes carved into its half-timbers, the hearts and initials of those who had lingered over the centuries on the shiny, yellowing oak seats.

The great weight of the church's oak door creaked on its hinges as he pushed it open, the echoing dimness smelling of mice and damp hymnbooks, and polish, the praise of a roster of village women, the white altar linen at the end of the nave a starched glow in the light from its window.

A hand-printed leaflet told him that St Swithin's, like Batch Castle, was Norman with Saxon beginnings. That the font, decorated with carved Norman chevrons and horseshoes, had once been part of a pillar from the old Roman town of Uriconium, on the other side of the county, a Christian stone plundered from Roman ruins and still in use today.

He was told that he was standing on quarried red sandstone flags under a hammerbeam roof with quatrefoils and owls and otters carved into its timbers. That the pinnacled tower was largely Norman, with angels for gargoyles and a string course of grotesque animal heads along its battlements. And that its bells, carrying on their sides the names of saints, squires and parsons, rhymes and prayers, rang out across this valley before the Reformation.

He learnt that the two-decker pulpit was seventeenth century, that the squire's box-pew below it, with its little benches and the faded Strange family's blue and gold escutcheon painted on the wall, was Jacobean, and the altar table Elizabethan.

The windows in the chancel were mediaeval, windows of the crucifixion and Christ in Glory, and the life of Paul, under dragon-red skies, the figures in cobalt blue and gold and emerald, and with pale flames in their gilded hair.

There was a Bethlehem scene in the nave with

adoring angels, and a window of Welsh saints to the barons of the Marches. And St George in shining white and gold, and behind the altar a head of Our Lord ringed with flowers the colour of gemstones.

And on a lime-washed wall, a dozen plain wooden crosses from the makeshift graves of local men who fell in the Great War, and who lie still in France, facing the sea and home.

And framed beneath them, in copperplate, sepia script, two stanzas from Houseman's *A Shropshire Lad*.

> *Into my heart an air that kills*
> *From yon far country blows:*
> *What are those blue remembered hills,*
> *What spires, what farms are those?*

> *That is the land of lost content,*
> *I see it shining plain.*
> *The happy highways where I went*
> *And cannot come again.*

There were memorials to other wars, and other lives lost, to the Strange family and a service to Empire, the Peninsula, India, the Sudan and Egypt, and a plaque to the General's two brothers who also died in France, and to his son in the last war. And among them, among the roll call of names on stone and marble, a brass of a lone mounted bugler calling.

In the south transept Humphrey, as Sir Humphrey, found his beginnings, the high seventeenth-century tomb of the first baronet, Sir Richard Strange, awarded for his loyalty to Charles I.

An alabaster figure in plate armour, his shield of arms painted on his breast, his head resting on his helmet and his feet on a lion. His sword and his Welsh wife, Lady Hawis, by his side, and their four children playing below them, looked over by angels and guarded by deerhounds. His family and hounds gathered to him again.

And at one end of the tomb, their enamelled coat-of-arms, a castle with a lion and otter rampant, and the Strange family motto: *Beati qui durant.* "Blessed are they who endure."

And that's just what he was trying to do. Endure, survive. And in a world that had, like, you know, grown up a bit since then. With problems that needed something a bit more complex than hitting them with a goddam sword. He felt beleaguered, besieged by ghosts. The past was everywhere in this goddam place. Following him like the eyes of the portraits lining the main staircase in the Hall, watching him go to bed in the evening, and down again in the morning, to plot the future.

Well, he had news for them. All that was history. And history wouldn't pay seventy-five percent death duties or get the goddam roofs fixed!

His ears were burning as he stormed out of the door of the church – "Late sixteenth century, made of oak, with crescent hinges and a great closing ring. Above it is a Saxon tympanum depicting a hunting scene, and the marks of bullets from the Civil War may be seen in its wood and stone surround."

Humphrey banged it shut behind him.

CHAPTER 16

In the tweed pocket of what, as an ex-army man, he called a change coat, Colonel Ash fingered the bowl of a pipe manners forbade him to light in the presence of a lady, and agreed with Miss Wyndham that, while it was indeed a beautiful day at present, quite splendid, he, also, wouldn't be at all surprised were it to cloud over later. Wouldn't be at all surprised.

And then Miss Wyndham, while privately of the opinion that the species in question was otherwise, specifically Small Earth, agreed that the colonel was undoubtedly right. That the bumble bee bumping its way through the flowerbeds outside the village hall, was, without question, the Small Garden variety.

This morning they were in a mood to be magnanimous.

With other members of the regatta committee, they were waiting for one of the press photographers to do something complicated with his camera concerning the light.

In the kitchen of the village hall, the chipped

white enamel teapot was standing upside down on the draining board, with the plates that had held digestive biscuits: the regatta committee had voted.

The result of which would now be made known to the wider world via representatives of the press, the three local reporters and their photographers who'd been kicking their heels outside.

For the first time in living memory, Batch Magna Regatta and Show would not be opened by the squire. Sarah, the General's granddaughter, it had been voted by a majority of five to three, would officiate.

The vested interest of Dilly Browne, landlady of the Steamer Inn, and one of the three who had voted for the new Sir Humphrey, by way, she said, of welcoming him to Batch Magna, was clear. And Dilly, being Dilly, putting her case with a smile which made it plain she really couldn't care less what they thought, had never really pretended otherwise.

But bed and breakfast were the words which sprung to most minds when listening to the two other members who, while claiming impartiality, endorsed Dilly's view. Well, the new Batch Magna may be on the doorstep but for now, as far as the majority of the regatta committee was concerned, it would just have to wait.

After snapping the committee, and noting names and the interesting division in comment, the news-hounds hotfooted it for their cars and Batch Hall, to get the new squire's reaction to the news. This one had Story written all over it.

Meanwhile, the new squire was just up the road from them, eating an extra-large raspberry ripple ice-cream in the shop, and talking to Mr Pugh. Humphrey was on his way to the paddlers again.

He hadn't made it after leaving the church yesterday. He'd gone back first for lunch, for one of Mr Stretch's homemade pork pies, as big as a dinner plate.

And on his way out again, had found the Hall had an outside he hadn't even *started* looking at yet. The stables and tack rooms, a forge, game room, dairy, an orangery. And a coach house, where he'd discovered a trap with a broken shaft, and a rather grand, ancient-looking motorcar he'd sat in, poop-pooping the lodge for the gates to be run back.

And the overgrown gardens, skirting the presence of a couple of peacocks claiming one of the lawns, with their ruined walls and abandoned glass-houses. And a mood then which had taken him by surprise, wandering among their neglect, and seeing as if for the first time the shabbiness of the Hall standing over it.

He couldn't blame the General. He, Humphrey, of all people knew how little money had been available. But it was about time *something* was done. And it was a good job that now something *would* be done.

Something would be done now, all right! he'd

said. And then said it again. But still couldn't seem to rally any enthusiasm for the idea. For the first time since the plans had been laid for the future of the place, the thought of that future left him flat.

He didn't know why that was, and he didn't spend too long wondering about it. If Humphrey didn't understand a thing, he simply moved on to the next. Which in this case, he found down by the river.

Poking about in undergrowth there, he discovered a creek, tunnelled with trees and leading to a boathouse, with upended skiffs and sailing and rowing dinghies, and a punt in it, and two fine-looking mahogany rowing boats under canvas on a slip.

He uncovered one of them, and pulled it down to the water. And working out what went where, and reminding himself, just in case, that he could swim, rowed slowly and awkwardly upstream, and discovered the hidden world of the river.

He was out of sight for long stretches of it, cut off behind stands of reeds and sedges and summer-high hemlock. Rowing past weeping willows with their boughs in the water, and the bare rooty earth of banks, like small cliffs under ancient oaks and sycamores, with the mysteries of caves for small riverbank animals tunnelled into them.

The fish he suddenly spotted, and mallards, upending themselves to feed, and a heron, motionless in the shallows, and ducking his head under the wings of swallows as they swooped, twittering with excitement, over the water. And once, cursing when his oars wouldn't behave, a blossom-white swan, gliding out imperially from behind a clump of rushes to see what all the vulgar noise was about. And emerald water meadows shining like fresh paint in the sun, where cattle grazed and horses tossed their heads and cantered down to watch him pull by.

He managed to turn the boat round without capsizing it, and on his way back, rounding a bend in the river, came on Batch Hall as if seeing it for the first time, standing as remote and as beguiling as a house in a storybook.

And he had felt even more of a stranger, an intruder, after hauling the boat back up on to the slip, and crossing the lawns to the house. Approaching it from the rear, from the river, as only a friend would – or an enemy.

After that it had been near enough time for a bath and dinner. And in the morning, with the houseboats still unvisited, he toyed with the idea of not doing it at all – you don't *have* to go. You're not *obliged* to, he told himself.

But it was no good. He knew that he *should* go. And having decided that he would, then couldn't find anything else that needed doing or looking at first.

And he was in the shop because he had forgotten to ask Mrs Thomas which one of the paddlers was the Owens', and thought it only right he speak to Annie first. The ice-cream had been a treat, a present to himself. Humphrey loved to be loved, and any minute now knew he was likely to be shouted at.

Although he didn't know it, Annie Owen was also in the shop, out of sight behind the postcard stand, idly looking at the new stock just in – including, ironically, one of the Hall, the Hall she had bicycled up to countless times, bathed in the light of happier days.

She had Worcester sauce in her wire basket, for Owain's breakfast, a few other bits of shopping, and half a dozen eggs, the first time for a long time she'd had to buy other people's.

There were only a couple of her birds laying at the moment. Three of them had been killed by a fox, after she'd failed to secure their door properly one evening, and another two had gone broody on her. They were currently shut up in one of the old railway containers, sitting on goose eggs, doing something for their keep. Reared by mother hens, there would at least in future be a few better behaved geese about the plot.

It was at that moment that Humphrey asked Mr Pugh the way to her boat, and Mr Pugh told him she was in the shop somewhere, and nodded in her direction when Annie emerged from behind the postcard stand. And she saw him, Old Chapel Face, with the American, their heads together in what looked like a right old gossip session.

Annie's eyes spat sudden and furious fire and her hand closed on the eggs.

Hisht! Dignity, my girl. Dignity, she chided herself, echoes of her mother, as she walked up to them with a smile which prompted Mr Pugh to suddenly consider his shelves needed an urgent tidying.

Annie plonked the wire basket down on the counter, said something which Humphrey didn't understand but took to be Welsh, and with a backward glance at them like a curse, flung open the door and left.

It hadn't been Welsh, but English, of a sort. Annie couldn't say what she wanted to say because she hadn't thought of it. Which hadn't stopped her trying to say it.

She thought of it now, outside the shop. She should have said, in a sweetly reasonable voice, of course: 'Do you two gentlemen want to speak to me? No? Of course not. You only say what you've got to say behind people's backs, don't you!' And then swept out. Or: 'I thought gossip was something only old ladies did, not gentlemen. But of course' – and with a pointed look at the American here – 'but of course you're not really *gentlemen*, are you.' And then, leaving with a scornful laugh: 'In fact, you're not really *men!*'

She was still saying what she should have said when she reached home, her face almost giving off sparks with temper.

Phineas, on the deck of the *Cluny Belle*, fed the last of his toast over the side to the ducks, his mind elsewhere, busy plotting the loud demise of a Chinese gang boss.

He had just finished a late breakfast after a couple of hours of cricket practice with his son, a last knock-up together. Daniel, originally staying for only a few days, was still with him some weeks later. He hadn't even made the French trip he'd talked about. Phineas had no idea why, and neither, when he'd spoken to her on the phone, had Daniel's mother. And now Daniel had decided it was time he went home. And that was probably all either parent was going to get.

Daniel was in the village now, seeing his friends before leaving. He and Phineas had already done that, said goodbye, on the cricket pitch. Father and son taking it in turns at the crease while the other bowled. There had hardly been need to say anything more after that.

Phineas sat at his work table under the Martini sunshade and lit a Gauloise. In the current chapter of *Breakfast at Mr Chow's*, he had a Triad Dragon holed up in a Chinatown gaming club, while members of a rival gang debated the best way to send him to his ancestors.

Phineas had decided on a bomb. Five hundred pounds of plastic high explosive ticking away in a steel barrel, part of a regular delivery of beer to the club. He was looking forward to it.

Then Lucy the barmaid ran up the gangway.

'What?' Phineas said plaintively, as she paused

dramatically on deck. There were times when the Welsh could be very tiresome.

And she was the third interruption in the space of an hour. First the Commander, wanting to know if he had a lump hammer, in aid of some bit of pottiness about firing the *Castle* up again, and then Jasmine, to borrow a fiver.

Phineas sighed. 'Look, Lucy,' he said, getting heavily to his feet, 'I don't mean to be rude, but—'

'I've left him!' she cried, and rushing to Phineas, clasped him around the chest and held on.

'Who?' Phineas asked, knowing who.

Just when you think the past has been tidied neatly away, somebody opens a cupboard and out it all falls.

'Carl,' Lucy said, and heaved a couple of loud sobs into his shirt front.

'He accused me of making eyes at some man. And said if I ever went with anybody else he'd kill me and them,' Lucy snuffled, while Phineas patted her back as if bringing up wind, and stared anxiously at the gangway.

Lucy looked up at him. 'As if he owns me! Well, he don't, see. I told him that, as well.' She pressed her head against Phineas's chest as if listening to his heart. 'I told him about us.'

Lucy hugged him as if in tearful goodbye, a man on his way to duty and danger. While Phineas let himself be hugged, and waited for the chef to come up the gangway.

With Sally in mind, he had kept his distance

from Lucy since that night, and to his relief Lucy seemed to want to do the same. In fact, watching her and Patrick, the landlord, when at the till together or sneaking looks across the optics, he had the distinct impression that Lucy had moved on. And for that he gave thanks.

He had once watched Carl de-winging chickens in the pub's kitchen with a meat cleaver, and doing so with an energy that Phineas, layman in these matters as he might be, couldn't see was entirely called for, the bright steel twinkling with brutal and unerring precision.

And now he was on his way here. Pausing first no doubt only to weigh up the respective merits of a cleaver and boning knife.

'Lucy,' he said sharply, his hands on her arms. 'Lucy,' he said on a gentler note, 'Lucy, I think it's best if—'

'I'm not going back to him!'

'No, of course not,' he said with a little laugh at the idea. 'It's just that . . .'

Her arms tightened around him, holding him there, holding him to her.

'I told him I love you. I told him I'd rather *die* with you than live with him.'

'What did he say to that?' Phineas asked, horribly fascinated despite himself.

'I don't suppose he knows, not yet,' she sniffed. 'That was earlier, at my place. I've put it all in a note I left for him in the pub kitchen.'

'Ah – *Ah*,' Phineas said, relief dawning. 'Ah, well,

in that case all we have to do is to get the note back – for now, Lucy, just for now,' he added quickly, getting her moving, guiding her towards the gangway. 'We can always send him another one later, by post. So how long have we got, Lucy? When does he start work?'

Lucy sniffed and looked at her watch. 'Should be there now,' she said.

'Ah,' Phineas said again

He was no good at fighting, he never had been. He had always shrunk with distaste from the thought of brawling. Even at school, where getting the worse of it behind one of the sports pavilions had been looked on as character forming. Besides, not only was Carl large and the athletic type, he was also clearly deranged. And it was no good looking to Sikes. Sikes's reaction to a couple of humans rolling about would be to bark a lot and then try and mount one of them.

'Right. Right, well in *that* case,' he said, peering over in the direction of the pub, 'in that case, we need to give him time to cool down. Are you off today?' he asked, taking charge, while Lucy leant against him.

'No,' she said, playing with one of his shirt buttons. 'No, but I don't start till twelve. Patrick's opening up this morning.'

'Right. Right, well, we'll disappear till then. Hole up somewhere.'

'All right, love.' She smiled up at him. 'Whatever you say.'

'We'll go for a drive,' he decided, looking up at the hills and the shelter of woods.

'All right, darling,' Lucy said coyly, her eyes agreeing with what she took him to really have in mind. In Lucy's experience, it was men who said one thing and meant another.

He took her firmly by the arm, and telling Sikes, sprawled under the work table, where he'd returned after a desultory sniffing of Lucy's leg, unnecessarily to stay, propelled her down the gangway. 'We'll just *drive*,' he emphasised. 'Give the dust time to settle. These things sometimes—'

She put a hand on his arm. 'Shhh!'

Phineas heard it as well then.

'That's him,' Lucy said. 'That's the brute. He's not sure which boat is yours. Just listen to the pig!'

Carl's bellowing out in Upper Ham somewhere put Phineas in mind of the Hereford bull penned up at Home Farm at the height of summer, goaded by testosterone and the heat.

'What are you going to do, love?' Lucy asked hopefully, eyes wide at the thought of them fighting over her.

Phineas knew precisely what he was going to do. It was just a question of which direction he was going to do it in.

'Quick! The dinghy,' he said, grabbing her hand, and pulling her down to the bank at the stern of the paddler.

He heaved the mooring peg out, thankful he always left oars and rowlocks on board, and never padlocked it. No one locked boats, or doors, in Batch Magna. Something else, no doubt, which was about to change.

He pushed off from the bank with an oar as soon as Lucy got gingerly in. And then, watched by a small audience of coots and ducks, almost immediately fell out again, losing her balance and flopping untidily over the side.

'For god's sake!' Phineas snapped, as she surfaced and made a panicky grab for the dinghy.

Lucy hung there, gasping and spluttering, as Carl, coming up the plot of the paddler by the sound of it, roared her name again.

'Come on!' Phineas urged, pulling at her, balancing the boat and fearing capsize as he grabbed a leg and helped her scramble aboard.

Lucy, oozing water and plastered with silt, opened her mouth to wail and he clamped a hand over it.

'*Shhh*!' he whispered fiercely, and jabbed a finger in the direction of the plot.

Turning the dinghy towards the *Belle*, he started to pull slowly and quietly for her stern, while Lucy sat in a muddy puddle on the floor, her hands wiping with ineffectual disgust at the silt on her, the stink of it, exposed to the air, blooming.

Carl bawled again then, on the gangway or the deck this time, Phineas judged, and Sikes started barking.

Phineas knew what his dog would be doing. He'd be standing there, looking up at the intruder, one end barking while the other end wagged. There were times when he was forced to wonder what Sikes was for.

He kept as tight to the stern of the *Belle* as the oars of the dinghy would allow, and followed it round, expecting discovery at any moment, followed by the heavy Underwood, or even Carl himself, with a boning knife between his teeth.

The chef shouted again, and Phineas guessed that he'd gone inside, the kitchen or the living room, and then, of course, the bedroom.

They were getting away with it, they were pulling it off, he told himself, glancing up at the deck. Just as Sikes stuck his head through one of the gaps in the rail, and looked down at them in a small, startled avalanche of jowls.

The dog started forward, and peered intently down as if making sure that it really was, unexpectedly, Phineas. And then started to wag his tail at the game.

Phineas flapped his hands urgently at him, shooing him away. Sikes wagged even harder, and lowered his chest, his front paws spread, inviting play.

'No – No! Quiet! *Qui-et*,' Phineas growled, baring his teeth at him, knowing what was coming next.

Sikes snapped off a couple of quick ones first, as if testing. And then threw himself into it, his body moving after each bark like the recoil of cannon.

Phineas, the need for stealth gone now, pushed off hurriedly from the hull of the paddler with an oar, and Lucy, fearing another ducking, clutched at the side of the dinghy and made little mewing sounds as it pitched and rocked on its way out to midstream.

Phineas glanced over at his dog barking away on deck as if seeing off an intruder. Seeing off Phineas, seeing off his master from his master's boat, his master's home, their home. He could see the curry stains on his white snout, the extra helping of chicken madras he'd made last night, just for him, because it was his favourite.

And he watched as Carl suddenly appeared next to him, holding a plastic bag up and shouting something Phineas couldn't catch. His dog barking at him. Standing with his enemy and barking at him. Treachery could not wear a more monstrous face.

'*You're dead. I'm going to get a gun and come back and kill you, Sikes!*' he roared, while Lucy sat in her puddle of river water and silt and snivelled miserably.

CHAPTER 17

Having only caught glimpses of the paddlers from the road, Humphrey hadn't known what to expect when, after a second extra-large raspberry ripple in the shop, while he wondered if there was something else he should be looking at first, he finally made his reluctant way down to Lower Ham.

Something from his childhood, perhaps, when he rode the big stern-wheelers in storybooks, with Huckleberry Finn and escaping Negro slaves in the Mississippi night. A gambler, known from St Louis to New Orleans, in a white hat and linen starched as a new deck of cards, with Southern belles fluttering admiringly at his shoulder and a derringer holstered in his well-cut sleeve.

What he found, when he stepped through the Owens' gate, was the *Felicity H*, and what looked like a junkyard. There were scratching chickens and ducks, and geese kicking up a fuss, and a goat, chewing the cud and looking at him in a know-it-all sort of way, tethered well away from a line of washing, the sails of what he took to be Mr Owen's shirts filling gently in a river breeze.

Alongside the *Robert E Lee* or the *Natchez*, the *Felicity H* would have looked like a tug.

She was tied fore and aft with old rope cables, her living quarters piled on deck like a Chinese junk. But it was obvious she'd had a fresh coat of paint recently, the stovepipe funnel, which was probably now a chimney, ringed with dark blue and gold, the flourishes of her name and the other ornate decorations on the port paddlebox, as jolly looking as a Coney Island ride.

Humphrey took a deep breath and started up the gangway.

There was nothing jolly looking about Annie Owen, waiting for him on deck with her arms folded.

'And what do you want?' she said.

Humphrey opened his mouth to speak, and then closed it again. Annie hadn't finished yet.

'I don't remember inviting you aboard. You wouldn't just walk into somebody's house, would you? Not without being invited.' Annie nodded at the gangway. 'Well, that's our front door, that is.'

Humphrey, embarrassed, glanced at the gangway and hesitated, wondering whether to go back, and maybe knock a couple of times on the side of the paddler first, or something.

'I suppose you thought it didn't matter, not with us, not with the gypsies. Well, let me tell you something, mister. They may not be proper houses, these boats, with proper doors, but they're homes. *Our* homes. And we wouldn't thank you for any other, see. We're neighbours and friends and family, all rolled into one, we are, on this river,' she told him, and was surprised to discover that out of nowhere a couple of fat slow tears were sliding down her cheeks.

She wiped them away impatiently. 'Other people are welcome to what they've got, we don't want it. Because the way we see it, mister, is that if we don't have it then it's not worth having.'

Something else that surprised her, something she'd never articulated before, had barely been aware she had thought it. Waking in summer to a mist on the water, the valley a pool of still green silence made deeper by birdsong, days when life is moved outdoors and there's the river to cool off in. And winters snug around the stove, with the sound of owls in the frosty dark or when a wind blows and there's rain on the roof.

She laughed abruptly at her thoughts, a laugh with scorn and triumph in it, from a place he could never reach nor understand.

'What do you and that old hypocrite know!' she said tossing her head in the direction of the shop. 'It's people, mister, *people*, that matter. How they behave. Not who they are, or how much they've got, or where they live.'

She held up her left hand, showing a wedding ring of Welsh gold. 'I'm a respectable married woman, I am, mister. And this boat, same as the other boats here, and the people on them, is as respectable as anything you'll get with a privet hedge around it, I can tell you. We've nothing to hide here, we haven't, behind *net curtains*,' she added, disdainfully underlining the last couple of words.

But Humphrey's attention had wandered. He was gazing across at the starboard side of the paddler, the riverside. Watching with his mouth open as a drowned-looking blonde, carrying a shoe and mumbling wretchedly to herself, fumbled with a gate in the rail, and opening it, hobbled through onto the deck.

Ffion Owen, in her bedroom in the uptops, discovered she wasn't pregnant at the same time that Phineas was tying up the dinghy to the ladder one side of the *Felicity's* paddlebox.

Fleeing downriver with Lucy, he had pulled alongside the *Cluny Queen* first. And after finding that Jasmine had gone to a bring-and-buy sale at the village hall with the fiver he'd lent her, had then pushed off for the *Castle*. He knew that the Commander was messing about upriver with Tom Parr, but he had hoped that Priny, unflappable Priny, might be there.

She hadn't been, and pulling nearer to the *Felicity*, Phineas was relieved to hear Annie's voice. He steadied the dinghy as Lucy, with one shoe lost, and obstinately refusing to let him chuck the other in after it, climbed awkwardly up the paddlebox ladder.

Turning his face away from the drips falling from

her sodden denim skirt, and telling her that it was simple enough, for God's sake, when she had trouble opening the child-safety lock on the gate, he followed her up onto the deck.

Annie and Humphrey both stared at them.

'Good morning, good morning,' Phineas beamed, holding his hands up in a mixture of apology and reassurance, while Lucy trailed behind him, snuffling quietly.

'Annie, it's a long story, but what it boils down to is this,' he went on briskly, glancing over at Lower Ham and the Owens' gate.

'Carl—' He looked at Annie. 'Carl, yes? Right, well, not to put too fine a point on it, Annie, Carl now knows that Lucy and I – er – slept together.'

'I told him,' Lucy sniffed.

'She told him. And—'

'And now he wants to kill us.'

'Carl is Lucy's boyfriend, and quite frankly not all there,' Phineas explained to Humphrey, a stranger to him, but given their intrusion, he felt he was owed something.

'A madman, he is,' Lucy added, half-heartedly trying to wring out her skirt.

'He's chasing us. Hot on our heels,' Phineas said, taking another peek in the direction of Lower Ham. 'That's how Lucy fell in.'

'Phineas rescued me. Saved me, he did,' Lucy said, the heroine of the piece.

'He was after us with a cleaver, or a boning knife, or something,' Phineas added to Humphrey, and made a face indicating how ridiculous the whole thing was.

'Anyway, Annie, if—' he'd got out, when Ffion ran up.

Waking after a lie-in on her day off, Ffion had also been relieved to hear Annie's voice on deck. Overnight she had been given her life back. She was sixteen and free again, and bursting to tell somebody.

A few minutes later, wearing only the T-shirt she slept in and a pair of knickers, she ran down the companionway and along the deck to her mother.

'Mam! Mam! I'm not pregnant!' she cried. 'I'm not, I'm not, I'm not!'

Annie looked at Humphrey, whose mouth was still open. And with a smile which held in it a memory of her own mother, and visitors to the best parlour, said the first thing that came into her head.

'Would you like,' she asked him, brightly genteel, 'a cup of tea?'

Before Humphrey could answer, Bryn the collie ran up the gangway, followed by Owain and Sion, with Snipe bringing up the rear.

They had been rough shooting over Home Farm, the morning punctuated for the past couple of hours by the dry cough of their guns. To Snipe it had been a call sounded from his youth, and he had ran to it, gamely, if much slower now and none too steadily, with his tail flying again.

Sion had left his gun in his Ford pick-up on

Lower Ham along with most of the bag, on its way to a butcher's shop across the border. Owain was carrying his broken over one arm and a couple of rabbits for the pot by their hind legs, blood dribbling still from their nostrils.

'How do,' he said, taking in the small gathering.

His daughter rushed to him and hugged him. 'Da! Da! I'm not pregnant – I'm not!'

'I'll explain later,' Annie said quickly, flapping a hand at him.

She had been relieved by the news but not surprised by what it meant. She just wished her husband could have been kept out of it. They'd have to listen to it all now. Thunder from a chapel he'd read comics in as a boy, and hadn't put a foot inside since, and ranting of murder when, pregnant or not pregnant, he caught the man who'd lain with his baby, his little Ffion. And then tearful breast beatings over his failure as a father, and finally cuddles and probably a bottle of the same perfume he bought Ffion whatever the occasion.

Owain moved his head like a bull pestered by flies. But if he understood nothing else he understood the word pregnant, and he narrowed his eyes at Humphrey, a young male stranger, and one looking even more ill at ease under his gaze.

'This is . . .' Annie faltered.

Humphrey glanced at the shotgun, and stood up straight.

'Mr Owen,' he said, getting it over with, 'Mr Owen, I am—'

'A Canadian!' Annie finished for him. 'He's a Canadian. Staying at the pub. With his family. And just having a look round, like. On holiday, he is,' she added, nodding at Humphrey as if that were obvious. He was no longer wearing his Brooks Brothers executive suit of yesterday, but tartan seersucker trousers and a shirt blooming with large red, yellow and white hibiscus flowers.

'I see,' Owain said cautiously, picking up something here, if not sure what.

'This is my husband,' Annie said, trying to warn Humphrey with her eyes, 'and our eldest son, Sion.'

Sion grinned cheerfully at him. Humphrey frowned at Annie. And then turned to Owain. 'Mist—'

Annie drew a sudden, deep breath, as if choking on something, getting everyone's attention.

'*What* are we thinking of! Standing here, nattering, while Lucy catches her death. Fell in, Owain, she did, poor girl. Nearly drowned. Touch and go, it was for a while. If it hadn't been for Phineas she'd have been done for, most likely.'

Phineas, who'd been keeping an eye on the gate to the plot, smiled modestly, and shrugged it off.

Owain eyed his dry clothes. 'He don't look very wet to me.'

'I fished her out from the dinghy.' Phineas shook his head. 'It's a long story, Owain. It involves *Carl*,' he said with a sigh.

'I see,' Owain said again, not sounding as if he did entirely.

194

He turned to Humphrey. 'And so you—'

'Well, don't just *stand* there, Ffion!' Annie broke in, suddenly aghast. 'Show Lucy where the shower is. And then get the poor girl some clothes. She can't go home like that. Whatever next! We'd better just hope she don't die on us. Looks half there already, she does.'

'You couldn't be in better hands,' Phineas told her encouragingly, as Ffion carefully guided Lucy, dripping and forlorn looking, towards the shower in the stern.

'Well, better get going, I suppose,' he said to the others. 'I've – er – I've got things to do. In Kingham,' he decided, if he could reach the Frogeye in one piece.

'See you all later.' He nodded at Humphrey. 'Nice to have met you, Mr . . . er . . .'

Humphrey addressed himself again to Owain. 'Mr Owen. I—' he started firmly, when Carl bawled for Lucy from below.

Phineas closed his eyes, and then opened them. And saw Carl pounding up the gangway, carrying in a plastic bag, no doubt, a small selection from the knife rack.

'Where's Lucy?' he demanded.

He matched Phineas's height but was much broader where it mattered, and it seemed to Phineas that up close even his brow was muscular.

Phineas smiled weakly. 'Lucy . . .?'

'Hey!' Owain said, glaring at Carl. 'Who bloody well invited you aboard?'

'I'm not talking to you. I'm talking to *him*' Carl said, stabbing a finger at Phineas.

Sion got there before his father.

'What did you say, boy?' he wanted to know, stepping in front of Carl, who was a good head taller. 'If you can't behave yourself you'd better leave, hadn't you?'

Sion's voice was casual sounding and light for his frame, his chest the size of his father's, and with broader shoulders, but there was a warning in it, his dark eyes quite cheerful with menace.

'There are two ways to leave this boat, matey,' he informed Carl. 'The civil way, the way you got on it, uninvited. Or that way,' Sion added, indicating the river.

'Any bloody chucking off to be done here, *I'll* bloody do it!' Owain told his son, while Annie, glancing at Humphrey, trilled a laugh at this bit of local banter.

But Carl wasn't there to fight the Owens, or Phineas.

'Here,' he said, thrusting the plastic bag at him. 'She left a few of her things in my room. You're welcome to her, mate – if you don't mind sharing. And the best of bleeding luck. You'll need it!'

'Language!' Owain roared after him, as Carl stormed off back down the gangway.

'Can I leave them with you, Annie, please?' Phineas asked, and then smiled his goodbyes again, and nodded at Humphrey. 'Enjoy your holiday, Mr . . . er . . .'

'The name's—' Humphrey started.

'*Take* the gentleman with you, Phineas!' Annie said before he could finish. '*Show* him your boat. Show him the *Belle*. He'll like that, being on holiday. And you don't have to rush off, not now Carl's not going to do anything.'

Phineas made a scornful sound. 'My dear Annie, I can assure you—'

Annie turned to Humphrey. 'They're historical, these paddlers. Used to be on the Thames in London, and then here, up and down to Shrewsbury. And now houseboats, little homes – for now,' she couldn't resist adding, and Humphrey stiffened with new resolve and turned to Owain for another attempt.

But Annie got there first again.

'Now off you *go*, Phineas. Can't stand here all day, talking. Got things to do,' she said, pushing both men towards the gangway. 'Goodbye Mr . . . er . . . Nice meeting you. Have a nice holiday,' she said, waving them off, while Owain looked on, vague suspicion lurking still.

'Yes, come on, old chap. I'll give you the tour,' Phineas said expansively, leading the way down the gangway. He felt a new man now it was all over. One for a start who was still alive.

Ffion pregnant! Or not pregnant – which almost came to the same thing. He wondered if it could be Daniel's doing. But thinking about it, he could hardly remember seeing the two of them together since Daniel's arrival. And as cool as they are, surely even young people still have to actually get together to do it? And was it possible, given the times involved?

He'd ask Sally. Sally would know. Good old *Sal*. It was true he'd managed somehow to take a wrong turning. And he'd be the first to admit that he hadn't gone very far before doing so. But he was back on the right road now.

From now on things would be *very* different, he told himself with breezy vagueness.

He paused at the foot of the gangway and took a deep breath, as if of the air on that new right road, and beamed at a glum-looking Humphrey, who was still travelling the old one, still carrying the burden of who he really was.

'Come along, old man. We'll take the shortcut,' he said cheerily, slapping him on the back.

'There are four paddlers,' Phineas said, striding out into Lower Ham and heading for the rear of the pub. 'There were five originally, when they were working boats. The old squire here, General Strange, who died recently, god love him, his father started the company. The Owens – the people you've just met – their paddler, the *Felicity*, was the flagship of the company, named after his wife, the General's mother. The Cluny Steamboat Company, it was called. It used to ply between here and, as Annie said, Shrewsbury. You may have seen the old photographs and other stuff from that time in the pub. Anyway, the old General died recently, as I say, and a great nephew – a neighbour of yours, by the way, an American, he inherited. And wasted no time in giving us all the old slingers. Harry Slingers,' Phineas translated. 'Fired us. Gave us notice to quit. Which is due any minute now. This way,' he added, climbing over the pub's crumbling, ivy covered boundary wall, and waiting for Humphrey to do the same.

'The holiday, I'm afraid, is coming to an end,' Phineas went on, leading the way across the back of the pub, past the hire boats pulled up on the slip and the terrace of summer chairs and tables above them. 'And it was like that – and note the past tense – like being on holiday, when everybody else had gone back. Splashing happily away still, while for the rest of the world, somewhere beyond those hills there, it was Monday morning again. Anyway, enough of the violins. I'm Phineas, by the way. Phineas Cook.'

Humphrey toyed for a moment with the idea of giving a false name. Then conscience stiffened his back.

'Right,' he said decisively. 'Right. OK, Phineas. Well – well, *I* am—'

'*Shhh*!' Phineas hissed, coming to an abrupt halt and shooting up a hand, listening to the unmistakable sound of a Morris Minor, travelling along the High Street.

Then he heard it turn off, and pulling Humphrey behind the cover of a crack willow which appeared to be growing out of the boundary wall that side,

199

watched as Sally's green Morris saloon blew its way down and along Upper Ham, and pulled up outside the *Belle*.

'Blast!' he said.

'Trouble?' Humphrey asked. In the brief time he'd spent on the river, trouble was something he was starting to get used to.

'That depends,' Phineas said slowly, watching Sally leave the car.

On how long Sally stays. Which depends on whether Daniel, if he's back yet, offers her coffee, and if Sally accepts. And then if Lucy, told by Annie that Carl's removed himself from the running, decides to rejoin him on the *Belle* while Sally is still there.

Phineas went over it again, making sure he hadn't missed anything.

Sally's car stayed where it was.

Phineas patted Humphrey's arm. 'Look, old man, I'm going to have to make a run for it. It was nice meeting you, and all that. And no doubt I'll be seeing you again before you move on. Perhaps I could show you the *Belle* then,' he said, scrambling over the wall into Upper Ham. 'Bring the family, kids an' all, if you like,' he added, on his way to the Frogeye parked on the verge.

The top was down and the keys in, as he had left it after returning from cricket. He was about to switch on when he glanced up to find that the Canadian had followed him.

'Gee,' Humphrey said. 'Nice car.'

'Well, thank you,' Phineas beamed, fond as a parent. 'Ginny. Her name's Ginny. She's a Frogeye. An Austin Healey Sprite. It would be ungallant of me to tell you her age, but what I *don't* think she'd mind me telling you is what she gets up to on the road. Flat out, she'll do . . .' And then he remembered Sally.

'Look,' he said, glancing towards the entrance to the *Belle,* 'I'm terribly sorry, but I *must* go.'

Humphrey nodded, and raised his hand with a small forlorn-looking smile.

He had, for that brief time, enjoyed not being Sir Humphrey, despoiling things and selling his birthright for a mess of pottage and all that. Had enjoyed for that brief while having a friend.

Phineas looked at him and sighed.

'Look, would you like a quick spin in her?'

Humphrey nodded enthusiastically. 'Yeah – yeah, I would. *Thanks.*'

Phineas leaned across and opened the passenger door. 'Hop in, then,' he said, one eye on his entrance gate.

Humphrey hesitated. And then shook his head firmly. 'Phineas, I think you ought to know . . .'

'For God's sake, man – get *in* if you're going to!' Phineas yelled over the sound of the engine firing. It was unlike him to shout at anybody, particularly a stranger, but any minute now he had a feeling the place would be stiff with complications.

Humphrey got in.

Phineas reversed at speed until the road was

wide enough to turn in, and then shot up past the pub and into the High Street.

Humphrey said something above the noise of the engine, and Phineas, not catching it, inclined his head towards him. Humphrey hesitated again, but this time smiled, and shook his head, indicating that it didn't matter.

Phineas lifted a hand to acknowledge it, as the canary-yellow car roared on through the village. The gesture like a pilot's salute, with a clear sky ahead and not an enemy in sight.

CHAPTER 18

Sally was still aboard the *Cluny Belle*, having coffee with Daniel, when Lucy walked up the gangway to be reunited with Phineas.

Not long before that, Daniel had been tucking into a fried egg sandwich, with dollops of tomato sauce on doorsteps of the white bread he was denied at home, when Ffion Owen rang.

Mysteriously, and out of the blue, she wanted to know if he was still on for trying the new club in Kingham. As she had turned him down once, and hadn't appeared to be at all interested since, he took some pleasure in telling her that he was sorry, but he was going back today.

But she wouldn't go away, an image of her figure still there with him in the kitchen, her tanned bare legs and the movement of her breasts, her dark eyes beckoning. And such was his surrender that he phoned her back before finishing his egg sandwich.

He had just put the phone down, and was wondering if his father had a clean shirt and another pair of jeans he could borrow, as well as the Frogeye for the evening, when he heard Sally call out on deck.

She said that Phineas's car was there, and Daniel pointed out that as Sikes was as well, and a sheet of A4 waiting in the Underwood, he had probably just nipped up to the shop.

He offered her coffee while she was waiting, and they took it out on deck, sitting at what Phineas called his off-duty table, another selection from Patio Living.

He noticed Sally's hair almost as soon as she took her uniform hat off.

She'd had it cut short and streaked with high-lights. She had decided that she'd give just the merest suggestion, whether Phineas asked or not, of avoiding the real reason for it. And she planned the odd, sudden, unexplained unavailability, with just a hint that, whatever else she might be doing that evening, it wouldn't be washing her hair or taking an ante-natal class.

Sally knew where Phineas thought their relation-ship was going, his feet plonked on her lap when watching television the other night demonstrated that. And now, if she had anything to do with its direction, he was going to learn where it was actu-ally going.

She fluffed out her hair, shook it, and asked Daniel did he think it suited her? Daniel thought she looked smashing.

He talked about Ffion, and Sally teased him about marriage. Daniel became serious. As she knew, he said, his father had been married three times. He, Daniel, didn't intend making the same sort of mistake.

Sally hadn't known. She knew that he'd been married but had assumed, from the way he'd talked, that he had only done it once. He seemed to have overlooked the other two.

When Daniel expanded on his father's marital background Sally, while pleased that he was opening up to her in this way – that he felt he *could* open up to her in this way – also felt she oughtn't to let him.

You really shouldn't be listening to this, she told herself again a while later, avidly and shamelessly all ears by then.

Daniel was talking about Phineas's first marriage, to Daniel's mother. 'Dad was only nineteen, mum two years younger. They had a bedsit in Chelsea then. Dad was writing the Great Novel – or, according to mum, more like talking about it in the local pubs. She was working as a waitress at the time, and bringing supper home in her handbag. Anyway, they got divorced when I was two.'

'Oh,' Sally said.

Daniel shrugged. 'Yeah, well . . . Anyway, not long after, he married Serena, the sculptress I mentioned. She was half-Polish, and completely potty. They used to chase each other up and down the Fulham Road. Dad had another son, Jamie, from that marriage. That didn't quite make a year.'

'Have you met him, Jamie?' she asked.

'No. She married a doctor from the place she used to check into for her nervous breakdowns, and they moved to America. And then after that dad met Diana. That one lasted nearly three years. There were two children from that marriage, a boy and a girl.'

'I see,' Sally said neutrally, noting that Phineas seemed, it might be said, to have sort of got better at it as he went. She decided that that was encouraging.

'Diana was rich, an heiress.'

'Oh,' Sally said.

'But that wasn't the reason he married her,' Daniel assured her solemnly.

'No. No, I can believe that,' she said, although not altogether sure why. Something to do perhaps with not being able to see Phineas being quite that definite about anything.

'They lived in Hampstead. Had a large Georgian house there.'

'And what happened to that marriage?'

Daniel smiled again. 'Dad happened to it. It started well. Mum says all his marriages do that. He's always in love and this one is always going to be the one, and he could see now where he'd gone wrong before. A failed romantic, mum calls him. Looking for something he'll never find, because he doesn't know what it is he's looking for. But, well, he was much younger then,' he felt obliged to add, remembering who he was talking to.

'Mmm,' was all Sally said.

'The trouble was that Diana was into opera, and gallery openings and first nights, and smart dinner parties, all that sort of thing. Dad was just into parties. He kept open house there. Couldn't see why he shouldn't, with all those bedrooms going spare, as he put it. Some of his bohemian friends from Chelsea and Soho virtually lived there with him.'

'And she'd had enough,' Sally said, her tone suggesting she could quite see why.

'I just think they both had in the end. Mum said if he'd just kept tapping away quietly at his potboilers he could still be there now. But he didn't *want* to be there in the end. That's the thing. He told mum on a visit that he found marriage a terrible *strain*.' Daniel laughed and shook his head. 'I have to wonder about my father sometimes.'

Sally smiled, and then said, 'Does he still see them? The kids, I mean?'

Daniel hesitated, and then said, 'No. No, I don't think so. I think I'm the only one he sees. I don't know, maybe it's because I'm the first or something. He visited me regularly at home, until mum met Richard, my stepdad. She was good about that. He used to tuck me up and read to me, and then just disappear again,' Daniel said, shaking his head again over his father, over a memory he still didn't fully understand.

'It was odd, really, I suppose. I don't know how

mum felt about it, but I liked it, as a kid, you know, so . . .'

Daniel asked her if she'd like another coffee and Sally hesitated. While the nurse in her nagged that she was due to look at Mrs Gower's leg, the woman, with the possibilities of more revelations to come, wasn't at all keen on leaving. The woman won almost immediately.

And over fresh coffee they moved on from Phineas to Daniel's university place. He had, as she'd remarked before, Phineas's eyes, if of a rather more serious blue, and his father was there also in his looks and some of his mannerisms. Which left her pondering the mysteries of genetics, not the least of which was where, or rather from whom, to bring Phineas into it again, did he get the sort of brains needed for applied mathematics.

She was nodding thoughtfully, listening, she hoped, with an intelligent air to him enthusing about algebraic topology, when they heard footsteps hurrying up the gangway.

She touched quickly at her hair with her fingers, her smile drying when Lucy the barmaid appeared on deck, fresh from the shower and a talk about love and men in Ffion's bedroom, her lips glossy with Ffion's deep pink lipstick.

Sikes, slumbering on, innocently, under his master's work table, opened an eye to take in the visitor, and when he saw who it was closed it again. He'd already done that one.

She barely glanced at them, mere extras in the drama.

'Phineas. Where's Phineas?' she cried, addressing the air.

'He's not here, Lucy,' Daniel said. His father had explained the Sally and Lucy thing, shaking his head over the wrong turning he'd taken when he was on the road to somewhere completely different, as he'd put it, as if blaming a map.

Did he live like this all the time? he wondered, looking nervously from one woman to the other. 'We don't know where he is. We thought he might have gone to the shop, didn't we, Sally,' he said, bringing Sally into the conversation with a sort of anxious social air, while Sally sat looking at Lucy.

'Is his car still there, by the way?' he asked. It occurred to him now that it might have been the Frogeye he'd heard while making the first lot of coffee and talking to Sally in the kitchen.

Lucy shook her head, her shining blonde hair swinging prettily. 'No – I don't know. I didn't notice,' she added, as if wondering how she could be expected to.

'Not in the pub?' Sally suggested helpfully. She hadn't heard about a wrong turning, from Phineas or anyone else, but she didn't need to.

Lucy shook her head again. 'I don't know. I haven't been in yet,' she said, frowning at Sally.

Sally smiled brightly at her. 'I'm Phineas's girl-friend, Lucy. You remember me. The dry white wine.'

Lucy drew back her head as if about to spit.

'Girlfriend!' she scorned. 'That's for teenagers, that is, for children. We almost died, we did. Died for our love.'

'Heart attack, was it, in his case?' Sally said. 'I thought that might happen one day, the way he smokes and drinks. And of course he's that much older, isn't he? Have you noticed the way his hair's receding?' That was for Phineas, even though he wasn't there, a bit of steam let off. Inside, Sally was boiling.

'I nearly drowned,' Lucy said, above such pettiness. 'While we were fleeing from Carl. I told him about Phineas, told him about our love. He wanted to kill me, he did. He was insane with jealousy. Phineas saved me.'

'Really?' Sally said, and wondered who would save Phineas when she caught up with him.

Lucy lifted her head, stubborn and proud with love. 'Even Carl has seen now that it's no use. He's given us his blessing.'

'Couldn't wait to get shut of you, more like,' Sally muttered, putting on her cap. 'Well, you can add my blessing to his,' she said, standing. 'And the best of luck to both of you.'

'Are you going, Sally?' Daniel said, standing, unhappily, with her, while Lucy eyed her suspiciously.

'Yes, I must go. Thank you for the coffee, Daniel. And the chat. I enjoyed it.' She smiled at him. 'And I wish you well in everything you do.'

'You might as well know that I'll be moving in here later today,' Lucy told her, holding her plastic bag of things left in Carl's bedroom ready for Phineas's, and standing by the gangway as if waiting to see Sally off the boat.

And out of nowhere, Sally, casting around in her mind for something to throw at her, some parting shot that would wipe that look off her silly blonde face, was inspired.

'Oh, well, in that case,' she said crisply, in her best nurse's voice, 'do make sure that, as well as the pills, he keeps on with the ointment on his you-know-what. It's out of my hands now,' she said, and never one to overlook a double entendre, had to stifle a wild giggle she hoped wasn't the beginning of hysteria. 'It's what's called a public health issue,' she managed to get out. 'Which means regular checks at the clinic. So, if only for your own sake, you need to make absolutely sure that he keeps those appointments, and keeps on with the medication.'

'I don't believe you,' Lucy said, sounding not at all sure.

'It's true, Lucy,' Daniel put in, lying this time on Sally's behalf. 'I've been doing that, making sure dad keeps up the medication and all that.'

'Daniel,' Sally said, smiling her thanks at him, 'has been very good about everything.'

Lucy looked doubtfully from Sally to Daniel and back to Sally.

Then footsteps sounded again on the gangway.

Sally's eyes trained on it like gun sights.

But instead of Phineas, the three local reporters and their photographers filed onto the deck.

The eldest of the three, a man in a crumpled business suit, with a rolled up copy of a newspaper in his pocket, grinned round at them. 'Where is he, then?'

'Where's who?' Daniel said. 'And who are you?'

'Local press,' the reporter said, and warily watched six stone of white boxer ambling over to them. 'Here to put Sir Humphrey's side of things regarding the opening of the regatta. The break with tradition. The twentieth century arrives in Batch Magna, that sort of thing,' he went on, as Sikes sniffed a few legs, and then wandered back to his slumbers under the table.

'Sir Humphrey . . .?' Daniel said blankly.

'Sir Humphrey. Sir Humphrey Strange. The new horseless squire. The future flying in from the New World.' He grinned in the direction of the living quarters. 'In there, is he?'

A second reporter, a pair of sunglasses perched on her head, and wearing a portable tape recorder like a shoulder bag, pushed in front of her colleague. 'This *is* the *Cluny Belle*?' she demanded.

Daniel nodded dumbly.

'Do you mean the American?' Sally asked. ''Cept he wasn't—'

'Yes, the American!' the third representative of the press, a youth with greasy hair and angry-looking pimples, said, impatiently suspicious.

'Perhaps you wouldn't mind asking him to come out, and say a few words. If, that is, it's not too much trouble. He owes the people that, at least.'

'What are you talking about?' Daniel said. 'There's no American here.'

'Oh, no?' the pimply youth sneered, and sucked insultingly on a corner of his mouth.

'There was an American earlier. Only he turned out to be a Canadian,' Lucy offered. 'On the *Felicity H.* The Owens' boat.'

'Well, that's who said he was here!' the girl reporter said. 'Mrs Owen. Said he'd come here with somebody called Phineas Cook.'

'Phineas?' Sally said wonderingly.

'Mrs Thomas, the housekeeper at Batch Hall, said Sir Humphrey was visiting the houseboat the *Felicity H.* And Mrs Owen said he was here, on the *Cluny Belle.* That was our chain of intelligence,' the girl said, pushing her sunglasses further back on her head.

The older reporter was looking amused.

'Tell me, who said he was a Canadian? Did he say he was? *Sir Humphrey?*' He spoke the name deliberately, revealing the true identity of the alleged Canadian.

Lucy shook her head. 'No. No, she did, Mrs Owen. He's a Canadian, staying with his family at the pub, she said. On holiday. I remember that clear as day.'

'What on earth has Phineas to do with it?' Sally said, more to herself.

213

The reporter smiled encouragement at Lucy. 'And did her husband, perchance, happen to be there when Mrs Owen said it?'

Lucy's eyes grew wide. 'Yes . . . Yes, he was. In fact, come to think of it, it was him she said it to!'

'I knew it. I *knew* it,' the reporter said, shaking his head fondly. He was also a tabloid stringer, and in the fifteen years of doing that job humanity had rarely let him down.

'The old hanky-panky. I knew it. The way she got rid of us, in all of a hurry before hubby came out. Blimey,' he said on a laugh, 'don't waste much time, this American, does he. No sooner unpacked than he's off after a bit of *droit du seigneur.*'

He rubbed his hands together briskly, and peered over at the living quarters. 'Right, so where is he then? Papering the wardrobe, is he? Under the bed till you give him the nod?' he said, cheerfully cynical, a man who didn't in the least mind people lying to him, as long as they didn't mind being found out.

'He's not ill, is he?' the girl asked then, Sally's uniform having registered with her, and with an eye to the human angle. 'Is that what it is? Taken ill suddenly, was he? That's it, isn't it?' she said to Sally. 'Go on, you can tell me.'

'It won't go any further,' the older reporter chuckled.

'I don't know!' Sally said. 'I've never met him.'

Daniel shrugged. 'Me, neither.'

'*I've* met him, of course,' Lucy said. The elusive

Sir Humphrey, last seen disguised as a Canadian tourist.

'Good looking, is he?' the girl reporter wanted to know. 'Rugged, was how the housekeeper at Batch Hall described him. A big rugged man, she said.' That's not all Mrs Thomas had said. 'And rolling in it, he is,' the reporter added.

'What's that got to do with anything!' the pimply youth, who worked for a paper with socialist leanings, snarled.

'Made his pile on Wall Street, apparently,' the older reporter said. 'A highflier who came out of the sun on enough deals to keep him in Club Class for life. Lucky barstool. But meanwhile, I've still got a mortgage to pay. So, he's not here then, is that what you're saying?'

Daniel sighed. 'We've told you enough times–no! No, he's not here.'

'And this whatsit Cook, I suppose he's not here either? Nobody here but us chickens, eh?' he said, and winked at his colleagues.

'That happens to be my father,' Daniel said.

'Who?' the pimply youth asked quickly, as if trying to catch him out.

'Phin . . . look, if you don't mind, I've got things to do.'

Sally glanced at her watch. 'Yes, so have I.'

'Going so soon?' the youth sneered insinuatingly.

The girl tried a smile and her eyes on Daniel. 'Do you know where we might find Sir Humphrey and your father, then? Please?'

Daniel shook his head. 'I'm sorry, I don't. Haven't the foggiest.'

'We're wasting our time here,' she said dismissively.

'Right, so what do we do now, then?' one of the photographers asked, sounding put-upon and bored.

'The pub. The local,' the older reporter said. 'When in doubt, try the village pump. That's my excuse, anyway. Who'd be a journo, eh?' he added by way of saying goodbye, and winked.

'I thought you'd come about the drowning,' Lucy said.

The reporter popped his head back round the top of the gangway. 'Drowning?'

'Well, I nearly drowned.'

Sally, after saying goodbye again to Daniel, smiled sweetly at Lucy as she left. 'Yes, unfortunately I got here too late.'

Lucy ignored it. 'It was touch and go for a while, it was. I was being chased by a jealous ex-lover, Carl. He was trying to kill us. Kill a love that couldn't be parted. With a meat cleaver. Me and Phineas Cook, the man you're looking for. Though you probably know him by a different name altogether,' she added coyly.

She watched with satisfaction as the others scrambled back on deck.

'He was consumed with jealously. Mad with passion, Carl was. I nearly drowned, escaping from his insane clutches. Phineas saved me. Phineas Cook. Known to thousands as Warren Chase, the famous crime writer.'

216

Eyeing the cameras, Lucy leaned her back against one of the gangway's stanchions, one foot raised and pressing into it, pushing her breasts out, and pouted pinkly.

'We're in love,' she revealed. 'A love we almost died for. A love that in the end was bigger than hate.'

While Daniel stood glumly at the rail, listening to Sally drive away, out of his father's life, and wondered where the hell he'd got to.

CHAPTER 19

His father at that moment was up in the hills above the river, changing down for another narrow bend with a blast on his horn, and then roaring throatily out of it. Up one hill and down another, stampeding grazing sheep and cattle used to having the hills, the world, to themselves.

A few of the lanes, as Humphrey had managed to glimpse, were clearly signposted as being unsuitable for motor vehicles, and it was round a bend along one of those that the Frogeye almost ran into a tractor and trailer pulling out of a field gate.

Phineas braked hard, and the Sprite slewed across the road and came to rest with the front wheels halfway up a bank, and with a clump of bellflower poking up prettily from behind her bumper.

'Sorry, Ginny,' Phineas said in the stalled silence.

And then he leapt out and peered anxiously under the front of the car. Humphrey joined him, standing in the road and looking vaguely solicitous as the tractor driver, a bulky figure in a blue boiler suit and a tweed hat the shape of an upturned flowerpot, came over to them.

'Lo, Phin,' he said.

'There's nothing leaking,' Phineas said doubtfully. 'Lo, Ken.'

'All right, is her?' Ken asked.

Phineas got to his feet. 'Yes, I think so.'

'I thought we'd had it, like, for a minute there.'

'It was a close run thing, Ken,' Phineas agreed.

He reached in and tried the ignition. The engine coughed a couple of times as if clearing the mud and grass from its throat, and then caught and purred into new life.

'Ah. Listen to her,' Phineas said fondly. 'What a girl!'

Humphrey patted her bonnet. 'She's a game lady.'

'It was my fault, I reckon,' Ken said. 'I was looking the other way, like. Seeing that the trailer was coming right. There's not a lot of room there.'

'No, Ken. It was my fault. My fault entirely. I was going too fast. *Much* too fast,' Phineas said, as if talking about someone else's speed.

'Still, all's well that ends well, eh?' He beamed at the Frogeye. 'She's a good sport.'

'We was sorry to hear about you having to leave the paddlers, and that, Phin,' Ken said. 'Won't be the same round here, it won't.'

'Thanks, Ken. Nice of you to say so.'

'Well, it won't. And what's going to happen to 'em? What's going to happen to the old boats?' Ken asked indignantly. 'He tell you that, did he, this new bloke?'

Phineas switched off the engine. 'The only thing he's told us, Ken, is to hop it.'

Ken frowned hard, as if squeezing out his thoughts.

'Bloody American!' he snapped then. 'Coming here! Something should be done about the bugger.' He looked earnestly at them. 'That's what the old man reckons. Reckons he should be shot. Reckons someone should shoot him.'

'That's been suggested as well,' Phineas said. 'And drowning. And blowing him up. Poisoning him. Running him over. Doing his brakes. Mugging him with tragic consequences. Dropping a loose flag from the Hall's dodgy roofs on his head. There's plenty of ideas, Ken, it's the victim we're short of. The blighter hasn't shown his face here since he fired us. That's the American I told you about,' he said in an aside to Humphrey, who was smiling fixedly at it. 'Sorry,' he added, 'I should have introduced you two. Ken, this is . . .'

'A poker, that's what our Wendy said,' Ken broke in. 'Do him with a poker. That's what her reckons. In the Hall, at night, like. Make it look a burglar's been disturbed.'

Phineas looked at him. 'I'd take care not to get on the wrong side of your Wendy, Ken, if I were you. She has only put her pretty little finger on the least traceable method of all of them – even if I do say so myself. Because that,' he was able to tell them, 'was *precisely* my contribution.'

'Get away!' Ken said.

Phineas went through on it on his fingers. 'Somebody who'd visited the Hall before, to account for anything inadvertently left behind. No fingerprints on the weapon because most country house burglars, being pros, wear gloves – so that wouldn't work against the disturbed burglary theory. Murder weapon left in situ, thrown down as if in panic at what the burglar had done, backing *up* that theory. And in my plot,' he added, after a pause, 'there'd be little risk of forensically contaminating the assailant's clothes or car.'

He leaned in closer. 'Because my murderer, me dears,' he said, lowering his voice, 'would be naked. The deed done in the skin. A nightmare waiting in the library or drawing room. And then a quick wash,' he added briskly, 'dressed, and off home to hearth and slippers.' Phineas smiled on Ken. 'Yes, apart from the stripping off bit, Wendy and I think alike on this caper.'

Ken beamed proudly at it. 'Well! Wait till I tell her. Her *will* be pleased.' Ken and his wife, both regular library users, knew who the real brains behind Inspector MacNail was.

'Haven't seen you in the pub lately, Ken,' Phineas said then. 'Not Wendy's doing, I hope. Start as you mean to go on, that's what I say. Ken's newly married,' he told Humphrey, who was smiling on as if he'd forgotten it was there. 'But I have to admit she's an absolute smasher, so we mustn't be too hard on him.'

'No, too busy, Phin, that's what it is. Too much

on, mate.' He turned to Humphrey, a fresh audience. 'People don't realise the work involved.'

Phineas tried again. 'Ken, this is . . . er . . .'

'How do,' Ken said briefly, not stopping. 'The sort of wet weather we've been having lately, the stuff comes up in rush, like. We've already started on the flax and winter oats. Then there's the ewes. They need extra work this time of year, before they're grazed out on the good stuff for the breeding, like. You'd be surprised at what needs doing. Oh, yes. People just don't realise. And you have to check for gum udder, foot rot, maggot fly, broken—'

'God!' Phineas cried suddenly, shooting a glance at his watch. 'Look at the time. We've got to go, old man,' he said to Humphrey. 'We're miles late, as it is. Sorry, Ken.'

'Ah, I'd better get on as well, I 'spose I won't be knocking off much before ten tonight, as it is. And there's no overtime on a small family farm, there in't. No time and a quarter, and double time on Sunday, and all that. Or holiday pay, or sick pay, or pension schemes, or a canteen. People just don't realise . . .' Ken went on, helping them push the Frogeye off the bank.

'Here, I almost forgot,' he said then, when Phineas was back behind the wheel. 'I saw the Blurford team practising earlier. Having a knock-up on one of Dudley Knowles's fields.'

'What's wrong with their own field?'

'Ah!' Ken winked. 'Too public, in't. All tucked away there, they are, like.'

'Tucked away? Why?' Phineas asked.

'Their secret weapon, in't.'

'Secret weapon?'

'Ah, Lobby Wright. He's batting for 'em, the bugger.'

'Lobby Wright? Big Lobby Wright? Lobby Wright the fencer?'

Ken nodded. 'That's him. That's the one. Something should be done about it, I reckon.'

'But he plays for Nether Myddle.'

'Not no more he don't. Obviously.'

'He can't do that!' Phineas said, aghast. 'It's against the rules. Lobby Wright lives nowhere near Blurford.'

'Well, he's doing it. Not half he ain't. Running the field knackered, he was. Dudley's took his horses out. To give him a bit more room, like.'

Phineas turned the ignition. 'Hop in,' he told Humphrey, his voice tight with purpose.

Humphrey, who'd been listening to the conversation with polite incomprehension, was still hopping in, fumbling with the door to shut it, as Phineas, who'd been impatiently building up the revs, shouted goodbye to Ken and took off with a backward salute and his foot down.

Fifty yards down the road the Frogeye screeched to a halt.

Phineas reversed back at speed, to where Ken

was standing in the middle of the road, a perplexed frown clouding his moon features.

Phineas looked up at him with a small smile of anticlimax.

'I forgot to ask you which one.'

'Ah,' Ken said, the frown dissolving in a grin. 'I was wondering how you knew, seeing as I hadn't told you. They're next to Brookwell. Go down here to Hales Lane, turn up where the postbox is, and follow the road round. You can use our gate there, first up on the left. It's not locked. Go directly across, towards the boundary spinney. They're on the other side. It's a bit muddy, mind, now, Brookwell. Rough ground, see, and in a dip anyway, and what with the rain we've had lately. Half of it is, anyroad. We've started ploughing it for sheep feed.' Ken shook his head. 'People just don't realise. They think grass is grass, but you try telling that to the cows or sheep. So we're sowing part of—'

Phineas shot up a hand as if to the traffic. 'Ken, I'm sorry, old man, but we have to go. It's imperative we get the full strength of this back to the skipper. The coming match may depend on it.'

'Yeah, right, right, Phin. Don't want that bloody Blurford lot walking off with it again. Cocky lot of buggers. That umpire of theirs should be shot. Along with the American. That's what I reckon. Bye, Phin. Bye, Mr . . . er . . .' Ken said to himself, the little yellow sports car already on its way.

★   ★   ★

224

A few minutes later Phineas was leaning on Ken's gate with Humphrey, the air disturbed by nothing more vigorous than the cooing of woodpigeons from the boundary spinney.

Perhaps they've gone. Perhaps Lobby Wright had been bowled on the knuckles by Wilf "Bones" Powell, a fate Phineas had himself once suffered, or by one of Wilf's corkscrew or shoulder breakers, and turned into a spectator for the rest of the season.

Then he heard it. A bat hitting a ball with a crack as clean as a rifle shot, and with the same promise of distance in it.

'Look,' he said to Humphrey, 'there's no need for you to come as well. I won't be long. Then I'll run you back to the pub. Your family must be wondering where you are. And besides,' he added, nodding at the turned field beyond the green, 'there's that lot to plod through to get there.'

'Oh, there's plenty of time,' Humphrey said with a wave of his hand, a man on holiday. 'And I don't mind a bit of dirt.'

'Well, all right. Come on then,' Phineas said, opening the gate.

'Ironically,' he went on, 'if this field belonged to Dudley Knowles – he's the skipper of the Blurford cricket team, Batch Magna's old enemy – we'd have had nice headlands, strips of grass along the edges, to walk round on. Because Dudley likes a few partridges to bang away at.' Phineas knew this because Owain had delighted in relieving the

Blurford skipper of a few of his birds in the past. 'And he also likes to be thought keen on conservation. As well as being unspeakably underhand and secretive when it comes to cricket.'

Phineas shook his head gravely. 'If what Ken says is true, I'm afraid one will be driven to question whether or not Dudley actually *is* English.'

They were strolling across the meadow, the uneven ground deep in coarse grass, and coloured here and there with purple self-heal and white clover. A summer stroll in the sun, with the wood-pigeons calling and swallows and house martins hunting the air above them, and a couple of copper-winged butterflies chasing each other around a clump of pink and white bindweed.

Humphrey sniffed the air appreciatively.

'Pleasant, isn't it,' Phineas said.

Halfway to the spinney the meadow turned to ploughed earth, the piled ridges, the yellow clay in them, like exposed muscle, gleaming in the sun.

Phineas looked at Humphrey's soft leather slip-ons, and his own blue canvas deck shoes worn without socks, and hesitated.

And then he heard it again. The thwack of leather on willow.

'Wait there, old chap,' he said decisively. 'I won't be long. There's no sense in both of us getting muddy.'

It was worse than it looked.

He moved quickly and gingerly, in a sideways sort of hop, trying to keep off the furrow ridges, and still sunk in a couple of times. He had to stop then, to scrape off some of the mud piling up on his soles, cleaning one shoe on the other, and he glanced back and saw with a mixture of surprise and irritation that the Canadian had started out after him.

The man had stopped when Phineas had, and he nodded a sort of idiotic, encouraging half-smile at him. And Phineas was put in mind of Sikes, when told to stay and following on at a hopeful distance, the same sort of plodding, obstinate amiability about his meaty features.

'Well, *come* on then, if you're coming,' Phineas called.

When he looked again further on the Canadian was balancing shakily on one leg, retrieving a slip-on left behind in the mud.

He swayed as if buffeted by a sudden wind, clutching the shoe in one hand, the lifted leg peddling away at nothing for a moment, before he staggered and fell heavily.

Sitting up, he put his head back and opened his mouth, like a toddler who'd just fallen and was about to give himself up to the experience as loudly as he knew how.

Phineas watched fascinated. But instead of tears, Humphrey started laughing, sitting in the mud, head back and laughing.

'For God's sake!' Phineas muttered.

Out of sight behind the spinney, he heard again the defeat of Batch Magna being measured by Lobby Wright's bat and more runs off the long

227

grass. 'I've got to go on!' he called sharply, and almost immediately got a foot stuck.

He was still pulling at it as Humphrey, making heavy weather of it, and finding it all very amusing by the sound of it, caught up.

'Hey, you didn't say this was gonna be fun!' he said, grinning. He had mud all over him, even in his hair.

Phineas's lips pursed.

He accepted that, as a foreigner, the man couldn't reasonably be expected to fully understand the seriousness of the matter, involving as it did not only cricket but *village* cricket. But even so . . .

'I have no wish to be offensive,' he said with quiet dignity, 'but if you have nothing more constructive than that to contribute, I would rather you said nothing at all.'

He'd been pulling at his foot while telling Humphrey this, and he freed it now, but then found that the other was stuck, buried up past his ankle. He set his face and heaved at it, while a chastened Humphrey hovered at his elbow, ready to help.

The foot came out abruptly, with an escaping plop of air, catching both men off balance and sending them sprawling.

Phineas got up first. He wiped half-heartedly a couple of times at the mud on him, before giving up in disgust. Then he found that he'd lost the shoe from that foot.

'That's what happened to me,' Humphrey told him. 'Sucked clean off. Near broke an ankle. And

I had to take a pound of mud out when I did find it. It'll be in there somewhere, all right,' he offered encouragingly, watching Phineas on his knees, digging for it with a hand.

Phineas pulled the shoe out and stood scraping at it with his fingers. Then he tried to flick the clay from him, before resignedly wiping it off on his jeans and shirt front.

He looked at Humphrey. 'What a lark, eh?'

'Jeez!' Humphrey said, and shook his head.

'*What* a state!' Phineas said, looking down at himself.

Humphrey looked down at himself as well, and tutted and shook his head again.

Unsure what to do with the sodden canvas shoe, Phineas pulled it on again, grimacing as he pushed his bare foot into it.

He stood looking across at the spinney for a moment. And then at Humphrey.

'Bet I can get there before you.'

'Yeah?' Humphrey said.

'Yeah.'

'Go!' Humphrey said suddenly, already moving, hoping to get the edge, the way he used to play it at school.

They ran with the freedom of having enough mud on them for any more not to matter. They ran, laughing when the other got stuck, hopping and stumbling, clog-footed on platforms of mud, an obstacle race, with Humphrey coming in panting two furrows ahead of Phineas.

They scraped the worse of it off their shoes on a fence post. And stepping over a few sagging strands of rusty barbed wire, moved through the gloom of the spinney like poachers, a snapped fallen branch sending a woodpigeon volleying out of an ash above them.

They crouched behind more barbed wire, in much better condition on Dudley Knowles's side of things, screened by a rash of flowering nettle, dock and thistle, sprouting from a dunging area used by his horses.

Phineas could see why Dudley considered Lobby needed the room.

They watched the bowler running up and Lobby, a redheaded giant of a man with his hair on fire in the sun and with a stick of willow in his hands, smiting the ball again.

'Not bad!' Humphrey said. 'Baseball's my game but a hitter's a hitter. He's not bad.'

Phineas gave up counting the runs Lobby would have made.

'He's a fencer,' he told Humphrey, 'with his son. Stock fencing, mostly. His son holds the posts upright and Lobby bangs them in with a sledge-hammer. That's where he gets his eye. And his shoulders. I really don't want to see anymore.'

Lobby, looking bored, was still waiting for the ball to be returned.

'Yeah, right,' Humphrey said understandingly. 'We'll get on then, huh?'

⋆　⋆　⋆

'Well, that *was* fun, wasn't it,' Phineas said, sitting muddily back in the Frogeye. 'Right, well, I can't think of any more treats for you, so straight back to your family, I should think. Hmm?'

'Yeah, right,' Humphrey said.

'Let them know you're still alive, and get a bath and a change of clothes. And then on with your holiday.'

'Yeah,' Humphrey said.

Phineas paused, his hand on the ignition key, and looked speculatively at him.

'Forgive me, but you don't seem to be in all that much of a hurry to get back to them, old man, if you don't mind my saying so. Haven't murdered them, have you? Left 'em for Dilly to find when she pops in to change the sheets?'

Humphrey laughed with him. 'No, nothing like that. It's just that, well, you know, it's good to have a break sometimes from—well, from . . .'

'From women!' Phineas finished for him, banging the steering wheel in agreement. 'There's nothing wrong with women, but . . .'

'No, I'm not saying . . .'

'But when there is, it's best not to be in the same room. Got you in one! Right, well, let's see . . . Ah, I know. Seeing as we're just up the road from her, we could call in on Dotty Snape's, home of the local cider. That's a touristy sort of thing to do. And you could tell your other half you slipped in the mud there. There's enough of it. It's no good mentioning cricket, not to a woman. The

231

word doesn't mean the same thing at all in their language.'

It hardly meant anything in Humphrey's language either, but that didn't stop him beaming with pleasure at being included like that.

'Good, eh?' Phineas said, taking it for appreciation of his cleverness. He asked Humphrey if his wife liked a drink. Humphrey decided she did.

'Well, there you are, then! You can say you'd heard about Dotty Snape's famous perry for ladies, and went to buy her some. You walked there, but found it further than you thought. How's that sound? Covers you for both time *and* the state you're in.'

Humphrey nodded.

With no family waiting at the pub or anywhere else, and with his failure to do what he'd set out to do on the paddlers, and none of the phone calls he was supposed to have made this morning, made, why not?

That, he told Phineas, sounded great.

The iron ghosts of long-abandoned farm machinery sat rusting in the mud of the smallholding on the hill, and there were rusty corrugated sheets patching up the fencing and on top of the old stone lean-tos in the yard, the low, tight roofs of the big ancient barn and house like caps pulled down hard against winds.

Dotty, a tiny bony woman, as alert as a bird, in a battered brown trilby and wellingtons that looked too big for her, the cuffs of a hacking jacket turned back, was in the cider shed. A dim flagged building, piled with barrels and smelling of apples and the sweet casky ripeness of wood aged in their juices.

'Hello, Phineas! Come to see us, have you? How are you, then? How have you been? Hello, dear, how are you?' she added to Humphrey, on the same chattering note, her small, bright darting eyes constantly in flight. 'Look who's here, Dad. Look who's come to see us. It's Phineas. With a friend, he's brought a friend,' she said, and Dotty's aged father stirred and muttered in the corner he'd retired to some years back.

One of the several customers there, perched on wooden kegs, grinned in the gloom. 'Blimey, look what the cat's dragged in.'

Phineas peered over at him.

'Ah, Derek. Just the man. What's this, then, about Lobby Wright batting for you?'

'I ain't saying he is and I ain't saying he ain't,' Derek said, and sucked on a smile. Derek kept wicket for Blurford.

'Well, it so happens that I *know* he is. And he can't,' Phineas said, as if that were the end of the matter. 'Because I *also* happen to know that he lives the other side of Nether Myddle. Which means that while he may play for Church and Nether Myddle, he may *not* play for Blurford. Look it up!' He was still holding on to the small hope that Lobby still lived the other side of Nether Myddle,

233

and that somehow that had been overlooked. But not for long.

'Moved, hasn't he, Phineas. Got a council house now, he has. In Over Hale. Quarter of a mile our side of the parish boundary hedge. Sorry, matey,' Derek said, looking nothing of the sort.

'Yes, well, I hope we never need to win that badly, Derek. Lobby's not a batsman, he's a blunt instrument. What he does isn't cricket, it's fencing – horizontally. With a bat and ball.' He shook his head. 'Typical Blurford approach to the game. Win at any cost,' he said, while Derek smiled sympathetically.

'You English and your cricket! I wouldn't mind if you were any bloody good at it.'

Dai, who had been leaving for the past hour, his two collies getting up each time expectantly, sat down again. 'Look at your national team. A joke, they are. A bloody joke, man.'

'You must be thinking of the Welsh back line, Dai. 'Cept they're beyond a joke,' a third man put in. 'Look at 'em the last time out, against New Zealand. Talk about—'

'Ah. But look at the ref, isn't it? English, he was. *Eng*lish!'

'A byword for fair play on any field of sporting endeavour, Dai,' Phineas, about to introduce Humphrey to Dotty, paused to tell him, and then he looked at Humphrey and laughed.

'My dear chap, I still don't know your *name*!'

Humphrey straightened, ready to confess, almost

by now out of habit. But then, with Phineas and Dotty looking expectantly at him, his nerve, this time, failed him.

'Frank,' he said, grabbing at the name. 'The name's Frank. Frank Smith.'

'Right. Well, Mr Frank Smith, allow me to introduce you to Miss Dotty Snape – *the* Miss Dotty Snape. Saint Dotty of the Orchards, to her legion of acolytes, among whom it is my good fortune, and indeed my honour, to be numbered. There are other makers of cider and perry, Frank, in this valley, and I implore you here and now, in the name of excellence and your taste buds, not to mention your stomach, to have nothing to do with their wares. Compared to Dotty they are mere pickers and mashers, mere rude mechanics of the trade. What Dotty does owes more to Merlin than to ladders and a press. She assures me she does not work by moonlight, but after taking the first enchanted sip of her potions one would be forgiven for thinking that she must. She is a sorceress, Frank, a siren of the orchards, an alchemist among the barrels,' he went on, while Dotty looked away from it, twittering and shaking her head in small quick movements, distancing herself from such extravagance.

He told Humphrey that he could not – *would* not – allow him to move on from this place before tasting that king of ciders, that aqua vitae of the apple, a nectar fit for Olympus and called Sheepsnout on the sound principle that it didn't matter what you called it, because such an essence was beyond description, Shakespeare no longer being with us.

'No it wasn't, no it wasn't,' Dotty told Humphrey. 'You take no notice of him. It's just the name of the cider that was always made here, that's why, from the apple called that, called Sheepsnout. Don't you listen to him, don't you listen to Phineas, he's always saying things.'

Phineas clapped a hand on Humphrey's shoulder. 'And there's a world of difference, Frank, between the cider then and the cider now. And that world, Frank, is called Dotty Snape,' he said solemnly, and turned what he considered to be his most beguiling smile on her, and then adding a slow seductive wink to go with it, furtively mimed scribbling something on his palm.

There were several notices in the shed warning against asking for credit, one of them facing him above a large, scarred pine table which served as an office, with another stating that cheques weren't accepted: "In God We Trust – Everyone Else Pays Cash". They had been there since Dotty's father bought the place after the war, and went with the other signs he'd lost no time in putting up. The Private Property and No Trespassing and Trespassers Will Be Prosecuted and Keep Out and Beware of the Dog signs, and the No Hawkers No Peddlers, No Circulars, and No Canvassers or Solicitors littering the house gate and front door, those and the Customer Parking sign above the hard-standing in the yard, and one pointing to

Sales and Office, a balance struck between keeping the world out and letting enough of it in to make a living.

Dotty, with a look as if reluctantly giving him the benefit of the doubt, turned to the cider barrel behind her table and a tray of pint glass tankards on a wooden keg in front of it, the Sheepsnout green-tinged in the naked overhead light, running from the tap as clean looking as shallows.

Phineas often had credit there and knew that she would oblige. He also knew that he'd have to sing a little for it first. It would be bad manners on his part to assume otherwise, and disrespect on Dotty's, to her father and his signs, if she didn't at least appear to need swaying first.

And besides, she enjoyed the brief dance beforehand, the quick whirl around the floor by Phineas, even if it did always end up at the cider barrel.

Phineas lifted his pint to toast Humphrey's onward journey and then introduced him to the others.

'Frank's a Canadian,' he told them. 'Here on holiday with his family.'

'Working holiday, is it?' Dai said, peering over at the state of him.

'It's a long story, Dai,' Phineas said.

'Will you be staying on, Phin?' he was asked then, after the new squire and his plans had been discussed, during which Humphrey had bought another round, and stood with his pint trying to look inconspicuous while hearing all about himself.

Phineas shrugged. 'I don't know, Ernie. No,' he

said more honestly. 'No, I don't think so. It wouldn't be the same.'

Dotty's eyes, already bright with indignation at the changes about to visit Batch Magna, grew brighter.

'Well, he'd better not come round here, that American! That's all I've got to say. He'd better not come round here.'

Her father, hunched over his china mug of cider like a bowl of workhouse soup, stirred again in the corner. 'Bloody Yanks. Coming over here, chucking their money about,' he said with an old man's memory.

An obliging, vague mumble of agreement broke out, and Humphrey joined in, muttering with them.

And then he looked at his watch abruptly, as if suddenly remembering something, and saw off the last of his cider.

'Quite right, old man,' Phineas said, and emptied his own glass. 'Frank's got a wife waiting,' he explained.

Phineas said he'd take him the pretty way back to Batch Magna, and they were about a couple of miles from the village, the little yellow sports car bowling cheerfully along, its flight as bright as a canary in the sun, when the engine coughed a couple of times and they spluttered to a halt.

Humphrey looked at Phineas. Phineas looked at the petrol gauge.

'Daniel! My son. He's a clever blighter, but when

it comes to the working of the internal combustion engine his knowledge seems to stop at the bit about it needing petrol. Well, there's nothing for it, old chap, I'm afraid. We'll have to walk. If we wait for a lift around here they'll find only our bones.'

'Yeah, well, it's a nice day for it,' Humphrey said, getting out with him, carrying the gallon container of Dotty Snape's famous perry for ladies Phineas had to remind him to buy before leaving.

'Yes, that's the ticket. It won't take us long, couple of sound-winded blokes like us.'

'Phew!' Humphrey said after they'd covered fifty yards or so. 'Warm, isn't it.'

'You're telling me,' Phineas agreed.

He joined Humphrey on a bank, sitting under a hedge oak on a cushion of ground ivy and dead leaves, and sucked on a blade of grass, his face lifted to the warmth of the sun. From somewhere on the other side of the valley the sound of a chainsaw reared in the distant, still air.

'Somebody's busy,' he said approvingly.

Humphrey cleared his throat.

'Phineas – Phineas,' he said, starting again, sitting up straight, back stiffened by two pints of Sheepsnout. 'Phineas, I am not who you think I am.'

'None of us are, Frank,' Phineas murmured, in the mood with the sun on his face to be philosophical. 'Who we think we or others are, or appear to be. And who are we anyway?' He thought about it. 'Something like that.'

'What I mean is,' Humphrey said determinedly, 'is that my name is not Frank Smith.'

'Oh?' Phineas said, interested now, aliases being up Warren Chase's street.

'My name is Humphrey – Humph. Sir Humph. Sir Humphrey. Sir Humphrey Strange,' he said, as if getting as much off his chest as he could. 'I am not a Canadian. I'm an American. From New York. *The* American.'

'*What?*' Phineas laughed.

'The one you all want to kill,' Humphrey added dolefully.

'Is this a joke?' Phineas asked. Sheepsnout could sometimes have that effect on people.

Humphrey shook his head determinedly. 'No. No, it's not a joke. I'll show you.'

He took his wallet from his shirt breast pocket, and carefully removed the return half of a flight ticket.

He passed it to Phineas.

Phineas peered at it, and spat out the blade of grass.

'Crikey!' he said, staring at Humphrey. 'So you are.'

Humphrey took the evidence from him and put it back. 'I'm sorry,' he said.

'Well, I'll be blowed,' Phineas said. 'Well, I'll be *blowed.*'

CHAPTER 20

Humphrey was drenched in misery. 'I should have told you sooner. I *tried* to tell you sooner. I tried to tell Mr Owen, on the boat. And again you, when you offered me a spin. And then in . . . Anyway, I'm sorry.'

'Well, I'll be blowed!'

Phineas laughed incredulously. 'And there I was, wheeling you about the place. Showing you the sights, drinking with you – *introducing* you to people.'

'Yeah, well, as I said, I . . . Anyway, I guess that's it. I'll – er – I'll get back. I'll see you.'

Humphrey walked away, shoulders slumped.

Phineas watched him trudge on, past the lane that would take him to Batch Magna and the Hall, his head down dejectedly on the road that would eventually take him out of the valley and onto the Kingham road.

And serve you damn well right, he thought.

And then he sighed, a man put-upon. And picking up the perry Humphrey had left behind set off after him.

'You're going the wrong way!' he called from the lane leading in the direction of the village.

Humphrey turned, and walked slowly back.

Phineas shook his head. Take these bloated plutocrats out from behind their big desks and they're not the same thing at all.

'Come on,' he said impatiently. 'It's this way. That road would have taken you out of the valley. Appropriately enough, some might say – and I'd be among the first to say it. But I brought you here, and I'll take you back. Alive,' he added pointedly.

'Yeah, well, thanks. It was good of you,' Humphrey said, after they'd walked in silence for some yards. 'You could have just let me walk on.'

'It is not in my nature to be churlish – *Humphrey*,' Phineas said loftily, and emphasising his real name. 'And I suppose, *Humphrey*, that this means there is no little woman, no Mrs *Smith*, waiting at the inn?'

Humphrey said he was a Humph, not a Humphrey. That's what people called him, Humph. And yeah, yeah, Phineas got it, there was no little woman called Smith, or anything else, waiting for him at the inn.

Wordlessly, Phineas handed him the plastic container of Dotty Snape's famous perry for ladies.

Phineas couldn't resist asking about the fate of the houseboats, once Humphrey had finished chucking people off them. Humphrey said they'd be turned into eateries, with an historical paddle steamer theme. All uptown sort of places, of course, like the proposed holiday village.

Exclusive catering, Humphrey puffed, was a

business he happened to have extensive executive experience of. They had no plans for the estate housing stock, he said evasively.

He said he wasn't sure about the Hall, an hotel or country club, something like that. Whatever promised the best returns.

'But what people don't seem to understand here,' he hurried on, 'is that I'm not a rich man. I don't have a choice in it. I *have* to do it.'

'Yes, well, whatever the truth of the matter might be, don't expect people to thank you for it, that's all.'

'That *is* the truth!' Humphrey said indignantly.

'Emm? Oh, I daresay,' Phineas said, looking bored and unconvinced.

Humphrey came to an abrupt halt.

'I am not a liar! I'm broke. Broke to the goddam wide! I've had to mortgage the old place to invest in it. Something you probably wouldn't understand.' He still wasn't sure he understood it himself, even after Frank had gone over it yet again. 'I'm bringing jobs and money into the place. I'm – aw, to hell with it!' he said, and dumped himself down among the corn parsley on a bank.

'What would *you* do then, if you're so goddam smart? Yeah. Yeah, I thought so,' he said, when Phineas didn't answer. 'Everybody knows what I *shouldn't* do but nobody tells me what I *should* do. Well, if you and everybody else are such goddam hotshots, why aren't you rich? That's what I'd like to know,' he muttered to himself.

Phineas, who'd stopped, and was wondering whether to carry on and leave him there, sighed and walked back.

'Are you coming, or are you just going to sit there?'

'I'm just gonna sit here! I'm just gonna sit here and drink this,' Humphrey decided, and opened the perry.

'Right. OK. Well, I've got to get back.'

'Yeah, right. You just do that,' Humphrey said, and helped himself to a large swig of perry.

Phineas hesitated. 'Look, Humphrey . . .'

'Humph,' Humphrey said, and wiped at his mouth.

'Humph. Look, maybe you are just doing what you think has to be done. I don't know. I'm not a businessman. All I—'

'Neither am I,' Humphrey said.

'What?'

'Neither am I not a businessman.'

'Well, whatever it is you call yourself. What I—'

'I'm not a businessman or anything else. Don't know the first thing about business. Haven't the *faintest* idea about it,' Humphrey said with airy indifference, as if, and what's more he couldn't care less.

'Not a businessman?' Phineas said, sitting down. 'What about the plans for the river? What about mortgages and investing, and all that sort of thing? What about—'

'That's *Frank*!' Humphrey looked at him as if

he couldn't believe how slow Phineas was. 'Uncle Frank, for godsakes! The real Frank. Left to me it would be a total goddam mess.' Humphrey laughed wildly, and made a face indicating the size of mess he was capable of.

'Have a drink,' he added gloomily, handing Phineas the container.

Phineas lifted the perry and then paused. 'What about the extensive executive experience in the exclusive catering business you happen to have had? What about that, then?' he asked suspiciously.

Humphrey laughed again. 'I was a short-order cook in a goddam diner. Downtown. For eight whole weeks. Even then I went before I was pushed. Burnt too many burgers.'

'Well, I'll be blowed.'

'Where people get the idea from that I'm some sort of millionaire, I don't know,' Humphrey said plaintively.

'Yes, I do!' he said then. 'Yes, I do know where people got the idea I'm a millionaire from. *I* gave it to them. I gave them the idea. That's where they got it from.'

He drew a sharp breath, and looked suddenly and tearfully resolute. 'I am never ever going to lie and boast about anything again. Ever! I'm not a go-getter. That was my dad. I'm the failure. The no-hoper. When it comes to the freeway of life, I'm the one who ends up on a farm track.'

Phineas, who wouldn't have got on a freeway, or

any other road that was in that much of a hurry, in the first place, nevertheless nodded sympathetically.

And then said, 'Now, come along, Humphrey—'

'Humph,' Humphrey reminded him from his misery, and took another swig of perry.

'Humph. Chin up. I mean, I'd hardly call a baronetcy and what you have down there a farm track. So what if your dad's—' .

'My dad's dead,' Humphrey said.

'Ah,' Phineas said, after taking his turn and handing the perry back. 'And this Uncle Frank, what is . . .?'

'He's not an uncle. Not my uncle, anyway. He's somebody else who saw fit to fire me.' Humphrey laughed briefly, a man with the upper hand. 'And now he works for me!' he said with a flash of the old Humphrey, before remembering the new. 'Well, he doesn't really work for me. In fact,' he insisted, 'he doesn't work for me at *all*.'

The perry container passing between them, Humphrey told Phineas the rest then, about what happened before Frank, and what happened afterwards, the money that went down over Wall Street, and life as a short-order cook.

'Then out of nowhere comes all this. And I go from a grease shoveller who goes home to his mom every night, to a baronet with an ancestral home in the old country, and the kind of girl he could only dream about. I mean, it's a movie, right? With one of those big, Technicolor endings, the sort that when you leave the theatre you don't mind that it's

246

raining outside. Then we get the paperwork. My mom says right, and rings Frank, and Frank looks at the figures . . . the death duties, the income that's not coming in, and the outgoings that have gotta go out . . .' Humphrey's voice was dreary with reality, with all that a happy ending is not supposed to be about.

'Anyway, he reads me the bottom line. I can't afford it. But, well, the thought of selling it, some complete outsider coming in and—'

'Turning the river into a holiday camp,' Phineas said, 'and the Hall into god knows what, all that sort of thing. Yes, I know.'

'Yeah, yeah, very funny. Well, don't forget the money and the jobs, will you. And what would you have done, huh? What would you have done?'

Phineas would have stayed and muddled through somehow. He wouldn't have let this place go. He knew that now in a way he had never quite known it before, now he was about to lose it. He wasn't entirely sure he could explain it all, even to himself, and with so much to say, and to someone he doubted would understand any of it, he said nothing.

Humphrey nodded. 'Hard one, right? Yeah, right. Take the money and run, that's what I was tempted to do – that's what I was gonna do at first. And I could have, too. There's no one in line so the entailment's broken. I can sell what the heck I like. And the money would be dandy, thank you very much. But, well, don't ask me why, but I couldn't do it.'

247

He said that Home Farm would have to be sold to meet death duty. They were short-term tenants who wanted to move on anyway, but if planning permission wasn't granted it wouldn't just be Home Farm, everything would have to go. 'I have to get a salary out of it – and a good one – or sell. That's the bottom line. I have to. Apart from anything else, I'm engaged to the most beautiful and desirable girl in New York. Sylvia. That's her name, Syl-via,' he said, as if about to start singing.

'That's the girl you went home to instead of mum, huh?' Phineas said, getting involved in the story.

'Well, we haven't – you know – done anything yet, but, yeah, that's her. That's Sylvia. That's *Sylvia*, all right,' Humphrey said, and grinned goofily at nothing. 'I met her through Frank. She's a financial whiz kid, an Upper East Sider out of Vassar. And, well, I know I'm no movie star, that maybe the title helped, but believe me, I gotta have a bit more in my pocket than that. She's a princess in her own right, Wall Street royalty. The sort of girl who's always out there, in the front of the parade, and expects you to keep up. Only winners need apply – these Vassar girls have got that written all over 'em. Know what I mean?'

Phineas wasn't at all sure he did. He wasn't sure he knew anyone quite like that. It didn't even sound like his last wife, Diana.

Which didn't stop him advising Humphrey on

how to deal with her. Something he was still doing when Ken pulled up in a Land Rover.

'You found it then,' Ken said, grinning at the muddied state of them. And then he frowned. 'Here, I saw Ginny back there. Her didn't break down after all, did her?'

'No, Ken, old man. We ran out of petrol, that's all,' Phineas said cheerfully. He waved the perry container at him in invitation, and then shaking it, discovered it was empty.

Ken said he wouldn't anyway, thanks, not with what he had on, but he could give them a lift in if they wanted.

'I have to pick up some bread for Wendy's tea. Got to be brown, it has. Her's on a diet. I don't know why her wants to do that,' Ken went on, as his two passengers squeezed in next to him on the bench seat. 'Her's not fat or anything.'

'The woman, Ken,' Phineas pontificated, 'who is satisfied with the way she looks does not exist. Simply does *not* exist.'

'That's what I reckon, as well.' Ken, one hand on the gear stick, paused and narrowed his eyes at them.

'Something else I reckon, too,' he added suspiciously, and Humphrey waited, looking suddenly exhausted, a man who could run no further.

Ken laughed. 'I reckon you buggers have had a drink or two, that's what I reckon.'

CHAPTER 21

Phineas got Ken to drop them at the Steamer Inn, to get the lie of the land, as he put it. Lucy, who'd changed into a mini skirt and off-the-shoulder sweater, was on her way back to the kitchen after serving a couple of lunches.

He wasn't sure what he'd been expecting, but what he got was an indifferent sort of smile and the menu.

'There's only chips and things, if you want to eat – egg and chips, sausage and chips, ham and chips, turkey breast and chips, steak pie and chips, hamburger and chips, and green salad. Baked beans optional,' she reeled off, one increasingly interested eye on Humphrey, as she recognised him despite his disguise this time as some sort of labourer. 'No chef,' she added briefly, by way of explanation.

'Hello, Sir Humphrey. Remember me, Lucy?' she said, and wriggled her shoulders at him. 'Saw you earlier, I did.'

'Humph, please,' Humphrey mumbled, clutching the empty container of perry, the long road to confession and two pints of Sheepsnout, plus half a gallon of Dotty Snape's famous perry for ladies, catching up with him.

'No chef?' Phineas said, trying to work out what that might mean.

'No. Carl's gone. For good, he has. To London.' She nodded at Humphrey. 'He all right, is he?'

'Gone to London?' Phineas said.

Lucy nodded cheerfully. 'Took the twelve-fifteen from Church Myddle. Said he'd had enough. Said he couldn't take any more, he couldn't. Patrick's doing the kitchen, and Dilly's on the phone now, trying to get a replacement.'

Phineas was still taking this in when Lucy said carelessly, 'Oh, and by the way, Phineas, I don't know when I'll be able to see you again. I'll be very busy from now on. The chief reporter from the *Kingham News* has discovered me. I'm starring in their next Local Beauty Spots page. I'm doing what we call a photo-shoot tonight. He wants me to bring a bikini,' she said, sharing that in a throaty aside with Sir Humphrey.

And then she looked at Phineas, yesterday's news. 'Sorry,' she said, not even bothering to sound as if she meant it. And turning on her heel, brushed him off with a sweep of her eyelashes.

Phineas stared after her in disbelief.

He hadn't wanted to get further involved with her, and it was obviously a good job he hadn't. He saw now what Carl had meant. As soon as his back was turned, she was off with another man. He could scarcely credit it.

251

And he'd forgotten to ask her if she had met Sally.

He had John, the lunchtime barman, chalk him up a couple of pints of Black Boy, as he had work to do, a much milder brew than Sheepsnout, Dotty Snape's famous perry for ladies, or anything else from Dotty's fermenting barrels.

He then sat Humphrey down at a table and went over it with him.

Lucy, he told him, had left the *Felicity H* sometime after Sally had arrived at the *Belle*. Sometime after that again, Lucy arrived at the pub and Carl had left it. That much was known. It was the bit in between that was missing. When Sally was on the *Belle* and Lucy had left the *Felicity H*. Had they met?

Humphrey smiled gently at it, as if listening to a favourite story, his eyes lifted to a spot somewhere on the ceiling opposite.

Phineas left him there, and rang Daniel from the pub's pay phone. He learned that they *had* met. And now there was no Sally, either.

Phineas moved briskly on to the stranded Frogeye. He told his son that if he didn't want to be keelhauled, he'd enlist the help of one of his mates with a motorbike and take Ginny a can of petrol. That was something he *could* blame somebody else for.

When Phineas sat down again, Humphrey stood up and said he was off to see Annie Owen. Phineas told him to sit down. He said he'd ring Annie and try and get her to come up and see them. He really didn't think he could go through all that again.

Owain wasn't there, but Annie still saw no reason to pop up and see Sir Humphrey. Until Phineas said that if she didn't then he, Sir Humphrey, would be popping down to see her. And besides, he added, it wasn't really as they had thought. He hated to admit it, but he really didn't see that the man had much choice. And he told her all that Humphrey had told him.

Annie had relented then, as he guessed she would, and sighing over it, the imposition on her good nature, said she'd be up as soon as she could.

He thought he might as well give Jasmine a ring then, and Jasmine said she'd be there right away. Then he rang Priny, who said she'd nip down to the *Sabrina* and fetch the Commander and Tom Parr.

And by the time he'd got back to the table, Humphrey, cuddling his empty container of Dotty Snape's famous perry for ladies, head back on the settle and his mouth open, was sound asleep.

Jasmine and her brood turned up first. It was her mam's day to slop over the baby, across the border in Bannog, she said, but she'd had to bring the rest with her. And while she and Phineas were at the bar, sorting out drinks and crisps and packets of scratchings, the twins, lured by his size and the gaudy attractions of his shirt, clambered onto Humphrey's lap, and as he snored and rumbled in his sleep, poked at him, and pulled at his hair, and stuck exploding fingers in his ears, until pulled off by their mother.

When Annie arrived she looked at Humphrey aghast. '*What* have you done with him?'

'I haven't done anything with him!' Phineas said indignantly.

'He didn't look like that earlier. All clean and smart he was then. And look at that nice holiday shirt of his!'

'He's not actually on holiday, Annie,' Phineas pointedly reminded her. 'He's here to evict us.'

'Well, I know *that*. But he's explained all that. You said. I knew it must be something like that. Knew it. He looks all in, he does, poor love,' she said, smiling at his sleeping head.

Phineas laughed incredulously. 'We were plotting his demise only last week.'

'*Shhh!*' Annie said. 'He might hear.'

'Bagged him, have you, Phineas?' the Commander said, when he arrived a while later with Priny and Tom Parr, both men with their sleeves rolled up and mucky from a morning messing about on the *Sabrina*.

'Mind you, somebody was bound to, walking about in that shirt. Well, not that I like to criticise, my boy, but what exactly do you expect us to do with him? And where's all the mud come from?'

'It's a long story, James,' Phineas said.

'Is he dead then?' Tom Parr asked over the Commander's shoulder.

'No, of course he's not dead,' Phineas said.

'Only sleeping,' Jasmine said, as if reading it off a headstone, and hissed at one of the twins, who was trying to get some of the attention by climbing on Humphrey's lap again.

Tom Parr prodded Humphrey with a finger, and then stood back, startled, as he jerked suddenly in his sleep. 'Her's right! He's alive, all right. Big bloke, too, en't he? Nasty-looking brute, he is.'

'Oh, I don't get anything like that from him, Tom,' Jasmine said.

'Now, what's everyone drinking?' Phineas said expansively. 'I'm in the chair.'

For Phineas, any sort of credit had a liberating headiness to it, as if he were no longer playing at real life but with paper money, like Monopoly. Consequently, his credit at the Steamer Inn, along with that at Dotty's and other establishments in the area, had a strict limit imposed on it.

But he had plenty of that left still, and no doubt another royalty cheque was due any day now, if not sooner.

'No, I don't get anything *nasty* from him,' Jasmine went on, frowning hard at a spot a couple of inches above Humphrey's dishevelled and muddied head. 'Confusion, that's what I'm getting so far,' she said slowly. 'Definitely. An aura of confusion.'

'That's hardly surprising,' Priny said. 'Apart from anything else, he's been with Phineas for most of the morning.'

The Commander, a restorative pint of

Sheepsnout in front of him, considered the muddy condition of the two men, and was given to wonder if an attempt hadn't been made to bury the American.

'Could it be,' he said slowly, his good eye tilted at Phineas, 'that he was taken for dead by an assailant when he had only been stunned? That that assailant, seizing, perhaps, the unguarded moment, and without thought for the next, struck him a terrible blow with a beer bottle?'

'We were drinking perry. In a plastic container,' Phineas pointed out gravely, and indicated as evidence the container Humphrey still clutched in his sleep.

'Can one strike a terrible blow with a beer bottle?' Priny wanted to know, screwing a cigarette into her holder. 'They're such small things usually, aren't they?'

The Commander was not to be diverted.

'And did that assailant dig a hasty shallow grave? And then, when filling it in, did he hear a groan as the first clods broke on flesh. Or watch even, as if in a nightmare, as the body stirred, and then threw off its earth like the bedclothes?' The Commander's good eye seemed to stare at the horror of it. In the glass one, Turner's *Sunrise*, went up in yellow flames over Norham Castle.

Phineas looked both amused and exasperated.

'I haven't knocked him out, tried to bury him, or done anything else to him. If it wasn't for me he'd be in Kingham by now.'

He told them how they'd met, and how he had learned only later that his companion was Sir Humphrey Strange. For much of their time together he was under the impression that Humphrey was a Canadian called Frank.

'On holiday,' Annie put in.

'The damned humbug!' the Commander huffed.

'What's he going to do with the old paddlers, then, Phineas? Afterwards, like? He tell you that, did he? You know, while you were talking?'

Tom Parr spoke as if only for Phineas's ears, and with almost desperate casualness. Almost from the beginning he had guiltily nursed the hope that after the evictions the boats would be refitted and put to ply the river again. And that then they would need someone who knew how they worked.

When Phineas told him, Tom was unforgiving. 'We ought to drag him out now an' dump him in the bloody river!' he said with an old man's sudden anger. 'Hit him with a spade and drop him off the back here! We ought to murder the bugger, an' that's a fact.'

'It's too late for that now, Tom. We're compromised now. We've been seen together. No, we're stuck with him now, I'm afraid,' the Commander said, and looked accusingly at Phineas.

''ere! He didn't say anything about chucking us out as well, did he?' it suddenly occurred to Tom.

Phineas shook his head. 'No, nothing like that, Tom. But don't be surprised if you have to start paying rent.'

'Oh, I guessed that. I guessed that would happen. We all did. Well, at least now they'll have to do some work on 'em. At least now we might get the leaks in the blame roofs fixed. At least we still have a home,' Tom added with a tremor in his voice, and looked at Annie.

She reached across and squeezed his hand.

'I know it's hard,' she said to them. 'And sad, it is, too. The old Hall, as well. But he'd no choice, see. Not really. Not as it stands. Tell them, Phineas. Tell them what you told me,' she urged, and immediately started to tell them herself.

'So he's doing it because he has to. That's what it comes down to. Anyway, if it wasn't him doing it, it'd be somebody else. And it's not him, really, it's his Uncle Frank. And he's not even an uncle. Well, not his uncle, anyway.'

The Commander wasn't sure he understood that, and nor did he want to.

'Well, no matter who did or who didn't do what, we're still left with this fellow. Not to mention his taste in shirts,' he said, and busied himself, suddenly and furiously, with scraping out his pipe.

Not to mention the evictions. Not to mention that we won't be meeting many more times like this. Not to mention that soon we'll be saying goodbye to it, to all this, to our lives together on the river. That's what he had really meant, and didn't have to say, not here, among friends.

Phineas was about to suggest another round to

cheer things up when Owain came through the door, mopping at his neck and face with a large khaki handkerchief.

With a pair of the late General's braces straining over a sweat-stained cotton vest, and wearing a battered-looking straw hat, Owain had been following the river from Water Lacy on Annie's bicycle with a loud hailer. He'd been lending rhythm and encouragement to Sion and three other scullers, all built like young Shire horses and crewing a Cluny gig, a racing quad that, it was hoped, in the main event on regatta day, would carry the honour of Batch Magna home on its blades.

To Owain, the cricket match with Blurford was only cricket. The annual race with Water Lacy was war.

The Hall had come between him and the boat on the home stretch, and he decided that they could pull the rest without him, the thought of a pint driving him on along the High Street to the welcoming open doors and malty, stone-cool interior of the pub.

'How do!' he said, looking with cheerful surprise at them all sitting there, and then peering across at the sleeping Humphrey. Before remembering where he'd seen him before.

'Hello, that's the . . .'

'Owain, sit down,' Annie said firmly. 'We've got something to tell you.'

* * *

259

Humphrey woke to find some old guy staring at him with one blue and one yellow eye, and sat up with a start.

'Ah! He's awake,' Phineas said, and with a proprietorial air formally introduced Sir Humphrey to his tenants. 'Or Humphrey, as I think we can now call him,' he added, beaming at him.

'Humph,' Humphrey mumbled, looking cornered.

'We was talking about drowning you,' Owain told him. 'Pouring a gallon of cider down your neck, and then chucking you in off the back here. Drowned when drunk.'

'*Owain!*' Annie protested, and smiled at Humphrey. 'You take no notice of him, dear.'

'My idea was to give you a couple of whacks with a spade first, then tip you in,' Tom Parr added.

And then it was the Commander's turn. He would like, he said, a word with him.

Scorning any reference to their own misfortunes, he sighted Humphrey like a target with his good eye, and firing on passion and Sheepsnout, let him have it, a brief but pungent lecture on the despoiling of rural England, the landscapes of Cotman, Palmer and Crome, all turned into miniature when worn in his other eye. And threw in Shakespeare in his orchard close and Blake's lambs gambolling under Constable's skies, and the light that Turner painted, while Humphrey sat with his mouth open.

'And what, sir,' the Commander wanted to know when he'd finished, 'have you to say about your proposed contribution to this vandalism?'

Humphrey had nothing to say about it, but Owain had, and had been waiting impatiently to say it.

'What about Wales, man?' he demanded of the Commander. '*What* about the glories of Wales? What about its mountains and castles? And its choirs, the voice of its valleys? Wales, land of my fathers. The Eden of bloody bards!' he said with sudden heat, remembering another bit from a recent TV programme on the country. 'The land that gave the world poetry and song.'

'But not the word for penis,' Phineas put in. 'There is not such word for penis, or any of its many synonyms, in the Welsh language. The Welsh for penis is little leg,' he was able to tell them, indebted for that to Sion, tittering over it together then like a couple of school kids.

'Is this right, Owain?' the Commander said, as if demanding an explanation.

'Little leg,' Phineas repeated.

'Coes bach,' Owain growled at him.

'And the female part is ffwrch,' Annie put in. 'It is!' she assured a sceptical-looking Priny. 'Ffwrch,' she said again, the word almost drowned out by an explosion of laughter from Jasmine.

Owen glared at his wife. 'A good honest Welsh word, that is, my girl! Means furrow. Seed bed.'

'Little legs in seed beds,' Phineas said, walking two fingers across the table in Jasmine's direction, and setting her off again.

'It's you lot! It's the English that have all the

261

bloody words for it!' Owain roared above the laughter. 'They're all there, for any *respectable* person to see, on the walls of your public bloody conveniences!'

'Graffiti is universal and timeless,' Phineas pronounced.

'Not in bloody Wales, it's not!'

'Not in *Welsh*, you mean, Owain,' the Commander said pedantically. 'At least, not the sort under discussion.'

Absently patting one of the twins, who was using his lap as a short cut, Humphrey looked round the table, at the bickering and the laughter, while he sat among them like a friend, these people whose homes he was taking.

Emotion swelled in him. He didn't deserve it. *They* didn't deserve it.

He banged the table with a fist.

'You'll all be paid compensation,' he heard himself say. 'Three thousand pounds sterling,' he decided, as the table fell silent. 'For you and . . .' and remembered in time that he wasn't supposed to be evicting the estate pensioners.

'For each eviction. I know money can't buy what we're taking from you. But for what it's worth . . .' he offered, and sitting back, embraced them all with a near-tearful look.

Now all he had to do was to tell Frank.

CHAPTER 22

A week after that, Priny was in Kingham, paying another visit to the hairdresser's. At times when a bit of swank was called for, the Commander flew the flag in his left eye, and Priny had her hair done.

The Commander was in the wardroom, puffing on a briar over a table spread with an ancient depth chart showing the sunken island of Atlantis, and graphs of the area illustrating isotherm and isoseismal patterns, the tides of the Gulf Stream and the theory of continental drift.

He was considering evidence that at eight pm, on 5th June, 8498 BC, a vast asteroid had struck the vulnerable crust of the Bermuda Triangle like the fist of God, at a speed relative to Earth of twelve miles per second. That the asteroid, which the Commander on his record of events had designated *Genesis*, had punched a hole into a fracture zone of the Atlantic Ridge, triggering off a cosmic explosion equal to the force of 30,000 hydrogen bombs, which had obliterated an island civilisation called Atlantis.

But his heart wasn't in it.

Through the open door he could hear the rooks in the sycamores in Mawr Wood, and from there or from the island a green woodpecker laughed again.

He limped back down the steps of the wardroom to the deck.

The day was dull and grey looking, a bloom of moisture on the air above the river like the sweat on fruit. The call of a green woodpecker was supposed to mean rain. But he knew it wasn't going to do that. He knew his river, his valley.

He stood at the rail, pipe clamped in his mouth, his good leg out, braced as if against a sudden heave of a bridge plate, staring out over the water.

It was some time since he had last looked for the otter. Because he was convinced now that it hadn't been an otter at all he'd seen that day, but a mink, another interloper. It had been a mink, that's all. And besides, he had other things to think about these days.

He wasn't sure if Priny thought they were actually going to *get* the promised three thousand pounds compensation. He'd believe it when he saw the cheque.

But the American had also, perhaps more realistically, said that the estate would buy back the *Castle*, along with the dinghy, at the price they had paid for it, which was a relief, as Priny had said, and as he'd agreed. Both of them being sensible about it, and both thinking about what that would mean. The old PS *Batch Castle*, boarded by tourists eating beef burgers and wearing plastic hats with Captain written on them.

The Commander almost bit through the stem of his briar at the thought of it.

He watched a pair of wagtails feeding above the river, a sudden fluttering, lemon-yellow brightness on the air, flying low and erratically downstream, and knew that flies were hatching from the water. Owain had taught him that, on their first day on the *Castle*, on the river, drinking Annie's home-made brew, the wine of their welcome. And he remembered the years since, other days and times on the river.

He would miss it, no doubt of that. Miss it all dreadfully . . .

He wiped at a corner of his good eye with a finger, and then cleared his throat sharply. That would *never* do.

Besides, he told himself briskly, snapping open his fob watch from a trouser pocket, the match with Blurford waited.

The Commander was entitled to wear the blazer, its stripes somewhat faded now, of I Zingari, a cricket side he'd batted for in days when his arms were stronger and one good eye was enough. The black, red and gold colours of I Zingari, which he also sported on the hatband of his Panama, signified that light came, out of the darkness, through fire. Their motto, "Keep your temper, keep your promise, and throughout the game of life keep up your wickets".

The Commander went in to change for cricket.

Batch Magna failed to keep up their first wicket five minutes after winning the toss and going into bat, the ball sending the bails flying and flattening the off-stump.

Robin Beddows, next on, and the nearest they could field to a Lobby Wright, lifted hopes with a brisk thirty-four runs, before taking one of Wilf "Bones" Powell's full pitches on his elbow, and sent on his way in the company of the secretary to Kingham General Hospital.

Daniel, playing as a visitor, stonewalled a slow ten, before running himself out, and his father, his left pad on first, after the great Denis Compton, went all out for sixes, pulled off a boundary four, then a three, and chopped a couple through the slips. And then, full of himself after belting one over a boundary hedge, fell like a complete and utter novice for one of Bobby Henley's googlies, and had to suffer playground jeers, and what passes for wit in Blurford cricketing circles.

He met Humphrey on the way in.

Humphrey was also not happy.

For a start, he could not *believe* the number of people in the village who knew about the private offer of compensation he'd made. And not only was it now common knowledge, it had also been added to. When last he'd heard, the offer – *his* offer, an offer, if anybody was damn well interested, that even Frank didn't know about yet – was running at ten thousand pounds per eviction.

And then he had met Clem Wroxley.

Ffion Owen had introduced them. 'The Honourable Clementine Wroxley,' she'd said, swanking it up, 'Sir Humphrey Strange.'

Ffion's feelings towards the American, after the drama of her pregnancy and proposed exile had left the stage empty for them, had swung from hissing hatred to finding herself liking him, and then, because of it, hating him again. She was liking him at present, a change of heart not un-affected by her parents' promise to buy her a horse out of the compensation. Neither Annie nor Owain entirely believed that they'd actually *get* the three thousand pounds but that hadn't stopped them spending it, if only on paper.

'Hi!' Humphrey had said cheerfully, grinning at Clem. 'It's Humph. Call me Humph.'

He had been immediately taken with her. A big, sunshiny sort of girl, her blue eyes smiling breezily at him from under a wide-brimmed straw hat with a pink silk rose, and looking cool and summery in white.

Until she heard who he was, and then the weather turned.

'So, you're Sir Humphrey? Well, you should jolly well be ashamed of yourself!' were her first words to him. 'You have betrayed not only people like Ffion's parents, but the memory of the General.

You have betrayed your own history, your own family name.'

She'd been *waiting* to say that to him. 'You are nothing but a bounder, sir. A *cad*!' she said, echoes of her late father, the baron, and his morning explosions over *The Times*.

Humphrey's ears were on fire.

'No. No, what I am, lady,' he managed then, 'what I am, is somebody trying to bring jobs and money to the place. That's what I *am*!'

Clem smiled without warmth, and as if he hadn't spoken. 'I do hope we shan't meet again,' she said, dismissing him.

But Humphrey stayed where he was, glaring at her, while Clem glared back from under her summer brim. And Ffion, standing in their large, serious shadows, wondered if Sir Humphrey was any good at arm-wrestling, and tried not to giggle.

'Never seen the woman in my life before – and I sure as hell don't want to see her again!' he told Phineas hotly. 'I've had it with these people. I'm either Rockefeller or Public Enemy Number-goddam-One around here. Well, I'm off. Tomorrow, if I can get a flight. Let the agent deal with the planning committee. I wasn't gonna come here at all today. But then I thought, to hell with it, it's my team, too. Well, I've had all that. They're doing a good enough job of losing without me. I'm gonna go back to the Hall now. And stay there until it's time to leave this goddam place. For *good*!'

'Women!' Phineas said, not out of any particular

sympathy, but simply taking his own humiliation at the wicket out on somebody, anybody.

And while Humphrey stomped on his way off to the Hall, Phineas stomped on his way to the changing room, and almost walked into Sally, on her way into the pavilion with a couple of large slabs of Madeira cake.

'Ah,' Phineas said.

'Hello, Phineas!' Sally said brightly.

'Lo, Sally,' he said. And it was as if Bobby Henley's googly had never happened.

'Daniel asked me to come and watch him play,' she said, seeing Phineas arrive at *almost* the wrong conclusion. Daniel *had* asked her, and it was all very sweet, and just as transparent. And it hadn't taken her at all long to agree.

'Ah,' Phineas said on a lower note.

'And well, I could hardly say no.'

'No, no, of course not.'

Sally indicated the cake she was holding. 'And then I got roped in to help with the tea. I work with the wife of your secretary.'

'Ah,' Phineas said again. 'I rang you, you know,' he said then. 'A few times.'

'I know. I got the messages.'

Phineas was silent. Sally helped him out. 'And I never phoned you back.'

'No. Right, well . . .'

'I'm surprised you had the time, having to keep up with Lucy,' she said, and after telling herself that if she saw him she wouldn't even mention it.

An incident, as she told Annie Owen, she no longer had the slightest interest in.

'Oh, that,' Phineas said.

'Emm, that,' Sally said.

'Yes, I'm sorry about that. I don't *quite* know how it happened.'

'I do,' Sally said with a little laugh. 'Anyway, it's really none of my business. It's not as if we were married, or anything. Well, I've got teas to prepare.'

'Look here, Sally,' Phineas said abruptly. 'Look, this business with Lucy. It meant nothing to me, you know. It was just a . . . Anyway, it's over now.'

'Oh, you finished with her, did you?' she asked, showing polite interest, while knowing he hadn't. Annie had told her how successful she'd been there.

Phineas hesitated. 'Well, no, not exactly. She did, really, I suppose.'

'Oh, dear,' Sally said innocently. It was her secret, hers and Annie's. Lucy, as Sally had guessed she would, was keeping equally quiet about it.

'Not that there was ever anything to . . . Anyway, I thought we could go for a drink or something, that's all.'

'Just good friends, you mean?'

Phineas looked doubtful. 'Well, yes, something like that.'

'Well, I suppose so. Although I'm busy this weekend. And for most, if not all, of next week.'

'Ah,' Phineas said. 'Well, what about next weekend? It's the regatta then.'

'Yes, I know. I think I'm supposed to be making up a foursome for it.'

Phineas looked offended. 'Well, you'd have much more fun where we'll be, on the *Belle*. And a better view. Still . . . And who's the rest of the foursome, then? Not of course that it's any of my business.'

He wondered if that was it, another man, the something that Annie had referred to when she'd told him that Sally had had her hair cut short. Always a sign of something going on in a woman's life, that is, Phineas, she'd said.

No, Sally agreed, it was none of his business.

There was pause.

'And it will probably be the last regatta, as well,' Phineas said plaintively.

Sally sighed, at him and herself. She'd meant to hold out a bit longer than this. 'Well, you could ring me, I suppose. On Friday. Friday evening. I'll see how things are then. Now, I'm not saying . . .'

'No, no, of course, not,' Phineas said quickly. 'I'll ring you then. Friday evening. Right. OK.'

'Now I must go,' she said.

'Yes, yes, of course. Right, well, I'll see you then. Your hair looks nice, Sal,' he said then, as Sally was disappearing into the pavilion.

She turned with a quick movement of her head and smiled at him. 'Why, thank you, Phineas,' she said, sounding surprised.

After tea, Daniel took a wicket with a low ball, despite ignoring all his father had taught him about

271

pitch, spin, length and body swing. Which was more than his father managed when he had the ball, despite all he knew about pitch, spin, length and body swing.

And then John Beecher, the team's fast bowler, who had a coal yard in the village, a man who knew nothing about pitch, spin, length and body swing, and didn't need to, sent two batsmen off with flattened stumps in the same over.

Batch Magna had gone into tea all out for eighty-nine. Blurford had lost four wickets for only forty runs, and eight of those byes off John Beecher's ball.

And then the Blurford skipper produced Lobby Wright. And as Lobby came out, his sleeves rolled up, walking to the wicket as if to work, so did the sun, breaking out from an overcast sky, suddenly, like a round of applause.

The Batch Magna skipper put John Beecher on again.

John turned a broad back, bowed slightly by years of coal heaving, on the wicket, and with the ball lost in a hand like a ham, plodded steadily on to get good run back.

Lobby, moving his body as if about to address a fence post with the sledgehammer, waited.

Working on the principle that Lobby's eye wasn't in yet, John tried a yorker.

Lobby caught it high on his blade and cut it through the slips for two. He hit the second, fast, yorker, meant for his leg stump, on the full pitch and sent it out to long-leg for four, and with unnerving ease hooked John's next delivery into the long grass beyond square-leg. Lobby had got his eye in.

And then the Blurford batsman piled on twos and threes, and boundaries and sixes, until his team stood a mere five runs behind Batch Magna.

After trying men expert in the subtleties of googlies and good-length balls, the Batch Magna skipper reached again for a good strong, honest tool, and called John Beecher.

Pushing sweat back from his forehead, John turned for the run back and sent down all he had, as true and as hard as he knew how. A blur of red at full toss, which Lobby came out to meet with a straight bat, and smote, walloping it clean over a boundary hedge for six.

The Blurford supporters went wild. Their team had done it for the third year running. And there were those, Miss Wyndham and Tom Parr among them, who felt it no longer much mattered.

They were the old Batch Magna, and they had already been defeated. Not by the sort of enemy they would have met and fought, on their river and in the High Street, with whatever came to hand, and to the last of them, but by change, bewilderingly made. By progress, and bloodless talk of balance sheets, and words like positive economic impact and area regeneration, at the public meetings in the village hall.

That was the new Batch Magna; and they were

the past. And since the death of the General, of the world as they had always known it, and the arrival of the American and his plans for their future, whatever was said, and however necessary it all might be, they felt it was no longer their village, no longer their world.

CHAPTER 23

The standard bearer of the new and future Batch Magna was still in bed, looking greatly reduced and staring wretchedly at the ceiling when Mrs Thomas arrived on Monday morning.

He had been fine only yesterday. He'd cleaned his breakfast plate and spent the rest of the day whistling about the place, happily pottering around outside, even hauling one of the rowing boats down onto the river again. Making sure, of course, to return in time for the Sunday roast Mrs Thomas had promised him, beef with Yorkshire pudding and all the trimmings, followed by jam roly-poly.

Unable to get a Sunday flight, he had told her he'd be flying out today, and she'd arrived with fresh supplies of eggs, and Mr Stretch's best cured back bacon and pork sausages to feed him up for the journey. And when Sir Humph – as a squire he was a temporary and unlikely figure, but he was still the squire, and that, in answer to his invitation to call him Humph, was as informal as Mrs Thomas could bring herself to be – turned doleful eyes on her, and said he didn't think he could touch a thing today, thank you all the same, you could have knocked Mrs Thomas down with a feather.

He didn't know what was wrong with him, he told her faintly from the bed, while Mrs Thomas held a hand to his brow and felt his pulse. It had just come on, he said, as he was about to get up, a kind of sudden, awful tiredness.

Mrs Thomas, who kept a well-thumbed *Home Doctor* in her kitchen, tried a few symptoms out on him, and Humphrey, shaking his head miserably, said, no, he didn't have that, or that, or that one, either.

Having eliminated several major illnesses, Mrs Thomas studied him with a perplexed frown.

Humphrey feebly lifted his head from the pillow and said that, whatever it was, he had to get up, he had a flight to catch. Mrs Thomas indignantly told him that he'd do no such thing, he'd stay where he was, and tucked him firmly in.

She persuaded him to try a lightly boiled egg and brought it up to him on a bed tray, and sat him up, and plumped his pillows, and took the top of his egg off for him. She said she'd have to get some work done now but that she wouldn't be far away and would pop in now and then to see how he was.

Humphrey thanked her with a wan smile, and lifted a toast soldier to show willing.

He rallied sufficiently to finish what was on the tray, and an hour later, checking the time and working out that he could still catch his flight, told himself again that he ought to get up.

And then, when he tried to, discovered that he was losing the use of his limbs.

He'd read about a case like it in a book on the medically weird and unexplained, of a man who'd sat down one day to read a newspaper and when he tried to get up again, couldn't. Twenty years later, Humphrey had learned in a sombre footnote, the man remained trapped, a prisoner of his own body.

And that, Humphrey knew with certainty, with utter dread, was what was happening to him.

Panic drained the last of his strength as he tried to lift first one limb, then another. They were useless, dead weights, trapping him there, a prisoner of his own body.

He opened his mouth in a dry croak to call out, to summon Mrs T. And then closed it.

He thought it must be delirium.

Then she called again. From downstairs. He'd know that voice anywhere. It was Sylvia. Here. In Batch Magna. In Batch Hall.

He almost fell out of the bed. He scrambled out onto the landing and peered down over the balustrade.

It was Sylvia, all right, paying off a taxi driver in the hall. Sylvia, with a pink cashmere sweater tied round the waist of her slacks, a Vassar alumna in pearls, her sunglasses pushed back on her head. Sylvia. His Sylvie.

Humphrey scrambled back into the bedroom.

'Humphrey, darling!' she called when she saw him. She had made it clear from the start of their relationship that under no circumstances would she be calling him Humph.

She pushed freshly-pinked lips out in his direction in a kiss, and went on dabbing toilet water on her neck and wrists as Humphrey, calling her name again, lumbered in barefooted haste down the rest of the stairs.

Sylvia shoved the toilet water back into a crocodile shoulder bag on the hall table and slumped her shoulders.

'I am *so* exhausted. This place is so *remote*.'

'I can't believe it! I can*not* believe it,' Humphrey said.

'Just a flying visit,' she warned him. 'Have to be back on Wednesday.'

Humphrey slowed. 'Wednesday? This Wednesday?'

Sylvia nodded. 'Have to be back at my desk. You can't win if you're not in, right?' A mantra from another world, a world he realised that lately he'd forgotten about.

'Yeah, right, right,' Humphrey agreed, guiltily catching up.

With a small, amused frown, Sylvia took in the dressing gown he was still trying to tie over an expanse of T-shirt and bullfighter boxer shorts. 'And who hasn't been sticking to his *di–et*?' she said on a singsong note.

'Yeah, well, what with one thing and another,' Humphrey said, and wondered where he'd heard that before. He waved a hand at his Yankees dressing gown. 'I'm sorry about this. I've only just gotten up. I wasn't feeling too good.'

Humphrey grinned. 'I feel great now, though!'

Sylvia smiled at his enthusiasm, and offered her face.

Humphrey fell on her as if he hadn't eaten for a week.

'I thought maybe you weren't here,' she said, coming out of the embrace looking as if she'd been in a pillow fight, and retrieving her sunglasses and tidying her hair with a hand.

'I tried ringing earlier. Twice, in fact. Some woman answered the second time and said you weren't available.' Sylvia sniffed tearfully, mock spurned. 'So I've been replaced by an English girl, have I?'

'No-oh!' Humphrey said with a laugh at the idea of anyone replacing Sylvie. 'That would be Mrs T, Mrs Thomas, the housekeeper. I was in bed then. She was just being . . . And I wouldn't have heard up there. There's only one phone, in the hall here.'

'One phone?' Sylvia said incredulously. 'Amazing!' She looked around her, at the hall. 'It is *so* old. I thought it would be bigger, you know? It looked it in the photographs. But I can see what Frank meant, though. It's the ideal prototype. The fireplace there, and the staircase, and all that panelling, and the pictures. And with the pool and tennis courts in. Yeah, yeah,' she said, nodding. 'I like. I like. I told you I was buying in, right? Equity shareholding? Name on the board with yours after we're married? Executive design veto? ' Sylvia rattled off the deal.

'Yeah, yeah, you did,' Humphrey said, smiling on at her, not really listening, just looking.

When she asked how the planning application was going, he sighed and made a face, indicating what he was up against.

'Well, you hurry back,' she said fondly, while at the same time managing to convey that when he did, she expected it to be with planning approval. Humphrey decided not to mention that he'd been thinking of doing just that, hurrying back. 'And you have to keep *after* the agent,' she added. 'You're too *easy* with people sometimes.'

'He's got Home Farm on the market,' he offered helpfully. 'With a nice photo to go with it.'

Sylvia obviously thought that not worth commenting on.

'We've got to get this moving, Humphrey. The money's looking good back home, the ad's out for a UK business manager, we've a London interior design company for this place, and even designs in for the river eateries. We've got all the various quotes in now, and as soon as those people are off the houseboats we've got marine architects and surveyors on line. But there's a whole bunch of stuff we need to do yet. We cannot afford this guy to sit there, holding up the traffic, right? He's gotta push, push, push. Gotta get a few butts moving up at the planning office. OK? Humphrey?'

Humphrey looked at her with awe. And she'd only just got here. 'Yeah,' he said. 'Yeah, right.'

Sylvia pulled at the front of his gown, straightening it. 'Well, you make sure he does just that. OK?'

'You bet!' Humphrey said. And then, 'Gee, Sylvie, it's good to see you.'

He was about to fall on her again when Mrs Thomas came in with flowers she'd picked for the hall table. Humphrey, who, when it was time for bed, hoped the arrangements would change, gave her a hand taking up Sylvia's airport ensemble of Louis Vuitton luggage to one of the more habitable bedrooms.

Humphrey then gave her a tour of the Hall, apologising one minute for it, boasting about it the next, while Sylvia nodded coolly and missed nothing.

Afterwards, he ushered her into the kitchen, where Mrs Thomas was ready to put the kettle on. Sylvia, who, when tea was mentioned, had thought vaguely along the lines of a pot of Earl Grey and crumpets, served from old crested silver in the drawing room, watched as Mrs Thomas got the tea bags and Shropshire Dunks out.

Humphrey, knowing Sylvia's opinion of the more colourful aspects of his wardrobe, had changed into jeans and the only quiet shirt he had with him, his white suit shirt. Sitting at the kitchen table with Sylvia, he shook his head in bemused delight and said again that he couldn't believe she was there. Actually sitting there, just across from him.

Sylvia told him that she'd been here since Saturday.

Humphrey's mouth dropped open. 'Here?'

'Well, no, not here, in Batch Magna. I wasn't even in Shropshire.'

'The borders. We're in the Welsh borders here, Sylvie,' Humphrey said automatically, echoing Owain's insistence on that, particularly the Welsh part of it, when the conversation had gone on that day in the pub.

'We're in England here, Sir Humph! In Shropshire.' Mrs Thomas, who'd been openly listening while waiting for the kettle to boil, had him know. 'Batch Hall is in Shropshire. And don't let some people round here tell you no different. This is Shropshire, this is. England. Every bit of this estate is in England. Except for the bit that's in Wales. But that's mostly been sold off now. So that don't count no more.'

'And the village is Welsh except when it's English,' Humphrey said, following Owain's map again, and his grudging surrender to English postcodes.

Mrs Thomas folded her arms. 'Excuse me, Sir Humphrey, but the village is *English*, except when it's Welsh.'

'OK, OK, Mrs T,' Humphrey said, holding up his hands.

Sylvia had been waiting patiently. 'Anyway, as I was saying, I wasn't in Shropshire, the Welsh borders, or anywhere else. The people I was with, I doubt they'd even heard of the borders – they weren't even sure where Shropshire was.'

Sylvia had addressed herself solely to Humphrey, but this last bit was aimed at Mrs Thomas, the hired help, who was beginning to get on her nerves.

Not that it bothered Mrs Thomas. She was like that herself. She had no idea where anywhere was, beyond Church Myddle or Kingham one way, and Penycwn or Bannog the other, and Tenby for holidays in the caravan.

'Where were you then, Sylvie?' Humphrey wanted to know.

'London,' Sylvia said, as if where else?

'London? Oh, well!' Mrs Thomas said, and sniffed.

Sylvia moved in her chair, showing the house-keeper her back.

'It was a spur of the moment thing,' she told Humphrey. 'I didn't really have a lot of chance to let you know at the time. A party of us flew over for a wedding. One of our traders married British, and a bunch of us hired a jet for the weekend. The others flew back in it last night.'

Sylvia tinkled a laugh at his expression, and to Humphrey it had in it the sound of such things. Jets hired like limos for the weekend, an apartment with a uniformed doorman on the Upper East Side, and a house in East Hampton on the beach. 'People like us, Humphrey,' Sylvia had once told him, 'don't go on vacation. We either visit or we live there.'

'Gee,' Humphrey said, gazing at Sylvia. 'Gee.'

'Well, I never!' Mrs Thomas was moved to say.

'I tried ringing you on Saturday,' Sylvia said. 'And again on Sunday.'

'Yeah, well, I was probably busy somewhere,' Humphrey said evasively.

'And I could have been doing anything,' Mrs Thomas said, sounding defensive. 'Feeding the pea fowl. Putting the washing out. Anything.'

'I could have been outside somewhere. Or upstairs maybe, assessing fabric damage,' Humphrey said, a phrase he'd picked up from the agent.

'Or I might have been fetching the washing in. Same difference,' Mrs Thomas added.

Humphrey told Sylvia about the press interview he'd done last week, when the local news hounds had finally found him at home. 'I used it to put our side of things. You know, how we're bringing jobs and money and all that to the area,' he said, while Sylvia frowned at the idea of Humphrey putting their "side of things".

'They were all going on about it in the shop,' Mrs Thomas said. 'Quite famous, our Sir Humph is.'

'I'll show you the press cutting later, honey. I've got them put away somewhere. Remind me to dig them out before you go,' Humphrey said hurriedly, in case Mrs Thomas mentioned what else they might have been going on about in the shop. Like compensation running at twenty thousand pounds per eviction, the last he'd heard.

'Have a Shropshire Dunk, dear,' was all Mrs

Thomas said, pushing the plate in Sylvia's direction.

Sylvia shook her head with a little smile, seeming to find even the idea of eating such a thing amusing. And then watched as Humphrey reached for them.

In honour of the guest, Mrs Thomas had brewed the tea in a pot. 'Having a cuppa with us, Mrs T?' Humphrey asked cheerfully as she was pouring, and laughed. It was a word that still made him feel like breaking out in a knees-up, or whatever it was called.

Sylvia, with a small bright smile, said she was sure Mrs Thomas had things she wanted to do, and Mrs Thomas said yes, that was right, dear, she hadn't finished the dusting yet, bless Sir Humph's heart for asking, him and his cuppas, and what did he want her to do about dinner? 'She means lunch,' Humphrey told Sylvia.

Sylvia said that before she could even begin to think about anything she *had* to have a shower. She'd had to change trains three times to reach here. *Three* times. 'God! Talk about a backwater. And then there was no taxi at the station, at Church . . .'

'Myddle,' Humphrey supplied.

Sylvia shook her head, seeming to find even the name at fault. 'Amazing – not one taxi. At a rail station! Would you believe? I had to wait ages. I mean,' she added on a laugh, 'is that outrageous, or what?' She looked at Mrs Thomas as if challenging her with it.

Mrs Thomas said she couldn't agree more. 'You should have tried the betting shop, dear. They're never out of there. There or the Red Lion.'

Humphrey made a face. 'Honey, I have to tell you, we don't have a shower. We've got a bath tub, though,' he added, and looked at Mrs Thomas, as if to back him up.

'Oh, yes, we've got a bath,' Mrs Thomas said airily. 'We've got two bathrooms in fact, if you count the one off the master bedroom. Only the ceiling's come in on that.'

Sylvia found the absence of a shower amazing as well, but her heart no longer seemed to be altogether in it.

She sighed. 'Well, it will just have to be a quick tub, then.'

Sylvia took a sip of tea and started to rise, her expression suggesting it would be no loss to leave the rest of it there.

'You can't have it *yet*, dear,' Mrs Thomas said with a little laugh at the idea. 'We have to put the immersion on first!'

Sylvia, with massive patience, sat down again.

Humphrey smiled at her. 'It doesn't take long, Sylvie.'

'Oh, no,' Mrs Thomas agreed. 'Be nice and hot in about an hour – hour and a half. I'll put it on in a minute.'

'Good. And I'll have it later. Thank you, Mrs Thomas,' Sylvia said, dismissing her. 'We'll have lunch first,' she told Humphrey. 'We'll eat out somewhere. Wherever you recommend.' And where she could keep an eye on his diet.

Humphrey frowned heavily, seeming to be thinking about it, although the several trips he'd made to the cake trolley in the Church Myddle tea shop made up the extent of any eating out.

'You could always try the pub,' Mrs Thomas suggested, and Sylvia glanced sharply at her, making it clear she was surprised, even astonished, to find her still there. 'Though I don't know what the food's like now, I'm sure,' Mrs Thomas went blithely on, 'now Carl's not there. He was supposed to be a good cook, he was.'

'The pub chef,' Humphrey told Sylvia. 'He left, over his girlfriend. She had an affair with . . .'

'An affair, Sir Humph? An affair? *One* affair?'

Mrs Thomas had to sit down.

'We stopped counting at five. And all in the space of a few weeks. I doubt that little trollop has even heard of the word, 'no' – in Welsh or English.'

Mrs Thomas lifted the teapot lid to see if there was enough left, and got up to get a cup for herself.

'I'm as broadminded as the next person, anybody will tell you that' she said, sitting back down. 'It's no business of mine what people get up to. Live and let live, that's my motto. But some of the things I've heard about that one!'

'Yeah, but how it came to a head, Mrs T,' Humphrey said, pushing the sugar across to her, 'was over Phineas Cook – one of the guys off the paddlers, the houseboats,' he added to Sylvia. 'You see, Phin and Sally—'

'That's Phineas Cook's girlfriend, dear,' Mrs Thomas told her.

'Right. They were going out together, see, when Phin went with Lucy, and Carl found out—'

'And then Sally did,' Mrs Thomas put in.

'And then Sally did. But before that, Carl did. That's the main thing, Mrs T. That's how Carl got to leave, right?'

'Not before trying to murder 'em, he didn't,' Mrs Thomas said, helping herself to a Shropshire Dunk.

'Not Sally,' Humphrey said.

'Well, no. Not Sally,' Mrs Thomas grudgingly agreed. 'It was just that Lucy. And Phineas Cook.'

'And I don't think he tried to murder them, Mrs T. He just went round to—'

Mrs Thomas was having none of it. 'Oh, yes, he did, Sir Humph! With an axe, from the pub's wood shed. Everybody knows that.'

'Yeah, well, anyway. You see, Sylvia,' Humphrey began, and then came up against Sylvia's expression.

'Well, it's a long story,' he added lamely, and wondered why that, too, sounded familiar.

Sylvia led the way out of the kitchen, followed by Humphrey and then Mrs Thomas, hastily finishing her tea, after Sylvia, smiling with terrible, implacable sweetness, said she was sure she wanted to get on with her dusting.

'It's all go, Mrs T,' Humphrey grinned, until Sylvia put him to work as well, suggesting that while she was upstairs getting her bag he give the agent another call.

And this time remind him that he wasn't being paid for sitting on his butt.

The agent, sounding quite excited about it, said he was glad Humphrey had phoned, because the planning application was very definitely on the move. And while it was still involved in the various procedural subcommittees necessary for the second provisional submission stage, there was every reason to believe that final processing for the formal submission for approval by the Planning Committee proper was imminent.

This was the third time Humphrey had spoken to the agent and he still wasn't entirely sure what had been said, but whatever it was, he couldn't help thinking that the agent said it, more or less, in a different sort of way, each time.

Humphrey thanked him doubtfully, and replaced the receiver.

And then, hearing Sylvia on the stairs, picked it up again, and bawled out the dialling tone. 'Look, buddy, just remember who's paying your salary, right!' he snarled at it. 'You're not dealing with local no-hopers here. Where we're from, if you haven't got your foot down you're in the way. So either hit the gas or get off the goddam freeway!'

Scowling, Humphrey banged down the phone, and was about to follow Sylvia out to the car when it rang.

It was a gunsmiths in Shrewsbury, some old guy, by the sound of it, on about a pair of shotguns the late General had put in for repair. And how, since somebody called young Mr Tomkins had retired, error, he was sorry to have to relate, had, on occasion, been allowed to creep into the back room. It had, the voice regretted to tell him, done so in this case. A slip of the pen, a *lapsus calami*, during the transcription of details from invoice to trigger-guard labels, and, in consequence, the pieces had been consigned to the wrong bench. In short, sir, instead of dispatch, they had gone into store. And it was a matter of further regret that there they had remained, undisturbed, and unfortunately undelivered, for the past year.

They would, Sir Humphrey should be assured, be dispatched forthwith, with the most sincere of apologies, and of course without charge attached.

Humphrey could not believe it. He couldn't wait to tell Sylvia. She *really* wouldn't be able to believe it.

Talk about a backwater! The whole place needs a rocket up its butt, he said, telling her about it in the car.

'Amazing,' he said, tutting and shaking his head over it. '*Amazing!*'

CHAPTER 24

The following morning, Humphrey stood at the large, leaded bow window of the master bedroom, with its frieze of armorial colours running along the top panes, gazing out in a glum sort of way at Batch Magna and the hills beyond. He didn't know what it was he felt, only that he wished he wasn't feeling it. He had felt it before while here, and could only guess that it must be homesickness.

He heard Mrs T pottering below, rattling the morning bucket of maize for the peafowl. He'd miss her cooking – not that his mom wasn't a much better cook, he told himself loyally, and dishonestly. But his mom couldn't nip over to Mr Stretch's for home-made sausages and cured back bacon, and well-hung beef, and tender-sweet lamb and belly pork with crackling you could sharpen your teeth on, and shop-filled pies the size of dinner plates.

He was wondering vaguely what the cost might be of shipping supplies of Mr Stretch's goods over to New York, when Sylvia knocked on his door to say she was ready, as she had knocked

291

on his door last night, and looking just as desirable.

The relationship had yet to get to bed, and he'd hoped that last night might do the trick. A New York girl, alone with him in an empty house, full of ancient shadows and things that go bump. And with all that silence and dark outside, and the owls hooting like in a ghost story. And if she didn't want somebody to cuddle up to with all that going on, then Humphrey did.

He was dithering with lust and indecision, wondering whether to knock on her door under the guise of a little manly reassurance, when she knocked on his to wish him goodnight. She was wearing a black silk nightdress and a negligee trimmed with lace, which showed little and so promised more, her body scented and mysterious in it, her skin under the diaphanous material warm to his touch when he kissed her.

She had pulled away as if unable to trust herself, her fingers curled in a small regretful wave at the door, her gaze holding his as she closed it slowly, lingeringly, behind her.

She'd said when they'd first met that she wanted sex between them to be special for both, to be something they shared only in marriage. It was ridiculously old-fashioned, she knew, but that was how she was. And Humphrey had nodded dumbly, and said how much he admired her for it. And he was still admiring her for it last night, grimly, for a good hour after she'd left him, alone and unsleeping in that big bed.

Yesterday evening they had eaten nouvelle cuisine in a restaurant in Kingham, and earlier this morning, while Sylvia, fresh from a run and a bath, had nibbled on fruit in the breakfast-room, Humphrey had started his diet. He'd had two slices of wholemeal and some of the low-fat spread of a bilious-looking yellow Sylvia had bought that afternoon in a health food shop in Church Myddle, while Mr Stretch's parcels of goods languished downstairs in the kitchen fridge.

This morning they were going riding. Humphrey was in jeans again, and to please Sylvia, another quiet shirt, one of the General's Viyellas Mrs Thomas had found in the airing cupboard. Sylvia, carrying a crop and black velvet riding hat, was in the lemon jodhpurs she'd brought with her, and a tailored black velvet coat, a white silk stock falling between her small, high breasts, the coat swinging open in a way which invited arms around her waist. Humphrey groaned inwardly.

Mrs Thomas said the nearest stables she knew of were those of the Batch Valley Chase, the other side of the village, and on the way there in the hired Ford Sylvia had him drive along the Hams first so that she could look at the site for the holiday village.

Stopping in Upper Ham, and hoping Phineas or no one else was about, Humphrey also pointed out the five Masters' Cottages, the remains, with the Keeper's Cottage, of the estate's housing stock. Only four were inhabited, the fifth was letting in the weather through a hole in its roof and was badly in need of repair.

Sylvia knew all about them. 'And as soon as we get planning permission,' she said, prepared to consider no alternative, 'and we don't have to worry about upsetting any locals that might matter, the notices can go out on all four of them. Then we can talk selling. We need the capital.'

Humphrey thought about his promise to spend a good chunk of that capital in compensation, and was silent. He must, he thought, remember to ring Frank and tell him.

'And we'll also need some figures in on them. Like, whether there's more profit in upgrading them for the open market, or fixing the fifth cottage and selling them on as they are. That's the agent's job. And I suggest that if he's not on the same page as us by the end of the week we fire him. Get someone who can hack it.'

'Give him the old Harry Slingers. Right,' Humphrey muttered, nodding grim agreement.

'One of them's a shorthold tenancy, right?' Sylvia said as Humphrey drove on.

'A young village couple.' Humphrey made a face. 'With a new baby.'

'And two months left on the tenancy,' Sylvia said, surprising him again with her grasp of detail. 'So what's the problem? They've had four months paying next to no rent. And the others are old people. Paying zilch rent.' She laughed briefly at such a thing. 'Yeah?'

'They're estate pensioners, Sylvie. That's the way the General—'

'Yeah, right. Well, that was yesterday. That's the past, Humphrey. We're the future. Let local government pick up the tab for them. Let them give them a home. They've paid their taxes. Right?'

'Yeah, right,' Humphrey said.

When they drove up past the pub and down into Lower Ham to look at the plot of the last houseboat, the *Felicity H*, Sylvia said the place looked like a junkyard. That had also been Humphrey's first impression.

'That's where Owain Owen lives,' he said with some indignation. 'The guy I told you about last night, the one who knows all about the shooting and fishing and that around here. In fact,' Humphrey went on, boasting on Owain's behalf, 'there's not a heck of a lot Owain *doesn't* know – about anything!'

Last night in the restaurant Sylvia had told him what had finally been decided about Batch Hall. It would be turned into an hotel, the flagship of a proposed chain of such hotels, combining top London and New York hotel standards with an English country house ambience. And which, starting with the Hall, would include the lucrative sidelines of shooting and fishing. With bits of old England, in the shape of country houses, regularly coming under the hammer, the idea was to extend this, targeting at first the American and Japanese markets in this country, and then seeking an international profile.

And Humphrey, listening to it all, felt he had an international profile already. A mover and shaker at last, sitting back at the table with a cigar and the champagne he'd ordered to go with their future.

It was nearly feeding time in the kennels when the Ford drew into the hunt's front yard, and the hounds knew it.

They stood, panting with frantic stillness, quiveringly alert for the familiar squeak and rattle over the cobbles of a barrow piled with raw meat, before dashing off and back again, jumping up at the bars of the lodges, yelping and clambering over each other, their coats glowing, honey and white, in the sun.

In the small backyard beyond, the headless carcasses of a couple of cows and a sheep lay, flayed and guttered on the cobbles, their blood washed down to a drain in the front yard by Ffion Owen with buckets of water and a bass broom.

When Sylvia and Humphrey got out of the car, Ffion greeted Humphrey but her eyes were on his companion, the stranger with him, frankly and admiringly missing nothing, down to the exquisite hand-stitching on Sylvia's soft black leather boots.

Clem was just leaving the battered caravan that served as an office after taking a phone call there.

She'd been working in the backyard, and her boots and the plastic apron she was wearing were stained with blood. Sunlight winked on the bloodied blade of the large butcher's knife she'd taken in with her, and blood was drying on her bare arms and was even smeared across her forehead where she'd wiped off sweat.

But Humphrey recognised her immediately.

He slowed to a halt and waited, a nervous smile hovering.

'We'd like to hire two mounts for the morning. Can you do that?' Sylvia said, getting down to business, and frowning slightly at the smell and the din.

'I don't mind what I sit but Sir Humphrey here must have something quiet. He's a novice.'

Clem smiled vaguely at her, and brushing hair from her face with the back of her hand, said to Humphrey: 'I was going to ring you, Sir Humphrey. To apologise for Saturday. After talking to Ffion Owen I realised that – well, that things weren't quite that simple. Anyway, I had no right to say what I said. It was appallingly rude of me, and I apologise unreservedly,' she added gruffly, another echo of her father. 'I hope you feel able to accept it.'

Humphrey looked embarrassed. 'Yeah! Of course!' he said, sweeping it away with a large hand. 'We had a few words,' he explained to

Sylvia, and laughed. 'She had my ears burning all day.'

Humphrey grinned on at Clem, before remembering Sylvia.

'Hey, I'm sorry! This is Sylvia, Sylvia Warner, and this is the . . . er . . . Honourable . . .'

'Clem will do.'

She smiled politely at Sylvia, and despaired.

She knew she would never look like that in a riding outfit, no matter how much she paid for it. And how did she do that with her make-up? How did she manage to look as if she wasn't wearing any, while at the same time it was perfectly obvious that she was?

Clem thought of the ruin of her own make-up, glimpsed in a mirror in the caravan. And for the first time in the five years of doing the job was uncomfortably aware of how she looked in her working clothes.

She wiped at her hair again with the back of her hand, and slid the knife further out of sight behind her.

Sylvia nodded at the introduction and said, '*Do you have two mounts we can hire?*'

'Well,' Clem said, 'we're the local hunt's stables and kennels. We do have guest mounts, but . . .'

'Better make mine a big 'un,' Humphrey said, patting his substantial frame. 'A cart horse – no, wait. Better make that *two* cart horses. And a cart,' he added, encouraged by Clem's response.

Ffion, eavesdropping while busy sweeping at

nothing a few yards from them, looked at her friend with interest. Humour had never been Clem's strong suit, nor, judging by what she'd heard, was it Sir Humphrey's. But there they were, nearly having hysterics together.

Sylvia smiled in a strained sort of way, and then tried again. 'Do you . . .?'

Clem composed herself. But Humphrey had spotted the knife. He pointed at it in mock horror, and threw his hands up, something else they both found irresistible.

Sylvia already felt obscurely wrong-footed by Humphrey knowing Clem, a yard worker with that accent, and a title, and now this. She felt that the joke, whatever it was, was somehow on her.

'Or would you like me to report you!' Her voice cut through the laughter.

'What?' Clem said, pulling herself together, and not sure if she'd heard correctly.

'Perhaps you don't need our money.'

'Report me?' Clem asked, puzzled. 'What for?'

Sylvia wasn't at all sure, but she had gone too far now. 'For rudeness,' she snapped.

She looked round the yard with distaste. 'Who's in charge here? Who pays your wages?'

'Sylvie!' Humphrey protested feebly.

'As joint master of the hunt on today, I'm in charge, I suppose,' Clem told her. 'These yards belong to the hunt, as I believe I've said. The hunt members pay my wages through their subscriptions.'

She stared at Sylvia, and blew upwards, hard, at a stray wisp of hair.

'The hunt,' Sylvia sneered. 'Damned British snobbery and elitism!' A remark which, coming from Sylvia, sent Humphrey's eyebrows up. Apart from anything else, she had, he knew, hunted herself in the past with a cousin of hers in Virginia.

'Balls!' Clem said deliberately. She had learned her language in the hunting field as well as the yards. 'The other joint master happens to be a man called John Beecher. John is a coalman.'

The two women glared at each other, and then Sylvia turned on her heel. 'I'd like to go now, Humphrey,' she said abruptly.

'Oh, I should,' Clem said. 'You don't want to get that smart outfit of yours dirty, do you. And anyway, I doubt we've got anything posh enough for your bum!'

It hadn't quite come out as she meant it to, and she glanced sharply at Ffion, who very obviously was only pretending to work, and just as obviously had found it very amusing.

'Yeah, well, bye,' Humphrey said, glumly preparing to follow Sylvia and hesitating over it.

'Humphrey,' Sylvia called, pausing impatiently.

'Goodbye, Sir Humphrey,' Clem said, sounding stiff, formal, cold even. Which wasn't at all what she meant.

'Humphrey!' Sylvia said sharply.

'Humph, please,' Humphrey said to Clem. 'Call me Humph.'

Clem bobbed her head awkwardly, with a sudden shyness. 'Goodbye. Humph,' she said solemnly.

'Yeah. Yeah, bye, Clem,' he said, not moving, just standing there, grinning at her.

'*Hum-phrey*!' Sylvia complained from the Ford.

CHAPTER 25

They had met for drinks on the morning of the regatta as they usually did, this time on the *Belle*. Another morning of sun and mist, a haze on the hills lingering on under a starched blue sky.

They were there on their own, crew only as the Commander put it. Apart from Jasmine's baby daughter, that is, asleep in the fringed shade of her pram, the rest of Jasmine's clan safely in the custody of their usual babysitter from the village. Daniel, staying on for the fun, had taken the Frogeye, with Bill Sikes sitting up in the passenger seat, into Kingham, and it was a good hour yet before Sally and other people would start arriving. They lifted their glasses to each other.

It was ten o'clock, the yardarm, as the Commander also had put it, lowered for the regatta. And they were drinking champagne, because it would be the last time they would be doing this.

'Sham pain,' Phineas said, 'to your real friends. Real pain to your sham friends.'

They drank to that.

'Nice weather for it,' Priny observed, waving at

the day with her cigarette holder, viewing it from behind a pair of large white-framed sunglasses. She was wearing a wide-brimmed pink raffia hat, with a pink chiffon scarf trailing down the back, and a faultlessly pressed cream shirt and wide-legged trousers, with red deck shoes the colour of her lipstick and nail extensions, the air around her scented with Guerlain.

'Lovely day, it is. *Lovely*,' Owain said.

And it was as if he'd had it all to himself earlier, out in the pram dinghy at dawn, going over the course the racing gigs would take from Water Lacy. Looking, perhaps, for overnight skulduggery in a mist which muffled his oars, with only a few feeding mallards and swans for company, and a silence broken now and then by the abrupt splashing of bickering coots in and out of the trailing willows, and the odd squeal and hiss of a water rail in the reed beds.

Owain laughed. 'Bet the boys won't think so, though. Pulling away later in it.'

'Sion had a good breakfast, I trust,' the Commander said, the smoke from his briar drifting over the river, the colour of the haze on the hills. 'Plenty of carbohydrates?'

'Plenty of eggs and bacon, if that's what you mean,' Owain said. 'The bugger cleaned us out, he did.'

'And beans,' Annie said. 'And sausages, toms and black pudding, and toast.' She had made the most of getting her hands on a son living away from home.

'Just the job,' the Commander approved. 'He'll need it.'

'I'm on a diet, I am,' Jasmine said, provoked. 'One slice of rotten old brown bread and tea without milk – as well as no sugar. Duw!'

The Commander looked aghast. 'What! Today, Jasmine?'

Jasmine looked no less aghast. 'No! Not today, I'm not. No. Go back on it tomorrow, I will,' she said, and finished her champagne off to show intent.

Phineas lifted the bottle from the silver-plated wine cooler and stand – "guaranteed to impress at dinner parties" – from another of Bryony's catalogues.

They would believe the promised compensation when they'd started spending it, which most of them had done almost immediately after being promised it, making plans for it in their heads. But with it or without it, the future still waited, and they talked about that now.

Jasmine and her family were moving to a local authority house in her home town of Bannog, and Priny and the Commander, after their sensible daughter had been busy, to Church Myddle, to something called sheltered housing – or leeward homes, as they preferred. Annie and Owain had found a place to rent through a cousin, a cottage in Little Batch, with room for the three children still at home.

Phineas was asked if he knew where he was going yet. He said he didn't. Hadn't the faintest idea.

The *Belle* had been let furnished, so when his time was up he had simply to pack his things and go, leave as he had arrived. If he stayed in the area it would only be because of Sally, and he wasn't sure he wanted that now, or wanted it enough. Or something.

He wasn't sure what he wanted, if he couldn't have their world, their river back. A place safe for one thing from having to make hardly any decisions at all. He could *think* about things, all sorts of things. He could be as decisive and purposeful as he liked, without having to actually *do* anything about it.

By the river, on it or in it, it doesn't matter. Nothing seems really to matter, or not matter very much, and that's the charm of it, as Ratty knew. Whether you get away, or whether you don't, whether you arrive at your destination or whether you reach somewhere else, or whether you never get anywhere at all. That was their river, that was their world, all right, and they didn't want any other.

And now they were losing it. Had already lost it. If planning permission wasn't given, then Humphrey would have to sell. So if it wasn't Humphrey it would be somebody else. The door had been opened now on that world, and would stay open.

What they needed, Owain had said, was somebody like them, only rich.

'People do not get rich, darling,' Priny had pointed out, 'by being like us.'

'Funny how we don't seem to hate him,' Phineas

said, bearing a fresh bottle from the fridge. 'Or even dislike him particularly.'

The Commander looked surprised by the remark. 'There's nothing *funny* about it, at all. We're all civilised, reasonable people here. Not without a certain sympathy for his position. And it was bound, after all, to have happened sooner or later. As I have pointed out, it's the times, my boy, the way of the world. Our little lot here of no consequence in the great scheme of these things, and soon forgotten. Soon lost to memory. Like a few yards of motorway where once a farmhouse stood.' The Commander, in the mood to be philosophical, paused to relight his pipe. 'Indeed, if we look at Sir Humphrey as that motorway . . .'

'Well, he's the right sort of size,' Priny agreed. 'Like one of the wide bits, say, on the M1.'

'If we look at Sir Humphrey as that motorway,' the Commander continued patiently, while his wife giggled with Jasmine, 'we begin to see it the right way up. While we may rightly deplore the forces that made that motorway, the modern logic which drove it so wantonly through our past, we do not call the thing itself to account, accuse its mute stone and tarmacadam. No, as reasonable people, we take the view—'

Phineas had heard enough. 'We were plotting to murder him only a week or so ago,' he reminded him.

The Commander looked amused. 'Oh, *that*.'

'Yes, that. We were talking of bumping him off. That was the sort of civilised and reasonable view we were taking then.'

'I don't think any of it was actually *meant*, darling,' Priny said.

'Course it wasn't!' Owain scoffed. 'It was just us being a bit angry, like, about things, that's all. Natural enough, isn't it? We don't have to *like* it as well, do we?' he enquired of Phineas with a wounded sort of air.

Owain still seemed sometimes not to have entirely grasped the reasons for them having to leave the river. He'd stopped running his head against the idea but could still look both puzzled and wounded by it, like a bull having finally to accept a brick wall while still not fully understanding why.

'That's not what you said then.' Annie, who'd been grinning and coo-cooing at Jasmine's daughter, sat down again and looked at her husband. 'Or you, James,' she added to the Commander. 'Mad keen you were to bump him off then. A bomb under his car, if I remember right.'

'And what about you, then?' Owain shot back. 'Miss Goody Two-Shoes! What about you and your anonymous present of fruit, poisoned with a syringe of rat killer? Stones and glasshouses, my girl, stones and glasshouses!' Owain's voice shook righteously.

'Still, we're not going to kill him now, are we? So that's all right then, isn't it,' Jasmine said with a placatory smile.

'Wouldn't be a lot of point now, would there,' Phineas said. 'There'd still be Uncle Frank. And if it wasn't this Uncle Frank, it would be some other.' He shook his head. 'There's no shortage of Uncle Franks in the world.'

'Though I still think Sarah would have inherited if Sir Humph *had* got knocked off,' Jasmine added. 'Then we could all have stayed here, and not have to go. And nothing would change. Ever.'

And Jasmine, who loved a happy ending, held her glass to her generous, giving bosom, and smiled fondly at the thought.

Shortly after that, Annie took her entries in the family Land Rover along to the field on which the show part of the Batch Magna Regatta and Show, to give it its full title, was to be held.

Miss Wyndham, as a member of the subcommittee – church fete and flower – of the regatta committee, was busily on hand with her clipboard to give her the exact time of the judging for the home-made wine and spirits section.

Later, Miss Wyndham, as she did every year, would watch the races from the *Cluny Belle*, the nearest paddler to the finishing line. It was another thing to look forward to on a day of things to look forward to. And Miss Wyndham intended that neither thoughts of the past nor of the future should interfere with that.

More people were arriving on the ground, most of them strangers, which added to the excitement, the cars directed, with a great deal of whistle blowing and hand signalling, to an adjacent field by the Church Myddle Scout Troop. The big grain trailer, from which Sarah would later open events, was being dressed with newly-laundered red, white and blue bunting and the flags of two countries, and more bunting was strung across the field on poles, along with fairy lights ready for the evening, and the sound system tested again.

All this, and the fun on the river, the crowning of the Regatta Princess, and the jazz band and funfair still to come. Miss Wyndham hummed with a surge of pleasure and anticipation.

She decided next to follow Annie to the marquee which would house the horticultural show, with relays of fruit and flowers, boxes and baskets, bottles and jars, vegetables, watering cans and dust sheets disappearing into it.

She wanted, among other things, to see if Mrs Llewellyn, the winner last year of the Davies Cup for most points in the flower section, had surpassed herself again this year, and to get a look at the marrows Tom Parr had been boasting about for the past couple of weeks, winking in the shop and going on about having to get Pickfords in to move them. And, despite herself, what Colonel Ash had finally decided to submit, and whether Miss Armitage was likely to triumph again in the flower-arranging section.

They were on Taddlebrook Leasow, a long stretch of Home Farm pasture running down to the Cluny.

Later the marquee would turn into a beer tent, with something like a small county show then on the ground, and in the evening the jazz band on the grain trailer, and down at the river end the annual funfair lighting the summer darkness.

By midday, families from the village and from miles around both sides of the border had turned the river into the seaside.

They sunbathed on its banks, and sat with ice-cream and hotdogs, sandwiches, flasks of tea and bottles of beer and wine. They swam and paddled in it, and boated, where they could find space, the water boisterous with children on inflatable rubber and tractor tyres and home-made rafts, clambering all over it like some large, amiable pet.

And Sally, arriving on the crowded deck of the *Belle*, thought she had never seen Phineas looking quite so dashing. He was in white flannels, in need of a press, she thought, but quite clean, a shirt with broad red stripes, and an ancient-looking straw hat, its red ribbon dressed with flowers from the Cunninghams' garden.

Phineas, after putting a glass of Chablis in her hand, introduced her to a couple of friends from Chelsea days, up for the regatta. Jeremy Bryant, who was also a crime writer, in a boater and a green-and-white blazer striped like a deckchair, and Jack Norton, a painter. Jeremy was too busy with Jack's girlfriend to do anything but nod, but Jack seemed immediately to take to her. He said he'd like to paint her. Naked, he decided. At first light in a Home Counties garden. An English rose among roses, opening herself to the sun. He would call it Aurora.

'Jack's an old roué,' Phineas said. 'Past it now, of course. Be kind to him, Sal.'

Sally just thought how uncomfortable it sounded.

Ignoring Phineas, Jack looked deep into her eyes and said he'd like to make her his muse, and spend the rest of his life painting only her.

And then moved on to say more or less the same thing to Clem Wroxley. While Jack's girlfriend, a dark sultry girl in a leopard print bikini top and tight red shorts, a tattooed snake entwined around one leg from her ankle, its head nestling on her inner thigh, was leaning against the deck wall of the living room with Jeremy Bryant, her arms trailing from his neck.

Phineas was talking to Sally by a couple of Annie's trestle tables, loaded with food and drink. Jeremy, closely followed by his wife, Roz, breezed in, and removing his boater as if about to start crooning to her, or to ask for her hand, introduced himself with a little joke about being otherwise engaged when Sally had first arrived.

Looking amused by it, he explained that Delphine, Jack's girlfriend, was, extraordinarily enough as it turned out, a fan of his work. 'She insists that I walk the same mean streets as Chandler and Dashiel Hammett,' Jeremy said with a modest laugh at the idea, and glancing at Phineas.

While Roz, furiously spooning a second bowl of strawberries and cream she'd grimly helped herself to, hissed at Sally, 'Never marry a bloody writer – they're total arses! Absolute bloody *bastards*!'

Sally was saved from having to find something to say to that by the sound of a motor launch and loud hailer on the river. And then the public address system, sitting on the stewards' table on Taddlebrook Bank, crackled into life, adding to the call for the water to be cleared.

The two racing gigs were on the home stretch from Water Lacy.

CHAPTER 26

The two boats looked neck and neck, coming round a bend in the river. Phineas, glasses glued to his eyes, saw the Trafalgar blue and gold singlets of Batch Magna, and the black and red of Water Lacy, and watched their bright oars rising and falling, shining briefly in the sun.

He could almost hear their grunts, could almost feel the growing drag of water in their arms as they pulled on, heads down and blinded with sweat.

There was no cox to tell them how near they might be, when the torture might end. The Cluny gigs were coxwainless, a tradition dating back to 1905, when the Batch Magna cox – an Englishman, as Owain had observed – slipped overboard on the home stretch to lighten the boat, immediately followed when spotted by the Water Lacy cox.

For Phineas, they carried memories of school-days on their oars, the best of his time there. Even in winter, scarf tucked into his rowing blazer, hands caned with the cold, the river had meant escape.

But when he thought of that time now it was

always summer in his memory, summer and an early morning Thames at Windsor, when voices echoed again from the boathouse slips and called on the water, sculling through its green shade in boats as nimble and as frail looking as dragonflies, the spires of Eton slipping away behind them.

And it was that as much as anything, a memory lit with a single scene of summer and the river, that he would salute when the gigs crossed the finishing line astern of the *Belle*, lifting an ancient-looking straw boater decked with flowers.

The prize the victors of the regatta's main event would carry off was called the Cluny Challenge Cup. Which wasn't a cup at all, but a battered red fire bucket with a brass plate with that name on it and the date it was first won, and stencilled on it in white the name of the paddle steamer it was taken off, the PS *Sabrina*.

The cup, which Water Lacy won last year, and which, until that morning, had sat in its honoured place behind the bar of the Waterman Arms there, waited now, filled with Black Boy bitter, on the stewards' table.

The gigs were still neck and neck, the roar from their supporters growing as they pulled for the finishing line, a white-painted rope bobbing gently on the surface, strung across the water between two skiffs.

The Batch Magna gig was on the Mawr Wood side of the river, the Water Lacy boat on the village side. And each year there was a body of opinion which held afterwards that whichever side the winning crew had been on, that was the side with the natural advantage.

This year it would be the Mawr Wood side.

Somehow, agonisingly, out of nowhere, the Batch Magna crew started to inch ahead. Determined, perhaps, not to lose this time, particularly this time. Determined that if this was to be the last regatta, then the cup, this time, would come back to Batch Magna.

And Owain, leaning over the stern rail of the *Belle*, and unable to stand the excitement any longer, put his head in his hands and then watched through his fingers as the Batch Magna gig, skippered by the son he'd taught to row almost before he could walk, surged first across the line. Followed, only a few strokes later, by the Water Lacy boat, the oarsmen slumping, steaming like horses, over their sculls.

The crews jumped in to cool off, and pushed their gigs in to Taddlebrook Bank, where Sion, two-handed and with ease, lifted the prize and held it up to renewed cheering from their supporters, before taking the first, deep, quenching drink, beer dribbling over his chin.

The cup had come home.

After the main event came the Vaughan-Powell Schools Cup, Monmouth College and Shrewsbury School this year, the parents swanking on picnic blankets, eating poached salmon salads and punnets of strawberries, and drinking river-cooled Veuve Clicquot. And then the Shrewsbury Challenge Cup, originally a trophy raced for by rival glove and shoe factories outside that town, and now a prize sought yearly by rowing clubs from a furniture depository and a bedding warehouse. And a cup for other clubs, from both sides of the border, followed finally by the Ladies Challenge Cup, open to anyone fit enough to get into a boat. And then the fun began.

First came the paddleboats, the fancy dress entries, among them a giant yellow plastic duck with a pantomime Mother Goose waving from it, an Edwardian bobby puffing away on a bike, and a pram, the baby in it an eighteen-year-old blonde, showing her frilly knickers and sucking on a dummy. And then the floats, one from Church Myddle fire station, a mock-up bright red engine, with ladders and a big brass bell, and a pump drawing river water, and spraying it in bursts at the spectators. And a float called the Tarts' Parlour, on which members of Penycwn rugby club, reclined enticingly, and showed a bit more muscular, fishnet-stocking thigh for the approach.

There was a four-poster bed, a department store float, towed down from Shrewsbury by road that morning, with two buxom girls in baby doll nighties pillow fighting on it, and one from Kingham General, with nurses dressed as nurses in male dreams should be dressed. The agricultural college near Llandovey had entered a tractor this year, with straw-sucking yokels in smocks, and there were two floats with papier-mâché castle turrets, one flying the flag of Wales, the other St George. The air of Batch Magna loud again with an old battle, fought with wooden swords and shields, and ending as usual in both sides getting a ducking.

After that came the tug-of-war across the river, the final event of the regatta, and then people went back on the water or started to drift off to see what was happening on Taddlebrook Leasow.

Jasmine was already there, in the bell tent she used for outside events. Owain was listed to race a couple of his hob ferrets, and Jack Norton had rushed back for his sketch pad, the pages of it soon rapturously filled with the leaping thighs and calves of a troupe of female Morris Dancers in Lincoln-green silk shorts and singlets. And Miss Wyndham and Priny were at the funfair, tittering like teenagers behind a wooden cut-out apiece, their heads where the heads of two bathing beauties should be, giving them skimpy bikinis and figures of saucy-postcard proportions.

There was a goat and a dog show, children's sports and field events, a fire-eater, a falconer and an escapologist. The Regatta Princess was crowned, and with three of her attendants, all in Tudor dress, did her lap of honour, waving as if born to it from the back of John Beecher's decorated wagonette, pulled by a pair of plaited and beribboned glossy Welsh cobs.

And the Church Myddle Stompers started to warm up on the grain trailer, and the fairy lights, and the lights of the funfair, grew brighter, and the rooks quietened in the sycamores on the edge of Mawr Wood as dusk fell, and the midges swarmed over the river.

CHAPTER 27

Humphrey had said goodbye to Batch Hall, inside and out, wandering about the place in his Brooks Brothers executive suit while the regatta went by his back lawns, feeling more of a visitor than ever.

He was flying out tomorrow, and in his mind he was already on his way, had already travelled a good distance from this place, from Batch Magna. On the freeway at last with his foot down.

He had heard that morning that subject to a few alterations regarding drainage, the planning application for the riverside holiday village had been successful.

Now all he had to do was to tell the paddlers.

Now all he had to do was to dash any lingering hope there might have been of a last-minute reprieve. For the moment, as far as Batch Magna was concerned, only he knew about it, and he wanted them to hear it from him first.

He should have told them right after the agent had phoned him. He knew that. He'd been through all that, what he should have done. And he should have told the pensioners in person that they were being given notice. And he should have told Frank about the compensation he'd promised. And if he'd told Frank, and got that OK'd first, it would have made it easier for him to tell the pensioners, he knew that, as well. He still hadn't told the pensioners but he would be telling Frank the minute he got back. But right at this moment he had enough to goddam do telling the houseboats, in person, face to face.

After, that is, he'd had his tea. And then checked again the inventories he'd been working on for most of the week with the agent, inventories that had to be done, no matter what the outcome of the planning application. The list of things put aside for Sarah, and the list of things that were to stay, and the list of things to be chucked. Leaving the door open for more strangers, his last act as Sir Humphrey of Batch Hall.

And he knew all about that as well. And if anybody in his position could do any better, then let them goddam do it. That's all he had to say. That's all he *had* been saying since arriving. And the sooner he was leaving the better!

It was late evening when Humphrey walked out to the hired Ford, because he'd stayed for his dinner as well, a last plateful of Mr Stretch's cold cuts, a pork pie and salad, left in the fridge by Mrs T. And he was still wearing his Brooks Brothers executive suit because today he felt nearer to his dad than he had ever felt.

He'd had one hopeful eye on his memory from

the beginning. And now, after he must have disappointed him so many times, he felt that, at last, he might have won his approval.

And this time he would not fail him. This time he would touch down with it or die trying.

He had to. He'd mortgaged his inheritance to get his stake in it, putting all that fate had already given him on this one spin of the wheel. If he didn't end up a winner this time he'd be back burning burgers.

Humphrey paused by the Ford, the lights of the funfair down by the Cluny bruising the sky above it a tender yellow, the sound of the fun reaching him on the night air.

He drove past Taddlebrook Leasow with scarcely a glance and at the junction on the edge of the village turned down into Upper Ham.

He'd had enough of Batch Magna and its river to last him a lifetime. He couldn't believe that on this visit he'd been here for a mere two weeks and a bit. It felt much, much longer than that. He felt aged in the place, in its petty squabbles and dramas, its drinking, and gossip. He felt sometimes that he had always been here.

Bill Sikes barked at him from the darkened deck of the *Belle*, and he could see from the lane that only the underway lamps were burning on the *Batch Castle*, green for starboard, red for port. For a journey, any journey, that would now never be made.

Jasmine's babysitter told him she was reading

futures at the show, and in Lower Ham the Owens'
young son, Iwan, standing at the top of the
gangway of the *Felicity H*, with the sound of
giggling from the dark of the deck behind him,
said his parents had gone to the pub.

But they weren't there, nor were any of the
others, and he tried to keep his eyes off Lucy
the barmaid's breasts, more out of her dress than
in it, as she told him that the river lot *had* been in
earlier but had left, probably for the fair. And how
smart he looked, like an FBI agent, or somebody,
off the telly, he did, and handsome, too, as ever,
and wanted to know what he was having, her
smile and tone making it clear that, whatever it
was, if she had it, he was welcome to it.

Humphrey, about to leave with the news he had
still to deliver, hesitated, feeling wanted there.

He settled on Sheepsnout. An appropriate
drink, he considered, with which to say goodbye.
A half, he said.

Lucy drew him off a pint and told him she'd
heard he was going back tomorrow, which surprised
him, because he'd only decided it himself that
morning. She waved his protests at the measure,
and then his money, away.

'Dilly said if you come in, it's on the house.'

Humphrey nodded, acknowledging his due from
another business person, and told Lucy to thank
her for him.

'She's in the other bar, the gossip shop. John's
doing the beer tent, see, staying on for the fair.

So's Patrick, to make sure John don't fiddle. That's why there's no piano tonight.'

Humphrey lit a cigar to go with his Brooks Brothers executive suit, watched admiringly by Lucy.

'I like a man who smokes cigars,' she confided, leaning on the bar, her arms pushing her breasts up, watching him complacently blowing out smoke, before moving away with a lingering look at him to serve another customer.

Humphrey adjusted his Atlantic Sports Club tie, worn with his red Wall Street suspenders, in the mirrored glass behind the bar, and raised his drink in a salute to himself.

He felt he had come a long way since that day in Dotty Snape's cider shed. That had been another Humph, it seemed to him now. A much weaker, vacillating Humph, sneaking about behind an alias. Tonight, he was coming through the front door, in a suit.

He felt it wasn't just planning permission he'd been given but the green light for success. The green and red light. Underway on the SS *Sylvia*, bound for the future. He drank to that.

He watched as Lucy lifted a glass to the whisky optic, showing as much tanned bare back as front, and a good deal of thigh as she reached up in the short lemon silk dress.

She was wasted here. He'd have a word with Frank when he got back, get him to speak with the guy who'd be doing the hiring this side of the pond, see what could be done for her. He'd already pencilled Owain in for the hotel shoot and the fishing, and he decided he'd see what he could do for the others as well, while he was at it.

Humphrey stood with one hand on his lapel, cigar in the other, looking benignly about him. A man with influence, a man with better futures all round in his pocket.

'Lucy,' he insisted when she'd finished serving, 'have a drink.'

Then he had one sent through for Dilly, and decided to have another one for himself, for the road. Dilly, her hair piled up and dressed in Saturday night royal blue satin and stilettos, trailing perfume and her two miniature poodles, looked in to raise her pennyworth of gin to him, and winked.

Humphrey raised his pint, the only measure Lucy seemed to know how to pour, and winked back.

Lucy bit her lip when she told him about giving her foolish heart to the chief reporter of the Kingham News, only to have it cruelly broken when she found him in bed with the next week's subject of the Local Beauty Spot.

'My love meant nothing to him. It was something to be used, and then shown the door,' she said forlornly, before cheering up and telling Humphrey about her new boyfriend.

'He's got a car showroom in Kingham. Drives a Mercedes Benz.' She shook her wrist, jingling with slender gold hoops. 'Brought me these, he did. It was fate, him being in Kingham and me in his local paper. Written in the stars, it was. A love with our names on it. A match made in heaven,' she said, as if reading it off a packet.

She said that Phineas Cook had that Sally with him when he came in. 'Phineas said he'd seen me in the paper, and congratulated me, that's all – but talk about *daggers*, from that Sally! She said she'd seen it as well, said she'd had her fish and chips in it the next night. Jealous, see,' Lucy confided, and smiled understandingly. 'Well, at that age . . .'

Lucy said she'd seen his piece in the Church Myddle paper, and asked suggestively if he'd seen hers. '*Almost* in a bikini, I am.' And when Humphrey said that he was sorry, but he didn't think he had seen it, she said she'd show it to him, if he wanted.

'When it's a bit more private, like,' she promised in a low voice, and shook her breasts at him.

Lucy took an order for a couple of pints of Black Boy, and gripped the beer pump handle with a fall of slender bracelets down her bare arm.

Her eyes holding Humphrey's, she slid a shapely, scarlet-tipped hand, slowly, down the handle, and ran the moist tip of her tongue over her top lip.

Humphrey stared as if mesmerised, and gulped down the rest of his drink.

He let her take his empty glass, his eyes following her to the barrel of Sheepsnout. She stooped to it, and then glancing back over her shoulder, wriggled her hips at him.

'No. No, no, Lucy.' He protested feebly, as she started to pour. 'No, I got things to *do*,' he remembered.

Lucy ignored him. She gave him the drink and rested her arms again on the bar in front of him. And then leaned closer, her perfume a sudden intimacy between them.

Humphrey came forward as if pulled, slowly, by his Atlantic Sports Club necktie, his eyes drawn to the creamy depths of the valley between breasts that seemed to have been oiled by the sun.

'Still,' she purred up at him, 'always open to offers, I am. Silly to close the door *and* bolt it. Pint of mild, is it, Mr Spence?' she said then brightly, interrupted by another customer, and before going off to pull it, shook her breasts again briefly at Humphrey.

Lucy looked at him, her tongue coming out again and her hand sliding slowly down the pump handle, and up again this time, and then down, and up again. With only an evening to work on him, she didn't have time for anything more subtle.

She wouldn't at all mind being Lady Lucy. Now Sir Humph had got planning permission it wouldn't stop there, you mark my words, Mrs T had told her. Power mad, he is. He'll end up buying the entire village out. Mrs T knew that for a fact, and Lucy quite fancied Lady Mucking it over people like Dilly and that dentist's wife. He's a multi-millionaire, money to burn, he has, Mrs T knew that for a fact, as well. *Thirty thousand pounds* compensation per eviction, he's paying – for doing what Mrs T said the council had been about to do for nothing.

She knew she'd be up against it with that Sylvia, she'd recognised that immediately, on seeing her in the shop one day. But Sylvia was no longer here. Sylvia had gone back to America; everybody knew that.

After serving a few more customers, Lucy took the glass Humphrey was barely aware he'd emptied, and filled it again without asking.

'Oh, yes, almost forgot, Dilly said to tell you congrats, as well.' And seeing his expression, she added: 'On getting your planning permission. For the holiday village, like.'

Humphrey was shocked.

'How did she know about that . . .!'

'Mrs T, Mrs Thomas. She told us. She wondered what it was about, like, when you had the phone call this morning. Then she heard you ring somebody afterwards – in New York, would it be? – and tell them. And she told us,' Lucy explained, while Humphrey stood there with his mouth open.

'That's how she knew you're going back tomorrow, as well, see. Heard you making the booking then, she did. She was amazed you could do that, book a flight on a *Sunday*. Never travelled, see. Tenby, that's about as far as she's been, Mrs T. But what got me was Air India. Air India to New York, that's what she said,' Lucy went on, obviously still wondering, as Mrs T had, if Mrs T had got that bit of it right. '*Air India*, to *America*. Well, doesn't sound right, somehow, does it?' Lucy said to Humphrey, as if inviting his view. 'Not that it's any of my business, of course,' she added.

Humphrey was glad that some people considered his business to be none of their goddam business.

'What did she do then, Mrs T, huh? What did she do, come straight here after leaving the Hall? Couldn't wait, was that it?' He could not believe this.

'No-o,' Lucy laughed, amused at the thought of Mrs T holding on to a bit of gossip for that long. 'She phoned. Only about half an hour after leaving here. She cleans here in the morning first, see, before the Hall – not that you'd notice much, mind, half the time. Before we opened, it was. I was on my own here – well, apart from Mrs P.' She lifted her eyes at the name. 'In for a change, she was. But she left then – in a hurry, like,' Lucy added with a laugh. 'I was filling the shelves here when the phone went. Mrs T was ringing to tell Dilly, really, sucking up, see. But Dilly was upstairs still, so she told me, and then I rang up and told Dilly.'

'And then who did Dilly del – tell? Who,' Humphrey went on more carefully, 'who else – who's Mrs P?' it suddenly occurred to him.

'You *know* – Mrs Pugh, at the post office. Oh, no, Dilly wouldn't tell anybody,' Lucy assured him. 'Plays her cards very close to her chest, Dilly does, when it comes to business. She phoned Mrs T then, after I rang her, and after telling me not to say anything, and told Mrs T not to say anything, either.'

The call for Mrs T, from her "cousin". Humphrey shook his head at the sheer duplicity involved.

'Then Dilly phoned down and told me again,' Lucy went on, 'she said I've told Mrs T, and now I'm telling you. She said it again, then, when she come down. Not a word to anybody, she said, so I didn't. And Mrs T wouldn't dare, not after Dilly had told her not to. Be more than her job's worth, that would.'

Humphrey frowned hard, thinking about it. And then with a sort of wild shrewdness in his eyes, said, 'And what about Mrs P? What about her, then, huh?'

'She was gone before Dilly come down,' Lucy said. 'Not that it'd have mattered what Dilly told her. I said as much to Dilly, I told her, I did, but she was too busy getting a bottle of champagne up to celebrate. Not that I got a glass. Thinks I've been trying to get off with Patrick, Dilly does. She should be looking at that dentist's wife, the one who thinks she's better than anybody else. Throws herself at him, she does. Everybody knows what's going on there.'

Humphrey nodded absently at it, and finished his drink. He intended this time to be on his way. But he wanted to make sure he had it right first, and stood muttering to himself, going over it.

And then, when Lucy had finished serving again, went over it with her.

'So,' he began, 'Mrs T heard the agent phone me, and me phone the States, and make the booking, and then she phoned Dilly. Right?'

Lucy nodded. 'And I answered, and *I* phoned Dilly.'

'And Dilly phoned Mrs T and told—'

'Dilly told *me* first, not to say anything. And *then* phoned Mrs T and told her. And then phoned me. And told me *again*, then, when she come down. Not a word about this to anyone, Lucy, she said. And I haven't. Haven't said a word to a soul, I haven't.'

Lucy breathed on a glass she was polishing and looked hurt.

'No, of course you haven't, Lucy. Of course you haven't. And thank you for that, Lucy. Thank you,' he said, almost tearful with gratitude.

He said he was leaving, he was going now, Lucy. But he wanted to buy her another drink before he did so, a double, he insisted, and Dilly, send her another one through, and didn't seem to notice then, when Lucy went ahead and included him in the round.

'Lucy,' he said, lifting his glass to her. 'Lucy, Lucy-Lou, here's to you.'

And then somebody introduced himself as George Bishop, bed and breakfast proprietor, slapped Humphrey on the back, said well done, and insisted on buying him a drink. Humphrey then bought George and his wife a drink, slapped George on the back, gave him a cigar, and winked at his wife.

'*Tattydar*, Sir Humph!' Lucy cried cheerily, toasting him with another glass of something purple, decorated with a cherry and a coloured umbrella.

He watched her, up at the optics again, smiling fondly at the dimples behind her knees, and the sprinkling of freckles across her bare back, and at the thought of her breasts. He was seeing her in that big empty bed in Batch Hall. Snuggled up with her in the dark, listening to the owls with Lucy.

Humphrey finished his drink determinedly. 'Lucy,' he said, smacking the counter, 'Gotta go.'

'Oh! You off, then?' she pouted.

'Ah, but I'll be back.' Humphrey winked at her. 'I'll be back, Lucy.'

'Oh, yes, what you off to get, then?' she asked coyly.

Humphrey, who'd started for the door, turned back to the bar.

'I have to tell them, Lucy. I owe them that. I *owe* it them,' he said, gazing earnestly at her, his hands spread as if in appeal.

'Owe who what, Sir Humph?' She'd been so taken with it she almost forgot to ask. He was like whatshisname in the film last week at the Odeon, and with his American accent, and all.

'The paddlers, Lucy. All those on the paddlers.

I have to tell them the planning application went through. I *have* to, Lucy,' Humphrey said, looking almost tearful again.

Lucy was frowning. 'The paddlers? But they'll know already.' She laughed at his expression. '*Course* they will! Mrs P, she was here, wasn't she?' There were times when she wondered if Sir Humph was the full shilling. 'It'd have been all over the village – all over the valley, by the time she shut. Be in Penycwn and Kingham, by now, as well, if it wasn't for early closing.'

Humphrey looked shocked for the second time that evening.

'But how did Mrs P know? How did *she* know?'

Lucy sighed. 'Mrs P was here when Mrs T rang,' she explained patiently. 'Mrs T told me, and I told Dilly, and Mrs P *heard* me tell her – I told you, I said, that's why Mrs P left in such a hurry. Couldn't wait to start telling people, could she. Right old gossip, she is. Come in for a Guinness, then, she did, after they'd closed, to celebrate, like. Seeing as how they'll benefit. On her own, of course – well, Mr Pugh don't come in pubs, does he, him being chapel and all. Don't drink, old Ding-aling, don't. Except in his storeroom, like. That's where he hides his bottles of Bells. Behind the tinned food with his dirty books. Everybody knows that.'

CHAPTER 28

Humphrey got into his car after leaving the pub, and sat for a few moments in the passenger seat, wondering where the steering wheel had gone, before getting out again.

He thought he'd better walk back to the Hall, clear his head.

Straight back and straight to bed. And stay there this time, until it was time to leave.

He felt he'd been mugged by Batch Magna, by gossip and Sheepsnout, and Lucy's perfume. They go through your pockets and read your mail, and then bat their eyelashes at you. They mug you, and then smile and hand you your wallet back with nothing in it but horse feathers.

Humphrey went on like that, not making a lot of sense, and not caring. *He* knew what he meant, he told himself hotly, getting into more of a temper about it, and making even less sense.

He trudged on along the unlit High Street, across the junction, muttering and mumbling, and arguing with himself, and shooting up a New York finger now and then, and yelling, *Loser!* at the odd warning toot of a horn from a passing vehicle.

To hell with them. To hell with them all! And tomorrow, baby, bye-bye. Tomorrow he'll be on his way back to New York. And boy! he could not *wait*.

'*I'm heading for tomorrow and I'm never coming back!*' he sang, tunelessly and loudly serenading the night, and almost walked into Clem Wroxley.

He hadn't noticed the hunt Land Rover, which had pulled up on the grass verge by the entrance to Taddlebrook Leasow. The two men who'd been riding on the back had jumped down and were standing on the road by the time Clem left the cab, followed by Ffion Owen.

'Hello,' Clem said, looking amused. 'So it *was* you I saw back there.'

Humphrey mumbled something even he didn't catch, and waved a vague hand back in the direction of the pub.

'I see,' Clem said, looking even more amused.

She was wearing jeans that hugged her hips, and what looked like a man's check shirt, her fair hair shining like straw in the reflected light from the show ground.

Phineas's son, Daniel, one of the two men on the road, looked towards the ground as the Church Myddle Stompers swung into "Home Sweet Home".

'They've got a jazz band. Great!'

Humphrey saw the second man, a few years older than Daniel, slip a familiar arm around Clem's waist, and move it up to her breast. And he experienced a sudden, and unexpected, lowering of spirits.

Clem abruptly shrugged the arm off and muttered something in a low, furious voice. A lovers' tiff, Humphrey thought.

'I don't think you've met,' she said then to Humphrey. 'Mr Giles Heatherington – Sir Humphrey Strange.'

'Ah, the baronet from the States,' Giles drawled, his expression making it clear what he thought of that particular import. 'Over to flog off the family silver.'

'Take no notice of him, Sir Humphrey. Giles's family did all that a long time ago,' Clem said.

'Humph,' Humphrey reminded her, and hiccupped gently.

He was looking at Giles, watching him toss his hair back like Rupert goddam Brook, or whoever the hell it was. He had every intention of taking notice of him. Another remark like that and Rupert Brook would find himself dumped on his high-falutin' ass.

'Indeed,' Giles said. 'Along with almost everything else they could lay hands on.' He smiled when he said it, but it was a smile he had still not learned to like the taste of. 'Leaving one to rough it in a caravan instead of a decent hotel, within smelling distance of the hounds, and listening to them barking at nothing half the night.'

'And you snoring,' Clem said.

Humphrey wasn't interested in hearing them

going on like an old married couple, nor in watching Giles slip an arm around Clem's waist again, and then cupping a breast.

And Clem, this time, placing her hands, tenderly, on his.

He had just started to say goodnight when his words were drowned in a sudden scream of pain.

Clem had taken Giles's hand in hers and was calmly bending his fingers back.

'She warned him about that,' Ffion told Humphrey cheerfully. 'She did that last week to a bloke in a club in Kingham. Stuck his hand, he did, where he shouldn't. She brought *him* to his knees,' she said, sounding disappointed as Clem gave Giles his hand back.

Ffion lowered her voice now that the yelling had stopped. 'Giles is her cousin, here for the regatta. Invited himself into her caravan, and then wanted the bed, with her in it.' She laughed. 'He didn't get it. He ended up on the floor, under a horse blanket. She can arm-wrestle, as well, Clem can,' Ffion added with a proprietorial air, watching Giles, his face frozen in agony, staring at his hand, and moving the fingers with the utmost care, testing for breaks.

'Even John Beecher and Sion, my brother, have their work cut out with her, they do. Isn't that right, Dan?'

Daniel nodded wryly. Challenging Clem earlier to a bout in order to impress Ffion had seemed like a good idea at the time.

'I'm sorry about that,' Clem said, smiling politely at Humphrey, a hostess apologising for a minor social hiccup. 'But Giles can be a very naughty boy. Can't you, Giles?'

Giles found his voice. 'There was no bloody need for that!' he said, sounding near to tears.

'I warned you,' Clem casually reminded him. 'I said something nasty would happen to you if you did it again. And it has,' she added unnecessarily.

Ffion, now that bit of fun was over, was impatient to get into the ground, and wanted to know were they going in or were they just going to stand there? Humphrey said that, for his part, he had to get back, that he was flying out to the States tomorrow, and had to make an early start.

Giles, his hands shaking, flicked a lighter at a cigarette, shooting hot reproachful looks over it at Clem, before trailing after Ffion and Daniel.

Clem looked at Humphrey. Humphrey looked at Clem.

'You coming, Clem, or what?' Giles called, pulling furiously on his cigarette, waiting, sulkily aggrieved, at the gateway.

'You don't need me, Giles. The caravan's open, and you're welcome to stay again. Now you know the rules,' Clem said.

'Well . . .' she added to Humphrey.

'Yeah . . .' Humphrey said.

'Well . . . goodnight,' Clem said.

'Yeah, goodnight,' Humphrey said.

And then several pints of Sheepsnout cider came to the rescue of both of them.

'*Hey*!' Humphrey said then, as if he wasn't letting her get away with that – as if *he* wasn't going to get away with it. 'How about a coffee? How about you and me getting a coffee? What's wrong with that?' he demanded, as if Clem had put up an argument.

But all Clem was doing was nodding. 'Yes,' she said. 'Yes.'

'Clem!' Giles called again.

'Bugger off, Giles,' Clem said happily, looking at Humphrey.

'Yeah, bugger off, Giles,' Humphrey said, grinning at Clem.

They had their coffee at a stall near enough to the grain trailer to listen to the jazz, and stood without speaking, a sudden awkwardness between them.

Humphrey tapped a foot to "Way Down Yonder", and said he liked that. Clem said she liked it as well, and went even further, and said she thought it was *really* good. Humphrey asked her if she'd like another coffee, and Clem asked if he was having one. Humphrey said he would, and he'd take it black again, because of his head. It was stuffed with horse feathers, he told her, and waggled his eyebrows.

Humphrey wasn't altogether sure what he'd meant, and Clem had no idea at all. Which didn't stop either of them from finding it so funny they couldn't speak at all then for laughing.

They decided to forget about the coffee, and made their way down to the funfair. The air smelt of hotdog onions and diesel, and was loud with rock and roll from the rides and the throb of generators, and screams from the big wheel, its spokes of light turning in the darkness high above them.

They went on the Octopus first, where Humphrey had reason to be glad he hadn't succumbed to a stick of pink candyfloss or a toffee apple, as their chair hurtled out into space and back again.

And then they bumped each other on the dodgems, and chased each other round on Ben Hur chariots. They went on the Super Disco Waltzer, Noah's Ark Swing, a Supersonic Skid, and then a Galloper, on enamel and gilded horses with manes flying and panic painted into their eyes.

Humphrey couldn't remember when he'd had so much fun.

They went on the big wheel then. And it was the same Clem who, for a bet last winter, in the dark and without touching the ladders, had skimmed up the outside of scaffolding erected for repairs to the tower of St Swithin's, who now screamed with fright and clung, helplessly, to Humphrey as they plunged to earth, and then rushed the sky again.

The valley spread out below them for that moment, its hills and reaped fields, and its river, the glimmer of reflected light at its heart like something buried and shining there.

Later, they wandered down to Taddlebrook

Bank, where the owls could be heard calling in Mawr Wood against the background of noise from the fair, and a punt glided dreamlike upstream. And there were other craft, unseen, tied up in the shadows under banks or in the darker caves of overhanging willow fronds.

They sat on the bank down on the river, Clem with the coat of Humphrey's Brooks Brothers executive suit around her shoulders. And he told her about his life, his *real* life, and she told him about hers, a daughter of a house on the other side of the county, minor aristocracy on its uppers.

'They still live there, in a flat, as caretakers. The National Trust own it now. Mum and dad tried most things to keep it going. Opening the house to the public, gift shops' – Clem laughed at some memory – 'even a small zoo. But, well, they weren't terribly good at that sort of thing. No head for business, you know?' She smiled at Humphrey, knowing now that he did, and Humphrey smiled back, not having now to pretend.

'Anyway,' Clem went on, moving as if to make herself more comfortable, and ending up lying down.

'Anyway, what I mean is . . .' she said. And forgot whatever it was she had meant then, when he leaned over and brushed her hair back from her face, and traced her lightly broken nose with a finger.

And then Humphrey also made himself more comfortable.

'Jeez!' he said. 'Look at that . . . look at those stars.'

Big, fat summer stars the colour of cider, their brilliance staining the sky. Stars, and the smell of summer and night on the river, and Clem's perfume, her head next to his.

And when he kissed her the night exploded, and it rained stars. The sky whistling and crackling, and shook rigid with flashes of light, and more stars bloomed and fell, bursts of stars, falling in coloured showers on Batch Magna.

'Wow!' Humphrey said, as more giant rockets and Big Bertha sky bombs were fired off at the annual midnight display in the castle keep.

'*Wow!*' he said, and kissed her again.

CHAPTER 29

Humphrey was back in Frank's office, where Strange Enterprises, Inc., the company that, it was hoped, would one day be an international hotel chain, was saving on office rent. And from where, eleven floors above Wall Street, Humphrey had once fallen from grace, exiled from America's dollar heart and his own dreams, sent to turn burgers in a downtown diner.

He even had his old desk back, by the photocopier, within sight of Frank's office. The door of which, with Humphrey once again on the premises, Frank kept firmly open.

Humphrey, in his current capacity as liaison executive of Strange Enterprises, with special responsibility for the UK, was on the phone.

He'd taken a call from the new land agent there, the old one having been fired, a corporate decision taken by Frank at a board meeting of two, immediately Humphrey got back. The new agent, recommended by their Kingham solicitors as an up-and-coming young thruster and go-getter, had even got the builder's price for refurbishment of the Hall – a price already accepted by Frank as financial executive – reduced.

And after sweating, as he put it, the new costings, to see if he could lose a few pounds there as well, the agent was now suggesting the price could be further reduced by stripping the roofs – the damage to which was found to be more extensive than first thought – of their sandstone flags and completely re-roofing them in slate.

And how did that grab Sir Humphrey?

It didn't grab Sir Humphrey at all. In fact Sir Humphrey, already not in the sunniest of moods, found himself outraged.

With one eye on Frank's office, and keeping his voice down, because it was the sort of thing to grab Frank, Humphrey took a corporate decision at a board meeting, convened there and then, of one.

Where, he wanted to know, was the agent's sense of goddam history? Stone had been used when they first roofed the place, and stone would continue to be used. Use stone, goddammit! And muttering something dimly remembered about a mess of pottage, slammed down the phone.

Humphrey's desk was piled with paper, concertinaed sheets of it sliding off or about to slide off. Sheets which, once he'd spread them, he could never refold properly, and after each unsuccessful attempt would sit, breathing hard and glaring at them.

They contained reams of figures, profit and loss

stories over the past five years of similar enterprises in the international market. And compiled from them, and frequently buried under them, was what Frank had called a graphical trend analysis, a projection he'd suggested Humphrey put together of the route Strange Enterprises, Inc., might be expected to travel in the future. Using different coloured pencils, his tongue protruding with concentration, Humphrey was desperately determined to get it right.

Frank had no need of such a projection. And neither had Sylvia. They were money professionals, who'd armed themselves with that sort of data before setting out on the journey in the first place. In the current climate the idea had a reasonable chance of reaching that future, after that it was wait and see.

The projection, along with the other figures Frank had given Humphrey to play with since arriving back, was simply to keep him harmlessly employed and where he could see him, while Frank got on with the grown-up stuff.

But if Strange Enterprises did go down, Humphrey would find himself on his own. Neither Sylvia nor Frank intended getting mugged over it. And Sylvia would even come away with a title, which of course was what she'd been after in the first place.

And it amazed and amused Frank still that Humphrey had ever thought otherwise.

Humphrey had told him when he inherited that he felt his life had turned into a movie. Well, from where Frank was sitting, it was a movie that for Humphrey had only one probable ending. At some stage he was likely to wake up and find that not only was the movie over but that he hadn't even got the taxi fare home. If playing in the international market didn't do it – and Frank, for Frank's sake, hoped of course that it wouldn't – then Sylvia would.

Frank had persuaded Humphrey to put Batch Hall and what was left of the estate up as collateral on a loan, to get things moving. He'd told Humphrey that he and Sylvia were putting in the same amount, something which he and Sylvia had decided beforehand to tell him. Neither intended putting anything into it, not until it promised to be worth it. Both considered that their contributions of financial expertise and their contacts were quite enough for now. But that was something else they weren't telling Humphrey. That was something else that had been decided beforehand.

Humphrey, when he had last sat at that desk, had cost Frank, both in money and reputation. If Strange Enterprises, Inc. went south, Humphrey would be travelling with it. Poetic justice, Frank believed it was called. And if it did happen, then in his opinion it wouldn't be before time.

Humphrey had pulled loose the Atlantic Sports Club member's tie he had nagged Frank to get him the first time round, and he had a dull ache over one eye. And the photocopier was being used again, making those groaning and dragging noises. It was about time Frank got the goddam thing serviced, along with the air conditioning.

From eleven storeys below the odd honk of a horn, the odd bubble of sound, broke now and then from the constant river of traffic.

Humphrey tossed the new Biro Frank had given him earlier onto the mess on his desk, and started again for Frank's office.

He had made the trip several times already that morning, coming away with the right time by Frank's watch, a box of paperclips, and the new Biro. This time he would ask for what he really wanted.

It was his fourth day back in New York, and he had still to tell Frank about the offer he'd made of compensation. This time he would do it.

Humphrey went in without knocking, and sat without waiting to be invited.

Frank had also loosened his tie, and sat tapping figures into a calculator at his desk. In a corner of his office, next to a water dispenser, more figures curled up on the carpet, chattering out of a telex machine.

Frank started shaking his head almost immediately Humphrey started talking.

The investors would never greenlight it. *He* wouldn't – *couldn't* – greenlight it. Hey! he understood why Humphrey wanted to do it. *He*, Frank, would want to do it in Humphrey's place, right?

But where would they be then? Frank wanted

to know, and leaning back in his brown leather captain's chair waited for Humphrey to tell him. And when Humphrey appeared not to be able to, Frank told him.

Humphrey looked older and wiser when he left Frank's office, carrying, as Frank must carry, the burdens of fenced dollar allotments, margin awareness, profit curve predictors, and encroachment monitors.

Now all he had to do was to explain it all to the paddlers.

The Kingham solicitors could tell the pensioners, who by now would have received their notices to quit, and be expecting the same sort of windfall as those on the houseboats. And knowing Batch Magna as he now knew the goddam place that could be running at any sort of cockamamie figure.

Humphrey took out his address book. And then put it away, and sat with head in his hands.

And when he did finally get round to it, he phoned Phineas first, who made it worse by appearing not to be at all surprised, and then offering to tell not only the rest of the paddlers but the pensioners as well. He even wished Humphrey well in his new life.

Humphrey quietly put down the phone.

After lunch, which, following Frank's example, Humphrey had at his desk from a nearby sandwich bar, Frank brought across the studio photographs Sylvia and Humphrey had sat for yesterday.

They were to be used to illustrate the hotel

brochures, a picture of Sir Humphrey and Lady Strange on the front, under the caption, A Special Relationship, a play on words echoed by the blurb, which described the New World-Old World emphasis of Strange Hotels. A framed copy of the photograph would also feature in the reception area of each new hotel.

Frank put a hand on Humphrey's shoulder, and told him again that he was one lucky guy. And Humphrey said again that he knew it.

He was just thankful he hadn't thrown it all away. That he hadn't messed up that night with Clem. That it hadn't gone further than a couple of kisses. A couple of kisses by the river and then he'd walked her home, back to her caravan, and left her there.

A couple of kisses by the river and all hell broke loose, you mean! he told himself, grinning at the memory of it again.

And then he started guiltily, as if he'd been caught doing it, and began thinking about Sylvia instead.

And why was it that, when he started thinking about Sylvia, he always seemed to end up thinking about Clem? Humphrey asked himself, before determinedly thinking about Sylvia again.

They'd booked a table for that evening at a new French restaurant that had been opened in SoHo by an internationally renowned, award-winning chef. 'Good cook, huh?' Humphrey had said, rubbing his hands at the thought of the treat, while

Sylvia looked at him as if wondering what on earth that had to do with it.

He hadn't bought Sylvia an engagement ring yet, and being French it would have been a good place to do it, just right for slipping one into a glass of champagne, like he'd seen in a movie once.

If, that is, he *had* a ring – if, that is, he had the money to *buy* a ring. He could ask Frank for an advance on the salary that Frank, as financial executive, was allowing him to pay himself. But if he didn't want to come away with another Biro or a box of paperclips, that would have to wait until next week now, after the compensation business – if, that is, the old agent, with the spotted tie and helpful smile, still hadn't got round by then to selling the General's shotguns for him.

Still, he hadn't had them a fortnight yet, which was nothing – absolutely *nothing* – over there. The gunsmiths in Shrewsbury had the goddam things for over a year before they got round to doing anything about them. It was Humphrey's opinion, given an edge to it by four days in Frank's office, that that place needed not one but a whole bunch of goddam rockets up its butt.

He knew the guns wouldn't be worth much; anything worth much had already been sold. All he wanted was enough to buy a ring for his girl.

Seated at their table in the restaurant, Humphrey had a good look round for his mom. He had to do that, even on a visit to somebody's house he had to make a note of things to tell her about afterwards – what colour was the curtains, carpets, what was the furniture like, what sort of coffee cups. While Sylvia was judiciously sampling her *crème vichyssoise*, Humphrey was having trouble deciding whether the napkins were pink or orange.

Sylvia sighed, and made a show of peering at her napkin, and then holding it up to the light, before telling him he could tell his mom it was salmon.

Over the main course, Sylvia was taking about falling equities, mergers and acquisition deals. Something like that. Humphrey, champing on tournedos in brandy, while nodding his head and saying, yeah, yeah, was only half listening.

It had occurred to him that as the new agent had been so aisydaisy about the roofs, he might be the same when it came to overseeing the work on the terraces. They needed to use stone from the lodge, or one of the ruined garden walls, and they needed to "age" the mortar with lime, the old agent had told him all about that.

Sylvia paused, and wanted to know if he was listening.

Humphrey smiled and nodded absently at her. And the walls, the same went for them. And seconds, mellow red bricks, must be used on repairs to the chimneys, to blend in. They were restoring the place, not just goddam repairing it.

Humphrey had to sit on an urge to ask for a

phone, there and then, and made a mental note to call the new agent *first* thing in the morning.

When Humphrey got home, a second-floor walk-up in the South Bronx, Shelly, his mom, was in the sitting room, shouting at the TV. 'He's a crumb! A horse's ass! Show him the goddam door, for Chrissake! What's with you – you dumb, as well as blonde!'

Shelly, who had done blonde and was now an exuberant shade of red, broke off long enough to say hi to her son, and tell him there was fresh coffee in the kitchen. And when she returned to the TV, to the patient understanding of a woman on one of the soaps, she could not believe it.

'Jee-*sus*! Give me . . .! *Don't* – what are y'doing, y'dumb cluck? Don't get his dinner, for Chrissakes – get a goddam lawyer!'

Shelly had had enough by the time Humphrey came in with his coffee. The television was off and she was searching behind the cushions and under the sofa, looking, her son guessed, for missing invoices. More invoices and chequebook stubs were spread on the rest of the sofa and on the coffee table in front of it. There were times when even Humphrey was given to wonder about the finances of the local small businesses and shops his mom kept the books for.

He told her about the meal and all the other details of the restaurant. He left out what Sylvia had been wearing. He didn't think she'd want to

351

know what Sylvia had been wearing. His mom, he knew, did not share his enthusiasm for Sylvia.

She had made that clear the first time they'd met. Like Humphrey, Shelly was no good at hiding her feelings, and when she tried to, it could be worse than showing them. And she tried that night, making small talk and grinning at Sylvia like some goddam mad woman, as Humphrey had complained afterwards.

Shelly had called her a piranha, and advised him to give her the goddam title, and run for it, and they ended up shouting at each other.

They were known for their shouting in the building. Old Mr Levin in the apartment above them, before he had his stroke, used to join in. 'Don't you talk to your ma like that, Humphie!' he'd yell down, banging on the floor with his stick.

Humphrey told his mom about his day at the office, casually dropping in terms like graphical trend analysis, profit curve predictors and encroachment monitors. Shelly looked suitably impressed, and smiled and nodded encouragement when he talked of the future he'd been charting for Strange Enterprises, Inc., as she had done at all his various ventures in the past, at all the dreams he'd brought home.

And this time, Humphrey thought, looking at her, this time I'm gonna keep her smiling.

The bookkeeping was his mom's new business after her mail-shot business. Before that there had been her lunchtime snacks to busy desk-workers business, her dried flowers business, her dress-making business, her proof-reading business, her advertising business, her job finding, office cleaning, and matrimonial agency businesses. And he was going to put a stop to it.

Not only was he going to take care of her future, he was also going to give her the past back, a time when she had never needed to lift a finger.

Humphrey stood up suddenly from the armchair, startling her, and going to her, held her face in his meaty hands.

'Mom, I know you've heard all this before,' he said, frowning down at her, fierce with love and determination. 'But this time, this time this really *is* it. This time I'm bringing home the bacon. I've promised dad that, in my mind. And now I'm promising you. This time, Mom, we're going back there. Back to the life you had once with dad – the life you would *still* have if dad hadn't died. That's what I'm gonna to do, Moms. I'm going to give you that life back.'

'Yeah, I know that, Humphie, I know that. You're a sweetheart, I know that,' Shelly said, looking embarrassed.

Humphrey shook his head. 'I've been lucky, that's all. It's been handed to me, the chance to do all this. Because of dad dying. See, the way I see it, Mom,' Humphrey said, sitting back again with his coffee, 'the way I see it is, I'm doing what dad would have done if he'd lived, right? And you know, inherited instead of me. Which means I'll be doing it for all of us, right?'

'Right,' Shelly said, and smiled vaguely.

Her son finished his coffee and stretched and yawned. 'Well, I'm for bed. Gotta give hell to a whole bunch of stuff again tomorrow,' he said, pulling a punch in the air.

'He didn't think he ever would inherit, being an American. That was something your dad never bothered dreaming about,' Shelly said, after he'd kissed her goodnight. 'I think he got it mixed up with a knighthood – like when the Queen gives it, but if you're not British you can't keep it?' Humphrey frowned, thinking about that. 'But it's funny to think that I might have been Lady Shelly.' She laughed. 'Nah. Makes me sound like a boutique. I could have lived in that house, though, I could have done that. Old Batch Hall,' she said, smiling at her memory of it. 'And Ralph, Ralph could have lived there – he *would* have lived there, the way he talked about it. You bet!'

Humphrey was nodding shrewdly. 'A UK base. Yeah, sure. Somewhere to entertain clients. Right. Makes sense. Yeah, well, that's for another time, Mom. That's down the road awhiles. But I'll get that as well for us. I'll get Batch Hall back, you'll see. And a house in the Hamptons. And an apartment for you, like the one we had in Manhattan. Don't you worry. We're going there, Moms, we're going there,' he promised, looking suddenly tired, as if at the thought of it, the distance he had to travel for them.

Shelly's heart went out to him.

'Humphie!' she said abruptly, stopping him at the door.

Humphrey waited.

His mother hesitated. 'Goodnight, sweetheart. Sleep well,' was all she said then. Which wasn't anything like what she'd meant to say, what she had come so near, after all this time, to saying.

She wanted only what he wanted for himself, and that he be happy in it. And now it looked as he was going to get it, the hard-nosed broad and all. She had never thought that that part of it would end in anything but tears. And now no longer believed, watching and listening to her son over the past few days, that he wanted it for himself any more.

And she couldn't help thinking that it was all her fault in the first place.

And whether or not she should own up to that after all these years, was what kept her awake well into the small hours. Whether or not it mattered now if she did or didn't tell him. Whether all it would do would be to show her to be a liar, to have used lies where there should have been faith.

And who said he'd be unhappy anyway? And if he was unhappy, he'd at least probably be rich. And rich was better than poor any day when it rained, as she knew well.

Let him be rich and unhappy, she decided at last, as if blessing him, and turning over, went to sleep.

CHAPTER 30

Shelly changed her mind again later that morning. Sitting with her son in the kitchen after breakfast she decided she would tell him, after all.

They had been talking about Humphrey's younger sister, Betty.

Betty had gone up in the world as far as she considered it decent for people like them to go, by marrying a druggist in Illinois, and thought Humphrey's new station in life a load of la-di-da poppycock. She thought he should drop the title, sell up, and share out the proceeds.

Everything else was so much applesauce, yet another of her doodle-brained brother's get-rich schemes.

She shared her mother's opinion of Sylvia but felt obliged, along with other members of the family, to ask when she phoned if a date had been set yet. Humphrey had looked embarrassed when Shelly mentioned this, and mumbled something about not having bought the engagement ring yet.

But it wasn't that that had made his mother change her mind. It was when she'd joked about the sex of her grandchildren in Illinois, the boys who had turned her into a grandmother twice, and prompted two new emergency hair dye jobs. She'd told Humphrey that she wanted him to produce two girls, to make the set.

It was then, something in her son's demeanour then, as he sat, almost sulkily, moving his empty coffee mug about. It was that which made her, although still not clear why, decide that she would tell him after all.

She fell silent, and when Humphrey looked up at her he was met with a smile of quite unnerving tenderness.

'What?' he asked, startled. 'What!'

She said in a rush, 'I still don't know if I was right to tell you what I told you in the first place and whether I'd be right to tell you what I think I ought to tell you now.'

She paused, as if she'd made it plain enough, and was waiting to see what he thought about it.

He looked blankly at her.

Shelly smiled at him again.

'What, Mom – *What*?' Humphrey said, irritated and a little alarmed.

She laughed briefly and nervously. 'Well,' she began carefully, 'well, you know that apartment we had when you and Betty were tiny?'

Humphrey nodded. 'The one in Manhattan. On the Upper East side, overlooking the park. With a doorman to keep the bums out.' He reeled off the familiar details. 'Yeah. What?'

'Well – well, we *did* live on the Upper East side. But not overlooking the park.' Shelly paused, as if that was all. *Wishing* that that was all. And then went on: 'No. No, what we really had, Humphie, what we really had, honey, was a service apartment. That's what we had. In the basement. Overlooking the garbage area. Your dad was a janitor there,' she said, and laughed again briefly.

Humphrey smiled politely and waited for the punch line.

'Humphrey,' she said, something she did sometimes, call him by his full name, when she was serious about something, or telling him off, or kidding him. 'Humphrey. Humphie – I lied to you. I lied to you, sweetheart, I lied to you. I made it all up.'

Humphrey was still waiting for the punch line.

'Is this a joke, Mom, or what?' he said then, inviting her to get on with it, and snapped off an executive glance at his watch. In five exactly he should be on his way out of here, gunning for Wall Street. Anything later than that for no good reason and he'd have to give himself a motivation check, the way Frank advised.

Shelly shook her head. 'No, it's no joke, honey. I made it up.'

Humphrey grinned at her. 'Dad, a *janitor*?' He laughed. 'Yeah, right!' he said, and it was his turn to shake his head then, looking at his mom and laughing and shaking his head, finding it funny, even if he didn't get it.

'Humphrey!' Shelly said sharply. 'It is not a joke. I made it up. I *lied* to you.'

'Are you serious, or what!' he scoffed. 'Dad a janitor – yeah, yeah. What is this?' he said, laughing, hands spread.

'Humph*reee!*' his mom growled warningly. 'I'll hit you with something in a minute. I am *serious*. And it's hard enough as it is. Listen to me. *Listen* to me, Humphrey – *I-made-it-up.* '

That got through to him. When she hit him with something, rolled up newspapers, magazines, a broom once, she was serious, no question.

Mother and son stared at each other.

Outside, 160th Street went past with a hiss of airbrakes, buses and delivery trucks grinding and banging over the potholes, horns blaring and a siren wailing up near the intersection, frantically beating its way through the morning traffic.

Humphrey spoke first.

'You're not kidding?' he said in a small, younger-sounding voice.

His mother shook her head. 'No, Humphie. I'm not kidding.'

'You made it up?'

'I made it up. I rewrote the past, honey.'

Humphrey's eyes widened. 'All of it?'

'Well, the big bucks part of it, anyway. The money bit. The swanky apartment. What your dad was – what he did. What I did. And I think you should know the truth now. I said I didn't know if I was right to lie to you. Well, I know now. I wasn't right. I was wrong. OK?'

'Dad was a *janitor* . . .?'

Shelly shrugged. 'Among other things. He was between fortunes, between dreams. Your dad janitored and I went out temping. The apartment went with his job.'

'He wasn't a hotshot, a go-getter, and everything? He wasn't rich? He didn't lose a fortune for being too trusting, and all that?'

His mom shook her head.

'He was a janitor,' Humphrey said to himself. 'My dad was a janitor. Among other things. He wasn't – What other things?'

'Things, things,' Shelly said impatiently. 'Door to door things, over the phone things, loading things, clerking things. Clearing snow for the City things. Whatever he could get things. Things.'

She got up from the table. 'Now, wanna another coffee before you go?'

'Clearing *snow*?'

'And a Santa Claus once. At Bloomies. You want the coffee?'

Shelly sighed and sat down again.

'Humphie . . . Humphie, look, your father didn't have a fortune to lose, that's true. But he *was* too trusting – like you. And he was a go-getter. It was just he never got, that's all. He was a dreamer, honey, like you. Till all this happened, that is. And I wonder how much of a blessing it will turn out

360

to be,' she said, looking at him almost accusingly, and sounding near to tears, her way of trying to shift some of the heat from herself.

But Humphrey wasn't listening. '*Santa Claus?*'

'Yeah. Not long after the war. Betty wasn't born but I took you to see him. You were just a kid then of course, barely walking.'

'My dad was a Santa Claus at Bloomingdale's,' Humphrey told himself.

'Had his own Santa Land up on the eighth floor. He was good at it, too. Looked the part, being big. Know what I mean? And *loud*? Jeez, you could hear him coming up in the elevator. *Haaaap-py* Christmas! Ho-Ho-Ho!' She laughed. 'He sat you on his lap and you bawled your head off. Got a picture of it somewhere. You bawled again then, when it was your turn to meet his playful elves. They were all midgets from Coney Island. And he had Rudolph the Red-Nosed Reindeer, a real reindeer from the Park. It was a winter *wonder*land, Humphie!' she said, as if urging him to stop sulking and get with the spirit of it. 'With an ice grotto and a log cabin, and snow and candle-lights, and the little playful elves singing a song with Frosty the Snowman in a top hat about Santa Claus's home in Lapland. And then Santa arriving on his sleigh, bells jing-alinging, with his big red sack of presents. Ho-Ho-Ho! You got a candy cane and an orange. Oh, and a colouring book,' she remembered, and smiled at him as if at a much younger Humphrey. 'Your dad loved that, handing out the presents, you could see it. *Loved* it. To some of the kids it was just store things in shiny paper and ribbon they were getting, you know? To Ralphie it was Christmas. He was giving Christmas. Haaap-py Christmas! Ho-Ho-Ho!'

Humphrey's head was wobbling in disbelief. 'I don't believe this. I just do *not* believe it.'

'Believe it,' his mom advised him. 'It's what it is. You want that coffee, or what?'

Humphrey's mouth opened and shut a couple of times on things he wanted to say, wanted to ask, and then he said, '*Why*? Why did you lie about it, Mom?'

Shelly flapped a hand at him. 'Because, because.'

Because she wanted him to believe that he could do it. Wanted him to think that if his dad could do it, so could he. That he didn't always have to be looking on, another loser at the feast. Because she didn't think he *could* do it, not without help. And lies were all she had to offer.

'Because I wanted to spur you on or something, honey, I don't know. I shouldn't have done it. That's what I know now. It sold you both short, and I'm sorry. All right? I'm saying I'm sorry. OK?'

Humphrey stared at her. 'So – let me get this straight here – so, there was no apartment over-looking Central Park. No uniformed doorman dressed like a Russian admiral. No maid called Bridget, who *adored* me,' he sneered, 'and no chauffeur called Louis. Right?'

362

Shelly sighed again. 'Yes, there was no any of that.'

'And no charity coffee mornings and lunches.'

'And no charity coffee mornings and lunches. That's right, you got it.'

'And no – what about the dogs?' he suddenly remembered. 'What about the two little dogs. The ones that *Louis* used to walk in the park. There were no dogs, either, were there? Not even a couple of dogs.'

No, she said. Not even a couple of dogs.

'We weren't allowed dogs as employees.'

They weren't allowed dogs in their present apartment, either, which was the reason, she'd told him, that she'd had to give away her Manhattan fashion accessory of two French butterfly dogs, when the dice sent them down the ladder to a walk-up in the Bronx.

Humphrey stared at her some more.

'And who knows about . . . what about Betty? Does Betty know about it?'

'No, she doesn't. And I'm not going to tell her. Neither are you. She's spent the last god knows how many years turning up her nose at it all. Or pretending to. It's really only because we didn't manage to keep any of it for her.'

Humphrey looked confused. 'But we didn't have any to keep. Did we?'

'No, of course we didn't. What have I been telling you? We just don't tell her we didn't, that's all. She's bad enough now, when she thinks we should

363

have. We'd never hear the end of it if she knows we couldn't have.'

Humphrey struggled with that for a moment, and then gave up.

'Well, who does know?'

'That he was or wasn't?'

Humphrey moved his head impatiently. 'That he wasn't. What about Frank? Does Frank know?' He had just remembered the number of times he'd boasted to Frank about what a hotshot his dad had been.

'Frank never met Ralph. It was all before Frank's time. I met him and his wife first through your Aunt Doris. And no, Doris doesn't know, either. I mean, she doesn't think he was, right? Nobody in either family knows – doesn't think he was, know what I mean?'

Humphrey didn't look as if he did altogether.

'What I mean is,' Shelly said, 'they know he *wasn't*, OK? And it wasn't easy, over the years, on family visits, and weddings and funerals, and all that, I can tell you. You can imagine, right?'

She sighed then, when Humphrey didn't respond, and said, 'Look, your dad was a good man. That's all you have to remember. He was a good man, and he was a rare one. Hell, I found that out long since.'

She laughed. Hadn't she just! That's what her laugh said. She had always said she'd marry again if the right man happened along, and she was still waiting.

'Remember Sergeant Daly, pride of the forty-second?' she asked, referring to one of her past dates, a cop who'd wanted to bring his handcuffs into the bedroom. Shelly laughed again. 'One kiss and he wants to arrest me!' That's what she'd told Humphrey. Her friends had got the full unedited version. 'Hey! I mean, come on here! What, I kiss that bad?'

But Humphrey wasn't to be cajoled.

He was frowning down at the table, the way he used to sit there with his school work, frowning over naming the main mountain ranges of America or some past president.

His mother smiled at him, briefly and unseen, a slight, wistful smile she was hardly aware of.

And then she reached across and put a hand on his. 'I thought I was helping you, honey,' she said, telling it to herself as well as him. 'I thought it was a place you wanted to go. Like when you were young, and I used to read to you. And you'd point at a picture, some place in a storybook, and say, wanna go there. It always sounded good to me, because you knew no matter what happened after that in the story, it would all come right on the last page. All end happily. Sure, I used to tell you, sure, we'll go there, all of us. We'll all go there. Do you remember that? Wanna go there, you'd say. Wanna go there.'

CHAPTER 31

That evening, after a meal largely eaten on Humphrey's part in silence, a friend of Shelly's from the neighbourhood, Rita, another merry widow, dropped in to visit.

Both women had sat gossiping and giggling over a special-offer litre of Valpolicella from the corner Italian grocery store, while Humphrey stayed in the kitchen.

He had further words to say regarding that morning's revelations, but they would wait until he had his mother's full and proper attention. Meanwhile, he sat on at the kitchen table, sternly going over work he'd brought home with him, and tutting now and then at the noise the two women were making in the other room.

After Rita had gone, Humphrey, still in his executive pants and Atlantic Sports Club tie, switched off the television his mom had just switched on, and stood with his back to it, as if to a Victorian fireplace, frowning at her.

He had, he announced, something to say. He had been giving that morning's matter a good deal of thought, and had decided to make allowances, for both his parents.

He paused, as if for thanks. Shelly, sucking on the inside of her cheek, examined her shirt front, carefully picking the odd bit of non-existent fluff from it.

Humphrey continued. He said that she had always exaggerated things, and invited her to look at where that had led her. Exaggeration, he was able to tell her, having been told it enough times himself in grade school, is first cousin to the lie. He hoped she would remember that in future.

As for his father, he, after all, had not been given the chance to do what he, Humphrey, was doing with the legacy. Humphrey had no doubt that, had he lived to inherit, his father would, at last, have made his dream come true. Would at last have climbed the same ladder to success that he, Humphrey, was at present busy climbing.

Humphrey was about to climb more ladders, to air again the future, the view from the top, when his mother snorted loudly, and tossed back the remains of her wine.

'Your father,' she told him, 'wouldn't have done anything of the goddam kind.' She laughed scornfully. 'That's not who he was. That's not who Ralphie was. Who he really was. That's why he never got there. And he never got there, to where he really wanted to go, because he was never sure where that was. Right?' she demanded.

Humphrey nodded his head, and then shook it, cancelling that. He had no idea what she was talking about, but whatever it was, he had a feeling it shouldn't be encouraged.

He opened his mouth to take back the conversation but his mom got there first.

'Your father never *cared* enough about money to make any. How about that, huh? And I'll tell you something else, *buddy* – neither did I!' she said defiantly, leaving Humphrey standing there with his mouth open. 'Which is why – which is why, wherever Ralphie *had* gone I'd have been there with him, and to hell with the rent! And do you know why? You wanna know why? I'll tell you why,' she went on without waiting. 'Because wherever it was – whatever it was – it wouldn't have been *boring*. No, not with your dad. Not with Ralphie,' she said firmly, and shaking her head as if Humphrey had suggested otherwise.

Humphrey hadn't. Humphrey hadn't said a word. He was too busy taking this new stuff in.

Shelly pointed her empty wine glass at him. 'You're telling me – *me* – what your father would have done. Well, I'll tell *you* what he'd have done,' she went on, as Humphrey opened and closed his mouth again. 'Your dad would have turned himself into the squire of little old Batch Magna for the sheer hell of it, that's what he'd have done. That's what Ralphie would have done. And I would have been mistress of Batch Hall – yes, *mistress*!' she cried, flinging her head back like she was in some goddam movie.

She wanted to know then what he had to say about that. He said he was going to bed, that's what he had to say about it. And *if* he had anything more to say about it, he'd say it to her in the morning, he said, and had to put up with her yelling after him not to be so goddam pompous.

There were football pendants on the walls of his bedroom, and a signed Yankees baseball bat and mitt, and a model of a Hurricane, one of the aircraft his dad had flown in the last war, suspended from the ceiling. And his collection of well-thumbed How to Succeed books, his maps to wealth and happiness, to that promised other country, and his place in the sun there.

He could not believe it. First his dad, now his mom. He could *not* believe it.

He hadn't brushed his teeth and he didn't care. His face was set determinedly, stubbornly, as he changed into his pyjamas and switched off the light, and then tossed this way and that.

He was going there, just you wait and see, he told himself, and them. He was going there, they all were. His mom and dad as well. Whether they wanted to or not.

CHAPTER 32

Frank was also thinking about the future, and he liked what he saw. He had the latest investment figures in for Strange Enterprises, and they were looking surprisingly good.

The past working for the future was how he'd billed it in the investment literature. And the future, with Frank taking the precaution of listing himself as chief executive in the legal papers Humphrey had signed in his usual slapdash way, was starting to look interesting.

He had now agreed all the tenders for the refurbishment and conversion of Batch Hall, and had appointed a UK business manager. Batch Magna was scheduled to start signposting the future, the march into Europe, next May, when the Hall, and the river eateries and holiday village – which would come under the leisure arm of the company, the first, as he saw it, of a portfolio of such villages – would open for business, and when the English countryside, and the half that was in Wales, would bloom and play its part.

At this rate even Humphrey could end up looking a winner – until, that is, Sylvia really happened to him. She was a piranha, only after his title, Shelly had said in a recent phone call to him. Well, of course she was. As anyone, as long as he wasn't called Humphrey, could see a mile off. It was a dance, and Sylvia was doing the leading, but so slowly and, for Humphrey, so subtly, he believed he was. She'd get an engagement ring any time now, and then marriage and the title, and her name prominently in the social pages.

And then one fine, rich day, with the sun in his eyes, with life shining away for him, whistling and grinning carelessly in that irritating Humphrey way of his, he'd walk straight into her lawyers.

Shelly had gone on about the sort of woman Humphrey needed. Frank knew what Humphrey needed. He needed a bit of maturity, that's what Humphrey needed. He needed to damn well grow up. He had nothing, owned nothing, only what luck had given him. He lived with his mom still, his car couldn't go two blocks without leaking and polluting the neighbourhood, and Frank's fifteen-year-old son had more in the bank then Humphrey had.

Frank didn't consider himself a vindictive man, and he tried not to gloat over the thought, but given Humphrey's attitude to life – by which Frank meant money and business – he would feel affronted if something like that *didn't* happen to him.

While Frank hummed tunelessly, and unaware he was doing so, at his work, Humphrey was sitting bored and fed up over his, his desk piled with graphs showing the latest share movements in the world markets, with particular reference to hotels.

Humphrey had had enough of world markets, share movements, hotels, and just about everything else today.

The old agent, with his wide local knowledge, had been left to deal with the sale of Home Farm, and had now done that, and to a local buyer who would meet the full asking price. It had given Humphrey no cheer at all. The money anyway would simply be moved from one account to another to pay the death duties, but it was much more than that. He no longer felt it had anything to do with him. He no longer felt that *any* of it had anything to do with him.

Which didn't stop him brooding about it. He put it down to sleeping badly, as he had been doing since arriving back in New York – and he put *that* down to sleeping alone, or discovering out of the blue that his mom and dad were a couple of goddam hippies, or pressure of business, or something.

He wasn't seeing Sylvia tonight. He wasn't seeing anybody tonight. He was heading straight home to his mom, who was going to cook spaghetti and meatballs, one of his favourite dishes, followed by apple cake. It was her way of saying sorry.

She'd said sorry with Maryland cookies last night, and baked Alaska the night before that. And made up a fresh batch of pickled relish, when she said she wouldn't again, not after he'd spooned the last lot straight from the jar, to go with Coney Island Specials, as she called them, ordinary hotdogs turned into something not at all ordinary when garnished with the relish, a family heirloom.

It wouldn't last long, of course, all this baking stuff, and relish making. But while it did Humphrey, as Mrs T used to advise him, was tucking in.

CHAPTER 33

In bed that night, after a large serving of spaghetti and meatballs, two extra helpings of apple cake, and too much coffee, Humphrey tossed and turned to a dream as busy as a circus ring.

There were paddle steamers and Gallopers, and Clem on a horse, and Frank telling jokes or something, and an usherette who turned out to be Sylvia, showing her legs and selling ice-cream. There was a Russian admiral with two small dogs, their tricks making him smile in his sleep, and an owl winking at him from a chimney pot, and one on a bicycle, who turned into Miss Wyndham, leaving him to wonder how it was done.

'Never you mind!' she huffed as he tried to keep up, while the steam whistles on the paddlers screamed louder and louder, until they turned into a peacock and Humphrey woke with a start.

He sat bolt upright, his heart thumping in the dark, listening to the phone ringing in the sitting room.

He fumbled for the bedside lamp and peered at the time. It had just gone four. It had just gone four in the morning, and the phone was ringing.

His mom would never hear it. Her bedroom was along the hall, on the other side of the bathroom, and she always slept with earplugs in against a neighbourhood that never stopped doing anything for long.

Expecting a family disaster, or at the least a drunk phoning for a cab, he found it was the agent again, the old agent. The one with the bowtie and helpful smile, calling cheerfully at four in the morning to find out what the weather was doing there.

Even knowing, as he now knew the English – not to mention the Welsh – preoccupation with the weather, Humphrey could not believe it.

Then the agent breezed on about trying Frank's office number first and getting no reply, and Humphrey knew what had happened. The darn fool had got the time difference the wrong way round.

It didn't matter to Humphrey that he couldn't be seen peering exaggeratedly out of the window to check what it was doing out there. Humphrey was in the right for once, and he was making the most of it.

He was about to suggest that, as it was still dark over here, the agent might like to ring him back when it was light. Then he, Humphrey, could be absolutely *sure* what it was doing out there, something biting like that, when the agent told him that the shotguns Humphrey had asked him to pick up from the Shrewsbury gunsmiths and then sell, had been sold.

There was a pause. 'What, sold for money sold?' Humphrey asked suspiciously, quite prepared to believe that it might mean something less positive in the agent's world.

They went under the hammer at Shrewsbury yesterday afternoon, the agent was happy to report. And Sir Humphrey wouldn't believe for how much. *He*, the agent, couldn't believe how much. And he wasn't the only one.

'There were others there, as well, who couldn't believe how much. You might be interested to know, Sir Humphrey, that the auctioneer himself said—'

'How much?' was all Humphrey wanted to know.

'—that even *he* couldn't believe how much. There was a London gun dealer there, Sir Humphrey,' the agent burbled on excitedly, 'who specialises in shotguns, and who said to me afterwards that he also couldn't believe how much they—'

'How *much*!' Humphrey almost shouted down the phone.

Advising him to take a pew first, the agent told him. And then had to ask if he was still there.

'*How* much?' Humphrey got out.

The agent, on ten per cent of it, chortled. 'Seventy-five thousand pounds sterling, old boy. Good as winning the pools.'

Humphrey's head reeled. He had been hoping for something between maybe three and five hundred pounds.

'Seventy-five thousand pounds sterling?' Humphrey said incredulously.

'Less commissions of course, for my offices and those of the auction house,' the agent said. 'But yes, old chap, seventy-five thousand.'

'Seventy-five thousand,' Humphrey echoed weakly.

The agent said he hadn't mentioned it to Sir Humphrey at the time, because he couldn't of course be sure, but he'd expected something in the order of around two and a half to three thousand. And then, having got some background on the pieces from Sarah, the late General's grand-daughter, and having consulted a couple of local gunsmiths, he had felt confident enough to put a reserve of eight thousand on them.

The agent laughed, delighted at how far out he'd been.

'And then, if they didn't make that, I intended seeking your permission to put them into one of the London houses – where, incidentally, I was assured by the London dealer that, as fine as they are, they wouldn't have made anywhere *near* as much. They're his-and-her guns, post First World War, bespoke Bosses, with chased silver engraving. Wedding presents, exchanged between the young General and his wife, and inscribed, I must say, rather touchingly as such. They're beautiful pieces in their own right, of course. But what got the bidding off quickly, and kept it moving, was strong local interest. Lord Erwynd, a Welsh peer and an old shooting friend of the General's, and a businessman, new to the area, had the field to themselves at the end. Then it reached the hammer price of seventy-five grand and his lordship blinked.'

The agent's sniff was audible. 'The businessman apparently wanted them to hang over the fireplace of a manor house he's just picked up.'

Humphrey was appalled.

It was in his bedroom that his doubts had always found him. Alone with his signed baseball bat and mitt, and the fighter plane his dad had flown, and where his How to Succeed books had waited for him like homework.

And it was there that he had doubted most since his last visit to Batch Magna. When he wasn't listening to Frank or Sylvia – when he *couldn't* listen to Frank or Sylvia. Alone with it then in his bed, with his thoughts of what he was doing – what he was *allowing* to be done. And now this.

He said he'd be robbing their graves next.

The agent laughed briefly and told him not to look at it like that. 'If the General had lived they'd have gone under the hammer anyway, so I'm told. Albeit reluctantly. The reason, his granddaughter imagines, he hadn't pressed for their return from the gunsmiths. But he apparently fully intended doing so, to pay for essential repairs to the roofs. Something which you have now undertaken yourself. So it comes to the same thing, as it were, in the end. The same difference, as they say, what?'

Humphrey said doubtfully that he guessed so.

'Well, there you are, then, Sir Humphrey. All's well that ends well, and all that, you know,' the agent finished briskly, and got down to business, arranging to take the two commissions out of the sale money and to forward the balance.

Humphrey put down the phone a rich man, and wondered if he should tell his mom.

As the apartment wasn't on fire he decided he'd better not, not even for this, and went back to bed instead.

He could pay compensation now, even include the pensioners in it. He could buy a ring for Sylvia and all sorts of things for his mom. A year's rent on a new apartment, if she wanted it. He'd send her on vacation first, while he got on with building the future. Santa Monica, maybe, or Malibu, somewhere big bucks and classy – though knowing his mom, it would be more like nickels and quarters, and a couple of weeks on the slots in Vegas. She even had a slot machine in the kitchen, her way of saving, she said. Which meant wondering aloud once a week how much was in there, and then asking him how much he thought was in there, before taking it out, counting it, and, no matter what it came to, stuffing it into her purse.

And they could get a new suite of furniture, and

a wash-dryer, one that worked *all* the time, and a car, a new car, put the old Plymouth out to grass, and a new TV.

The things you could do when you were rich, he told himself, and wondered why he didn't feel excited about it.

It was probably because it hadn't sunk in properly yet. He shut his eyes, as if when he opened them again it would have, and then turned this way and that. But it was no good, he couldn't get back to sleep.

He made coffee and wandered into the sitting room with it in his Yankees souvenir mug, and stood gazing out of the window.

A Sheffield Farms milk truck rattled past below, a friendly sound in the dark street. And there was a cleaner's light on in the auto-insurance office, and green neon burning still above Mac's Bar and Grill. There was the Puerto Rican barber shop on one side of that, and the One-Hour Cleaners on the other, and then Mrs Ambos's candy-and-cigarette store they used to steal from after school, the 160 Coffee Shop and the Frutas Tropicales store, the window of which, as a batter with the neighbourhood South Bronx Renegades, he'd once put in with a baseball.

All part of his past, his real past, and still there, if elsewhere the rest of the Bronx was changing, becoming fashionable. The *Bronx County Gazette* had talked glowingly about a new start, a new neighbourhood. His mom just complained about it going all preppy, when she wasn't on about the muggers in the old neighbourhood.

And he'd miss it, he guessed, was bound to, when he married Sylvia and moved away. And he wondered where that would be, the sort of neighbourhood they'd move to.

And it was while he was doing that, while he was thinking about Sylvia, that it occurred to him, completely out of the blue, that he could ring Phineas. It was far too early to ring Sylvia but he could ring Phineas and tell him about it.

Of *course* he could! He wondered why he hadn't thought of it before. He couldn't *think* why he hadn't thought of it before.

He'd do it now, immediately, right this minute, he told himself, searching the room for his address book, before finding it in the kitchen, humming and whistling away under his breath.

It was obviously beginning to sink in now. That was all he'd needed, somebody to tell, somebody to share it with. He wondered what the weather was doing over there.

Raining, Phineas told him, and Humphrey laughed. He'd have laughed at whatever Phineas had said right then. If Phineas had been there with him, he'd have hugged him, waltzed him round the room. He couldn't remember when he had last felt so happy. Boy! it was beginning to sink in now, all right.

Phineas asked was there anything else he wanted, apart from the weather report, as, with just two days to go before Humphrey's bailiffs turned up, he, Phineas, was busy leaving.

And Humphrey started telling him several things at once, and laughing again, even when talking about the gunsmiths needing a rocket up their butts, and about the sale of the shotguns, and how Phineas wouldn't believe how much they'd fetched, how the agent couldn't believe how much, how *he*, Humphrey, couldn't believe how much. And how he was now going to pay compensation all round, while trying to work it out in his head if he could afford to double it, triple it, quadruple it even. Even – well, whatever came after quadruple, and to hell with it.

And it was then, out of nowhere, when he was busy doing all that, busy looking the other way, as it were, busy thinking about things that had absolutely *nothing* to do with her. It was then that he surprised himself, *astonished* himself even, by asking Phineas if he had Clem Wroxley's phone number.

Humphrey's head had finally caught up with his heart.

CHAPTER 34

When he arrived back in Batch Valley the weather wasn't doing anything in particular. Just sort of sitting there, all grey and mardy, as Mrs T would say.

Skirting the edge of the wood where, when he was last there, he had scattered the pheasants, flustering them like elderly maiden aunts, the leaves of the horse chestnuts were touched here and there with the first yellows of the year.

He liked horse chestnuts, big, generous, handsome trees. He was proud of those on the lawns of the Hall. History had walked in their shades, lords and dukes and duchesses. Kings and queens, too, he wouldn't be surprised. Before remembering that that was the old Humphrey, and he wasn't going to do that sort of thing anymore.

Well, maybe a duke and a duchess or two, he allowed himself, on this day of all days.

And every fall those trees, he knew, were raided by foraging squirrels and small boys. Annie Owen had told him about the kids on his first visit. They plundered them for chestnuts – conkers – armoured in vinegar and swung in battle on the High Street and in local school playgrounds.

His first son would be doing that in time, no doubt. And Humphrey wouldn't be at all surprised if he ended up conker champion of champions. Wouldn't surprise him one bit.

He thought about the local custom of planting a tree to celebrate a birth, but he wasn't too sure about that. The first one, sure, they'd do that, all right, along with the party the whole valley would be invited to, and midnight fireworks of course at the castle – gotta have that! And he liked the thought of a new horse chestnut among the others on the lawns. New growth among the old, he liked that idea. But he doubted there'd be room for all the little trees he had planned, not without using the rest of the estate as well.

He took a deep breath, gathering in the scents of the valley through the open window of the car.

And then he grinned. A slow, wide grin, as if drawing it from deep within himself. And if asked to explain it, to explain what he felt, and why, he would have talked vaguely about the landscape and its people, and just as vaguely said something about the life he wanted to make down there, in the heart of the valley. And it would still only be a part of it.

But he knew what he meant, in that place where the grin had come from.

And if forced to admit it, then, yeah, all right, he would. It was better – yeah, yeah, better, even – than making first baseman for the Yankees.

And Humphrey could *not* say more than that.

He didn't need Miss Wyndham's directions this time, as he passed the spot where he'd met her that day. Miss Wyndham with her magnifying glass, hot on the case of Colonel Ash and the escaped alpine plant.

Humphrey turned first right, and then first left, and second right and then right again, catching a glimpse of the pinnacled tower of St Swithin's, before losing it behind a high-banked hedge. And then right, first left, and then another left, followed by a right, and then left again into Hollow Oak Hill, all the way down, all the way down, singing as he went.

'*I'm heading for tomorrow,*' he bellowed, accompanying himself with a few blasts on the horn, '*and I'm never coming back!*'

He had told Sylvia. He had even done it in person. He felt he owed her that.

He'd phoned her and she had finally agreed to leave her desk for ten minutes, and meet him in the Crash Coffee Shop on Wall Street. Where she had listened to him talking about anything but for most of that time, while waiting for what he really had to say.

She had cried at first, a controlled sort of sobbing, which left her mascara intact and

Humphrey not sure if he should offer one of the paper napkins or not.

She had paid for the coffee. She told him he'd need his money, marrying another loser, another no-hoper on the take. She'd said goodbye out on the street, where she'd delivered herself coolly of a few more thoughts on the subject of his future.

And telling him he was yesterday, turned on her heel and walked out of his life.

And then it was Frank's turn. He decided to phone him. Frank didn't cry or anything, he just sounded awfully tired. He argued about it at first, in a tired sort of way, and then sighed, and said he wasn't surprised. He even wished Humphrey well, in a tired sort of way.

Humphrey had thanked him and invited Frank over to stay at Batch Hall any time he liked, and meant it. He thought that by the sound of it Frank could do with the break.

He phoned Sarah then, a call he *had* been looking forward to. John, her husband, answered. Humphrey told him about coming back to live there, and how nobody would be evicted, now or ever. Jolly good, John had said, which is what John said about almost everything, and then went to fetch Sarah.

Humphrey asked her to tell the pensioners, because if she told them it was all right, they'd *know* it was all right. She said she'd be glad to and that she'd get the keys from the agent and open the Hall up ready for him. And that's all she said.

Before adding simply, after saying goodbye, 'Good chap,' and he guessed that was all he was going to get, ever. But for him, from Sarah, it was enough. When he put down the phone he was smiling.

Then he took care of business, as Frank would say, arranging to pay back the loan and interest to the bank. He'd have to pay the architect's and surveyor's fees, and all that sort of stuff, as well, Frank had pointed out, and had given him a rough idea of cost, which wasn't all that much. And of course he had his windfall, and even a bit left over from the sale of Home Farm after the death duties had been paid.

All of which meant, when Humphrey was doing the accounting, that in a way he'd be keeping most of the loan. And when you add that to the fact that the Hall's roofs needed doing anyway, he was really only paying the interest on it. So it was even better than the interest-free loan, or whatever it was called, that he'd read about somewhere. It was a loan-free interest, sort of loan.

There had been a small silence on the other end after that, and then the so-called loan executive had asked him would he mind saying all that again. And then *still* couldn't seem to grasp it.

He phoned the agent overseeing the work on the Hall next, and instructed him to finish when the roofs and chimneys had been done, shooting from the executive hip, as he had with the bank.

His dad would have been proud of him, he told

himself out of habit. Before remembering that he had a new dad now, and had a photograph to prove it, one with them together on it. And if Bloomingdale's, in their whole history, had had a better Santa Claus *ever*, than his dad, then he'd eat his best Yankees baseball cap.

And he was different, this new dad. The other dad, the old dad, well, he admired him. He was a hotshot and go-getter, and a decent guy, so what's not to admire? But he *liked* this new dad. To Humphrey he made much more sense. Sure, he'd have probably asked what the hell his son thought he was doing, how the hell was he going to live, and all that, like dads do. But he'd have soon kidded him out of that. His dad, his new dad, would have done just what he was doing. He knew that now. He had learned it just in time.

And now, as he saw it, they were doing it together. Travelling together, both free now.

And his mom, who was happily settling things in New York before following him over to live here, would have her moment as mistress of Batch Hall. Until, that is, he carried the real mistress through its doors. Because if he had any doubts at all about the past he'd turned his back on, he had none at all about the future.

They'll have Donald Duck and Goofy and the gang on the wallpaper ready for the first arrival in the nursery, the boy who would be conker champion, and the signed baseball bat and mitt, and his granddad's fighter plane suspended from the ceiling. And he'll coach him in baseball, and Phineas in cricket, and Owain will teach him to fish, and later shoot. Phineas would be one godparent, he'd decided, and Annie and Owain, and Jasmine, and the Commander and Priny, and Miss Wyndham and John Beecher, and Tom Parr, there'll be plenty to go round, enough new trees over the years.

And they'll grow up, their brood, like Jasmine's and the Owens', and there'll be all the Hall and the grounds to chase each other round in, and the river to explore, and picnics on it, and trips to its hidden places, and all that English countryside, and the half that was in Wales, to play in.

Humphrey clamped his cigar in his mouth, and scattered sheep feeding by a field gate with a couple more blasts on the horn, singing his way down Batch Valley.

The cigar was a large torpedo, hand-rolled Havana, and the shirt he'd worn for his return the most colourful of his Hawaiians. On it, a party was in full swing, an island festival, in combustible yellows and reds, blues and orange and tropical green, people eating and drinking and dancing. He'd bought it at the Five-O store, a Kamehameha Garment Company original, with polished coconut shell buttons, and never worn until now, because he'd been keeping it for a special occasion he'd never before been sure had arrived or not, until now.

And if now wasn't a special occasion, then would somebody kindly tell him what the heck would be.

He reached Monk's Bridge, the humpbacked bridge over the Cluny, and with another, long blast on the horn, stormed it like an invasion.

CHAPTER 35

Mr Pugh, on this, the last day of the house-boat eviction notices, was singing to himself about hailing to the Lord's anointed as he fiddled with the cardboard display sheets behind the half-glazed shop door.

Then he pushed his nose abruptly up against the glass.

There had been no mistaking the shirt and cigar. That was Sir Humphrey who had just shot past, taking aeroplanes from America like some people take the 10:37 bus from Shrewsbury. On his way to the river, no doubt, to chasten and plague the last of them. And speaking as one of the righteous, Mr Pugh was more than glad, he was almost giddy with it.

After decades, after centuries, when nothing ever happened here, nothing except the seasons ever changed, suddenly everything was happening, everything was changing.

The future in a hurry, that's what had just roared up the High Street. Progress and modernisation, the rallying cry of the new Batch Magna. And where the American led, Mr Pugh would not be far behind. After Sir Humphrey's successful planning application, Mr Pugh's proposed extension of the shop into the back garden would, he'd been assured, be deemed complementary and necessary.

It was, as he had learned to say, in the bag.

And Mr Pugh saw again the throng of customers and the tills ringing like Christmas, and the wanton girls who sat at them. And two in particular he had his eye on. One English, a sulky blonde, with her roots showing, he'd insist on that, the other valley Welsh, with a back-of-the-chapel laugh. And neither more wanton than in his storeroom after business hours, where they took turns to wait for him, that day's Special Offer, while Mrs Pugh sat upstairs with the telly.

While the shopkeeper dreamed again of the future, Humphrey, busy going the other way, as it were, was roaring off down the side of the pub into Upper Ham, ignoring, as everyone else did, the no-entry sign, and slowing then, when he saw the removal van outside the *Batch Castle*.

Phineas was standing by the Frogeye further down the lane, kicking the car's tyres.

A couple of suitcases, his Underwood typewriter, a bag of wine, and one of books, were strapped into the luggage space, and Bill Sikes was in the passenger seat, sitting resolutely upright, determined not to be left behind.

Not wanting to get under the feet of the others, who anyway had their own problems, Phineas was on his way to Sally's, until the compensation money arrived.

Daniel had gone back last week, not knowing where his father would end up this time. And his father had still been wondering that himself up to a couple of days ago, still not wanting to leave, and still not having the foggiest where he was going when he did go. But working out his finances, adding and taking away, and then going over it again, and frowning suspiciously at the total, he knew that wherever it was it wouldn't be far.

And then Humphrey had called from New York, and Phineas had felt free then, with a large cheque in the post, to take up Sally's offer of a bed. The way he drifted through life sometimes, following whatever current happened to be pulling the hardest at the time, he knew that anything longer than a couple of nights could end in a mortgage, and a suit and briefcase, and Sally waving him off to some office each morning. Women could be quite shameless about that sort of thing.

He'd checked the tyres and everything else he had to check, or could think of to check. He'd said his last goodbyes yesterday, and again, just now, to the dear old *Belle*.

So that was it. He was ready to go. He was, finally, about to leave the river. For the last time. For good.

And then a car pulled up with a squeal of brakes, and he blinked at the sudden rush of brightness in the air as Humphrey piled out.

The promise of compensation was about the only part of the phone call from New York that Phineas had understood. The others when he told them hadn't got too excited about it; they said they'd heard it all before. And Phineas hadn't got too excited about it then, either, and said he'd heard it before, as well. And then went ahead and believed it anyway.

He'd had his mail redirected to Sally's, but had been hoping the cheque would arrive before he left. And now it looked as if here it was, delivered by Humphrey in person.

Phineas beamed at him, and complimented him on his shirt, and hoped he'd had a good flight, not too bumpy, and all that.

Humphrey ignored it.

'Where the hell are you going, Phin?' he demanded, staring accusing at the loaded sports car.

'I'm leaving,' Phineas said, not looking too sure about it now. Last night had seen another farewell jolly, a combined one, after the farewell jolly for Jasmine a couple of nights back, and the one before that for the Owens. Saying goodbye had left him easily confused.

'But why? I said when I phoned, didn't I?' Humphrey said indignantly, although he could hardly remember afterwards what he had said.

Phineas had no idea what he was talking about, but he was beginning to suspect that whatever Humphrey was here to deliver, it wasn't a cheque.

But what Humphrey had to deliver turned out to be far more valuable than that.

And when Humphrey told him, saying again what he thought he'd said on the phone, Phineas asked him would he mind saying it again.

Humphrey sighed, and went through it again.

Phineas stared at him. 'Well, I'll be blowed.'

Humphrey glanced down the lane towards the *Castle*, at the removal van that Mr Pugh, sneaking down earlier to check on things, considered was probably wanted for the empties.

'You can stay, can't you? All of you?' It had occurred to him that he might be too late.

'Well, I'll be blowed,' Phineas said.

He took off his Gent's Superior Panama, and scratched briefly and furiously at his head. And then put it on again, as if he'd got things working up there now.

'Now let me get this straight, Humphrey.'

'Humph, Phin, Humph,' Humphrey reminded him, fretfully pulling at one of Bill Sikes's ears, and keeping an eye on the removal van.

'So— So, there's not now going to be a holiday village,' Phineas said, taking it a bit at a time. 'Nor floating whatnots on the river. Or pensioners out on the street. And you're coming back here to live at the Hall, which isn't now going to be an hotel. With Sylvia, presumably. I take it you'll be living there with Sylvia.'

Humphrey shook his head determinedly. 'No, not with Sylvia.'

Phineas studied him. 'Are you and she finished?' he asked doubtfully, remembering how Humphrey would almost burst into song at her name.

Humphrey nodded equally determinedly. 'Yes, we're finished.'

That, as Phineas knew, was something else that didn't always mean what it said. 'And what about later, if you make it up? What about—?'

'We won't *be* making it up. It's finished, Phin. It's over. Sylvia. Frank. Everything. It's *all* over. Believe me. I'll explain it all later, I'll tell it you all then,' Humphrey promised anxiously. 'But for now, I just want to know that you'll stay. That you'll all stay.'

Phineas studied him some more.

'So nothing, in fact, will change. Is that right?' he said slowly, still in the grip of everything suddenly changing.

'*Nothing* will change,' Humphrey assured him. Well, almost nothing, he thought, thinking of the visit he had yet to make.

'Phineas. Phin,' he said earnestly, 'listen to me. Please. I want Batch Magna, the river, and the Hall, and . . . and everything. I want it as it was . . . as it is. That's what I want. That's what I remembered in time. So don't tell me now that you can't stay. You and the Cunninghams, and everybody. *Please*?'

'Well, I'd be blowed,' was all Phineas said.

And then he laughed. 'Well, I'd be *blowed*!'

He stared at Humphrey, as if unsure whether to hug or hit him.

'Humphrey . . .'

'Humph, Phin,' Humphrey said happily, 'Humph. So you'll stay?'

'Stay, old chap, *stay*? Of *course* we'll stay! Of course! Of course! Of *course* we'll stay!'

'The others, as well? They'll stay?' Humphrey asked, getting excited with him.

'Of course! Of course!' Phineas started again, before remembering that half of them had already gone. 'Well, Annie and Owain, and Jasmine and her crew will have to come back first to stay, but . . .'

Humphrey was pulled up short. 'They've gone?'

'Yes. But of *course* they'll stay! They'll be back the second I put the phone down. If not sooner. You'll see. I've got their new numbers. I'll ring them. I'll tell them. They'll be back . . . they'll be *back* all right!'

'I'll pay all their removal costs. I'll meet all expenses.'

'Yes, yes,' Phineas said, nodding. 'Well!' he said. '*Well*!' he said again.

'Yeah!' Humphrey said, and laughed.

They stood grinning, gleefully, at each other, sharing it like a conspiracy, like two small boys who, whatever it was, had only *just* got away with it.

'I'll go and tell the Cunninghams,' Humphrey said, heading for the hire car.

'We'll have a jolly,' Phineas said.

'At the Hall. A party at the Hall. We'll take the dust sheets off. Open the old place up. Tell Jasmine to bring her guitar,' Humphrey called through the car window, bumping up on the verge for a U-turn, and grinning and sticking a thumb up, before roaring off again.

While Humphrey pulled up with another squeal of brakes behind the removal van, Phineas stood looking about him, at the hills, and the village, and the castle above it, and the river. As if checking that it was all still there, and finding it just as it had always been.

And then he looked at Bill Sikes, and grinned.

'Out,' he said.

Sikes shifted in the seat but stayed put, gazing steadily at his master.

And it wasn't until Phineas had made his phone calls. Had passed on the good news, news that Jasmine said she'd known was coming, she had, that's why she hadn't unpacked properly, and Annie, who had to sit down, and said she didn't believe a word of it, and then wanted to hear it again, from the beginning. And had then called Sally to tell her, and make sure she was free for the party tonight, feeling then such a rush of affection for her he wondered if it was love – felt free then to wonder if it was love.

It wasn't until he had done all that, and until all the stuff in the car had been off-loaded onto the verge, that Sikes felt it safe to leave it.

He followed Phineas and his two suitcases back up the gangway of the *Cluny Belle*, and once on deck slumped down, as if taking a well-earned rest from it all, home again.

Humphrey had suggested to the removal men that they wait until he had spoken to the Cunninghams before loading any more of their goods. And if, as he hoped, the move was cancelled, he'd pay the full cost of it.

The two men folded their arms. This would be the second irregularity since arriving. Then, the Cunninghams had asked for their goods to be put into store, instead of the delivery they'd booked to Church Myddle, and which was clearly docketed. And now this, and from a foreigner, in a shirt.

And then Humphrey mentioned a cash bonus each for their inconvenience, a universal language, instantly understood and just as quickly accepted.

Humphrey, diffidently going up the gangway, found the Cunninghams in the kitchen, with everything removed from it except that needed to make tea, which they were doing now, for themselves and the removal men. For the British, Humphrey thought, whatever the problem, the answer is tea, a cup of cha. Moving home, divorce, birth, death, bombs, and eviction notices – put the kettle on.

Priny, carefully made-up on this last morning, her hair done earlier, was wearing red-and-white toreador pants, one of her husband's old county check shirts for the business of packing, and her best pearls next to her skin. The Commander's glass eye, worn also in the face of so much defeat, was flying, out of pure swank, the Union Jack.

Humphrey knocked politely on the open door,

sending a black and white collie pup, who was sitting with biscuit crumbs on its snout, watching the Cunninghams' every move, barking dementedly.

Some hours before that, the Commander had been on the phone to the warden of leeward homes about the pup, a dog they'd called Stringbag, the Fleet Air Arm's old nickname for the Swordfish aircraft. He had been a farewell present from the Owens, one of the pups from a litter sired by Owain's Welsh collie, and the Commander had thought it only right to let the warden know that they now had an extra crew member.

The warden had news for them. Residents were not allowed dogs. Cats, yes. Dogs, no.

And when the Commander suggested that if that was the rule then it was damn silly one, he almost heard the man smile on the other end. He did not, the warden said with prim satisfaction, make the rules, and was there anything else? There was. The Commander hadn't finished yet.

That utterance, he was able to tell the warden, was the refuge of every jobsworth, every complacent, hypocritical, self-important, puffed-up Jack-in-office who ever polished his self-satisfied bum behind a desk. The Commander was able to tell him a few more things, as well, while he was at it, bringing in names like Duce, and Fuhrer, followed by a short lecture on the rise of Fascism.

While Priny, sitting with a cigarette and the *Telegraph*, had lifted her eyebrows now and then quizzically at him.

When her husband, who had effectively just torpedoed their future, put down the phone, he looked at her, and cleared his throat guiltily.

Priny grinned back at him.

'That was a close call,' she said, and the Commander was reminded again of just one of the reasons why he had married her.

'Yes, well, I'm afraid it does rather leave us without anywhere to run to, Number One, does leave us a bit at sea,' he said, looking about for his pipe. And then he regarded her solemnly. 'We could always, I suppose, give Stringbag back to the Owens.'

'Nonsense, Cunningham,' Priny said on a laugh. 'You don't suppose anything of the sort! Frankly, I can't think what possessed us in the first place. Sheltered housing, indeed. Whatever next!'

'We were simply limping in to the nearest port, Number One,' the Commander said, defending their seamanship. 'Badly holed, with a sea over our decks. Any bridge would have taken the same action.'

'And now what?' Priny asked cheerfully. This was *much* more the thing.

'Well, we've got marching money waiting for us in Kingham,' he said, referring to the papers of sale for the *Castle* and the dinghy drawn up ready for them in the solicitor's office there.

'And we've got the car. Our bits and bobs can go into store, and we'll just – just march,' Priny said, and grinned at it. Whatever happened to them, it surely couldn't be as *boring* as the ending she had seen waiting for them in leeward homes.

'Bows into the storm, and keep the wardroom open. Well *said*, Number One,' the Commander approved.

And then a few hours later Sir Humphrey had turned up, come striding, as the Commander put it, like Arthur, through the high, bright corn.

Last night in the small hours, when the green and red underway deck lamps burned in the darkness, they had stood unspeaking at the starboard rail, listening to the river noises, saying goodbye to their home. And now they stood together at the port rail, on the landward side, the storm suddenly, and most remarkably, over, listening to Humphrey doing racing changes up the High Street.

'My word,' Priny said mildly, as a tub of pink angel's trumpets and one of fuchsias nodded their way past her, carried back in again by one of the removal men. 'My word.'

Humphrey swept into the yards of the Batch Valley Chase, and at the very door of the woman he had come three thousand miles to marry, for the first time doubted.

It had occurred to him that he hadn't actually asked her yet.

He hadn't mentioned it when he'd phoned from New York, he was sure of that, he thought, frowning over it now. He hadn't even touched on the subject, as far as he could remember. Hadn't even hinted at it.

And now he was here.

And what if he had only got half of it right that night? What if what had happened to him hadn't happened to her?

What, he thought shrinkingly, if he was making a total horse's ass of himself?

Humphrey got slowly, reluctantly, out of the car, conscious for the first time since leaving New York of his shirt. He felt too loud, and too big and clumsy. And stupid, just plain stupid. And his cigar had gone out.

He dropped it, furtively, and thought of giving some other reason for being there. Or even just turning round and driving out again, as no one seemed to be about.

And then Clem, her two dogs at her heels, walked round the corner from the stable block.

She stopped dead when she saw him, a hand going up to her hair, and coming away with bits of straw. And the sleeve of her shirt was ripped, torn on a tack-room nail. And she had no make-up on, she'd been late getting up and hadn't bothered since.

And what on *earth* was he doing here?

She had no idea what he'd meant, when he'd called from New York. She had no idea what he'd meant one minute, and then hoped he'd meant what she thought he might just *possibly* have meant the next. And listening to it yet again in her head, to the things he hadn't said but might have meant, until she could no longer remember what he *had* said. And then getting furious with herself, behaving like a teenager, when all he wanted anyway was to see her on business, probably. And besides, he was getting married, even if she hadn't been wearing a ring in the yard that day, she'd remind herself – had only just *finished* reminding herself again, on her way round to the front yard.

And there he was.

Clem said hello, and asked how he was, and smiled politely, waiting for whatever it was he did want. And whatever it was, he might have had the bloody manners to phone first!

Humphrey said he was fine, thanks for asking, and asked how she was. Clem said she was fine as well, and thanked him for asking.

And watched by Ffion, who had followed her round from the stables, and John Beecher, strolling out of the backyard to see who had arrived in the car, his broad amiable face frank with curiosity, Clem stood smiling at Humphrey, and Humphrey stood smiling at Clem.

Humphrey opened his mouth to add something, feeling something more *should* be said, and was about to remark on the weather. And Clem, who also felt there was a gap to be filled, was about to ask how his flight had been.

And then, somehow – and they would disagree for years afterwards about who did what first –

somehow they sort of went to each other. They went to each other, and there were no more doubts.

And Clem, big Clem, with her broken nose and straw in her hair, who was always among the first in the field to put her mount at the riskiest hedges, and who could skin and joint like a butcher, and make Sion Owen and John Beecher work at arm wrestling, yielded to him.

And he put his arms tight around her, as if to carry her off. Or keep her there.

Humphrey had come home.

AN ENDING *AND* A BEGINNING . . .

Owain heard about the otter while standing glumly that day at the bar of the Plough in Little Batch.

The cottage they were renting in the village was roomier than the old boat, as Annie had lost no time pointing out on their first day there.

'And a proper home, too, it is, with a door knocker, and net curtains, and stairs with carpets on them,' she'd said, making the most of it for all of them.

'And look how neat and tidy it is, Fee,' she'd invited her daughter, who was trailing behind, scowling with boredom, and shooting the odd resentful look at her mother, as if she knew, if no one else did, who was to really to blame for all this. While Owain asked did she think it was all right for him to light his pipe.

They'd been there a week now, and outside of the bedroom he still had to take his coat off indoors. Sitting like a visitor, and on his own furniture, too, as Annie had reminded him, and keeping his voice down as if at the doctor's. Hadn't shouted, or raised it once, he hadn't, since they'd been there, and she'd started to get quite worried about it.

But if the cottage was bigger, the land was much smaller. They had no front garden and only a small back one. They'd had to leave everything behind on their old plot and sell the livestock, except for Megan the goat, who, before being tethered, had lost no time in browsing on the flowerbeds the owners had asked them to keep up.

It had come as no surprise to Owain to find that the village pub, our local, as Annie had called it, looking brightly about her on their first visit there, did not keep Sheepsnout cider. Owain had not expected it to, and the pub had not let him down.

But if their new local didn't sell Sheepsnout it did sell Black Boy bitter, and now Owain was sucking his pipe over a pint of it, to remind him of home, three miles up the road. Standing on his own, distanced by a gloom which sat over him, in that small, perfectly friendly bar, like the threat of rain on an otherwise pleasant day.

And then his ears, sharp as a water rat's when it suited him, as Annie had pointed out often enough, pricked up at the mention of an otter from a group of men also standing at the bar.

One of them was apparently a water bailiff at Horton Cross, and two months before, Owain heard, had trapped an otter, a bitch, which he'd then found was pregnant. Earlier that day he had gone to the pen he'd been keeping her in, intending to release her and the unborn cubs up on the Severn, well away from his beat.

He had found the pen empty. And he couldn't for the life of him, he said, see how she had got out.

She'd got out, Owain knew, because it was time to do so. And he lost no time in wondering how. Owain was border Welsh, and had learned as a child that otters have magical powers. Everybody knew that, unless they were English. Which the group at the bar were, so would know no better. The Commander was the only Englishman he had met who *really* understood otters. But then to Owain's mind, which had its own logic, the Commander wasn't really an Englishman but a Welsh man who just happened to be English.

Owain wasn't bothering about how she got out, only where she might have gone to, to give birth, puffing furiously at his pipe, the smoke piling up as if from his thoughts.

Horton Cross was six miles or so upstream from Batch Magna, but as he'd told the Commander at the time, an otter could be lying up anywhere within a fifteen mile stretch of river. The Commander's otter might have been the dog to the bitch, or the bitch herself, before she was caught, and having first driven off her mate after he'd done his piece.

She'd be due any day now, and if she was the Commander's otter, then she might well have already returned, gone back to the island to give birth in a familiar holt, in an old burrow or dug in under the roots of an ash or one of the hawthorns. The Commander wouldn't be able to see her yet, and certainly not the cubs. But it wouldn't be long, Owain thought, digging in a pocket for change for the pub phone, before remembering.

It didn't matter now. The river and the things that happened or didn't happen on it were none of their business now.

He returned to his pint, to the present and his own misery, and the memories he clung to in it. Owain was old Batch Magna, and all he was would live there still, stubbornly, no matter where they moved to, or *what* they said.

He could hardly bear to think about this new Batch Magna they talked about. And he couldn't bear to think at *all* about his river, his home. Couldn't bear to think that they would no longer open their doors to summer, and send up their companionable smoke on winter days, when the owls called as darkness fell and the lamps were lit.

Couldn't bear to think about it, but he did. And it looked for a moment as if the rain had arrived where Owain was, threatening to fall, there and then, in the pub, as he gave himself up to his loss.

And then the door of the bar opened, was flung open, and Annie, her face flushed, stood, framed dramatically, in the doorway.

Owain had the look of a man who could take

no more, but who knew he was going to get it anyway. It was Megan, the bloody goat, no doubt. She'd managed to get at the flowerbeds again, the beds that Annie had replanted, and had been diligently looking after since.

But as she made her way to him, Owain saw that whatever it was about it wasn't about flowerbeds, and hope leapt like a fish in him. Because whatever it *was* about, it was obviously good news of some sort and for Owain there couldn't *be* better news than that.

It was arithmetic done in his heart. Without adding up or taking away, without asking why or how, Owain, who believed in the magic of otters, allowed himself to believe in a happy ending.

And he was right.

Annie said it then, taking his hands in hers, her dark eyes, staring into his, almost saying it before she did.

'*Owain*,' she said, her voice low and fierce with it. '*Owain, we can go home.*'

The End – For now . . .